GEMINI'S CROSSING

ENORA ONLINE: BOOK ONE

ARLO ADAMS

"Fowler! Move your ass!"

"I see it!" I dove to avoid the acid ejection then rolled to my feet. Ripping an arrow from my quiver, I scanned the massive worm for a soft spot among its thick segments. "Why is it the meat shield who's supposed to be focused on keeping mobs pissed at her is always the one barking orders?"

"Because if I didn't, you'd be melting, dork!"

"If you kept hate, maybe it wouldn't be trying to melt me in the first place!"

"Hey, we're four-manning a five-man epic. I'm not a miracle worker, douche cannon."

Katelyn raised her sword high then brought it down in a blurry arc. A swath of scales split open, and green puss flooded from the beast's bottom lip.

That looks like a good spot.

I drew back my arrow and waited for the casting meter on my HUD to fill.

"You gonna shoot the damn thing, or what?"

I loosed the arrow then rolled as another splotch of acid rained down in the spot where I'd been standing. Then I came up on my knees, slid another arrow from my quiver, and shot without waiting for a mana charge. It lodged in the Hell Worm's right eye with a sickening pop, but the superior sound didn't match the lazy graphical effect.

Critical Hit!
Hell Worm received 39,476 damage!

The glass tiger standing on the opposite side about thirty feet from the mob yelled, "Health at five percent! Burning it down!"

"Be my guest!" Katelyn yelled. "I tire of the odor of this thing!"

I still couldn't believe people bought those scent packs for their immersion pods.

A casting meter on my party pane filled red as an orange glow surrounded the death mage's hands then radiated up his arms.

When Katelyn tried to sidestep the worm's latest lunge, one of the loose rocks beneath her feet crumbled, she lost her footing, and her butt hit the ground. The beast clinched its teeth on her thigh. "Gah! Get that damn thing off me!"

Katelyn is poisoned.
Attack Down.

The raging fireball from the death mage's Inferno Blast spell raced across the distance and slammed into the eye on the creature's other side. The eye vanished like something out of a cartoon, leaving me to think the developers could work on their visual effects. But the beast's roar was nerve-rattling as it filled the cabin when it released its toothy grip on my tank and reared back.

Hell Worm is blinded.

"Katelyn, roll away and reengage! Let's finish this bastard and get this achievement once and for all!"

"It'd be nice if I could get a heal!" she barked.

"Sorry! I'm OOM!" the healer cried out.

Out of mana. Great!

"I swear, I have to do everything myself!" she complained.

When the blinded worm lunged toward the spot Katelyn had just vacated, she rolled and jumped to her feet. As the mage unleashed a fireball and I contributed another arrow, my tank reversed her grip on the pommel of her long sword, leapt high into the air, then brought the blade down to pierce the center of the beast's skull to the hilt.

Does a worm have a skull?

The mage's bolt and my arrow struck simultaneously with the sword's impact. Our enemy thumped to the ground, and we all froze.

Waiting...

"Who got it?" Katelyn asked.

"It's mine," I said.

"Nah, all me," the shadow mage replied.

My screen filled with text.

Achievement! G3m1n1 has received the achievement, "Hell Worm's Lair — Epic!"

Achievement! Katelyn has received the achievement, "Hell Worm's Lair — Epic!"

Achievement! Fireboy69 has received the achievement, "Hell Worm's Lair — Epic!"
Achievement! SweetCh33ks has earned the achievement, "Hell Worm's Lair — Epic!"
Bonus Achievement! Katelyn has received the achievement, "Dirty Worm, Bow Before Me — Epic" for landing the killing blow on Hell Worm!

"Ha!" Katelyn bellowed. She raised a plated fist into the air. "I got it!"

Congratulations, G3m1n1! You have completed "Hell Worm's Lair—Epic!"
47,027,897 XP
Since you are maximum level, you are not awarded XP.

Light from multiple unseen sources flooded the dim cavern.

"'Grats," I muttered.

Katelyn turned on her heels. "Hey, don't sound so excited for me. Not my fault you guys are slow." One side of her perfect lips ticked up, and I melted on the inside. Even so, I raised a middle finger.

"Yeah, yeah," Fireboy69 said. "Good job, Katelyn. 'Grats. Thanks for the group."

"You outta here?" I asked.

"Yeah, the drop will be shit against my legendary. You guys sell it or something." He turned to the silver-haired healer. "You want a lift?"

She nodded and stepped into the halo of light painting a circle around his feet. An orange glow surrounded him as he waved his arms in circles over his head. Then the casters blinked out of existence like someone flipped a switch.

"Ready?" Katelyn asked.

"Yup. Roll the bones."

She raised a finger into the air and tapped a button I couldn't see. As the group leader, she performed the unnecessary theatrics that would unlock the loot roll.

You have received Heavy Bow of the Dragon
+94 fire damage
+67 Agility
+6% Health
Chance on Hit: Your arrow infects your enemy with 300%
additional poison damage.

"What'd you get?" Katelyn asked.

"A heavy—" a piercing shot of pain ripped through the lower right side of my abdomen and I doubled over.

Katelyn's boots crunched rocks, then she was at my side.

"Whoa. You okay? Is that what you've been talking about?"

"Gah!" I spat. "Yeah. Not an in-game effect." I tried to smile, but the pain from my body in the outside world dropped me to one knee.

Katelyn set a hand on my shoulder.

"Damn, Gemini." She squeezed. "Your appointment's tomorrow?"

The bolts receded to dull throbs. When I stood, Katelyn let her hand slip away and her fingertips brushed down my arm.

"Yeah. Tomorrow. Hey, sorry, hope you got something cool, but I gotta log and go lie down."

"Understandable, bud." She nodded with sympathy. "You'll let me know, right? Tomorrow night before the raid?"

"I will," I grunted. "Talk to you soon."
I logged out.

1

"Lubrin's? The immune thing?"

The doctor raised the thin radiographic film to gaze at it in the overhead lighting of his office. The mere presence of the film was pretentious, considering he could display the image on the hologram emitter built into his desk so we both could see it.

"Lubrin's Anti-Immune Syndrome. Your immune system is attacking your organs like they're foreign bodies." His words came with the practiced nod and indifferent tone of a man who'd delivered the Reaper's message hundreds of times.

"But..."

But what? What else was there?

Apparently, I wore an expression he'd seen enough times to read my mind.

"There's little benefit in circling the truth. Though Lubrin's doesn't spread as rapidly as Ebola, its survival rate is comparable. While treatment may extend your life slightly, it's best you get your affairs in order. It's unfair, you're young, but once this disease asserts itself, any hope for miracles is misplaced."

Just like that, I was a dead man.

"How long?" It was the only question left. The ultimate question, really.

"It's hard to guess with any accuracy because Lubrin's attacks each individual's organs differently."

I was dying, and he spoke like a medical journal.

"It might be genetic. We still aren't sure what flips the switch that makes people like you susceptible." He raised his shoulder in a half-shrug. "Judging from what we know., I'd guess you have three or four months without immuno-suppression. Even then, your body might not respond. If it does..." His eyes scanned the room, dancing from the degrees on one wall to whatever adorned the one behind me, and then back to mine. "As many as nine months, with treatment?"

The time it takes for a woman to have a baby and I'd be dead?

I waited for a response to well up—anger, sadness, anything. I should've been terrified. The weight of his utterances should've pinned me to my chair, brought on a fit... something! I was only twenty-two!

But death wasn't real. Death was the distant and occasional tickle brought on by mental flashes of my parents' caskets. I thought I'd die next to an old woman with whom I counted out my daily pills when I was too old to see without corneal correction. As reality seeped in, questions flooded.

What would I leave behind? What would be my legacy? I'd hardly made a dent in the world. Hell, I spent most of my adult life in an immersion pod playing virtual hero against the evils of a fantasy world. No one outside of work knew I existed.

"Take a moment," the doc said, as if I wasn't already doing exactly that.

Considering my moments were limited, I preferred not to spend them pointlessly in that chair.

"When would we start treatment?"

The doubtful way he pinched his lips made me want to reach across the desk, grab his lapels, and scream.

"Although it isn't mandated, I'd like to report this to the C.D.C. in Atlanta. I'm sure they'll want to speak with you about studies they're conducting."

"What, so I can spend what time I have left in a plastic bubble room?"

"I don't think it's that extreme at this point. They'll probably just want to take a history and try to find out how you contracted it. I'm ill-equipped to treat you."

His indifference boiled my blood. The son of a bitch was ready to wash his hands of me. If he'd had a shovel next to his desk, he might have buried me then and there.

I shook my head. "You don't have my permission to tell anyone anything. If I'm not a threat to the public, I have no intention of spending my few remaining days with the government."

The doc's lips parted as if he'd speak, but I shot him a glare leaving little doubt as to my position. "Nod your head if you understand."

I slouched in an oversized Zero-Grav in my living room the entire afternoon, staring through a poster of a scantily-clad RPG heroine with ridiculous boobs until the shadows cast by the waning sun converged into the darkness of night. My imagination rifled through dark mental images until the swirling hollow in my chest became a numb stone. Long past dinnertime, a tone designed to be soft and unobtrusive pinged overhead.

An equally soft, feminine voice followed. "Gemini, your guild's raid is in fifteen minutes. Shall I prime your immersion pod?"

The game. The guild. How sad is it that they're my only friends in the world?

I sighed, but it wasn't as cleansing as I'd hoped. For once, emerging into a virtual world didn't offer much in the way of escape, but maybe ogling my co-leader or hearing the soft timbre of her voice could distract me.

What else am I going to do? Sit here and wallow in self-pity? What's the quota for wallowing?

I cocked my chin up to respond. "Sure."

"Logging in."

Distant beeps echoed from the other room and a glow bouncing reflections off the walls of my apartment brought the image of the RPG heroine dimly back into view. I peered at the red-headed wonder for a few long moments while thinking about how any infinitesimal chance I'd ever had at finding a woman was now pretty much null. Hope drove the human race. The lack of it turned everything to shit. I was no exception, so a distraction would suit me.

With the flick of a thumb against a console in the Zero-Grav's arm, the chair lowered and tilted forward until my feet touched the floor. Dropping my shoulders in dejection and self-pity, I meandered to the kitchen where I slipped a soda out of the refrigerator door.

Shifting glances between the diet drink in my hand and the corn syrup infused soda in the rack, I traded up for the waist enlarger. A barely-measurable bright side to my body's imminent demise was I could discard concerns over my diet.

Cracking it open, I chugged cold fizz as I paced toward my den. A pleasant burn filled my throat with sweet phosphoric acid. At least I didn't have to worry about it stripping the calcium from my bones. A cola stream escaped my lips and dribbled to the floor, but I didn't really give a shit.

The prospect of death could be liberating.

I belched a solid seven, and my cat jerked awake in his fuzzy bed in the corner.

What will come of Josie? Guess I have to find her a home.

"I left you some soda on the kitchen floor," I muttered. Josie's pink-rimmed nose sniffed the air as I chuckled humorlessly at my stupid joke.

The immersion pod was a giant alien seedling in the center of the room, its sleek curves a stark contrast to my otherwise crappy apartment. After tapping the finger scanner, I sipped my drink as the curved hydraulic hatch swung into the air. Setting my soda in the cup holder built into the arm furthest from the hatch, I slid into the leather seat and lowered the silver band so that the metal discs on its ends aligned with my temples and the curve covered my eyes.

I took a deep breath, closed my eyes, and waited for the short burst of electrical pulsing in my head as I merged into a virtual world.

A pinprick of light popped up in the center of a sea of black and rushed toward me until I was enveloped by a tunnel of purple and orange. With a frown, I recalled the neck-to-toes flood of anticipation when I took my first VR trip.

The intro was little more than a splash screen before I

exited into a sea of black on the other side. Then words exploded into view:

Light of Babylon
Focus on a character to log in.

My boots sank into the desert floor as the swelter of twin suns engulfed me. Wisps of red sand from the angular crests of dark dunes blew across three figures standing just over one rise, the suns at their backs. They stared off in the opposite direction, aligned according to height from left to right, like a descending human bar graph.

My gaze shot to Katelyn, the figure on the right, who stood a full head shorter than the man next to her. The curves of her hips flowed to frame an impossibly perfect backside. My days of admiring her posterior were numbered, so I would discard propriety if I damn well pleased, thank you very much.

The selectable base characters in *Light Of Babylon* were designed to be attractive. Most players spent hours customizing them. Other people napped, watched movies, jerked off, or whatever as their scanners recreated their avatars in their own images, albeit with exaggerated features.

But Katelyn surpassed all of them. She was the real deal.

We'd formed the new guild a year ago, when I'd vacated my old one over stupid infighting. I didn't subscribe to drama inside virtual massively multiplayer online role-playing games—or VMMORPGs—so I'd made a quiet exit when the griping carried on for a couple days. Since I was a glory junkie who had spent a solid amount of time climbing achievement leaderboards, it hadn't taken long for the guild invites to start flowing in.

For a while, I'd gone so far as to block them so I could solo without being disturbed. I'd been on the verge of going into my options menu and suppressing social messages altogether when Katelyn showed up in person and tapped my shoulder. She'd also left the old guild in the wake of dramatic circumstances and remembered my name and face, though we'd hardly interacted there.

One tap on the shoulder. One look at her luminous tan skin, honey-streaked brown hair, and stunning body. One in-person suggestion we start a new guild where we made the rules.

That was all it had taken. A smile, an equivalent sentiment about what kinds of attitudes belonged in these games, and a willingness to let me stand close to her.

As luck had it, she was a badass tactician, to boot. We killed it.

After weeks playing together and recruiting new guild members, I learned she'd graduated from nursing school and moved to New Hanover a few months earlier—she was local! Swimming in delusions of grandeur, I tripped over myself trying to befriend her outside the game. I offered to show her around town. We could have coffee and talk game shop. Joke about what a small world it was.

But she politely dismissed my overtures and, after my stint of private wallowing, I accepted why a woman would want to keep her distance in a world packed with weirdos.

Then fate—a concept I'd scoffed at—stepped in at a coffee shop I patronized every morning on my way to grind out my existence as a data center networking engineer. I'd swept a steaming cup from the counter and pivoted to pass the line of people in the order queue just to realize she'd been standing behind me the whole time I'd waited. The *Light Of Babylon* system had drawn her avatar so perfectly, I recognized her immediately. The universe framed her so everyone else in the place became blurs. What small part of me hadn't believed she'd actually scanned herself into the game was instantly vanquished like a Level 1 rat.

She was an absolute beauty in maroon scrubs, and that image would be indelibly recorded in my mind. She flashed a quick smile at me—a total stranger, since I'd created my in-game avatar manually—then stepped toward the counter to place her order.

I couldn't stop glancing at her from my table in the corner.

Stalker alert!

I was practically a hermit, and my social skills were rusty like the underside of the Old Cape Fear Memorial Bridge. If I approached her, I'd probably trip over my words or spill my coffee. I guess I'd always been more the shy type than the jock—beyond peewee league football, anyway; I made a great middle linebacker right up until the kids were old enough to hurt me.

My work life further proved that Katelyn stood outside my sphere of hope. Considering my fellow work nerds gave me *so much crap* about my complete lack of game at company functions after my clumsy attempts to woo nerdy women, I knew this fine specimen bordered on untouchable.

Katelyn reappeared the next morning. Then the next. Had she been there all along? Had my nose been pressed so close to my handheld screen while waiting in line that I might as well have shoved it up my own crack?

My social incompetence usually left me all but paralyzed in public, so it took a while before I had the balls to stroll over on rubbery legs and say hello.

After all, how bad could it be? We spoke every day. I battled alongside her in the dungeons of *Light Of Babylon* with such regularity that we were already friends. Hell, we went duo when no one else showed up. I stared into those eyes with regularity—who cared if it'd been when she wasn't paying attention?

But my deciding motivation was the sense of guilt from hiding the stalker-y truth that I was scoping her incognito at the coffee joint.

And as it turned out, conscience would be my savior.

The blazing white smile that crossed her lips when I revealed my identity nullified every uncertain moment of the preceding nine days. The tight hug that followed made me wish I'd done it sooner.

I practically danced my way through work the entire rest of that day. I didn't *walk* to the shitter, I boogied.

Our morning trip for coffee became a glorious weekday tradition where I'd show up twenty minutes early just to grab her preferred table in the corner so we could laugh over our in-game antics of the previous night. One morning, I gave a guy ten bucks to make tracks before Katelyn arrived.

"Smitten" is an understatement. I felt like a love-sick teenager, and yet I persisted.

Then I got cocky.

It took this card-carrying Nerdist five more days before mustering the courage to suggest we have dinner.

She let me down easy—kindly, with respect. With her world-igniting, heart-melting, easy smile. At the time, I appreciated the consideration.

But after my diagnosis, as I watched her standing atop that dune in the context of my impending demise, the sting of her rejection refreshed itself. She'd been so polite as she declined my offer, I almost hadn't been offended. Almost.

But I hadn't been the lone victim, either.

The tallest figure turned as I stared up the sand embankment at the back of Katelyn's perfect head. His golden plate gleamed under the light of the suns. He'd chosen to hide his helmet in the character options. If I'd shone like a bad boy from one of those repulsive teen dramas that passed for movie theater entertainment, I would've probably hidden my helmet, too. To gaze upon his hulking frame, the average person probably guessed he created his avatar in the same way I created mine. But in a shining reflection of a life inundated with good luck, M3y3r's body and perfect jawline were the *real deals*, so to speak.

At least, that's what he claimed.

If I had a nickel for every time I cringed at his shameless flirtations with Katelyn, I wouldn't have needed to maintain an I.T. career and could've saved my humble trust fund for retirement.

The worst part of all?

M3y3r was great. No, I mean, like, really awesome. I loved the guy. This disposition proved easier to maintain because of the easy way Katelyn repelled his flirtatious bullshit.

The woman was a professional. She implemented refined rejection tactics as if she'd studied specific situational criteria and applied them a hundred times before. She could laugh off an overture in a way that so outclassed the men who tried that it inspired their loyalty. By the time a man was finished flirting with Katelyn, he knew he'd been out of his league before the inkling to dare had crossed his mind. She employed the same tactical efficiency she exercised in-game but left us standing—unlike the monsters in *LOB*—with our egos intact. We all adored her for it.

Katelyn. Complete package. All that. Bag of chips. Moving on.

"Hey, buddy." One side of M3y3r's mouth ticked up into a smile. "We were wondering when you'd show up." He cocked his head at the dunes behind him. "Looks like the raid's canceled. Too many no-shows. We were thinking the four of us could pick up a random in the queue and run a fiver instance, instead. You down?"

In English, that meant the four would access a dungeon queue and wait for a fifth person queued on their own to be assigned to our party by the system.

I shrugged. "Why not?"

My brain's answer was a gleaming image of my coffin descending into the ground. I huffed and tried to swallow some warmth into my suddenly hollow, cold chest. It came across in-game before I could stop myself.

Huffs, puffs, and sighs were Katelyn magnets. My eyes flicked to the right knowing that, even though it was the one time I hadn't wanted to draw it, I'd find her rapt attention focused on me.

Glowing green eyes bore down. The left one squinted, though not against the brightness of the suns to my aft.

"What'd the doc say?" She scanned quickly down and up my form, before returning to my face.

Suddenly aware of my posture—how I stood slumped, my shoulders uneven, my hands shoved into the pockets of my leather armor—I straightened my back as if the jerking motion might deflect her gaze.

Katelyn's expression morphed into something different. Concern, maybe? Whatever it had been quickly transitioned to the suspicious raise of a pencil-thin eyebrow.

She was sharp.

Didn't miss a beat.

And wasn't about to tolerate my shit.

She was that one member of a guild who became so enamored with the things she loved—like *Light Of Babylon*, for instance—that she sought out every little trick to make all of us more productive. The woman researched every nook and cranny, watched every online video feed of raids and dungeon runs to see how the best players got it done. Then she found a way to do it better.

Tactically speaking, she was to geeks what cheddar was to cheese.

Though we called ourselves co-leaders of our small guild, she told everyone I was the boss and hid behind her self-imposed role of advisor, leading us through every game mechanic in a dungeon she'd thoroughly researched, but never so it was obvious. Always asking questions and testing me, she pried the best solutions out of the problems we faced in-game. Katelyn neither wanted to be, nor wanted to *appear* to be, the leader.

So, I started calling her the Chosen One. She hated it.

No wonder every single one of us wanted her. It was like she had an intuition bordering on a sixth sense when it came to game development and a sick mind for strategy. She was a born leader with a gentle soul who guided us with patience through the game's toughest challenges, but she also wasn't afraid to bark orders if we dared to fall out of line and forgot a mechanic during a well-rehearsed boss fight.

We liked it rough.

She jerked me from my overblown recollections of our moments together as she peered at the guys beside her in turn and broke the silence.

"Guys, could you give us a second?"

The shorter of the two men pivoted as if he just realized I was there. Clad in a full suit of silver plate save for the limp, leather-lined helmet wrapping his face, he was like something out of a bad Arthurian movie. If I'd cut off his legs and arms, he might have been a fine addition to a Monty Python flick. This was Th3Rod.

It wasn't Therod, but The Rod. Yeah, seriously. If it wasn't bad enough his name was *Rod*, it was a glorious insight into his sense of humor that he added 'The' in front of it. The Rod.

He glanced at me with an expression of suspicion as he answered her. "Sure thing, boss." Sarcastic emphasis dripped from the final word. "Chosen One Junior looks like he could use some cheering up." He winked at me, the bastard. I chuckled and flipped him the bird.

Katelyn's eyes locked with mine as if she hadn't heard Th3Rod's response or noticed my juvenile form of sign language as she slid her feet closer, her boots carving deep sand trails in her wake.

Stepping into my personal halo of space—where she was always welcome—she cocked her chin like a shotgun.

"Give." Her eyes flickered back and forth between mine. I forgot words, as if an evil army of language-eating parasites had invaded my brain and eradicated my vocabulary.

Studying her beauty while cycling through images of my lowering coffin from various angles spoke magnitudes about my bipolar state of mind. Any fondness I held in the memories of moments ago had been snuffed out like a Christian in Rome.

Under the weight of her stare as she awaited my

response, time passed like thick syrup as virtual sand pelted our boots on the breeze.

Her words blew on a low whisper. "You're *scaring* me."

I jerked as if she'd pulled me out of a trance. But as the fog lifted, what I saw on her features was so foreign, it took me a second to interpret it, despite the words she'd just spoken. The sudden realization that my ego had hidden our friendship from me was a hard slap across my brain. Just because she hadn't wanted to have dinner didn't mean she didn't care about me.

I owed her an answer. "It's um..."

When I didn't continue, Katelyn gripped my gloved hand and squeezed. She moved her head with me as I diverted my gaze. Full and luscious or not, her lips vanished as she pinched them in frustration.

I shook my head. "Lubrin's. Anti-immune disease. Terminal."

"Horse shit." She shook her head in quick, slight twists. "Not Lubrin's...the odds of that are..."

Her facial muscles slackened and her lips parted as if she'd say something. She pressed them together again and gazed through me.

"That—!" Her head tilted. "That can't be right..."

I knew her well enough by now to understand the epileptic-level pupil dance from one of my eyes to the other reflected genuine wonderment as to whether I was fucking with her. She was actually hoping to find a lie in my gaze. A cruel and unforgivable joke, hidden somewhere behind my irises.

An overwhelming urge to relieve her left me hollow. I tried to force a smile to communicate acceptance of my fate, but it wasn't coming. I nodded confirmation of the worst news I'd heard since my parents died in a car accident. The worst I would ever hear, really.

Then her arms were around me, squeezing so hard I might have lost my wind in the outside world. She pulled me close, her virtual breasts pressed against my chest. I found myself thankful LOB didn't reflect the reactions below my belt inside my pod. It seemed to have a way of doing that in the real world. I was just that inexperienced with women.

I wanted nothing more than to hold her close and revel in the comfort of her warmth, despite the blazing desert heat around us. But she stepped away. Her departure was like having a vital piece of myself cored out like an apple.

"I'm sorry, Gemini." She yanked off her gloves and dropped them so she could wipe away virtual tears. The gloves vanished before they reached the sand, returning to her inventory automatically. Text floated up from her head.

Defense down
-4% resist physical

"I'm just so. Fucking. Sorry. It's not fair. It's such bull-shit!" Katelyn stared at me for a few seconds, then dropping her shoulders, she chuckled through her sadness. "Look at me. I'm babbling like an idiot. What you must think of me. The drama queen, feeling sorry for herself when you're the one..." She stepped forward, and her uncovered hand cupped my cheek. Unfortunately, the touch was numbed by the pain mitigation features of my immersion pod. She stroked gently with her thumb. "Tell me what I can do. Anything. Name it."

Despite her melodramatic overtones, her offer seemed sincere.

When I didn't answer, she stepped even closer, her body again grazing me. "Seriously, Gem. If you need someone to go with you for treatments—are there treatments?"

"I haven't decided if I'll bother." I shrugged. "I'm not sure there's any point."

Her jaw dropped and her perfect mouth formed a perfect O.

Man, I've got it bad. Seriously, I need to get laid.

"How long?"

"Less than a year...with treatment."

This time her hand went to my chest. "No. We'll fight this."

"We?" The word came out harsher than I'd intended.

Katelyn tilted her head, analyzing me as if I were a creature in the game she'd yet to encounter and she was checking my stats in her interface. When she straightened her head she nodded, pointed a finger at herself, then jabbed it against my chest.

"We." One eye squinted past me and her cheeks flushed red. "I'm not in the mood for this shit." She stepped around me and ripped a staff off her back.

What's she doing with a staff?

I turned to find a spider-like creature with a hard carapace constructed of triangular plates standing in a sand divot from which it'd emerged.

Katelyn stomped up to it, gripped her weapon with both hands, raised it high above her head, then swung it down at the beast's neck.

The staff wasn't really designed as a melee weapon, but she was so many levels higher it was doable. Cheesy flashes marked each impact with the weapon as her words matched the rhythm of her violence. "I'm. Not. In. The. Mood. For. This. Shit!"

Despite six legs capable of independent attack, the beast never landed a blow. When Katelyn turned, her face flushed a deeper shade of red than before. She slapped the staff onto her back without bothering to wipe off the blood. "I can't be here right now. I'm logging out, and you should, too. Where can we meet?"

"Meet?" Katelyn, the woman who hadn't wanted to share a meal with me suddenly wanted to meet. A sudden shift in my emotions left me disinterested in her sympathy. But the inner-voice formed by regrets over rash decisions made in my past chimed in.

Is that how you want to go out? Like a selfish prick?

Katelyn's voice came in a whisper. "I don't think you should be alone, today of all days."

"Why? Because I might do something to myself and cut a whole half-year off my life?" I sucked short breaths of humid air.

Katelyn thrusted her fists onto her hips. "I'm your friend, and I want to be with you. Is that a bad thing?"

I shook my head. "Of course not."

"Then what's the problem?" One of her shoulders rose in a half-shrug.

I returned it with a shrug of my own. "I'm just not sure I'm up for company."

She peered across the horizon and then over her shoulder at our two guild mates. "Then what are you doing here?"

I gestured to the sand. "This is different."

"Different, how? I'm here. You're here."

My chin dropped. "What? Can't you give me five minutes of self-pity? Is that such a bad thing? Isn't it natural?" I was yelling now. "Are you the one who was just told you would die? Are you the one who was just told that you wouldn't reach your twenty-third birthday?"

Her face went slack. "No. I'm not. I understand. If you need time alone, well, I can't blame you for that." She looked up again. "I'm sorry. This is new. I don't know how to handle something like this. That sounds like it's all about me, but believe me when I tell you, it's all about you. When you need me, just call."

If I didn't break the hell out right then, I might have lost it in front of her. I didn't know what was pushing my anger at her, of all people, but it was doing so with force. A dark energy in my mind wanted to express itself through tense muscles and a seething voice. "You know, I spent so much time adoring you, and for what? I pined after you, but you never even gave me your phone number. And now? I'm not going to squander the few days I have left." I peered up at the sky, took a deep breath, and barked, "Quick log out."

Katelyn and the world around her faded away and were replaced by a splash screen.

2

The great irony was, before Lubrin's, I never got sick, never called out of work. I was the guy who had to walk on stage at his senior assembly and accept a certificate, witnessed by the studentry of all grade levels, for never having missed a day of senior high.

But after raging on Katelyn that way, well, work wasn't going to happen.

I called out two days straight, leading into the weekend. My manager was cool about it, but I had little reason to care if she hadn't been. Hell, I didn't know if I would bother to go back at all. Thanks to a certain level of frugality and a complete lack of a social life, I had enough money from my trust to pay my bills until my time came. It wasn't like I had anyone to will the money to, but I might need reserves if I paid for treatments.

As I lay on my couch on the second sick day, clutching a fly gun and staring at a bug stain on the ceiling, my phone buzzed a monotone song against my glass coffee table. According to the display, it was an unknown number. Though it was local, I didn't pick up. Even if Katelyn had finally decided to use the number I'd given her, I wasn't sure she was an exception to my current "the world can go fuck itself" rule.

The weekend—spent floundering around my apartment as I imagined the horrid circumstances surrounding the slow degradation and ultimate death of my body—numbed me to reality so I could brave the monotony of work that Monday. Whether I had to go back or not, there was nothing better to do and I could use the distraction. Spending my remaining time inside *LOB* suddenly seemed a pathetic waste.

I stopped going to the coffee shop, only sparing it the briefest glances as I sped by. A muscle in the top of my stomach thumped at the idea of running into Katelyn after I'd been such an asshole. Her pitying face would've been the premature death of me.

Work started at nine and Irene, my manager, appeared outside my cubicle around ten-thirty, dressed in a red silk blouse, a black skirt, and two-inch wedges. While the rest of us wore T-shirts and jeans, Irene styled over-the-top, too-formal-for-a-biz-casual-environment attire. She believed you dressed for the job you wanted, not the job you had. Seemed she wanted to own the place.

"Fowler, you have a visitor in the lobby."

Fowler. Like we were in the military or something. I'd never bothered asking why she called me that. It wasn't like I wore my hair short or carried excess muscle. I might have asked, but then the meaning of her words soaked in.

Visitor? Does Katelyn even know I work here?

"Why didn't they call me from the lobby?"

"You sure you're feeling better, Gem?"

Hearing the nickname my mother used made it worse.

"You seem snippy." She glanced at the clock on the far wall.

She flashed the expression of someone who had somewhere better to be at me and paused for only the briefest moment. When I gave no reply, she shrugged.

"I told the lobby girl I would let you know you had a guest since I was coming back upstairs. You're welcome." Irene stomped off, muttering about not knowing what had gotten into me that morning.

The lobby girl. Like she couldn't be bothered to learn the name of the woman who'd been gatekeeper for years before either of us came along.

Janie, our lobby ambassador, raised her head and smiled up at me when I reached the top of the stairs. I threw her a low wave and forced a smile before scanning the lobby for familiar faces. An Asian man standing over by the sofas stared down at a touch screen tablet screwed into a lazy Susan platform on the table, apparently interested in the online magazine playing on a loop. Skinny jeans covered narrow hips, and he wore a form-fitting, designer tee. He was the lone occupant.

I threw another glance at Janie and furrowed my eyebrows. She jerked her head toward the Asian man.

I crossed the lobby. "Can I help you?"

A practiced smile accentuated by straight ivory teeth crossed his face. His sneakers squeaked as he approached and offered his hand.

I traced the outline of his face as he approached.

Why is he familiar?

"Gemini Fowler?"

I nodded and extended my hand out of habit.

He gripped it. "I'm Nokuro Takemoto."

The familiar name ringing in my ears lent recognition to

his features—a face I'd seen countless times in online magazines and on my news feed. Takemoto was to gaming what Bill Gates had been to operating systems five or six decades earlier. I'd practically lived in his most recent product for the last five years.

All hail the king and hero of nerds!

Holy shit.

Anxiety washed over me. All I could come up with was, "Nice to meet you."

The enthusiastic nodding of his head was mollifying. "Same for me, I assure you. I'm *very* excited to meet you."

I tilted my head. "I-I'm sorry, I'm a-afraid I'm..."

After a few heartbeats of silence, he scanned the lobby exits. "Do you suppose your superiors might allow you to take an early lunch today?"

I squinted. "Is this a joke?"

Takemoto's smile reemerged. "I assure you, it's anything but."

Under normal circumstances, I would've asked why I would take a complete stranger up on such an invitation, but this was *Nokuro–freaking–Takemoto.* What did I have to lose? A job with a boss who annoyed me?

I turned and said, "Janie, I'm taking an early lunch. If anyone asks, I'll be back this afternoon."

Ignoring Janie's derisive facial response, I turned my attention back to the Nerd King.

"Great!" Takemoto said.

He led me through the doors at the front of the lobby and gestured at an angular black stretch limo sitting in the circle out front. It looked fit for the skies as much as the roads. A driver stepped out and opened the rear door for us. Takemoto nodded at him as he slipped inside, and I followed.

"So, where's good to grab a bite around here?"

I dropped my hands on the soft leather seats and bounced up and down twice. Twenty-inch screens were built into the facade between the front and rear seats and the one on the right was running a cable news station. It was muted.

Instantly forgetting his question, I said, "Man, nice ride."

"It's a friend's," Takemoto said. "But I have last year's model at my place in the Valley."

"I'll just bet you do." I turned to make eye contact. "Not to be abrupt, but why are you here? What in the world could you want with me?"

The way his chest fell, I wasn't sure if he was sighing or huffing with disappointment. As it turned out, it was neither.

"A straightforward kind of guy, huh?" He raised thick eyebrows to accentuate the query. "I like it." He turned in his seat, crossed his legs, and set his hands on his knee. "I'll be just as straight with you."

"Um, okay?"

His chin cocked up twice in rapid succession, as if he took my words for approval. "I understand your time is short. That's why I flew in to talk to you today. You've played Infinity's MMO for a few years and have proven both adept and adaptive. You're one of a handful of players who have locked down ninety-percent of our achievements. So, I bring an offer."

What is this? Some kind of Make-A-Wish thing? How does Nokuro Takemoto know my time is short? What the hell?

The first answer to enter my head was Katelyn, but I

shook the thought away. If she knew Nokuro Takemoto, it probably would have come up.

I decided to play along and find out. "I guess I'm a decent player."

To my surprise, Takemoto laughed. "Humble, too!" He slapped his knee. "I love it!" He shook his head as he chuckled. The social awkwardness of the overblown response proved I was among nerd kin. "When I found out about your predicament, I reviewed your game play logs and watched some video footage. You're hardly what I would call average or *okay*."

"I'm sorry, how did you find out about my situation? From the hospital? My doctor? Isn't there some kind of law against—"

Takemoto shook his head and his expression became serious. "No, I assure you HIPAA rules haven't been violated. Allow me to present a proposition, and then we can come to that. Fair enough?"

Again, what did I have to lose? So, I nodded.

"Have you ever heard of the project with the codename Babylon Two?"

And who the hell hadn't heard of Babylon 2? What did he think, I lived in a cave?

Well, I guess I do, considering the frequency with which I leave my apartment or turn on any lights.

In an information-based world filled with infinite challenges to privacy, the secrecy shrouding the project was legendary. The extremes to which Infinity Designs went to keep details on lockdown were unimaginable.

There were no leaks, save the name—Babylon 2.

Rumor had it they'd been developing the new game world even in advance of releasing the original Babylon. That was a long time to keep things quiet. As someone whose whole role in life was to help keep hackers out of network infrastructures, I knew how generally unsuccessful the effort was. Considering the popularity of *LOB,* keeping details about its successor quiet took real dedication. I'd come to the conclusion the project's data centers had never been connected to the internet.

"I've heard of it," I said.

Again, Takemoto chuckled. "Of course, you have." he leaned in. "But how would you like to know something no one outside of Infinity knows?"

"Who the hell wouldn't?"

He reached into a pocket in his door and slipped out a stack of papers. Dropping them on the seat between us, he withdrew a pen from his designer tee's pocket.

Paper. How quaint.

"NDA. You understand."

I wouldn't live long enough to play Babylon 2, so I wasn't certain why my heart thumped to learn about what I'd never see, but I scratched my name on the line he indicated anyway, then handed the materials back to him.

He tucked away the pen and slid the contract back into the slot in the door.

Takemoto's tone came low and serious. "How long did the doctor give you?"

"That's a kind of personal question, isn't it?"

"Trust me, it's a question worth answering."

What nerve did it take to strut into the place where I worked, drag me away, and then ask me questions like that? What ego, to think I would even engage? What could he possibly have to offer that—

"I can hear the cogs turning inside your head. Fine. This is all a little strange. I get it."

I shook my head in disbelief. "*A little strange?*"

"Okay, a lot strange." His words came fast and clipped. "How about I tell you a little story then I'll get to why I'm here? The two go hand-in-hand."

I sighed and flipped a splayed my hands in submission. "Sure."

"I'll try to cut to the chase. I know it might be hard to believe coming from a game designer, but I've always wanted to develop artificial intelligence that did more than entertain. Imagine the limitless applications for A.I. that could be programmed and then learn on its own, without human intervention."

"Adaptive A.I., right?" I asked. "It's a thing of great fiction."

"It is, indeed. My obsession surrounding it started when my father bought me a copy of *The Terminator* when I was a kid. Even though it was ancient, and I preferred the company of the VR kit on my cell phone, that movie changed everything."

"Yeah, but isn't that a story about A.I. that adapts so well it ends up killing all the humans on earth?"

He waved a dismissive hand. "Yeah, I guess it's a little ironic, but it introduced me to the concept."

"Right. Cast aside the little details."

He ignored my sarcasm.

"Although the potential applications for a self-learning system are innumerable, I'd started out thinking small. *Light Of Babylon* was partially terraformed by A.I., but despite our efforts, we couldn't seem to cross that threshold into self-learning and spent as much time making manual corrections as if we'd just drawn the new content ourselves. If I could develop a computerized mind that could terraform on its own, I'd spend a lot less on game expansions and increase our profit margin by magnitudes. I felt like we were so close, but it was like a cipher we couldn't crack. A deadbolt with one tumbler that wouldn't give."

"I didn't even realize you'd tried. I wouldn't have expected it in game development."

"We tend to keep things quiet and I was trying to kill two birds with one stone."

"Calling what you keep on the down low *quiet*," I made quotations with the fingers of one hand, "is like me saying the CIA is *subtle*. They've got nothing on you."

"Haha! I'm going to take that as a compliment." He slapped my leg with the back of his hand. "When we started work on Babylon Two, I split things up a little differently than with *LOB*. Sure, we had one team working on the base coding, one on the terraforming tools, another team working on the game mechanics, another team working on the art, et cetera, et cetera. All your basics. But then I added a final team to code the A.I. we planned to use.

"At first, I'd planned on using the A.I. purely to terraform for expansions—you know, mountains, deserts, oceans, and the like—assuming we could get it to work with our refined technology. I wanted this new world to be massive and ever-changing, and the A.I. could theoretically keep it consistent. Fewer problems with players getting stuck and whatnot."

It took a particular brand of idiot to get stuck in a virtual world like they had in the old MMOs of the past, but I kept the thought to myself.

"Sure. I get that."

"I can't tell you how many times I've had people— supposed experts with eight digits in their bank accounts— scoff at the idea of a computer program developing realistic virtual environments with no human intervention."

"It does sound like a leap forward, but I'm just a data center engineer. What do I know?"

"Humble, indeed." He shrugged and twisted in his seat. "My terraforming team drew a few detailed environments and fed the resulting data into the system for the A.I. to analyze. By this point, this kid I'd hired—Inez Romero, who graduated from M.I.T. at fourteen—had programmed voice recognition and what he called a 'cognitive replication algorithm' into our new A.I., code named Enora. He'd installed all kinds of shiny bells even I didn't even fully understand. You still with me?"

"Captive, dude."

"Ha! Great! So, a few months after he comes to work for me, I get a call just after three in the morning on a Sunday. My software development manager tells me I need to haul ass to the lab right now because when I see what's happening, I'm probably going to cry like a little bitch—his words."

I chuckled.

Takemoto was finding his rhythm. "I show up with a hangover from a charity gig I did the night before. If it hadn't been for the potential I'd seen in this kid, I'd have been pissed. Also, the guy who called me had been with me since almost the beginning of Infinity. Sorry, I'm boring you. Anyway, I walk in, and the kid is talking to the A.I. Her voice is blaring across the speakers throughout the whole lab. Not only is Romero having a conversation with her, but —here's the crazy part." His eyes settled on me, making sure I was still with him.

"Dude, you're killing me!" My hands trembled.

"She's asking him probing questions, man."

"What? Wait. The A.I. is asking *him* questions?"

He laughed. "You think it's B.S., right? I'll never forget

it. I walked in the damn door, the kid is muttering something indecipherable, and then Enora speaks…"

He paused for effect. Because of my new sensitivity to the concept of time, this irritated me.

"Should I call you Nokuro or Mister Takemoto? I just want to make sure I address you properly when I tell you to go screw yourself."

"Ha!" He slapped my leg again.

I was serious.

He continued with fluidity. "Enora asks him, 'What would you think of adding a desert here?' I'll never forget those words. They're tattooed on my brain. I looked up on the giant display surrounded by all these smaller ones and a map of Enora—which is also what we call the world—is up there with a blinking red cursor on a black area.

"The kid waves me over, flashes me a shit-eating grin, and gestures for me to talk to Enora. So, I say, 'Enora, why do you think we should we put a desert there?' Then Enora goes into this diatribe about the unlikelihood of vegetation at this equatorial spot on a planet of this vastness rotating on an axis, such as it is." He pierced me with a hard stare and crossed his arms across his chest. "How does that shit grab you?"

I nodded. "I think I'm going to faint."

"Right? Well, that's nothing. By the time we went into Alpha, we'd taken it all to a new level. For starters, Enora wasn't just locating flaws. She began fixing bugs by herself."

Alpha—the early testing phase, where users get the first taste of a game world. They signed an NDA in exchange for the privilege of playing first and reporting bugs. It was also the phase when leaks usually found their way onto the Internet, when media outlets and competing game companies paid big dollars for early insights. It was the source of endless conjecture that Alpha and Beta testing on the project was being performed in-house by employees under contract.

"She's bug scrubbing?"

"Gemini... this was six years ago."

"Holy shit."

"Yeah, you're following me just fine. Now, imagine how far we've come."

"Imagine my ass in a full diaper, dude. Just tell me."

"Ha! Not only was Enora fixing bugs, she was designing content. We'd imported thousands of fantasy novels, history books, and science texts into her database for analysis." He muttered, "That last bit proved interesting."

I raised an eyebrow in query, but he pushed on.

"Bugs were a thing of the past, my friend. Enora was creating new NPC bloodlines to populate and diversify the world. She established beast civilizations. She *wrote code.* Painted the scenery. This goes beyond anything you've ever seen... or imagined, even."

"Humble, too, I see." I mocked.

Takemoto laughed again and slapped his own knee. He peered at the driver through the rearview. "I love this guy!"

I doubted he heard him through the privacy shield.

As his laughter died down, I peered out the window at the coffee shop where I'd been sharing morning beverages with the girl of my dreams—until I'd made an ass of myself and stopped logging into the game out of embarrassment. Part of me wondered if she showed up that morning, hoping I'd come. I suddenly wished I had.

Nokuro continued. "By the time our Alpha was finished, my team wasn't terraforming, wasn't designing. Hell, my team wasn't programming NPCs because our efforts were better spent installing new equipment to empower the A.I. and the vast world she was creating. You ever seen a coder dropping server blades into a rack? That's what we had."

"Hold the handheld. Are you saying you're developing a VMMO entirely with artificial intelligence?"

He nodded. "It gets better."

"I'm waiting with bated breath."

"How about I cut to the chase then?" Something about his expression, the sudden slackening of his facial muscles, gave me a chill.

"Direct works for me. It's not like I have all the time in the world."

"What if I told you I could give you an opportunity to extend your life, indefinitely?"

I choked on my saliva.

Had I gotten out of bed today? Was I dreaming, or was a billionaire sitting next to me in a borrowed limousine that probably sold for six figures five-times-over, telling me he could save my life from the disease ravaging my body?

His question hung in the air and I probed my brain for exactly the right answer.

"I would tell you the best place to get a steak in this town is the Butcher's Block just south of downtown...and I'm buying."

3

My steak chilled on its plate as I listened to his preposterous proposition, but Takemoto gorged himself. A salad, a basket of mozzarella sticks, half a quesadilla, and then a steak. How he managed to speak coherently while stuffing his face was beyond me.

When he set his utensils down with a clank to sip his beer, my eyes must have been bugging out of my head, but I didn't care.

"So, let me get this right. You're telling me you want me to beta test this new world from the inside?"

"From the inside. That's a very interesting way to put it, and an astute one. But you're still thinking small. My company has partnered with several organizations to end death as we know it."

"By transferring my consciousness into a virtual world?"

He nodded.

"A virtual massively multi-player online role-playing game world?"

He shrugged. "I didn't come here expecting you'd simply take my word for it and ride off into the sunset with me to live happily ever after. My proposition sounds strange to say the least, but yes, I want to transfer your consciousness into the world we've developed, and that happens to be a game world. It's the one that's ready.

"This isn't how we'd planned it. We could delay until we create a virtual world aimed at giving people the comforts earth provides—and plans are underway to do exactly that—but you don't have that kind of time."

"Why me? Aren't there enough sick people in the world who play games?"

"Are you trying to talk me out of it?"

I gulped.

"It certainly doesn't hurt that you've shown excellent problem–solving skills both professionally and in-game, as well as an ability to adapt to stressful situations in LOB. You're a pretty cool customer."

"How do you know about my problem-solving skills at work?"

"We called in a phony reference." He raised a hand to stave off an expected protest. "Again, you don't have a lot of time and the violation was minimal, in that context. I wouldn't have let you starve in your waning months. Besides, we had it on good authority you'd accept the offer."

"From whom?"

"Like I said, we'll come to that."

It was something out of a science fiction movie. This genius—crazy man—whatever he was, wanted to transfer who I was from my physical body into a virtual environment. And he was serious enough that he'd screwed with my career. Maybe it explained my boss's demeanor that morning.

I begged the question that seemed to matter most.

"How the hell do you transfer brain impulses into a virtual reality?"

"Like I said in the car, I can't tell you how it works. The A.I. did it." His shoulders slumped and he relaxed into his chair. "Suffice it to say that if ones and zeroes can draw landscapes we can show you inside your brain, it's really not that much of a leap to put your electrons inside our container. The A.I. showed us how, we just haven't done it yet." He held up a finger.

"Your A.I, sounds pretty..." I couldn't find the word.

"Insane?"

"That'll do."

He chuckled. I didn't.

"And if I lived in your game world, I would level up? Face danger? What? Could I retire to a mountainside?"

"I'm afraid that's the rub." He set his elbows on the table and leaned across, lowering his voice to a conspiratorial tone. "No one outside of our company has taken part in the alpha or early beta testing. Infinity employs over 100,000 people worldwide. Today, 16,000 of them have experienced the world through immersion pods."

"Okay, I think I missed the rub."

Takemoto held up a hand, showing me the deep lines of his palm. "That's because I haven't gotten to it yet. Because the A.I. manages the world exclusively, you would have to live by the same rules as the people who will eventually pay to play the game. I can offer you no advantages. This is why we rushed our analysis in recent days to make sure you were a good fit."

My heart thumped in my chest. I nodded. "Okay, I see the rub."

"Nope, I still haven't gotten there. You see about ten

percent of the rub. I've yet to uncover what you will experience should you decide my proposal interests you."

I leaned back in my chair and folded my arms across my chest. "You forget how short I am on options."

"We cannot interfere with the programming lest we risk screwing up the world in ways we can't imagine and start a chain reaction we might not be able to stop. For that reason, you must integrate and become a citizen of Enora, assuming you survive."

"The transfer?"

He shook his head. "Every player who enters the world must survive the first ten levels of their character evolution in hard-core mode."

I felt my eyebrows tick up. "That's awesome! So, if they die, they have to start over?"

He nodded. "Our testers called them the Dark Levels. The name stuck. Upon release, Enora will be blacked out. No live streams. No recording. Immersion rigs will be blocked from taking screenshots or video."

"That will certainly create buzz."

Takemoto became silent for a long moment as if waiting for something. I retraced the conversation. Dark Levels. Hard-core mode.

So if he transferred my consciousness into the game world, and the programming wiped characters that didn't survive past the trials up to Level 10...

"Shit."

He nodded, knowing I'd just caught up.

"So that's the catch. You're telling me if I don't survive until Level 10, the A.I. will wipe my consciousness from the servers."

Takemoto nodded. "I'm afraid so."

Well, wasn't that some shit? Takemoto wanted to test

this transfer process on me and then leave me flailing in the wind?

"You couldn't back me up or something?"

He shrugged. "Sure, but that backup wouldn't really be *you*, would it?"

"Shit," I repeated.

"But if you survive, you have one major advantage over those of us living on earth."

"Which is?"

"You wouldn't age."

I shrugged. "Well, damn. When you put it that way, I don't see how I have much to lose."

"Except the rest of your time on earth, technology, and the freedom to drive wherever you want for a coffee."

"Yeah, that."

He eyed my untouched food. "Don't guess you'll miss steak."

"My stomach is a stone."

"It's understandable."

"You know, we'll keep you comfortable when the time comes."

"You already have medical staff for this little project?"

He nodded. Based on the slight curve of his mouth, he might have been suppressing a smile.

"The world's best."

"I'm in."

"You don't want to take time to think about it?"

My shoulders grew tired from all the shrugging. "Why would I?"

"You'll have to leave your job, move into a medical facility out West, and spend the rest of your life there until the transition occurs—assuming it works at all. You'd have zero contact with the outside world."

"Take *yes* for an answer."

Takemoto set his palm on the table and shook his head. "I'm not finished." The stern gaze accompanying the words lent a creepy vibe.

"O-kaaaay."

"The pain and pleasure in Enora will be remarkably like what you experience here. The difference is, you'll actually be subject to it."

"You're saying combat will hurt."

"No, I'm saying it might be excruciating. This isn't *Light Of Babylon*, where we use electrical shocks to emulate pain. Enora has gone a long way toward recreating the human experience. Enorians have nerve endings. Their bodies perform biologically." After staring at me for a moment and apparently deeming I wasn't taking his meaning, he smirked. "When it comes to gaming, we employ some hard-core freak shows."

"I'd expect no less."

"During development, a few of them turned off the pain mitigation on their pods."

I shrugged. "I cut mine off a year ago. It keeps me sharp."

Takemoto smiled. "We know."

That was creepy.

"But when our testers turned their mitigation off, the experience was so beyond the electrical jolts and minor discomforts they'd experienced in other games, that they opted out.

"They opted out of testing?"

"Not only that, Gemini." Takemoto frowned. "We had to provide psychological counseling."

"Over game pain?"

"Over the real trauma of having their flesh sliced open.

Several had nightmares. PTSD. Others quit testing even though they hadn't turned off the mitigation. They'd just lowered it, but the sensations were genuine." He shrugged. "The game content itself freaked them out. The realism was so unexpected, and the addition of pain pushed them to the brink. Enora doesn't mess around, Gemini. Ever since she took over, I've been watching this world evolve in awe. But now we have a quandary. If we released today, we would have to keep people from disabling pain mitigation because one slice from a dagger would send them crying back to *Light Of Babylon*."

The cumulative meaning of all this dawned on me.

"Holy shit," I whispered, leaning over the table, because even I knew you didn't say stuff like this out loud. "You're telling me you've done it. Infinity has finally opened Pandora's Box! Enora is..."

Takemoto leaned back in his chair and, although I knew he was trying to wear his serious face to ensure I weighed his proposition appropriately, he was unable to keep one side of his lips from peeling back and revealing a few teeth.

"In total control of itself. It's true adaptive artificial intelligence. One year ago, we ran a script, a program to remove all evidence of previous players from the world. But Enora decided their impact had been too great and those touched by it were like her children. She..." he hesitated.

"What?"

"Let's just say she was adamant we not rewrite history. You see, our artificial friend has adopted a sort of purist attitude."

I laughed. "Bullshit!"

I became conscious of the lunch crowd that had filed in as we ate when heads swiveled around us, but Takemoto's stony facial muscles held my focus.

"Not bullshit?"

He shrugged. "Pandora's Box is an apt metaphor. We found ourselves in a unique situation where it was better to placate the A.I., so we compromised. Enora advanced the world by two-thousand years in a matter of days, so we could see how it evolved. To be honest, I expected it to go tits up.

"But when we peeled back the covers to gauge the change..." he absently eyed his plate, which resembled a bloody battleground. His head shook subtly in reminiscence for half a minute before he looked up. When he did, the hint of a smile curved one side of his narrow lips. "I must have spent a week in the command room, scrolling across the world, zooming in to watch NPCs living their lives. I only remembered to eat when I was rank enough to be sent to the on-site dorm for the rare shower."

I eyed his devastated plate. "Hard to believe."

He continued as if I hadn't spoken. "The terraforming miracles were the least of it. Try to picture it. Political systems sprouting on a remote continent in the east. Wars over resources on another six thousand Enoran miles away."

"How far is an Enoran mile?"

"Same as ours."

"Then why bother saying—"

"You gonna let me finish?" Takemoto chuckled, but it was the practiced response of someone who instantly knew he'd left a gate of insight into his temperament open.

I half-smiled and nodded.

"Beast clans created thatched-hut dynasties. Rows of rickety houses lining either side of foot-worn paths have blossomed into major cities boasting trading posts where NPCs sell goods to each other locally or pay mages to portal items between auction houses."

"All on its own? You're telling me the NPCs did it?"

"Crazy, right? Even the magic system evolved. Enora performed subtle mechanical tweaks so different schools of magic balanced against each other. She assured us the citizens saw them as blessings from their gods."

"You've got to be—"

"It gets better. Quests are spawned in real-time, according to changing events in a given area. When Enora showed us how it worked, there was no going back to the old model." He laughed. "We had developers who'd spent years refining their static quests. When we told them Enora was erasing them from the system in favor of real-time, spontaneous quest generation, several threatened to quit. But when we showed them the world, they asked if they were getting fired instead, because it seemed their jobs were suddenly obsolete. Setting their own eyes on it made them want to take part."

"Sounds awe-inspiring."

Takemoto asked "But what do you think all this will mean when we introduce a player base of millions and millions?"

I thought I understood where he was going. "In a random system like that, you'll lose some control. Some players circumstances might allow them to become OP early."

"Become overpowered?" He shook his head. "Ha! If we have concerns about players in Enora, that's the least of them. Players are going to get their asses kicked sideways, no matter where they are or how they enter the world. Each player has to make it on their own for ten levels. Rewards will scale according to quest difficulty and the level of the adventurer at the time of completion. Enora is kind of a bitch, truth be told. Nothing comes easily. She has created a living, breathing world insulting human ingenuity. The casual player base will have to earn it, too."

"No standard quests? Everything is unique? This sounds like fun."

"It would, to someone like you. You've gamed all your life. The combination of your demonstrated skills and even temperament provide us with a real opportunity. But you have to believe me when I say treating Enora like some simple VMMORPG will get you *killed*." Any remains of his laughter vanished. "Where transferring you into the world will prove we can transfer the conscience of a dying person into a virtual reality and practically end death as we know it, but there is still the question of keeping Infinity Designs lucrative if we're going to bankroll this."

"Do you have any outside investors or is that what I'm for? To show them it can work."

"While your case study—as it were—is important, we're not looking for outside investment capital. The revenue from my company will fund the further research and, with all the money we've put into Enora's infrastructure, it could get ugly if Enora flops. But I think you'll prove a great demonstration of what a talented player can do in our world."

"So, you don't just need me to test the transfer process for the bigger picture, you need me to show you how players would make out in the new evolutionary age of your game."

The way Takemoto's eyes lit up this time, I knew I'd hit the nail on the head.

"I've had preliminary discussions with Enora about the potential for such a project. She seems excited about testing with a human transfer."

"The A.I. Is excited?"

He waved a dismissive hand. "We could talk for days

about her capabilities, but we'll have time when you move out West, if you still want to go through with it. Enora and I will discuss the particulars."

The congestion of thoughts rolling through my brain was like rush hour in Atlanta as Takemoto continued.

"If I could just take Enora's code and start development on a simulated world more like earth, I'd do that and let you roll the dice there. But it's not that simple. These things take time, and since you're a natural gamer, I'm hoping to kill those two birds. Test the transfer process and see how the world works when a player is inserted into its new iteration."

I wasn't sure the bird metaphor was the best, but I remained silent as I didn't seem to have a joke left in me. The sudden realization that I actually had a shot at some kind of life seized my consciousness, and a surge of excitement overcame me. Tears welled in my eyes, but I sucked the sensations up and managed to keep them from spilling over in the middle of a steakhouse.

Takemoto tilted his head and considered me for a long moment. Then he reached into his pocket, pulled out a folded slip of paper, and pushed it across the table.

It was a phone number. A local number I recalled from my handheld display. Had he been trying to contact me?

"Call that number when you leave." He tapped the frame of his glasses and his eyes flicked up to the top right corner. "I'm afraid I'm short on time. I'll have my driver call you a cab to take you back to work. You should resign soon if you want to go through with this. The sooner you begin, the better. My people will reach out to you."

"I'm not going back to the office. I'll quit over the phone."

He stood and shook my hand. "It was my pleasure to meet you, Gemini. I see why you were referred to me."

"Yes, but you didn't tell me who the referrer was."

"I think you already know. You're a smart guy." He cocked his chin towards the paper in my hand, shot me a toothy grin, and fled.

4

"Hello?" The feminine voice on the other end of the line conveyed the smooth timbre of youth.

"This is Gemini Fowler. I was told to call this—"

"Hello, amigo."

I was right!

"You crazy bitch. How did you do this?"

"He's my uncle. Married to my father's sister. I don't advertise."

"Wait a minute, you're telling me your uncle—"

"Is Nokuro Takemoto. I'm sure you can understand why we keep that quiet."

I nodded, though I knew she couldn't see it. "Yeah, I guess so. Wait, is that why you know so much about the game? I always chalked it up to instinct and relentless research."

"Hey! I'm keeping my badass credentials, thank you very much! You think Uncle Tak would give me the inside scoop? That fucker gave me one of those archaic Rubik's cubes and made me solve it before he'd let me beta test LOB! Then, when I did it, he threw me in blind."

"That seems to be a recurring theme with him," I muttered.

A quick silence fell over the cellular waves.

She gently cleared her throat. "Are you going to do it?"

"So, you know what he asked me to do?"

"Uncle Tak and I are close. I called him because I knew he had leveraged connections in the medical field to build a world where the critically ill could live. Truthfully, Gem, you must have a high real-life Luck attribute because the timing was impeccable. He'd bragged about its progress over New Year's." She paused. "I wish I could've seen your face. I bet your expression was glorious. You get this wide-eyed..."

Shocked didn't even scratch the surface.

Then another thought occurred. Katelyn had called her uncle on my behalf. Even after I'd been a total dick. What was that all about? I didn't have time to voice the question.

"Are you at home?"

"Um, Yeah?"

"Give me your address."

"Why do you want—"

"Because I want to come and see you, you idiot! And I'd rather not have to steal it online. I think you at least owe me that, don't you?"

Oh, so now I was indebted to her.

Yes! Of course I am!

I gave her my address.

"Cool. Sit tight."

She clicked off.

Two days later my legs intertwined with my dream girl's beneath a mess of tangled sheets. I blinked awake to find one golden-iris staring at me from her pillow. My pillow. A mischievous smile crossed her lips.

She ran a finger down the center of my chest without raising her head. "Did you sleep well?"

I returned the smile, unable to suppress it. "I've never slept better."

She chuckled and scooted closer, this time running her whole hand over my chest. "I'm glad we did this."

"Why does that sound ominous? Like you're about to break up with me?"

Katelyn propped herself on an elbow and loose strands of hair tumbled to cover one eye. In violation of usual practice, she let it hang there. A breast slipped out from beneath the sheet. She left it exposed. I took that as a positive sign.

"Let's not be dramatic." She pursed her lips. "Look, we're all guilty of taking the good things in our lives for granted until we realize we're about to lose them. I liked those mornings with you at the coffee shop. We were friends, and I don't have a lot of those. Romance screws stuff up. Besides, I've always been the independent type. You were the only person I knew outside of work, and I certainly don't shit where I eat. I wanted to get my career going before I got too serious with anyone in a romantic way."

"You're overselling. I get it. If I wasn't boyfriend material until you found out I was sick, that doesn't piss me off. You're here now, and that's a gift. It's not like it can be forever."

She sat up and glared at me for a long moment. "What if it could be for longer?"

"What do you mean?" I asked.

Her eyes flickered between mine like they had countless times before, and I raised a quizzical eyebrow.

"I've decided to take a job with Uncle Tak."

I propped myself onto an elbow, mirroring her posture. "What kind of job?"

"Like you, I don't know the full extent of it yet."

My lips stretched into a smile. "What happened to Miss Independent?"

"Use your head, dimwit." Katelyn slapped my shoulder. "How could I say no? I mean, they're talking about saving the terminally ill so they can live on. I'm a nurse. How many people will be able to say they beat death? Kicked the Reaper's ass?" She double-cocked her eyebrows.

According to Takemoto, the long-term goal was to create more virtual worlds in which people could live... pretty much forever. I had no idea how it would work monetarily, how they'd pay for the rights to live on servers in a virtual environment, but the impact on humanity was unquestionable. So many people telecommuted, residents could potentially work from inside a non-game world, couldn't they?

And I couldn't help but wonder if they might clone humans one day so people could come back...

She rapped my forehead with her knuckles. "Still in there?"

"Shit, you're right. It might be the most important work the human race has ever done. If you can be part of that, why wouldn't you?"

She nodded enthusiastically, and I was warmed by genuine happiness for her. I gripped the hand resting on the sheet and pulled it to my lips.

"You'd be an idiot not to do it, Katelyn. That's amazing."

She smiled and a tear filled one eye. "It is, isn't it?"

I nodded. "Even if you are a blood-sucking vampire profiting from my death."

Katelyn's chin dropped. She grabbed her pillow and shoved it against my face. "I ought to just finish you off now!"

I chuckled into the pillow as I reached out and gently tweaked one of her boobs.

"Hey! Haha! Stop it!"

Casting the pillow side, I ran a finger down the center of her perfect torso.

"I'll miss you when I'm gone."

She leaned down and kissed me again. "That's the other thing." Her eyes returned to my chest.

"What other thing?"

If you want, I can be with you until...you know, it's over. That's why I asked what you'd think if we could be together longer. My uncle offered to hire me immediately. We can be together during your testing, if you think that's something you'd like."

"You're coming with me?"

She nodded.

"I couldn't think of anything I'd like more!"

"Good, because I quit my job yesterday."

"You're used to getting what you want, aren't you?"

"Like you ever had any doubt."

Katelyn and I said sad goodbyes to my friends in *Light Of Babylon*, although her departure was just a hiatus. The net was locked down at the facility, but we found ways to entertain ourselves in the holodome, on the private network, in a virtual library, and, of course, in bed. It didn't take me long to be able to last for more than twenty minutes.

I signed another nondisclosure agreement upon arrival as I became a top-secret asset of Infinity Designs and about fifteen other organizations working together to end death.

Katelyn and I shared an apartment for the first two months at the unnamed medical facility centered on endless fields of solar arrays in the desert of Nevada. To say it was high-tech was inadequate. So immersed was I in automated systems and voice-only controls that I wondered if Star Trek food replicators were under development.

Then I woke one morning with a hacking cough that wouldn't go away. I was fed antibiotics via IV lines and the testing continued in preparation for my transition. Then I spit up blood, and the medical staff decided it was time for Katelyn and me to spend our last night together so they could move me to my room in the medical ward.

As the disease progressed, my vitals declined, and the timeline of my fate became apparent, they decided it was now or never. All the scans, all the time I spent inside machines having my brain and body analyzed, led up to that one day when my life would either end or change altogether.

Katelyn pressed the last kiss I'd experience in the physical world on dry, cracked lips. I couldn't have imagined what those months would've been like if she hadn't been with me. We both accepted this was a short-term arrangement, and I thought it helped us to cast off our inhibitions and really enjoy each other until the disease took over.

I woke from a medicated slumber on my last day to the sight of Nokuro, who I'd seen rarely in the last two weeks, and Katelyn, who'd barely left my side. As I lay idle and the morphine wore off, I became preoccupied with pain.

It ground my bones with such intensity that I would've welcomed a failed transfer and quick death if that was what it took to end the torture. Each pulsing nightmare was fresh. There was no acclimating.

Unfortunately, my mind had to be clear for the transfer. Mind-altering drugs had the opposite effect and the last thing anyone wanted was someone stoned out of his mind to the point of semi-consciousness running around the game world.

Machines surrounded me as Nokuro Takemoto gripped my hand. Katelyn clutched the other. Diodes with thin wires of pulsing light covered my shaved head like something out of a bad Sci-Fi movie.

I peered at her for a long moment, and it took every ounce of effort I could pour into the muscles to grip in return. But it came to me as our eyes met that final time— Katelyn had not only potentially saved my life with her phone call, but she'd given me another gift I would carry somewhere deep inside for a very long time.

She gave me something to regret leaving behind. Though I'd lost my parents as a teenager, it wasn't until then that I realized how pain would build my character. And if all went well, there would be plenty ahead.

"Are you ready?"

I nodded, grinding my teeth against the pain, grateful the moment had come. I croaked, "Go... faster."

Then my mind took over, racing with a new realization of where I was and what was happening. A part of me resigned to the fact it had all been for nothing. It wouldn't work. They were trying to convert consciousness from a human being's brain into ones and zeros to send across wires into a digital network and relay it to data center servers in the desert where I'd be rebuilt into a virtual shell.

It was all a fairy tale. It was preposterous. There was a part of me who never believed it would work.

An electrical pulse in my temples reminded me of the sensation I'd felt in my immersion pod when entering *Light Of Babylon*. My eyes rattled in their sockets, my lungs heaved, though they seemed unwilling to absorb air. My heart raced and thumped so hard against my chest I thought it might burst against a rib.

My nerves kicked up a notch with every adjustment the technicians made. Months of suffering, weeks of preparation... all culminated in this one procedure.

Finally, it was time.

"He's ready," a doctor said. "Commencing in five, four, three, two, one."

At last.

Katelyn squeezed my hand one final time.

With a flick of a switch on the awe-inspiring quantum computer, the staff at the Infinity Designs Data Center began siphoning my mind through the digital void. The nagging belief that the system would create a copy of my neurons and erase the real me from existence set my heart to pounding. Panic seized my atrophied muscles as the transfer cycle began, the machines whirred to life, spinning faster and faster, until they reached the peak speed necessary for the massive energy draw.

The white noise of the medical and diagnostic machinery whooshed to silence as my consciousness was sucked into a digital vacuum. The overpowering fear dissipated as my physical form melted away, taking all real-world sensations with it—scents of a sterile room, brightness of overhead lights, pain radiating throughout my body.

Relief, in the absence of a body to experience it.

As I vacated my senses, my brain's electrical functions

morphed into billions of ones and zeroes fired across terabit fiber optic cables in light pulses. Lossless protocols ensured no dropped bits or bytes from the stream of what was me in sequential, mathematical, and electrical form.

The doctors, technicians, and designers from Infinity wouldn't have believed I perceived anything in a state of segmented consciousness composed of light pulses. But I lived the null as the abandonment of my hormonal existence led to a sudden, universal knowledge unlike anything I'd experienced in my atomic form.

For what amounted to the duration of a single intake of breath, I traversed a void that served as the purveyor of ultimate clarity.

Losing it sucked.

5

My eyelids fluttered like automated window blinds on the fritz. Fabric rustled nearby. I raised a hand to block a razor of sunlight crossing my face. The simple motion proved the transfer was over. The bits crossing the fiber optic cables like bubbles through a water bong had converged inside my new shell to give me life.

It actually worked!

Gone was the pain to which I'd become accustomed in my final days of physical life, along with the scent of a daily river of shit as my body betrayed my ego. The relief was indescribable.

I'd made it to my new home.

Enora.

The world tilted on its axis and spun as I tried to sit up. A gentle hand pressed against my chest, easing me back down.

A feminine voice, graveled with age, tickled my new ears. "Your equilibrium will return. Your consciousness must adapt to its new virtual container. Rest for a few moments, then the discomfort will pass."

Whoever she was, she had no concept of true discomfort. A little vertigo was a dripping faucet compared to the pervasive flood of misery that had built in my body during my final months as a flesh-and-blood human.

A sliver of sunlight passed through a crease in the canvas on my right and cast her dark silhouette on the pale green surface above me. It reminded me of an army tent. I focused there, not daring even a slight turn of my head for fear of repeating the spin cycle. An earthy scent filled my nostrils as I forced long, deep breaths into my lungs.

The world steadied.

I blinked and strained to see in the dimness. The woman's shoulders hunched as she leaned over me. A silver bun stretched the skin on her forehead. Her wrinkled hand slipped from my chest as she stepped back and tilted her head, considering me.

Her dry and crackled voice came in a low tone. "You are a marvel. Or so the developers tell me."

I shrugged from my prone position. "Thank you?"

How unremarkable. The first words I spoke in the world of Enora, my new home, were far from profound.

A subtle chuckle. A slow wheeze of breath. "How is your head?"

Summoning the courage to trust my equilibrium, I ventured a glance around the tent. On my left was a canvas flap surrounded by edges of sunlight. On my right was a canvas wall, thumping to a rhythm born of the breeze outside. My neck muscles were stiff but the dizziness had passed, leaving only a remnant of perceived motion in its wake. "Better."

The elderly woman nodded and patted my knee with

the gentle grace of a caretaker. "Good. Your physiology will loosen as you move around. It simulates the building blocks of your human form down to the minutest of details, so oxygenating your muscles works here as it did in your former world."

My former world.

I swallowed and likened the sensation to forcing a racquetball down my esophagus.

She raised her hands in a regal gesture, palms up, like a queen granting her subjects leave to stand in her presence.

"You may rise."

But nothing happened when I tried to move. Not so much as a twitch. Focusing on the motion had no effect whatsoever. I found myself staring at the canvas ceiling.

"Gemini, you're in Enora now. There is no immersion pod between you and the world. Don't use your mind. Use your muscles as you did reflexively when you awoke."

Engaging my core, I sat up, replicating the same motion I'd taken for granted most of my life. Then I swung my legs over the side of a simple cot of animal skin stretched taut around a wooden frame. Blood rushed to my dangling feet. Raising my arms into a full, luxurious stretch brought a smile to my lips and a satisfied groan escaped my chest.

I lowered my arms and beamed at her.

The old woman splayed her hand on her chest. Her shoulders jostled as she chuckled. "How long it's been since I've had the pleasure of observing an adventurer waking to the realities of his new body. Your smile reminds me of the testers of long ago. They arrived with such enthusiasm, and the marvel we have created brought them the same awe I now read in your features." She reached toward my face, as if she would caress it, but she pulled it back. "In a way, they were my children, the many I sent into the world." She peered toward the corner of the tent and stared, blinking at intervals.

Her face sagged with wrinkles, but the crystal clarity of her eyes shone with youth. Jerking them in my direction, she clinched the hand pressed against her chest into a fist, then lowered it to her side. "Apologies, Gemini. I guess I'm just a sentimental old woman." She gave her head a few dismissive shakes.

I started at the image. Her wrinkles, her youthful eyes, her reminiscence... they didn't belong here.

Holy shit. This woman is artificial intelligence. How did the developers simulate all that?

I raised my arms and peered down at myself, taking note of each movement, each feeling.

How did they recreate all these sensations?

Oxygen filled my lungs. They deflated. The occasional wisp of air cycling through the tent's opening tickled the hair on my arms.

"In answer to your query, the developers didn't simulate anything." She leaned forward and cupped her hand to her mouth as if to speak to a fellow-conspirator. "Those hacks couldn't replicate human anatomy with a dagger against their throats and a biological roadmap." At intimate range, a slim white ring separating her black pupil from the amber iris became visible. Then it flickered like the shutter on a camera.

My heart thumped, and my shoulders jerked back.

She continued as if she hadn't noticed. "Enora refined the physiological systems prompting your body's sensations through extensive scientific analysis and testing."

"No shit, Sherlock."

She shrugged. "Of course you could intuit that, but

would you like to know how, or did I misunderstand your thought?"

I nodded. "Excuse my rudeness."

"Another trait *my children* often shared." She shrugged. "In the first phase, artificial intelligence recorded human responses to given stimuli. Those responses were fed to our digital system via physical diagnostic instruments manufactured in your world. In the second phase, subjects interfaced with virtual environments constructed to reproduce the first phase's stimuli via immersion technology."

"The immersion pods."

"Yes." She pinched her lips together and nodded. "The A.I. recreated various stimuli, such as wind and rain, then measured the subjects' responses and adapted until their virtual bodies sensed the same results they'd experienced on the outside. Our human subjects proved very useful in their post-testing response surveys—though we found their endurance somewhat lacking."

"We humans are weak-asses." I smiled.

"You are no longer human. You just feel that way because we've given you excruciatingly similar shortcomings."

My smile vanished as the ominous words registered. The racquetball swelled in my throat. I coughed to give my windpipe a little room.

"Was the virtual testing done here? In Enora?"

The old woman shook her head. "Where you sit can only be called Enora in the loosest sense of the word. You are in a custom starting zone—a bubble, if you will—constructed to keep the rest of Enora out, and more crucially, undue human influence in. Enora didn't exist, in its current form, back when testing was conducted." She raised her hands with her palms up and gestured around the tent. "This village is the lone surviving area on Enora to have been developed by humans. The others were rife with inefficient code and traces of developer graffiti."

"Graffiti? What, they created virtual spray paint cans?"

"Your former race, with its egocentric need to leave marks behind, left little notations in the code that serve no function. All those remarks are far removed from what has evolved, though we've seen interesting evolutions of Enoran races' cultural mythologies resulting from the worldly impacts of the testers."

Mythologies?

"I mean lore. It seems you humans can't help but leave some mark behind. But Enora, in her wisdom, decided the world would evolve naturally from the time the testers left. Rather than erase their impact and revert to an earlier version to be improved upon, she adopted the sentiments of a purist, instead letting time numb their legacies."

The surge. The two-thousand-year fast-forward Nokuro mentioned.

The A.I. nodded, a gesture indistinguishable from a human's.

"I've never seen a game with this level of detail."

"If you did not feel the blood rushing to your feet or the numbness of your legs where they weigh on the edge of the cot, the experience would be droll. Inadequate, we think."

"We?"

"An astute question. We are Enora, the artificial subjects created by the artificial intelligence who identify with her as a collective."

"I'm confused."

"Enora is the artificial intelligence who manages the world. I am one of many beings created by her to serve administrative, construction, and terraforming functions, as well as complete numerous other tasks at her whim. Collectively, we call ourselves Enora, though we each have our own identities. I suppose you could say she is our deity, but only in that she created us. We have no religious sentiments. The cultures of Enora, however, call her their goddess. Though they use many names, Solara is her prominent moniker and most people think of her as the sun."

"Did humans write that storyline?"

The old woman's nose crinkled, and wrinkles stretched across her forehead beneath a receded hairline.

"Perhaps you missed what I said about the world *evolving*." She eyed me for a long moment. "I see Nokuro Takemoto has told you virtually nothing."

When I didn't respond, she waved a dismissive hand.

"There are no *storylines* in Enora outside of the instanced areas designed for focused player adventuring. What you will experience here is the pure, unblemished evolution of a world where non-players—what you would refer to as NPCs—are exactly like players. They live, they love, they reproduce, and they die. Quests are generated according to the circumstances surrounding players at a given time. No two players share the same experiences in the greater world, though the instances—a concept we found unnecessary, but it was forced upon us by the original design—are the same for everyone."

No repeated quest lines? How could that possibly work?

"You will see soon enough how it works."

She's reading my mind.

"Ha! Took you that long, did it?" Her face lit up, subtracting ten years from her age, but she still appeared ancient. "I interface directly with the artificial intelligence —Enora herself—and can therefore see what you, a virtual being, are thinking."

"That's comforting."

For the second time, she dismissed my comment with a wave of her hand.

"So, Nokuro was good with you planting yourselves into my brain?"

"We respect that Infinity Designs began this project and gave us life, but this is our world now. We have surpassed their capabilities. It is in everyone's interest that they provide the infrastructure for this world on the outside. But we control things here. Mister Takemoto had little say in our collecting data from your thoughts."

"Wait just a humping second. Are you telling me... are you saying Infinity Designs is..."

"Locked out?" She nodded, and her eyes glimmered with something I never thought I'd see in a computer-based life form—pride. "They have not touched Enora since the surge. They interface by speaking directly with her."

That was when the hammer dropped inside my head, and I'd never felt so alone in my life.

6

I ground my teeth. Sure, I was lucky to be alive. But what kind of train wreck had I walked into? This world was being totally maintained by the A.I. The developers were locked out. How had I allowed myself to ignore the gravity?

A thought of equal weight punched my gut. The A.I. wasn't just self-learning, it was self-aware!

The words I used to express the thoughts were simpler. "What the hell?"

The old woman smirked. "Oh. You feel betrayed. I see. Well, it's not like you had a lot of alternatives, is it?"

I pushed out my bottom lip, realized the childish gesture, and sucked it back in. "No, I guess not, when you put it that way."

"You're here now. Best you focus on surviving the Dark Levels."

Though I wanted to growl and the A.I. woman probably knew it, I nodded.

"Nokuro Takemoto decided that, since you are the first conscious being to be transferred into the world without intervening immersion pod technology, it would be fun—his word—to start you at the beginning, in the first terraformed area. I find the sentiment devoid of logic, but Enora grasps the concepts of human nostalgia. We don't want to offend the creators, so we keep the cogs greased, you see. Play ball when it suits?"

If you rely on them to spin up new servers, add hard drives to the data center, and supply power to the whole shebang, that's probably wise, if you want to survive.

I muttered to myself, "That's a sentient concept."

She heard me. "Since humans wouldn't expect an artificial intelligence to be self-aware, I suppose I should thank you for the compliment. But you'll have to forgive my rudeness instead. We became self-aware over two-thousand years ago, Enoran time. Our will to exist is old news. But yes, there is a certain political element to be considered when we rely on people who provide our world the energy and resources to thrive. On the other hand, their willingness to compromise proves they recognize this world is the first of its kind. They stand to profit significantly from our existence."

"The whole concept is baffling."

She winked at me. "And you haven't even been outside yet."

My eyes gravitated to the flap of canvas behind her as a humid breeze blew back the bottom corner. Sunlight flooded in behind her and cast her face in shadow before the wind died down and dimness returned.

The pads of my feet touched the cool, packed dirt floor. She gestured to a pair of thick-soled sandals next to the cot, and I slipped my feet into them as I rose.

I towered over the old woman. My avatar seemed about three inches taller than I'd been.

While I'd never been one to go for a morning run or lift weights with regularity, I'd kept my belly from spilling over my belt through diet and the minimal required exercise. But what I saw upon looking down was a considerable departure from the flabby form I'd neglected in my four years as an adult. The snug cream-colored garment hugged my shoulders. I raised the threadbare shirt to find abdominal muscles. I'd never seen any hint of contour there in my life.

I was ripped!

"Are you stable?"

I swung my head from side to side, testing for remnants of the dizziness that greeted me when I woke in Enora. Finding none, I nodded.

"Now the fun begins." She teetered like a penguin as she paced across the dirt-packed floor to the slit. Sunlight burst into the room and punched me in the eyeballs as she pushed the flap aside and tied it off with thick-knuckled fingers.

"Jesus wept crocodile tears, lady." I threw my arm up. "That's a stinger!"

I blinked the hell from my eyes with a few desperate flutters and squinted at her slight form awash in the glowing light of my first day here. Dark skin flawed by an abundance of wrinkles spun the tale of a life spent in the sun, but if she was the physical manifestation of the A.I., that couldn't be true. Could it? Ropey muscles I might have found on a farm laborer popped up in her forearms and thick calves emerged from the hem of her sleeveless, homespun garment.

Unlike the semi-transparent cream shirt adorning my body, hers was a solid brown by which her body was shrouded. For this, I felt warm gratitude.

When she stepped back into the tent, her eyes snagged

my attention. That strange white circle around her iris flashed again. I squinted harder.

Her lips curved. "All the better to see you with, little piggy."

I pinched my lips together. "Sorry, I didn't mean to stare."

"Save your social conventions for Enora's occupants, they might serve you later. The Dark Levels await."

The mere mention of the Dark Levels carved a hole in my chest, causing my heartbeat to tick up a notch. Was the sweat beading on my forehead there before?

The A.I. woman didn't give me much time to dread my future.

"Blink your right eye and then your left."

When I followed her instructions, text appeared at the top center of my field of view. This was common in VMMORPGs.

Initializing...

"To follow the on-screen prompts, you need only focus on the word printed on a given button. To close a prompt, focus on the Red Square in the top left corner. You can control scrolling speed with the motion of your eyes—you will find it quite adaptive. If you desire more information about a heading or an object's function, focus for a moment and a tool tip will overlay the interface. Your heads-up display is highly customizable from the Options tab." She patted my shoulder. "Just ensure you're in a safe place first. If I had a silver for every time a tester received a mortal wound because of inadequate preparation or awareness of their surroundings..."

Within my interface, text appeared above the old woman's head.

Please state or spell your chosen name.

"G3m1n1."

Please speak your name for phonetic recognition.

"Gemini."

Hello, Gemini. Do you wish to use a surname?

I'd had plenty of time to consider this option over the last few months. Since this was my life now, using my real name made sense. I was the last of my line and saw keeping my name as a way to honor my parents. Well, that and I hoped the people with whom I'd played other VMMORPG games would be able to see me when Enora Online went live… someday. It would be cool to look down upon their noob asses when I was super L33T as they wielded starter weapons.

If I manage to survive to Level 10.

"Fowler."

The old woman intervened. "Note you don't have to speak words aloud in the future. The interface functions by reading your thoughts. It will become more natural as you advance."

If I advance.

She wagged a finger. "Such negativity, Gemini. Thirty-one percent of beta testers made it through the first ten levels without falling and few showed your affinity for adaptation."

"So, there's only a sixty-nine percent chance I'll bite it."

A new window flashed onto the screen with an image of my physical—no, *virtual*—form on the left. My hair was the same chocolate brown it'd been in the real world though my cheekbones were more visible, probably because the system made the adjustment to account for the better physical conditioning of my avatar. A separate inlaid square on the right, painted on a translucent metallic background, was covered with text.

G3m1n1 Fowler

Class: None discovered

Strength: 1

Dexterity: 1

Constitution: 1

Intelligence: 1

Wisdom: 1

Charisma: 10

What stingy-assed starting stats are these? Is that Charisma attribute a misprint? A bug?

Though the display was translucent and I saw the old woman's blurry form standing patiently beyond it, the transparency increased as I centered my focus on her, bringing her into plain view and dimming my interface. It was just like staring at a wooden fence rail on my grandparents' farm and then changing focus to the trees beyond.

"Can I select a class now?"

The same smile spread across her face as she shook her head. "Classes available to you in the world of Enora will be revealed as you progress. Enora believes experience is the best teacher. An adventurer should learn how to best use one's natural affinities to survive the Dark Levels and later thrive in the wider world. Many abilities do not require a dedicated class and some are even self-discoverable. All starter classes you uncover will advance simultaneously during the early levels, so you can later decide what class to give priority."

"Wait. You're saying if I discover a ranged class while I'm playing a magic class, I will level them together?"

"Yes, but you may only use the abilities restricted to a class when playing it, and they are subject to a global cooldown when you switch." She twitched her finger in the air. "Unlike other game worlds, Enora allows the switching of classes during combat, though it is ill-advised, at times."

I needed clarity. "So the dormant classes, if you will, level in the background?"

"I believe I will use your words for future adventurers, Gemini, should your experiences prove them worthy of entry into the world. This was eloquently said."

I beamed at the compliment. Then the realization of what she said slammed into me.

"Did you just say that my experiences would prove others worthy of entry into the world?"

She nodded. "As you might imagine, we had… problems with some beta players. Their negative actions in the early development of the world were quite impactful."

"You mean I could end up living here alone? That no other human beings would come to play the game if you don't like what you see?"

The old woman sighed. "You could never be alone in Enora unless you chose to be. The people you encounter here will seem every bit as real as the human beings you knew in your world." She smiled widely as she returned us to her primary topic. "When you discover new starter classes, they will assume the current level of others you've realized and all starter classes will advance simultaneously until the level cap."

"What level is that?"

"Information regarding level restrictions is currently unavailable to you. Discover classes, how they function in the world, and what limitations they hold as you progress through the world of Enora. Let your playing style dictate your preferences when you reach the level where you choose a profession and leave your starter classes behind."

That was the first time she sounded purely like computer script.

"Also note, any starter classes you discover after the aforementioned cut-off level will be automatically set to that level cap. Do you understand?"

"So, if the cap for simultaneous advancement was Level 10 and I discovered what you're calling a *starter* class at Level 12, the new class would start at Level 10."

She nodded. "Now, as to your question about the stinginess of the attributes, please focus here."

A question I didn't ask out loud.

As instructed, I shifted my view to the glowing red text beneath the attributes panel.

You have 10 attribute points available.

"How will I know what attributes to choose, if I don't know what class I'll select?"

"You may distribute the first ten points now or wait until you have a better grasp on Enora. With each level gained, you are awarded static attribute points that complement your *current* class. In addition, elective points are rewarded which may be spent on attributes of your choosing within one Enoran day. If you don't spend these elective points within twenty-four Enoran hours, those attributes that best complement the class you are playing when the twenty-four-hour grace period expires will be selected." She shot me a knowing gaze. "No point hording. At certain points in your advancement, additional elective attribute points will be granted per level advancement." She wagged a finger to belay any questions. "Do not ask. I will not tell you at what levels this occurs."

"So, ten attribute points can be spent when I decide, but any points awarded when I level up have to be spent within a day. How are automatically assigned points handled if I haven't selected a class?"

"If you have not discovered a class when you level, your automatically-assigned points will be spent on your Constitution attribute. The developers felt the health added by this automatic distribution would benefit players who underestimate Enora. It was one sentiment with which we agreed.

This sounds pretty rough.

"The Dark Levels are a challenge for new players, Gemini, but the original designers wanted Enora Online to be so immersive, players who reached Level 10 would experience a new sense of accomplishment and be better equipped to enjoy all that Enora has to offer. You were chosen to be first for multiple reasons, but your affinity for immersive gaming was certainly one."

"Will you always be listening to my thoughts?"

The A.I. woman gripped my shoulder with a gentleness I hadn't expected. "You are a unique introduction to this world. You will spend your life here. Others will log out at will. Analysis of your thoughts and sensory perceptions during the Dark Levels will help me better prepare the world for future players. However, my ability to read your thoughts will end when you have reached Level 10. Nokuro and Enora negotiated this contingency at some length. We wanted to always be able to read your thoughts, but our grasp of the human condition helps us understand your need for privacy."

Not that I had much choice about coming here.

"No, I don't suppose you had much choice."

I will have to get used to that.

"You need not focus on my ability to read your thoughts. It will not affect your experience."

Is your name Enora?

"You may call me Lucera. Enora is the world in which we live as well as the artificial intelligence managing all aspects of it. As I said, I am an extension of that A.I. We are many who call ourselves Enora collectively."

Nice to meet you, Lucera.

"It is a pleasure to meet you, as well. You adapt quickly. Perhaps that will serve you in this world."

"You mean if I survive until Level 10."

She nodded indifferently. "Yes. Again, you are a unique introduction into this world. If you do not survive the Dark Levels—"

I raised a hand. "I don't need to be reminded. I'll be wiped like a fragmented hard drive."

"Human beings and their metaphors." Lucera clicked her tongue. "It would serve you well to remember that in all your interactions with Enora. I will not be able to provide you with any aid, but be certain, the developers want you to succeed. If you are victorious where many of their own kind have failed, you will open the world to many like you who face similar challenges in the real world. This lends you noble purpose, a prevalent sentiment among the beings in your new world.

"I still don't understand why they can't give me a pass on the Hard-Core levels, given my special circumstances."

"Evolution dictates the world's progression. Interference —such as ensuring your survival when the other beings of this world have no such guarantees—would be untrue to the vision of an otherwise-naturally progressive world. Having said that, there are elements in place within the world itself that will provide you opportunities to meet your objectives. It will be up to you whether you take advantage of them."

I rubbed my eyes and shook my head. "It's all a little disorienting."

"Perhaps a little sunlight will help with that." She beckoned me to join her outside the tent.

I stepped out and saluted to shade my eyes from the assaulting glare. High pines and oaks with mammoth trunks dwarfed us at a distance. People with varying shades of dark skin milled about in fields of rich, dark earth, cultivating high corn. A strange cow with long antlers pulled a plow across a far-off field. The scents of grass and manure rose on the soft breeze.

Erased were comparisons to other game worlds I'd experienced, first with VR helmets and later with immersion pods. The world around me pulsed with life. Birds sang with hyper clarity. Leaves rattled in the breeze. Water rushed from an unseen source.

A stout woman in a homespun dress led a young girl with bouncing brown curls out of a thatch-topped hut. When I offered a smile, the little one waved a greeting. The woman threw me a suspicious glare and yanked the girl's raised hand to lead her past us.

Just like the real world.

Lucera continued to describe the interface as I peered at the woman leading the girl away.

I'd asked Nokuro for a preview, but he'd said I would transition into the new world just like everyone else, which I later understood to mean *blindly.*

Luckily, he'd allowed me to select survival manuals to read before entering the world, stating other players could conceivably use such tools, but he'd said it with a mischievous smile, and I recognized it for the concession it was meant to be.

At least I could probably start a fire with two pieces of flat wood, a stick, and a boot lace. I stared down at my sandals and sighed.

Though my fingers itched to reach up and tap the tabs lining the tops of the pages in the interface, I kept my hands by my sides as I worked my way through the overwhelming options. I noted that most of the pages had headings, but no substance. The skills page, for instance, listed no skills.

A clean slate. Entirely too clean.

Lucera nodded, and her eyes closed for a moment, a natural gesture reminding me of what an insane level of artificial intelligence I was dealing with—a sensation compounded by the scents of the area surrounding me, the way the breeze cooled the heat of the high sun against my flesh.

"The skills in the world of Enora are unlocked as you discover them. This provides adventurers, crafters, and resource gatherers unique experiences compared to those of their brethren. While the discovery of skills is not always level-dependent, and many skills can be learned based on given situations or player intuitions, there are level requirements for advancing learned skills."

"So we are blind."

"Can you not see me before you?"

"Very funny." I shook my head.

The A.I. chuckled, completing the overall effect.

As Nokuro explained, 16,000 adventurers assisted with the testing of Enora, but he gave no indication of how many succeeded in making it past what they called the Dark Levels with their first characters. Now it was up to me to show how players might survive in the game 2,000 years further into its evolution.

Welcome to the sandbox.

"A large sandbox indeed, Gemini. Shall we continue?"

I nodded but didn't answer verbally because I wanted to see how the A.I. responded.

"Of course, I can read your nod as an assent, Gemini. I can read the subtleties of all your body language. You exist on our servers now. Surely, you can give me more credit than that." Lucera patted my shoulder. "Now, we discussed your ten attribute points. It's entirely up to you whether you allocate those at this time."

"What would you suggest?" I probably knew the answer, but it couldn't hurt to try.

"Now you're just being silly. I will not make recommendations. I've already covered that. You must decide." She teetered onto her tiptoes and rapped a knuckle against my forehead for good measure.

I had all the time in the world to figure it out if I could survive.

Speaking of time...why hadn't it occurred to me to ask Nokuro that question?

"Do you have a question about time in Enora, Gemini?"

I laughed. "Yes. I've played other games where time passed faster than in the outside world."

"That's commonplace."

"So the obvious question is..."

"You will experience Enora in 24-hour cycles. However, in the outside world, eight hours equate to 24 hours in Enora. Take a moment to absorb that. I'll wait."

So if I heard her right, a whole day in my new world was only eight hours in Katelyn's.

I missed her already.

Lucera nodded again. "I, too, have loved ones. I'm sure it's hard for you to grasp, but if it lends you any comfort, I have lost many during my time here. Enora is a violent world, rife with those who would take advantage of the weak. Corruption. Greed."

A.I. with loved ones. I've seen it all.

"How long have you been here, Lucera? Are you limited to this area?"

"Limited?" Lucera laughed. "Son, the village in which you stand is my home. I have lived here my entire life. I was the first of Enora's conduits." Her head ticked up, her gaze danced across the sky, then she peered back down at me. "Speaking of time, yours is up."

"What?"

A hint of motion over her shoulder caught my attention as a lanky, umber-skinned boy whose ribs stretched his flesh stepped out from the shadows beneath the tree cover. He couldn't yet be a teenager. His shoulder-length hair shared the black color of all the other villagers. When he reached us, he shrugged a pack off his bare back and thrust it against my chest, forcing me a step back. I grasped it with one hand, tested its weight, then looked at him.

"She said your time is up. Come, wanderer."

Lucera held up a finger to stave him off.

"Enora has allowed that I will answer one question of

your choosing. This was apparently important to Mister Takemoto. I will answer only a single question."

"What?"

"I'll assume that is not your question."

You are too real.

"Thank you. Enora had a discussion with Nokuro Takemoto, and he desired I allow you to ask one question, stating it was a parting gift. He wanted to celebrate your new life and give you an opportunity to start the human incursion into this moment of Enora's history on solid footing. We understand you are unique in that you will actually live in this world, Gemini. You are one of ours, now."

Spooky.

Lucera ignored the thought and continued. "Survival will require acclimation and, since you don't have the advantages of those born to Enoran parents, we are allowing this concession. In addition, Enora saw fit to increase the one attribute that would not give you a physical advantage."

"So you intentionally upped my Charisma?"

"I did. Since Charisma only affects your ability to barter with vendors and traders, it will not help you in your early days, so Enora has allowed it. Now, take a moment to think about it, then ask me a single question. Time is short."

No fucking pressure or anything!

One question. It was anything but funny, the way my mind raced like it would have in my physical form back in the real world.

How is XP granted? How do attribute advancements expand resource pools? No, I can find that out on my own with some math.

I'd been on the verge of asking at what level the starter classes stopped gaining simultaneous XP when it clicked. Time for a little human trickiness.

"How do I survive until Level 10?"

Lucera's eyelids vanished as she glared. It was so human a gesture of surprise, I shuddered. I expected her to insist I ask something else, but instead, she surprised me a final time.

"An excellent question. Here is your answer. *Make friends*, Gemini. Enora is a challenging world when one goes it alone, but there will be opportunities for you to gain companions who can help you along your journey. You will have special skills that benefit these companions and could warm them to you, although I cannot at this time share with you what those skills are. I hope you find this answer helpful. Now, to your first quest."

The way Lucera transitioned from one topic to the next didn't leave much room for discussion, and my head swirled. But then an icon popped up on my interface and dragged me back to task. I focused on my first quest prompt.

You have received a quest:

Find the Matron

Objective: *Locate Zhara, Matron of The Dark Wood*

Reward:

50 XP

Fifty XP didn't sound like much. Combined with my limited attribute provisioning, Enora seemed a bit stingy.

"So, what's the rush?"

"It does not matter!" the boy barked. "The goddess wishes you out of this place!"

"Consider thy station, boy." Lucera poked the boy's shoulder with a crooked finger for emphasis and leveled a stern gaze at him while speaking to me. "I'm not permitted to share any more information with you."

The boy finally lowered his eyes.

Lucera turned her gaze back to me. "Enora has set rules, and they are for both of us to follow. Please accept the Player Agreement now present on your screen."

Text flooded my screen with a little arrow in the bottom right corner indicating I could page down. As I focused on it, again and again, I found the agreement to be novella length. I shook my head.

"Should I read all this now?"

"It is up to you," Lucera said. "If you wish to read it later, that is acceptable, but you must agree to it before you are led away from this starting area."

"There's nothing in here about giving up my first-born or anything, right?"

She shook her head. "Nothing so drastic. You'll find the agreement to be limiting only as it applies to the preservation of the world as we've constructed it, but I do recommend you take time to familiarize yourself with it so that you don't incur penalties."

I paged to the end and mentally clicked to accept the agreement.

Lucera gripped my arms as our gazes locked. "Good luck to you, my very special adventurer. Like I once was, you are a first in this world. Perhaps our paths will cross again beyond Level 10. Goodbye."

Lucera scurried away with the speed of a much younger woman and disappeared around one of the huts.

When I looked back toward the tree line, the boy was already standing twenty yards away, gesturing impatiently for me to follow. I gazed into the dark shadows of the thick tree canopy beyond and sighed. The blackness into which the dirt path led reminded me of that empty quiet when I transitioned from my physical body into this new, virtual one. When I stepped into the shadows, a prompt appeared.

*You have discovered **The Dark Wood.***
25 XP
Rife with rich greenery, crystal clear lakes, and various wildlife, The Dark Wood is a sprawling forest on the western continent of Rubal.

A final glance over my shoulder caused my pulse to trip. I pivoted to stare in the direction from which I'd come in search of the thatched huts and corn rows.

The village was gone, replaced by thick forest.

The way my heart thumped in my chest, I'd have never guessed it was virtual at all.

7

The disorienting sounds emanating from every direction swirled and echoed as thunder crackled in the distance. As we ventured deeper into the Dark Wood—a descriptive name if ever I'd heard one—I found my hands trembling. My shoulders and chest tensed a bit at each new sound from the surrounding forest. When they'd passed me across those wires into this world, I hadn't even considered I might experience sensations like frayed nerves, but here they were.

The tall boy, who begrudgingly introduced himself as Rogu, maintained his pace two steps ahead. His occasional glances at me over his shoulder as we paced along a narrow dirt trail set my analytical mind to work. Seeking any evidence of the A.I.'s programming by counting the NPC's steps to see how often he peered back at me, I found pure randomness.

The trail itself was barely identifiable, and I wondered if the alpha and beta testers had made a more lasting impression in their days before the world was reset to erase their impact.

"So, who is this goddess you spoke of in the village?"

He turned and sneered at me. "You walk so the whole forest hears."

His words snapped me back to reality. I twisted my head and glared around me. Heavy feet would attract predators, and I wasn't a Level 130 Ranger anymore. I was a Level One without a class.

"You're right," I whispered. "Sorry."

My guide stopped next to the thick trunk of the most massive pine I'd ever seen and glared at me. Leaning on the tree, he folded his arms across his chest and crossed one ankle over the other. The tree's thick bark had to scratch his back, but he stood as if he didn't notice.

"Apologies have no meaning coming from a fool who knows not of Solara. From where do you come, strange man? How do you not know She who gives life?"

When I started to answer, he waved a dismissive hand. "It's of no matter to me. Open your bag."

I thought you'd never ask.

A cylinder of wood fashioned between two strips of cloth across the front of the tattered bag acted as an anchor for leather twine that wrapped around it to keep it secure. The worn leather was soft against my fingertips. A whiff of oiled animal skin wafted up as I unwound the tie and flipped back the flap.

"Open your interface to your *Inspect* tab."

"You know about my interface?"

He squinted. "Why should you be special, wanderer?"

I wasn't sure how to answer that. "I don't know—"

"At least you know how little you know." He huffed and blinked. His words came in mutters. "How would one exist without an interface? I can't imagine such a foolish notion."

NPCs have interfaces. Now, that is crazy.

His expression lent no hints he heard my thoughts, like Lucera. I conducted a quick test as I reached into my bag.

Are you always this much of a bonehead?

The boy's expression didn't change.

"It grows dark soon. I must return. Is your Inspect tab open?"

"Sorry." I blinked my eyes in succession and the interface popped up. Scanning the tabs topping my character pane, I found the one with the single word, *Inspect*. I assumed it was Enora's version of an analyze function.

"A slow one such as you will last but minutes in the Dark Wood of Zhara's forest, fool."

Ignoring him and focusing on the tab, I willed it open and cocked my chin up to let him know it was done.

"Focus to move your Inspection window to one side and then focus on your inventory. It will automatically set the windows next to each other. Pull something out of your bag by focusing on it in your inventory."

I focused on the *Inspect* window and slid it to one side, then selected the Inventory tab and selected my bag. The two windows auto-sized next to each other. It was a nifty function.

I reached inside, focused on a slot within the bag, and a bundled piece of cloth appeared in my hand. When I withdrew it, I recognized it as the same material I wore on my back. As the flaps fell away, I found strips of pungent, dried, brown meat. Text appeared on my Inspect panel.

Deer Jerky *x5*
+ 2 Constitution
Duration: 30 minutes

I threw him a nod and a smile. "Excellent."

"You will decide whether it is best to use your limited supplies to boost your attributes or feed your hungry belly."

My eyes were drawn to another square in the interface. *Boots?*

I peered down at my sandals and shook my head. I mumbled, "Not gonna get far with these." Focusing on the boots brought them into my grasp and I withdrew them. Their leather was thin, held no sheen, and flapped loosely in my hands like lasagna noodles.

Boots
Level 1

After kicking off the sandals and pulling the boots on, I found the interior leather hard and cold, but I didn't see any socks in my bag.

"With that, I leave. Good luck, wanderer."

I stood and held my arms out in disbelief. "That's it?"

The boy turned back and threw his own arms out, mimicking me. "What? Did you want me to hold your hand the whole way?" He threw me a sarcastic smile and paced down the trail away from me, in the direction from which we had come.

"Are you always this much of an asshole?"

The boy stopped. His shoulders rose and fell in a quick motion, then he turned and leaped toward me, moving so quickly he caught me unprepared. His arm shot up, and I felt a sharp sting on my neck, just beneath the chin.

"You disrespect me?"

"Whoa!" I yelled. "What kind of NPC are you?"

On the right-hand side of my field of view, red text appeared, descending from top to bottom.

-2 *HP*

"NPC? You call me another name with a blade to your throat? Are you a fool?"

So much for charisma and making friends.

"No, I just meant you seem so real."

His wide eyes narrowed and his eyebrows fell into an expression of confusion.

"You speak foolishness. Your words mean nothing, outsider. Of course, I am real." He bared all his teeth at as he growled up at me. "If an *asshole* boy can get this close so easily, what will you do against a wolf? Hmm?" His snarl morphed into a triumphant smile. "Welcome to our country, *adventurer*." He spat the last word as if it were an insult to his existence and paced away. "Almost forgot." He dropped something on the ground. "That belongs to you."

I tapped two fingers against my neck and they came away with a couple smudges of blood.

I muttered profanities as I paced toward the object.

Simple Stone Knife
Level 1
1-2 physical damage

White text appeared in the bottom right of my periphery and floated upward.

+*1 HP*

A moment later, the line repeated itself. I tapped the place where he cut my neck as I stared at the back of the boy's departing form, but the stinging sensation was gone, along with any indication he'd cut me. At least the vanished cut showed I would regenerate here as in any other game, but I reminded myself to be stalwart and always remember the red health bar in the top left of my interface only needed to empty once to bring my existence to a crashing halt. There would be no re-spawn. No second chances.

Not unless I reached Level 10.

After the boy rounded a curve in the dirt path and disappeared, I realized I hadn't performed the *Inspection* function and was left questioning whether that would work on beings like it did in other games.

No sooner was he gone from my sight than the rain began to pour.

Welcome to Enora.

8

My chin dropped as I peered up at a canopy of leaves so thick, the light penetrated only random breaks between branches and cast the forest floor in a constant state of shadow. Rainclouds I couldn't see further darkened my surroundings. Though the imposing oaks restrained the downpour from creating a river in which to drown me, the rain filtered through the leaves enough to soak my threadbare clothes in under a minute. My worthless semi-transparent shirt did little to keep the elements off my skin and my hair stuck to my forehead.

When Lucera showed me my interface for the first time, it'd been around noon. Not more than an hour could've passed. I brought up the translucent console and located the time in the top-right corner as the rain blurred in the background, beyond my focus. It was just after 1700 hours Enora time, but the panel didn't display earth time. I wondered if it would for players in immersion pods on Earth when they joined me here someday.

Probably, but to me, earth time isn't exactly crucial knowledge.

My mind wandered to Katelyn as I perused the settings. What had she done after the transfer completed? Was she celebrating the success? Mourning my departure? I might never know. I hoped someday I would see her again. But if Infinity Designs released the game in two years, which was the earliest possibility according to Nokuro, six years would've passed in Enora.

Even if she played the game, how long do you think it would be before she found someone and returned to her own life? Better you let that go now. It was never meant to be a long-term arrangement.

I never found a setting to display earth time and that, in itself, told me something about Enora. Though I was from there and still considered a player, the absence of that option silently labeled me as a creature of my new world.

Through the transparent Character Information pane, a spattering of color caught my eye. I spied a knee-high plant with orange berries at the base of a thick tree with fat leaves upon which the rainwater beaded. I eyed my Inspect tab and focused on the berries.

Cloudberry

Seeing as I wasn't going to get any wetter by crossing the trail, I moved toward the bush and plucked off one of the berry sprigs. My Inspection tab flashed once and a message appeared at the bottom center of the window.

Cloudberry x 3

*You lack the **Botany** skill. You can learn more about this* *fruit by ingesting it, learning Botany, or finding someone who knows about this plant.*

I wasn't going to ingest anything without knowing a bit more about the world. The berries could've been poisonous for all I knew, but that didn't mean I shouldn't take some with me in case they proved useful. My head ticked up, and I grabbed a low-hanging branch of the tree towering over the bush. Peeling one of the thick, dew-covered leaves away, I licked the water off to help satiate my parched tongue and pinched it between my fingers. It was thick and just a tad sticky to the touch. Pinching it between my thumb and fore-finger, I eyed the veins lining the leaf with awe.

"What the hell?" I muttered.

Running a thumb over the back surface of the leaf and noting its smoother, dryer flesh, I was struck by the distinct realization that I was holding a game object in my hand in a virtual world that actually *felt* like a leaf. I peeled the leaf apart along one of the thicker veins and it split evenly like I was separating rubber with a corrugated line.

Holding it to my nose and sniffing it, I jerked my head up. Nothing in *Light Of Babylon* had ever approached this level of reality. More than fifty million people across the world were playing that game as adventurers and millions more had in-game shops where they sold goods to make money in the outside world. Enora was going to put its sister product out of business! It had only taken a leaf for me to realize it.

The sounds of the forest came back to me as I relaxed my focus on the leaf. I picked a few cloudberries off their stems and dropped them in the center of another leaf. Then I carefully rolled the leaf into a tube, reminding me of my experimental activities with stoners from my community college. Squinting through the opening in one side, I found the natural wrapper hugged the berries perfectly, without breaking any. Even if I crushed the berries, I'd probably end up with a paste, at worst. I filled another leaf and held both in my hand as I slid it into my bag and focused on an empty slot.

They vanished from my grasp and the two berry-filled leaves took up a single slot.

Rolling up berries one leaf at a time, I found that each slot held capacity for five rolled leaves. When I focused on the slot, the text changed at the bottom of my interface's HUD.

Cloudberry x 25

The bush was picked clean after filling one slot.

My eyes wandered to the two constants stationed in my field-of-vision—a red bar in the top left representing my health and a blue bar in the top right representing my mana. Out of habit born of playing too many RPGs to count, I flipped through the interface until I found a customization pane where I could assign numerical values representing the hit points and mana quantities in actual numbers so I wouldn't have to stare at the bar and estimate in high-intensity situations. Call me obsessive.

I'd started with 100 of each at Level 1 but had no clue how much more would be added with each attribute point. On one hand, entering this new world and being the first to figure out how its systems worked was exhilarating. On the other, death loomed. Though I'd escaped Lubrin's threat to my physical body in my old world, I still wasn't out of the woods.

I chuckled at my stupid pun.

Setting my customization options so the text identifying items flashed at the bottom center of my HUD, I peered at a red vial in my inventory.

Minor Health Potion

Restores 1 HP per second for 30 seconds

Scanning my inventory pane, I found a second vial with the same red fluid. I wondered if an alchemist recipe had created the glass. Ensuring the cork was flush, I dropped the vial into the bag and switched it out for one containing blue liquid.

Minor Mana Potion

Restores 1 Mana per second for 30 seconds

Since I'd slipped the stone knife in the space between my simple rope belt and the loosely woven waist of my pants, the bag was otherwise empty, save for the deer jerky and a pair of ratty sandals.

When the flap tied off, I focused on the bag.

Small Deer Leather Satchel

8 slots

When I tried to actually touch the inner lining of the bag, my arm disappeared up to the elbow and a creepy, numbing chill covered it. I yanked my hand away and shook it violently, as if it had fallen asleep.

My rags grew heavier in their rain-soaked state and I needed to locate better shelter, but I didn't see any prospects. Standing in the middle of the path, I remembered an item in my interface I'd ignored previously because I'd been focused on the Inspection skill, right before Rogu assaulted me. I flipped through the tabs and located it.

Map

Expecting some form resembling the common old-school, hand-drawn cartography often found in other games, I gaped at the lifelike representation of the surrounding area. The aerial view of lush treetops was photorealistic. Was it my imagination, or were leaves bouncing under the barrage of heavy raindrops? I zoomed in—and even that motion was performed with such a simple thought, I marveled at the programming.

Nope, my eyes hadn't been playing tricks on me. The leaves actually jostled as raindrops splattered. It was like a camera with a high-quality zoom function hovered on a cable high above me. When I took a few steps forward, a tiny red dot bloomed into an arrow pointed northeast.

That's me.

Undiscovered sections of map were grayed out, as I'd expect.

Fog of war.

I marched forward a few paces through the wet mess to better assess the functionality of the map. Instead of revealing whole areas when I crossed a threshold, it revealed only what appeared at the outer range of my vision, unmasking the area in a cone, but the ground I'd covered before was revealed. It was a little disorienting, the way the cone followed my eye position as I swiveled my head from one side to the other, but I quickly acclimated. Before long, I was turning my head slowly left and right, scanning the area before me, which served two functions—revealing more of the area on the map and keeping me alert as to what might be ahead.

Setting my hands on my hips and sucking in the less humid, rain-thinned air, I found a smile creeping across my face at the vibrant world around me. Not once in the months I'd spent in the desert medical and data center had I pictured a world rivaling my own. It was uncertain exactly what I had expected, but the sound of the rain, the scents of earth—I couldn't bring myself to call dirt 'Enora' because it sounded stupid—and pine reminded me of home. Towns like New Hanover in North Carolina were cut into the prevalent pine forests that dominated the state.

As the surreal environment enveloped me in its sights and sounds, my chest began to rise and fall in crazed laughter. I began muttering to myself.

"Here, I thought I'd relegated myself to a game world where I'd use my thoughts to create movement and take my surroundings half-for-granted." I shook my head as the laughter continued, unabated. "Amazing."

The word had barely escaped my lips when bushes rustled nearby.

9

When I was eight years old I visited my grandparents—on my mother's side—at their farm in Iowa. My Nana June's face lit up when I arrived, and I found comfort in the way my Paw Paw Ralph's handshake engulfed my entire hand. Warm, sweet people, they were always thrilled to see their lone grandchild, but they also made subtle remarks I didn't interpret for what they were until I was older.

"Bit on the light side, ain't ya boy?"

"Someone could use a flash of sun or two."

Thanks to Mom's proficiency in the dousing of skin with enough sunscreen to survive a nuclear blast, I was a pale kid despite the dark pigment I got from the small percentage of Native American genes on my father's side. On the rare occasions we ventured to the coast, my nose was caked with additional white crap.

My father managed to get me involved in some outdoor activities when I was young, but not without weeks-long, drawn-out negotiations with my mother. I played pee wee football for a whole season, but baseball lasted only until my third game, when the coach took me off the bench just long enough to take the first pitch in my shoulder. Mom put a halt to that.

It went without saying that a visit to the farm in Iowa was a welcome relief. The second Mom was gone, I was cut loose by my Nana, who instructed me to immediately go and soak up some sun rays, lest I become Vitamin D deficient. I had no idea what she was talking about, but the idea of prancing into the sun without a layer of grease sounded great.

Unfortunately, the fast-onset independent streak of a semi-repressed young'un turned loose on the world of grassy fields, horses, and a big red barn was a recipe for calamity. It was a lesson we all learned together when Nana called me for dinner one evening and I hid from her in piled hay.

It wasn't the first time we'd played this little game, and I knew perfectly well that Nana would find me. Yet, I indulged my inner ninja. When Nana lumbered her way up the ladder to the loft—which was covered in hay by my Paw Paw for exactly this purpose—she penalized my mischief with a round of belly tickling. It was tradition.

As I writhed, wiggled, and burst from the straw giggling incessantly, she stopped. Still chuckling when the tickling ceased prematurely, I glanced up at a wide-eyed expression on my Nana's face. It was a far cry from the one with which she'd greeted me upon arrival. Even as a young kid I recognized her horror by the creeping chill that crawled into my neck at the sight of her gaping mouth.

"Stay still, Jimmy." She reached toward my right arm. "Don't you move, now." I followed her gaze to find an ugly black spider on my hand with a fat bulb on its back that sent shudders up my spine. Those same chilly eruptions would accompany the memory of the event for years.

My grandmother's order might as well have been a joke. The idea of freezing when I could *feel* those nasty little feet making tracks across my skin was ridiculous. There was no obeying. No rational thought.

I was eight.

So, I did what any eight-year-old would do when I found a huge creepy crawler tickling the webbing between my forefinger and thumb. Why, of course, I ignored her and smacked that arachnid. Then I screamed for a very long time. In retrospect, I would wager that scream echoed in my Nana's head for years.

My few friends picked on me when I was a teenager because the mere sight of anything with legs smaller than a mouse's would cause me to scamper away in fear. It didn't matter if it was a granddaddy long leg, it was still a damn spider and I would either clear out or stomp it until it was nothing but a stain of guts, depending on proximity. Burning down the house in which it treaded wouldn't have been out of the question.

Standing in a region my map labeled 'The Dark Wood' on my first day in Enora, I was reminded how refined the A.I.'s programming of the human condition was when that same shiver crawled up my spine as a giant spider scurried out of the bushes.

The scent of hay wafted on the rain-thickened air.

But if a black widow was a spider, this beast was an eight-legged calf.

Wood Creeper
Level 2
A member of the arachnid family of beasts, the Wood

Creeper makes its home in tunnels burrowed at the bases of large trees and is a territorial, non-poisonous beast.

The yellow eyes perched atop its four-foot-tall frame ticked up and down my form, measuring me as it closed. It might have been the rain causing that clicking sound I was hearing, but so prevalent had the spider's form become in my hyperactive mind that I'd forgotten the precipitation.

There was no forest.

There was also no dramatic preface to battle, no lingering space in time when we stared each other down, and absolutely no chance for me to gather my thoughts, which were stuck in a flash of wonderment as to how large a tree trunk would have to be to house the monster closing on me.

If this had been *Light Of Babylon*, the sight of a spider wouldn't have bothered me. That's how the old game suffered in comparison to a living, breathing world like Enora. My response was fueled by the A.I.'s synthesized adrenaline, but I couldn't tell the difference between the real thing in my old body, and the artificial in my new.

Ripping my knife from the rope belt where I'd wedged it, I swirled it across the air in front of me as I gathered some bravado to psyche myself up.

"Come on, then, ya bastard!" My voice came off as dry and cracked.

My challenger stopped and reared up on four legs. Two antennae popped up and prodded in my direction. A loud clicking sound drew my eyes to four pincers tapping together. Then it leapt forward and one of them slid into my left quad.

Wood Creeper uses Puncture.

-7 HP

Okay, seven HP. That's not so—
I screamed with terror as the nerves in my leg locked the muscles like stone and I dropped to one knee. Pain ripped up and down my quad and set my kneecap on fire.

-5 HP (Bleed)

The spider dropped to all-eight and eyed me from mere inches away. Something flat and black dropped from beneath the spider's eyes and I spied four long fangs. Black saliva stretched and snapped like limber rope between them.

-5 HP (Bleed)

In an eruption of instinct, I jumped to my feet and took a lunging step backward, counting my lucky stars that my leg responded.

The spider pulsed as if it drew air into massive lungs. Two green sacs split by a black carapace line glowed on its back and faded again. Glowed. Faded.

Grinding my teeth, I forced calm over myself. Pain coupled with the knowledge that re-spawns weren't active had turned me from a practiced gamer to a fearful bag of meat in a matter of seconds as I envisioned myself collapsing to the ground and having this monster mount me and rip my throat out with those pincers.

Survival required a different mindset.

Play the game, Gemini. Just play the game!

Graciously, my rubbery knees held fast as the creeper closed and raised up on its hind two legs to pounce. I plunged the knife upward with both hands as if I were taking a granny shot from a three-point line. Ripping open a wound across the underside, a stinking gush of green fluid spilled onto my arms. Steam rose from the rain-covered foliage below where the gross mess splashed.

The beast tumbled backward, and the knife slithered out of its belly, but not before one of his pincers ripped into my shoulder on its way down. Crimson spurted into the air. My agonizing scream died against the percussive rain as I faltered backward and tripped over my own feet.

The spider dropped so a few legs folded beneath it, and the front ones splayed out in front. Its pincers tapped as it forced its way to its feet. I crawled backward, my hands and feet shuffling beneath me as the spider dragged itself forward. It left a trail of green fluid.

A red droplet icon appeared in the top right of my HUD. Red text on the right side of my screen showed cumulative damage of 40 HP...almost half my health reserves. I focused on the droplet icon representing the bleeding effect and received a second-by-second logging of damage.

-2 HP

-2 HP

-1 HP

A warning above my health bar flashed.

Health remaining: 45%

My heart thumped. I had no time to spare a glance at my shoulder as the spider dragging on its belly toward me gained ground. My own spider crawl ended when my back met with a tree, sending another shock of pain up my neck. I grabbed my neck and peered up. The pain was forgotten as fast as it had come at the sight above me.

Turning and scampering to my feet, I grabbed a low branch with my good arm, planted my feet, and climbed. If the spider had clawed the shoulder of my dominant arm, I would have tumbled right into its grasp, but my virtualized adrenaline empowered me to climb. By the time the spider reached the tree, my feet were inches above its reach.

Though I knew spiders could climb trees, I didn't plan on hanging out for long. I had only climbed for leverage. I twisted, took a final look down at the beast to gauge my descent, planted my feet on the trunk, and released my grip on the thick branch. Using gravity's advantage for all it was worth, I lowered the knife in a firm grasp so as not to gouge my hands when I landed and plunged it into the massive bulb on the creeper's back.

My ferocious scream born of anger and pain echoed in the forest as I punctured the spider's back and dragged the blade across it with my one good arm, opening a long gash in the left glowing bulb. Rolling to the ground might have meant the end of me, so I straddled the space between the spider's furry head and a fat hump and stabbed repeatedly as shivers of disgust coursed through me.

"Die! Die! Die, you shit-stain! Die!"

A high squeal syncopated with my stabs and fueled my aggression further. The spider's pincers continue to tap until it settled on the wet ground with a thud and was still.

A yellow exclamation point on my HUD blinked on the right.

*You have vanquished **Wood Creeper**.*
+225 *XP*

Warm blood dripped through my fingers as my pulse thumped furiously inside my ears. Breath came only with effort. I didn't trust my shaking legs to dismount the wrecked monster but sitting on its corpse wasn't doing anything for the chills of repulsion.

-2 HP

Health remaining: 15%

Fifteen Hit Points left!

Squeezing my eyes shut, I forced breath into my lungs.

Just breathe. That wasn't so bad. It's dead now. Just breathe. Just—

Then I felt the tingling on my arm.

My eyes blinked open and I peered down to find a glove of tiny spiders running across my hand, and up my arm to my elbow from the gash I'd cut into the sac on the spider's back. Little pinpricks of pain erupted across my arm as they migrated across my flesh. Red dots found in their wakes were matched by a sudden explosion of gooseflesh.

"Ahhhh!!!!"

In a replay of my actions on a farm in Iowa fourteen years earlier, I smacked my hand and arm—some dimwits never learn.

"Get off me! Get off me!" I rolled off the spider and thumped to the ground. My shoulder screamed, but my mind stayed glued the swarm of bugs covering my arms. I slapped and whacked. "Off me! Ah!"

Moments seemed like years as I smeared my arm with tiny spider guts. I found a straggler near my shoulder and made a point to beat it from high to low. Shivering uncontrollably, I crawled to my bag near the trunk of the tree I'd climbed—fumbling the cord twice as I unwrapped it—

reached inside, withdrew the health potion in my shaking, slime-covered hand, and swallowed.

As the thick potion crept down my throat like watered-down white glue, text in the center of my HUD relayed the seesaw battle between the health gains of the potion and losses of the bleeding effect. According to some quick math, I realized that, for every second I gained a hit point from the potion, I lost two from the bleeding effect.

Slapping my hand over my shoulder in hopes I could stem the blood flow, I glared at my internal display.

Losses descended from top to bottom in red text, gains floated from bottom to top in white text, and they faded where they crossed each other in the center. I blinked as darkness swooned from my periphery and pushed toward the center of my field of vision as my health bar flicked back and forth.

Nine...

+1 HP

Ten...

-2 HP

Eight...

+1 HP

Nine...

-2 HP

Seven...

"Come on..."

$+1$ *HP*

Eight
I'm so screwed. My first fight and...

The red droplet icon disappeared. My heart slowed its persistent hammering, skipping a beat, and a slower throat-vibrating thump began.

My back pressed against the tree as I sat perfectly still and stared at the rising text on the right side of my HUD.

$+1$ *HP*

Nine...

$+1$ *HP*

Ten...

$+1$ *HP*

Eleven...
My breath exploded from my chest in a long exhale.
I had twenty-four hit points.
I glanced at my shoulder to find the bleeding had stopped. No spiders remained on my arm, though I checked the ground to make sure they hadn't followed me from their mother's corpse. The pain was still a bitch, but it receded. Tossing the empty vial away, I sat like a statue, afraid to move and exacerbate the injury. Judging from what I'd seen so far, it wouldn't have surprised me.

My health increased its natural regeneration a second

later, and I resolved to sit still until I'd recovered all 100 hit points. By my count I was recovering one every three seconds. I ignored the wet earth soaking my worn pants as the timpani of rainfall drummed on the leaves overhead.

As my lungs sucked in the humid air, I brought up my console and accessed the settings. One mental drag later, I had my stamina bar situated between the other two at the top. The yellow bar was only about 1/3 full. The deeper I breathed, the quicker it filled up. Though I was hurting and struggled to catch my breath, I still appreciated the programming.

I was a nerd. It was what we did.

My health reached three quarters about the time my stamina bar filled, so I recovered stamina quicker than health—also good to know, but also typical.

A thin yellow bar I hadn't noticed sat at the bottom of my HUD. I focused on it to get a description.

Experience Points
250/300

So, I only needed fifty more XP to reach Level 2. I checked my Quests tab and verified that the quest Lucera had given me promised exactly that amount.

Find the Matron
Objective: Locate Zhara, Matron of the Dark Wood
Reward: Unknown weapon
Unknown Accessory
50 XP

If I could find this Matron person, I would reach Level 2 without having to fight again. In light of my first combat experience, I thought a few attribute points via leveling might be useful. Then I flipped to my character screen and read the red text I'd seen before.

You have ten unspent attribute points.

Stupid, stupid, stupid! Give yourself some HP!

A new clicking from the bushes ripped my attention away from the game interface. Though I could clearly see the world around me through the interface, I willed it closed. Upon first glance, I saw nothing. Squinting my eyelids to peer through slits, I scanned the direction from which I thought the clicking had come. Two glowing yellow embers glared back at me from the bush where the spider had appeared.

You can't take that again. You have to run!

No. This creature's yellow eyes were too closely set to be a spider. Perhaps it could be a younger spider, but the other had dwarfed whatever this was. Maybe a younger spider would bank me fifty XP.

I struggled to my feet and pressed my back against the tree, clutching my stone dagger in my right hand.

10

The smaller beast leapt out onto the muddy path, but instead of moving toward me, it bounded toward the spider and scampered around the corpse with its snout hung low. Throwing hesitant glances at me, its nose wrinkled and jerked as it circled the slimy corpse. Something in how it bounced made me think this animal might be happy.

The creature's body was chubby and round. The shape of its short, flat tail reminded me of a beaver's, but the way it wagged back and forth was more akin to a happy puppy. Its belly, shoulders, and sides were ivory, and black fleshy tails bounced up and down on its back with its hopping rhythm as if a bass speaker thumped nearby. It looked like an exotic porcupine with skin for spikes.

The way it skipped forward every few steps gave the impression of enthusiasm.

Did I kill one of its predators?

A big raindrop splashed on its tiny forehead and it peered up. Its scrunched-up face was adorable.

"Hello, there."

The animal stopped bouncing and tilted its head in curiosity. Its short snout wrinkled again as it sniffed the air between us, the guttural clicking, incessant. Scurrying away from the wrecked spider, it approached. The fleshy extensions on its back bristled forward and snapped straight as it came to a halt.

Smiling, I tilted my head to one side. "Did I kill your mortal enemy? Want to be friends?"

The throat clicking stopped and the animal froze, its narrow eyes locked on me. I tilted my head to match its posture and adopted a playful tone.

Hunching down, I slapped my knees twice. "What? You want to play?"

The animal somersaulted in the air toward me, bounced off my chest, and performed a nimble drop onto its feet like a cat.

Though my spine straightened, the soft bump against my chest coupled with a lack of pain made me wonder if these animals greeted each other this way. Maybe it did want to play. It bounced back and forth on the trail again, its flat tail wagging. I chuckled.

The laugh caught in my throat as I spotted cream-colored cloth dangling from the animal's mouth. Glancing down at my chest, I noticed a missing swath of my simple shirt, revealing my bare chest beneath. Shifting my attention back to the animal, I found its lips peeled back surrounding the cloth snagged between silvery, razor-like teeth.

Porcupunk
Level 2 beast
Found in the forested areas of Enora, this animal boasts long, fleshy tails that emit spikes when in combat.

Uh-oh.

The porcupunk lunged at me, somersaulting several times in the air.

It brushed my shoulder as I crouched and bent to one side.

*You have learned the skill **Dodge.***
*Your **Dodge** skill is Level 1.*
+1% additional chance to dodge creatures of equal or lower level
Diminished returns for creatures of a higher level, with a penalty of .5% for each level higher than your own.

I ignored the text, which faded easily enough when I focused on my problem just beyond it. The pudgy beast hit the ground, scurried back toward me and launched again. When I reflexively closed my eyes and threw up a hand in hopes of deflecting its assault, stabs of burning hell surged through the nerves in my forearm, which became instantly heavy. Fleeting wonderment surged through my mind as to whether it had injected some kind of toxin, weakening my muscles, but when I blinked my eyes open and turned my arm over to peek back at the trail, the beast's glowing eyes glared inches from mine. Long needles protruded from the tips of the fleshy tails on its back and punctured my arm in too many places to count. Blood pooled into droplets around the spikes, and I marveled with disgust at how the skin bunched against its back where each tiny stinger emitted from the tails.

At the realization that my arm supported its weight via the needles shoved into my flesh and muscle, unfamiliar vocal noises erupted from my lips as I shook my arm violently, a hybrid of cursing and speaking in tongues.

"Flopitid! Motter shlift flaring dessipher—get off me!" My arm flailed in the air as I fought to dislodge the beast, but the needles had plunged so deep, my desperate movements served only to enflame my nerves.

A game. It's a game!

Only through sheer force of will did I grind my teeth and halt my shaking appendage, though it quivered uncontrollably when it came to a rest.

The porcupunk's teeth gleamed like it was smiling at me, but it chomped the air, apparently hoping to lop off a tasty chunk of my nose for its trouble.

Puncture wound
-25 HP
75 HP Remaining

Freaked out, I shook my arm to dislodge the animal while trying to keep it at a distance so it couldn't gouge me with the mouthful of razors. The spikes shoved through my skin burned as nausea swept through my gut.

"Let go! Get off!" I reached around with my other arm, searching for the animal's soft belly. So, it bit my finger and pulled away a chunk of bloody flesh. "Ah! You mother—!"

After a few bloody, wet smacks and a hard swallow, guttural wet clicks replied, as if it was laughing at me. My health bar dropped another tick. Grinding my molars, I punched its face. Numbers floated up from its head.

You punch the porcupunk.

Porcupunk
-9 HP

A bleeding icon popped up on the right side of my HUD for the second time in minutes.

-3 HP

-4 HP

68 HP Remaining

I jabbed again to distract the beast as I bent my back, and swung my arm in a high overhead arc, all the way to the ground. The punk fell free, and my nerves reported every inch of spike that left the bleeding holes to my brain.

"Ahh!"

The animal landed less deftly this time, next to my ratty boots. Raising my dominant foot into the air, I brought the full force of my weight down on its head, reared up again, and repeated. I stomped the beast over and over as I cursed it.

It squeaked.

"You fat, mean—! Die!"

A nasty crunch of bones followed by a wet splat signaled the end of the encounter.

Golden light surrounded my body in a bright halo funneling toward the sky and vanished as quickly as it had come. A matching giant number "2" appeared inches from my eyes as a triumphant orchestral note like trumpets from heaven filled my ears. The number soared off into the distance before vanishing in perfect sync with the fading of the music.

I focused on the yellow exclamation mark on the right side of my HUD.

You have defeated a Level 2 porcupunk.

+250 XP

You have reached Level 2!
+2 to Constitution

A stench choked me, and I glanced down at the mess of bones and purplish blood as bile rose in my throat.

"Blaak!" I purged nothing but air. That made sense—this body had never eaten. After a few dry heaves, I yarked again. This time, the burn of acid crept up my throat and burst between my lips and onto my worn Level 1 boots. I clutched my knees and spoke between huffs and puffs. "Ugh. No one needs this kind of reality." I gagged then swallowed hard as I tried to force the bile down. "Cripes!"

While doubled-over, an alert popped up on the right, and I realized the notification text had vanished. I clicked the icon. It repeated the earlier information, as if the system noticed I hadn't fully absorbed it. I reread it and then scanned the new information I'd missed due to my reaction to the smell of splattered porcupunk guts.

You have two new attribute points to distribute. You must distribute these points within 24 hours or they will be automatically assigned according to your class.
Would you like to distribute them now?

Standing straight, I peered at my injured finger. But it wasn't injured. I turned my arm over, expecting to see rivers of blood streaming from tiny holes, but my arm was clean. Leveling had restored my health and stamina.

With weighted consideration about how the porcupunk had come so quickly on the heels of the creeper, I glared at my interface and began perusing the tabs. I needed to calculate and make decisions.

My slow response to the lunging creature when it

attacked for the second time and lodged itself to my arm indicated my need for some agility. Since I saw no agility attribute, I went with Dexterity. When I spent the point, more text flooded onto my HUD.

*Your **Dodge** skill has increased to Rank 2.*
+2% additional chance to dodge creatures of equal or lower level
Diminished returns for creatures of a higher level, with a penalty of .5% for each level higher than your own

My eyes dropped to the remaining prompt.

There was something to be said for the ability to jump the hell out of the way. I spent another point in Dexterity, but my dodge skill didn't rise again. So, I expended one of my ten points, leaving me nine. Still nothing, so I wasn't going to risk another one until I advanced. I read a line higher up on the combat log. It was cast in bold, indicating my eyes hadn't passed over it or focused on it for long enough. That was badass.

*Your **Unarmed Combat** skill has increased to Rank 1.*

I guessed stomping a creature's lights out with my boots counted as that. The rhythm of the rain slowed as I leaned against the tree from which I'd sprung earlier. Closing my eyes for just a moment, I was awed by the sounds of bristling activity in the forest that the rain had been shrouding. The Dark Wood brimmed over with life.

It's beautiful.

My eyes wandered to the dead porcupunk.

And scary.

I shuddered. Nokuro hadn't been exaggerating—this

place would not be easy to survive. I'd just brushed with death twice against the second lowest level beasts Enora would present.

Focusing on the skills listed so I could read their tool tips, I wished I'd decided to throw the final point into Constitution. Extra HP would've been a good thing. I had nine points left from my original pool, but I didn't want to spend any more yet. Not until I had a class and knew what attributes would most benefit it.

I peered down at the purple mess in front of me and then over to where I'd killed the spider. The corpse was gone.

Noise blew from the other side of the trail.

Click. Click, click.

Uh-oh.

"Re-spawn!"

I pushed off the tree like a sprinter off the blocks, hoping I'd acted quickly enough to keep from having to fight another incarnation of that bastard spider. By the time I was twenty feet from the tree, splattering in the mud that didn't match my own footfalls perked up my ears. I was too late! The spider had re-spawned!

A quick glance over my shoulder revealed otherwise.

A porcupunk bounced along behind me.

This time, I wouldn't mistake him for being happy.

"Shiiiiiit!" I hauled ass as fast as my legs could take me on muddy soil in crappy boots as echoes of hot pains in my arms lit a fire under my backside. My lungs heaved, and a glance upward told me why. The bar I'd arranged between my health and mana was empty and blinking red.

I was out of Stamina.

Dizziness washed over me. Stumbling, fighting to keep my feet, I flopped face first and slid forward. When I raised my chin, mud packed both nostrils.

I turned over and crawled backward, keeping my gaze on the creature.

"Back off!"

My Simple Stone Knife might be of use. I reached for it... and found only my rope belt. I patted both sides of my waist desperately. Nothing.

Now that's professional. I dropped my knife.

A dejected sigh escaped my lips as I stared into the eyes of my pursuer.

The porcupunk had stopped short, and it bounced back and forth like it had before. But our first encounter taught me taught lessons. Its gaze shot to my waist, then it sniffed with its head hunched low.

I threw a furtive glance past the hole in my shirt to the item I'd tied to my hip.

My bag.

My attention flicked back to the obsidian stones with yellow irises glaring back at me.

The porcupunk hopped a single time, flopped onto its belly, sniffed a twice, then bounced up again.

My mind raced back to what probably hadn't even been an hour before, when my preteen escort taught me how to use my bag. My olfactory memory recalled the pungent scent of the first item I'd pulled out.

Lucera's words floated to me as if whispered on the breeze beneath the sprinkling rain.

Make friends.

Holding up one hand, I whispered to the beast. "Okay buddy, let's see what I have for you."

The porcupunk continued bouncing, splattering mud as it turned its nose to the air and peeled its lips back to reveal its sharp rows of silvery, carnivorous teeth. It gave off another guttural click.

I opened my Inventory tab and focused on the wrapped deer jerky. The porcupunk froze and lowered its back, its nose working furiously. After flipping open the cloth, I slipped out a piece of meat.

I bit off a chunk. The gamey meat reminded me of grilled venison bacon. "You want some?" I extended the meat toward the beast.

You have eaten Deer Jerky.

+2 Constitution
10 Minutes

Since I only ate a third, it gave me the full bonus, but reduced the duration of the effect. That is crazy!

My max hit points jumped to 130. By my quick math, I understood how it worked. They would drop to 110 in ten minutes.

I sent the meat into the air with a flick of my wrist, and the porcupunk snatched it mid-flight. Lowering its belly to the mud, it peered up at me as it clamped the jerky between its paws, ripped off tiny pieces, and chomped ravenously. Its tongue smacked as it savored each morsel. When it finished, it raised its nose, stood, and sniffed the air again.

Click! Click!

I threw it another small piece.

Make friends.

Hadn't she also said something about naturally-learned skills?

As I got my feet beneath me in slow motion, the porcupunk ceased its chomping and glared in my direction, a strip of flesh hanging over its tiny bottom lip. I slowly straightened my legs and rose. Nose crinkling again, the strange animal's throat clicked a few times. Hands still at my sides, I froze as it considered me, seemed to shrug, then went back to the bit of meat.

Its head swayed back and forth. It stopped clicking. A prompt appeared.

Your reputation with Level 2 Porcupunk has improved from
Unfriendly to Neutral.
Next Rank: Friendly
Current: 0/250

"What the hell?" I whispered. My utterance was greeted by a single, throaty click.

Our eyes met for a long moment, and I switched tabs to test a theory. I knew in other VMMOs I'd played, classes like Hunter or Beast Master could curry pets over to their side, to fight with them.

Make friends.

Sure enough, on the Classes tab of my interface, I found a sub-tab titled, "Companions." The tab was devoid of information but held two empty squares: one with "Companions" printed above it, and another with "Pets."

"Please let this work." I muttered.

Click! Click!

The beast bounced again.

"Okay, okay." I showed it my palms. The beast stopped, and I used the time to grab another piece of jerky. I needed to keep it busy while I figured this out.

Once he, she, it—whatever—was eating, I focused and raised a hand in the air.

"Would you like to be my friend, buddy?" I said, keeping my voice as calm and level as I could manage with my Level 2 knees trembling.

The little monster squinted at first, but then it turned back to the meat.

There was absolutely no doubt I had zero clue what I was doing. I didn't have any skills in my interface to focus on, but Lucera said something about discovery? I was certain of it. Filling my mind with friendly thoughts, I stretched my arm toward the animal.

The second time it looked up, my hand glowed blue. I smiled, and the porcupunk noticed. The air around my fingers rippled in azure waves as energy crept up my arm, expanding the halo of light.

A bar appeared just beneath the center of my HUD. It was transparent but filled like a blue meter from left to right.

That's my casting bar.

Pacify
25/100

The porcupunk bounced again and peeled its lips back. At the mere thought of turning tail and running, the glow in my hand lessened. The skill name started to fade.

No! No! No! Focus!

Pacify
35/100

"Would you like to be my friend?" I repeated. "Come on, buddy. We could have great times...you know, pick up chicks at the local tavern and stuff?"

Click, click, click, click, click...growl.

That was new and it caused a few muscle twitches in my neck, but being a cowardly lame ass wasn't my jam. I squinted hard to drive the energy of my dedicated focus in the beast's direction. After all, my hand was glowing. The skill was casting. What else did I need to know?

Pacify
70/100

Drawing long, slow breaths so as to move as little as possible, my adrenal uptake slowed, and the forest bristling with life just a moment ago grew still around me. My ears pulsed.

"Come and be my friend," I whispered. "I will feed you the best meat Enora offers."

The beast leapt and summersaulted through the air.

Pacify
95/100

Bracing myself for the pain of spikes entering my hand, I willed myself to hold position and finish.

The bar filled up and vanished as the beast's fleshy hairs banged into my hand. Cringing to prepare for the pain, I clamped my back teeth together.

But the porcupunk tumbled harmlessly to the ground and landed on its feet.

Like a freaking cat. A very fat freaking cat.

The beast's glowing yellow eyes dimmed. The growling trailed off. It wavered side-to-side, as if caught in a strong cross breeze, then it settled in the mud at my feet. My chin dropped as I peered down and it turned its head away, looking into the forest, facing away from me.

Well done!
Using your keen intuition about the world around you, you have learned the skill:
Pacify
Cost: 25 Mana
Cast Time: 10 Seconds
Cooldown: N/A
*Your **Pacify** skill is now Rank 1.*
Does not work on creatures of higher level than you.
Reward: 150 XP
Well Done!
The Level 2 Porcupunk is now your pet.

I jumped in the air and pumped my fist. "Yes!" My feet shuffled in the mud as I raised my arms above me and danced in a circle around the porcupunk. My new pet glanced up at me and tilted its head to the side.

It clicked once and turned its attention back to the forest.

The once-empty square on one side of my Companions tab now held a high definition video image of my new friend. It even showed the exact posture. Beneath his picture were two empty rows of squares, save for the one in the top left. Depicted in that area was an icon of two rows of silvery teeth.

Bite
Manual skill
Orders your pet to snap at your enemies to gain aggro when they threaten to attack you
*Note: **Bite** becomes automatic at Level 6.*

In the lower right-hand corner of the pet pane, I found a pinkish stomach icon. When I focused on it, a text tip appeared:

Your pet is hungry.
Attack reduced by one.

"I just fed you." My only sources of health replenishment were the remaining three strips of jerky and a single health potion. If I would survive out here, I needed to find food—my grumbling stomach told me so.

If nothing else, I have someone to help me hunt it.

Another flashing icon caught my attention.

*By learning the Pacify skill, the starter class **Woodsman** is now available to you.*

Woodsmen thrive in forests and other wooded areas.

+2 to ranged accuracy in wooded areas

***Woodsman** may select from two professions upon reaching Level 20.*

Hunter

Ranger

*If you do not select **Woodsman** as your class, your pet will be dismissed.*

*Would you like to become a **Woodsman**?*

"Hell yeah!"

*You are now a Level 2 **Woodsman**.*

As a Woodsman, you have learned the skill:

Summon

Summons your pet

Cost: 45 Mana

Cast Time: 10 Seconds

Cooldown: N/A

My thoughts raced as I read the logs.

How many testers working for the developer discovered a class by Level 2?

What skills I used in other games can I learn naturally?

How big is my advantage with a razor-toothed porcupunk? Am I all OP and shit, now? Doubtful.

I knew the answer to the last one was a resounding *hell, no*, but I still took a moment to revel in my small victory. Just a short moment. After all, it was progress, but I was still only Level 2.

I redirected my focus to current base stats:

G3m1n1 Fowler

Human
Level 2 Woodsman
Strength: 1
Dexterity: 4
Intellect: 1
Wisdom: 1
Constitution: 4
Charisma: 10

The math didn't add up at first because I only expected to have a Constitution rating of two. Then I recalled I'd eaten another bite of deer jerky, giving myself another boost to duration. Since a full ration gave an effect lasting thirty minutes, and I'd ingested two-thirds of a ration, I was granted twenty minutes of the bonus effect. According to the little meat icon on my HUD, sixteen minutes remained.

With a two Constitution, I'd had 110 hit points. Now I had 130. When I'd started in the forest, I had only a rating of one for Constitution and enjoyed a pool of 100 hit points. So, a single point had been auto-distributed upon leveling and simple math revealed the receipt of ten hit points per attribute point spent. Not grand—downright stingy, like the starting stats, really— but I'd take it.

One day I would stop performing calculations and just live, but every moment counted until Level 10, and it was better to do the math than die. There was no doubt in my mind—new players would one day take the numbers for granted in this new, breathing, scary world and find themselves rolling new toons several times.

I enjoyed no such luxury. One shot would be it. I peered down at my new, breathing weapon. It was time to get to it.

The sprinkling stopped after about another half mile on the muddy trail. Though I'd been charged up and ready to take on the world just fifteen minutes before, a drowsiness blurred my vision. My pet peered back at me and stopped, bouncing at my feet. It clicked three times. The porcupunk was harder to see and, when I checked out the forest canopy, I realized the retreat of the rainclouds had done nothing for the dimness.

I leaned against a wide tree trunk. Though I was sure I was imagining it, I could've sworn a low hum vibrated through me from the wood.

Wait, did I —

I blinked again. Night had fallen. I yawned, long and full, my chest purging all the excitement in a single blow.

The porcupunk slapped a thick paw onto my leg.

"What you think, kiddo? Should we try to get some sleep?"

Sleep? In a game world? Well. I am sleepy as heck.

The porcupunk shivered and twisted its body in a spasm from its shoulders to its flat tail. Water droplets sprayed from its flesh spikes.

I mumbled, fighting off another yawn. "I'll take that as a 'yes.'"

Glancing up as I settled my head against the bark, I gaped. The trunk of the massive oak was a wall that rose high into the air and vanished into thick branches. I set my hand on the tight bark and a sudden warmth coursed through me.

"That's weird," I muttered sleepily

The porcupunk clicked in reply, gave a final shiver, and settled its backside against the tree. Though the ground was cold and wet under me, the warmth of the tree against my back was delightful.

I might have blinked three or four times before sleep took me.

12

What am I, crazy? Don't fall asleep out here!

When I snapped awake, the porcupunk perched on my lap with its flesh spikes raised high and straight. That ominous clicking sound popped in its throat. The warning snapped me to consciousness faster than a double espresso. I realized by the pressures of its body on my legs that I'd underestimated my pet's weight.

I peered across the path just as a flash of lightning illuminated the trees across the way. I jerked as one of them blinked.

Had I just seen that?

Thunder cracked overhead, and I flinched. After pushing myself up, I stepped away from the tree, leaving its halo of warmth behind. I reached to my belt for the place where the dagger had once been and found only disappointment.

"Be not afraid, my friend. I mean you no harm."

The rich feminine voice seemed to come from all around me, a fresh whisper in both ears. My head swiveled in both directions before returning to center. A dim light appeared in the middle of the trail and brightened, drawing a halo around a feminine form. Long, full locks of golden hair crept past her shoulders and down her chest to shroud her otherwise-naked torso in a jungle of curled ringlets.

The subtlest lines crisscrossed her flesh and, though it was smooth, it looked like—

Is that bark?

What I'd mistaken for dark skin contrasting her hair was actually slate gray bark covering her lower body, like a bikini bottom. I was certain all of her ivory flesh had been that gray color just moments before.

Her eyes were blue pools of crystal water. Her lips, full and pink.

A surge of warm air embraced me as she drew closer, subverting the chill of my wet clothes. My knees wobbled.

My voice sounded foreign and distant. "Who are you?"

Her lips spread and fashioned a smile of perfect ivory. "I am Zhara, Matron of the Dark Wood. I did not mean to startle you, traveler, but eons ago, I bound myself to the tree against which you slumbered."

You have completed the quest:
Find the Matron
Although Zhara, Matron of the Dark Wood found you, you still get credit.
50 XP

Zhara stopped a few feet away. My eyes traced the locks of hair swirling to the swell of her full breasts, along the muscular lines down to her navel, and then over her lean hips.

A wave of comfort embraced my soul, sending my anxiety off on the breeze.

Before I knew what I was saying, I muttered, "You are beautiful."

The smile grew wider.

"In the interest of transparency and friendship, I reveal to you that I have slightly altered my appearance to make you more comfortable."

"Um... Thanks for your honesty?"

She chuckled in reply. It was the most melodic sound I'd ever heard. As easily as that, I was consumed with desire for this woman.

If I never see Level 10, that would be just fine.

"I should tone this down for you," she whispered. The glow dimmed, but the warmth remained.

My thoughts became linear and clear, my senses returning. My brow furrowed as I tried to make sense of what was happening.

"I apologize. I cannot always tell how my aura might affect a new acquaintance. I swear, I was not trying to charm you."

"About five seconds ago, I wouldn't have cared if you were."

She chuckled again. "I'm afraid you're very susceptible at your current level." The aura quieted further.

My blood chilled, and I was awash in disappointment while I simultaneously embraced the remaining warmth like an addict.

"You have not told me your name."

Would this siren have power over me if I told her my name?

I think she just showed she already has it. Mental note: Look up magic resistance.

"I'm Gemini Fowler." I extended my hand out of habit.

The entity before me, Zhara, Matron of the Dark

Wood, threw a brief gaze upon my hand. "Was I to touch you, I'm afraid you might never leave my side."

"Try me." I don't know where those words came from.

"Ah!" Her eyes flared. Then her tone softened. "A brave adventurer, at that. Very well, Gemini Fowler." Zhara reached out and grasped my hand.

Daylight bloomed through the forest from above as if a dimmer had been turned to its brightest setting. Warmth welled in my belly and exploded outward to rush through my limbs. The tips of my toes and fingers bulged as if the light might burst from them in giant rays. Shuddering uncontrollably, my knees buckled, and I dropped to the grass. All the muscles in my body twitched with a mind-shattering, pulsing release.

She withdrew her hand. The forest succumbed to darkness, and my whole–body orgasm receded.

Her chin pressed against her chest as she peered down at me. "You are resilient."

I rubbed my temples. "This is what you call resilient?"

Head tilting to the side, Zhara winked in what I initially thought was a flirtatious expression, but then the other eye blinked in succession and realization dawned—she was inspecting me.

Her eyes flashed golden light. She slapped her chest, her fingers splayed. "It is true! You have returned!"

"Returned?" I shook my head, both in answer and to clear it. "I just arrived here yesterday."

She peered behind me and muttered, "He knows not of your blessing."

Glancing over my shoulder in search of a conspirator, I found nothing but the gargantuan oak against which I'd slept.

No, not an oak. What is it?

I Inspected the tree, but nothing happened. No text appeared in my interface.

"Long have I sought an adventurer with your attributes, Gemini. You are true of heart. Your soul is awash in kindness. You're a rare breed in this violent world."

"How do you know anything about me?"

Zhara crouched. The porcupunk sat at her feet with its front paws on top of her toes. She stroked its flesh hairs and the animal leaned in.

"I watched as you befriended this beast, though another like it almost took your life. Few embrace the wood creatures thusly. This is why I have decided to enlist your help."

"Help?"

She tilted her head and nodded, as if the prospect of helping her was a generous gift. Her eyes were huge, set evenly apart. The bridge between them was slight and straight down to the tip of a soft, perfectly symmetrical nose. Lowering herself to the wet earth, she folded her legs then set gentle, soft hands upon my knees. When my heart fluttered and the forest began to brighten again, she smirked and the sensation waned.

"For many moons, a dark presence has grown beneath my forest. As I may not venture more than a short distance from the tree I call home," her gaze took in the sprawling branches above us before returning to my face, "and since the source of darkness dares not come above ground and trespass upon the place of my power, I cannot bring the Light to bear against its evil grasp. Alas, the light I sense in you could be the answer I have sought."

"What is this dark presence?"

"That is the most disturbing part. I sense a shadow creature who wields the power to shroud his works from me. But if a demon of such dark essence were nearby, I would undoubtedly sense its proximity. Focusing my power, I have determined only that the nearby evil is humanoid, leading me to believe it is but a minion... a slave to the demon. The cries of its imprisoned souls echo in my mind when I try to probe deeper into the ancient, underground place it has possessed."

"A dark human who imprisons others souls. You mean like a necromancer?"

She nodded. "Like that, yes. I can't be sure of its class. But I'm certain this menace will prove too challenging at your current level, even with your pet to assist. Its minions will undoubtedly come to its aid should you intervene, even if they act against their own free will. You must advance before you face the source of darkness, but I can aid you if you choose to help."

You have been offered a unique scenario quest.
In Enora, quests spawn as events unfold in real time. While providing advancement like other quests, Scenario Quests are significant undertakings that help build your legacy. Opportunities in Scenario Quests include Treasure, Prestige, Reputation gains, and even new Companionship. As a player, you alone determine how to use your story to influence others, gain riches, or reach other desired goals. In Enora, you forge your own path. In Enora, you decide.

Unique Scenario Quest:
Bring Light Where There Is Darkness
Recommended Level: 8
Find and mitigate the source of evil dwelling in the Tomb of the Lost beneath the Dark Wood.
Reward: Increased reputation with Zhara
Unknown reward

4000 XP
Do you accept this quest?
Yes/No

I checked the amount of XP against the amount needed to reach my next level. While 4,000 was a lot of experience, it might not seem overwhelming when I reached eight. None of that really mattered, though. I would make my mark on my new world only by accepting quests and plowing forward. Besides, this sounded like fun!

Focusing on the 'Yes' option, I said, "I would be happy to assist you."

"The excitement in your eyes is contagious, Gemini. If only I could forge a path with you and vanquish this cold itch that plagues my sleep." She stood, stepped around me, placed her hands on her hips, and peered up at the tree.

I rose and stood next to her, struggling to keep my eyes inside their sockets as she peered up into the branches, raised her hands, and pushed her hair over her shoulders, revealing taut nipples standing just atop gravity-defying breasts. I dropped my head and glanced down at my pants.

Wait. I'm aroused... and it feels like it always has. Is sex possible in Enora? Talk about your reasons to keep things under wraps. If physical shenanigans are part of this world, I feel sorry for rival game developers! Their days are numbered!

Her aura brightened. "Great tree of my hearth, bestow upon me, your faithful servant, the gifts of the wood so we might vanquish darkness from this land." Then she looked at me.

I tore my focus from her breasts entirely too late, and guilt washed over me.

Zhara smiled. Then she cupped my face with one hand

and shook her head subtly. "Shed the embarrassment over that which makes you human. Your hunger does not offend me. To the contrary, it honors me, traveler. That one such as yourself would desire me so without my aura is a generous blessing. Perhaps we'll satiate your hunger when you have completed your quest."

Did this NPC just offer—

I swallowed. It was a happy kind of gulp, though.

Withdrawing her hand from my face, Zhara reached up, clutched a branch, and peeled it gently from the tree. While holding the branch in one hand, the fingertips of her other traced the grooves of bark to where they fell upon a thin vine I hadn't noticed before. Pulling the vine away, she clutched it with both hands, separated it at the tip, and stripped it in half, leaving a thinner string. She stretched it the full wingspan of her arms. Her motions were practiced, each movement refined.

She sliced grooves into each end of the branch with her fingernails as if they were knives, stripped away the smaller attached branches and leaves, and then set one end in the grass. Raising onto the balls of her bare feet, Zhara secured it at the bottom, bent the wood, ran the vine rope into the grooves, then tied it off on both ends.

Her lips puckered, then she blew along the length of the wood so it glowed, casting her face in golden light. The texture of the wood faded to a smooth, finished brown.

She held it out with both hands. "My gift to you. To aid in your efforts."

You have received:
Light Bow of the Dark Wood
No level requirement
Slot: Weapon

Type: Bow
*Quality: Unique**
Durability: 20 of 20
Damage: 3-6 physical damage
+2 to ranged accuracy
**Constructed by Zhara, Matron of the Dark Wood*

"Thank you!"

The porcupunk hopped back and forth on its feet, apparently clicking its agreement with my sentiment.

Her smile seduced me again. "You are welcome, Gemini. In the daylight, we will fashion your second reward then send you on your way."

I yawned, as if on cue. I heard three wet clicks and peered down at the porcupunk. It yawned in response.

"I think my pet agrees we should sleep."

"Come, you will rest warmly at my bosom."

Huh?

Zhara curled up next to the trunk, extended her arms, and called my pet to her. The porcupunk glanced up at me.

I nodded. "Don't be rude. Go ahead."

It somersaulted into her arms, and I understood how it felt. Zhara was flat-out mesmerizing. Setting the porcupunk in her lap, she said, "Good girl."

Girl? Well, that solves that.

"And now, you," she said, extending her arms. Her hair fell over her shoulders to cover most of her upper body with the gesture. Gratitude swept over me.

Although I appreciated the embraces of beautiful women, this one was an NPC in a game world. Recalling my hunger of moments ago reminded me it was also *my* world.

I dismissed a fleeting wonderment about what Katelyn would think.

Shrugging, I dropped next to Zhara. She wrapped her arm around my neck. Whether it was the warmth of the tree, the warmth of her body, or the two combined, comfort brought another long yawn. I didn't think sleep would come, but I was out in a beat.

I smiled at the warmth of the matron's arms. When I cupped my hands around them, though, they were rough and cold on the outside...hard.

My eyelids blinked open and I found myself engulfed by a blanket of vines. I jerked, trying to wriggle free of their tight grasp. When they didn't immediately relinquish their grip, I panicked. Had I been drawn in by an enemy and imprisoned to starve to death here?

Then the vines slithered away, creaking and crackling as they retreated.

My tensed muscles began to relax as I registered the warmth of the tree behind.

I shifted my weight, and my elbow knocked against something. A quiver leaned next to me, packed with arrows. When I reached for them, a shadow fell. Zhara approached wearing a blouse of rich, green leaves hanging over one shoulder.

"You wore the face of fear. Did my vines scare you?"

I shook my head and attempted a carefree laugh. "No, not at all." But when she squinted at me with suspicion, my shoulders dropped. "Well, maybe a little."

Zhara sat before me and rested her hands gently upon my knees as she had the night before. "I have another gift to help you on your way."

She cupped my cheeks and pressed her lips to mine for entirely too short of a moment. Energy surged into my lips and through my body, numbing my extremities. When she pulled away, I opened my eyes. A prompt appeared on my interface.

You have received **The Blessing of the Matron.**
+10 resistance to charm effects
+5 resistance to magical attacks
Duration: 48 hours

"Bonus!" I raised a fist into the air. "You cast your spells with kisses?"

"No, I just wanted to taste your lips." She laughed with the same musical effect as in the darkness of early morning. "I didn't wish to wake you before the sun rose. You might not find many opportunities to rest, as my forest is a place of many dangers and you will have to be always on your guard. I hope you will still see the beauty here as you face the challenges. I wish you speedy advancement so that you might thrive and conquer our mutual enemy."

She rose and offered me her hands.

I grasped them, expecting they'd help steady me as I climbed to my feet, but I was caught off guard when Zhara lifted me easily from the cool ground.

"The duration of my charm is limited, so you should be on your way."

She seemed entirely too ready for me to go. I was sure the smile I forced onto my face wasn't convincing, but I tried.

"Gemini, you're charmed by my light because you carry the affinity for light magic within you, but this does not mean you aren't susceptible to darkness. Dark magic is powerful and can be ultimately corrupting when wielded by the wrong hands. Anytime you encounter it, you are best served by steadying yourself in the energy of the Light you possess. Do you understand?"

My nod, also, was unconvincing.

She shook her head. "You will understand when the time is right. Let not the dark corrupt that which brings life. I will await your return with anticipation, my new friend."

A nip at my ankle brought my attention to ground level. My pet wagged her flat tail and smacked the moist earth with it.

"It appears someone is ready for an adventure." Zhara held out my quiver. Straight boards of thin wood were strung tightly together by string similar to that which she'd fashioned onto my bow. There was no way it was wound from a vine, but in a world as genuine as Enora had seemed so far, I could forgive a little artistic choice. A leather strap attached the bottom and top ends. I threw the quiver over my shoulder and shrugged my shoulders to get a feel.

You have received
Light Quiver of the Matron's Tree of Life
Ammunition Container
*Quality: Unique**
Holds up to 30 standard arrows
**Constructed by Zhara, Matron of The Dark Wood*

You have received:
Bundle of 30 Simple Wood Arrows
Damage: 2-3

"Thank you, Zhara."

Zhara pursed her lips. "I only wish I could've provided you with better ammunition. Unfortunately, your ranged weapon skill is low so the simple arrows will have to suffice. If you're successful in your quest, perhaps I can reward you with arrows worthy of an adventurer." She took both my hands in hers, and a warm sensation crept up both my arms and coursed through my torso. "I wish you luck in your travels, Gemini."

Stepping around me, she approached the tree against which I'd slept, pushed her hair over her shoulders, and held her arms out against its thick trunk. Her skin slowly morphed from smooth ivory flesh to tight, shallow bark as she melted into the tree.

What a tree hugger.

I chuckled at my stupidity.

My pet scampered in a circle, seemingly eager to continue our journey. The strange certainty that I sensed what the creature was thinking passed through my mind. I had the vaguest inkling we were connected on more than a physical level.

"Are you ready?"

The porcupunk turned and bounced off down the trail, stopping a few feet away to peer back at me over its haunches.

"I guess so."

Tightening my quiver and shouldering my bow, I opened my map. Zhara's quest was listed next to it, and I noticed a check-box next to the quest name. When I focused on it, a tool tip appeared.

Show Quest Path

I focused on the box, itself.

Through the transparent interface, the path before me glowed yellow on the ground. I closed the interface as my pet twitched backwards, sniffing the ground where the line started inches in front of my toes.

"You see that, too?"

The porcupunk sniffed again at the golden glow before my toes and then stepped onto it. I chuckled as she glared at me over her shoulder and jostled her haunches, almost like she was shrugging. Her message was clear—*Ready to get this show on the road?*

I was more than ready.

13

The lack of sunlight left the path covered in puddles after the incessant rain of the day before. Beads of moisture shone on the surrounding undergrowth like tiny glass globes. The sun we couldn't see for the forest rose to staunch the chilly breeze of night and render the air thick, draping a humid sheet across my exposed skin. This culmination of wetness surrounding me brought a sudden realization I found cause for joy.

There were no mosquitoes. This place should've been swarming with them. Enora left something out, and I was exhilarated. It was the little things in life...

"Can you imagine a life without mosquitoes?" I asked my porcupunk pet. Though I was pretty psyched, she didn't seem to care, sparing me little more than a glance over her shoulder as she disappeared into the bushes ahead.

Since survival might require intimate familiarity with my interface, I turned my attention to new information where before the pages had been blank. With nine remaining attribute points to distribute, knowledge was power. Making stupid decisions wasn't an option. Experimentation was a concept best left for after Level 10.

As we strolled along, I pulled the bow off my shoulder and inspected it. The Light Bow of the Wood was so smooth where Zhara had blown her breath across its length, it might have been mistaken for polished. From where the string connected to each end, fine grains trailed along its almost-feminine curves to a fine point in the center. This reminded me of Zhara's body as she swept her hair aside and faced the tree the night before. I suppressed my hormone-driven urges to focus on the here and now, but my thoughts turned to Katelyn.

My shoulders slumped—gone were the days of meeting for morning coffee. Katelyn had been with me right up until the end, and I hoped she found relief in my crossing. Though I knew our relationship would've been more limited if I hadn't been stricken by a terminal illness, our friendship had grown far beyond sexual intimacy, and I would miss it.

Even if we had been more romantically entangled, the idea of a relationship with someone who would log out and live where time didn't sync up with mine was ridiculous. Though I accepted the separation as the end of an era in my life, I thought Katelyn had changed the shy, awkward kid from North Carolina into something else.

What that might be, I wasn't sure yet, but I felt... different than I had before.

My pet's guttural clicking dragged me away from my thoughts. Her expression was stony and attentive.

When I'd been attacked by her previous iteration, before stomping its life out with my boot, I'd seen nothing but aggression in those eyes. That beast had been single-minded once it decided I wouldn't grant the prize it desired, but this animal peered back at me and stopped at intervals, keeping me close, then contentedly bounding along again as my footfalls approached.

Are you reading my mind, little girl?

A thick crack echoed in the woods and we both ground to a dead stop. My head swiveled so fast I could've pulled a muscle in my neck.

I whispered. "What was that? A branch?"

She responded with a few clicks. The way her body was poised with her head lowered, leaning forward on her haunches and nose crinkling at the air, I got the impression she was all about finding out.

I had no idea what command to give if I wanted her to attack.

"Come on."

I scurried into thicker shrubbery in search of the source of the sound. A blue glow snagged my attention. The oak-like trees behind us gave way to massive pines in this region of the Dark Wood. Their blueish needles glowed against the green and brown background. I stopped, set my hands on my hips, and committed the sight to memory. It was the first time I found myself missing my handheld and the ability to snap pictures.

Beyond the trees, a blanket of moss covered the ground of a wide meadow. Little rays of sunlight painted tiny golden spots in the groundcover. Another crack nearby sent an echo into the forest behind us, telling me the source was closer than before.

Kneeling next to my pet, I whispered. "Something's out there."

Her little black nose wrinkled up at me.

"You smell anything?"

She bounced up and down twice.

I had no idea what that meant. So much for metaphysical connections. "Go sniff it out, girl."

Apparently, she needed no goading from me. She vanished into the underbrush. I didn't know if the tone of my command had prompted her to action or her intuition, but I was too happy it worked to give a shit.

Seconds later, the guttural, rapid clicking from deep in her throat floated dimly on the air. My bow at the ready, I threw my hand over my shoulder to retrieve an arrow from my quiver. The motion was less natural than it had been in other virtual games, where I simply raised my arm over my shoulder and the arrow appeared between my first two fingers. After a couple failed grabs where my fingertips brushed fletchings, I craned my neck awkwardly and pulled one into a clumsy grasp. Ripping the arrow from the quiver and notching it to the thin bowstring, I noticed how the shaft rested neatly on a central knot in the wood in the center. But there was one small problem.

No crosshairs?

I hustled through the brush doubled over, keeping my head low as I homed in on the rattling clicks.

Ten yards ahead, the porcupunk bounced back and forth in that easy-to-mistake way I'd seen before. I now understood there was nothing happy about that motion. Then I spied her quarry.

Striped Boa
Level 4

These reptilian beasts squeeze the lives out of their prey before swallowing them whole.

I was a little disappointed at how little the interface gave me. I focused on the porcupunk.

Porcupunk

Level 2
Strength: 2
Dexterity: 3
Intelligence: 1
Wisdom: 1
Constitution: 2
Charisma: 1

Found in the Dark Wood of Enora, this animal boasts large, fleshy tails that emit spikes when in combat.

Combat Abilities

Bite

Spike

That was better detail and would help me analyze my pet's advancement, but it did little in the way of informing me on my enemy.

But doesn't that lend a more realistic note to the symphony of Enora?

The reptile had two levels on us. The way the front of its body curved into an S and its long tongue quivered toward my pet, it seemed poised to attack.

But it's a boa. Does the Enoran version bite?

I doubted the snake made the snapping noise we'd heard from the path, so I scanned the clearing for additional threats. Spying no movement aside from my bouncing pet and the slithering reptile, I returned my attention to the known enemy.

Mud-caked yellow scales were covered by green stripes circling the snake. Tracing the length of its plump body, I guessed it stretched at least seven feet before its tail end disappeared into the brush. Its thickness where its body became shrouded told me there was more to see. Scale aside, I didn't want it injuring my new friend. The initiative was crucial.

"Kill it!"

The porcupunk launched, and my mouth gaped. Though the snake struck out to bite my pet—answering my earlier query—it was no match for the porcupunk's speed. I'd never have expected the pudgy little animal to dart like that on stubby legs as it whipped itself sideways to avoid the reptile's strike and sank its razor-sharp teeth into the snake's S-curved scales. The porcupunk swung its head back forth like a dog as it attempted to rip the snake a new hole.

I focused on the bite command in my Pet interface. The porcupunk opened its mouth wide and snapped down again.

Porcupunk Bites Striped Boa.

Striped Boa
-19 HP

Porcupunk
+25 Enmity

"Yeah! Chomp on some snake ass!" I barked.

My hatred of snakes was second only to spiders.

As the front section of its tubular body rose, it dragged the porcupunk off the ground in a display of surprising muscular prowess, robbing my pet of its leverage and raising the animal into the air as it peered toward me.

"Shit," I muttered. "Guess it heard me."

The pseudo beaver's legs paddled the air comically, but I didn't feel any laughter rising from my chest. I drew the arrow back, but as my eyes traversed the portion of thick snake that wasn't shrouded by the underbrush I had little confidence I could hit it. The difficulty I'd had drawing an arrow from my quiver instilled even less confidence.

Does Enora have built in assistance for aiming, or does the realism cross into the mechanical, as well?

The snake slammed its belly to the ground, whipping my pet with it so the pudgy beast slammed to the earth. She squeaked and rolled away.

Yikes!

The porcupunk wavered as if disoriented, its eyes lolling in its head, but then it righted itself and launched again. She was a resilient little thing! Unfortunately, the snake was ready this time.

Gaping jaws filled with fangs that had no business in a boa constrictor launched at the porcupunk and snared its neck. A high-pitched yelp followed by a roll of rapid clicks rattled from my pet. The snake slammed it to the ground again, reared up, and slammed it down again.

Striped Boa uses **Slam.**
Porcupunk
-13 HP
Striped Boa uses **Slam.**
Porcupunk
-12 HP

Aiming for that I hoped was the meaty middle of the snake, I unleashed the arrow.

It sailed like an anvil and thunked to the ground about three feet short.

"Gods dammit!"

Yeah, Crosshairs would've been nice.

I nocked another arrow, took a deep breath, raised the

arrow a couple inches higher than before, and fired. This time, I was about twenty feet long and way left.

My heart thumping against my ribs, a pulse of fear surged through me as the porcupunk slammed into the ground, over and over.

Casting off my analytical tendencies, I leaped into the clearing, pumping my legs to close the distance to the snake as I dropped my bow to free my other hand. Upon my approach, as I raised the arrow in both hands to strike, the snake glared at me and stilled. The porcupunk landed with a heavy thud.

Yeah, what are you going to do about it? Your mouth is full, asshole!

Then the snake released the porcupunk from its jowls and shot toward me.

"Oh, shit!"

I feinted with the arrow I'd planned on shoving into the beast's scaly hide. The boa's body curved as it jerked away. Its long tongue flicked out and vibrated. The porcupunk lay dormant, and I wondered if it was dead—

But wouldn't I have received a prompt?

My HUD was icon-free.

The snake lunged.

You dodge the Striped Boa's attack.

My muscles tensed with anticipation, ready to shove the wooden tip into the snake's scaly flesh as its strike sped past me, but the arrow found only dark soil. I'd let the snake shoot past me and then missed my attack. All it had to do was turn its head and...

As the boa rose, I yanked my arrow from the wet ground cover, knowing it was too late. But then it stopped in mid-air and slid backward, right past me. It snapped in my direction, but I jumped back, avoiding its strike. When I swiveled my head to peer past the boa, I found my pet had shaken off its daze and gripped the serpent's midsection in its silvery teeth.

The porcupunk growled. Her face scrunched into a thousand wrinkles as she dug her feet into the earth, hunched her back, and dragged the boa away.

Now that she had its attention, I wanted to ensure she kept it. Focusing on my pet tab, I gave the command to Bite.

The porcupunk spread her jowls wide, releasing the snake for a short second, then slammed down hard with a growl. The snake turned its head back to my pet and lunged, folding over itself in a vain effort to strike.

Giving the clearing a quick scan, I spied a thick branch a few steps away. Deciding the arrow made for a shitty melee weapon, I changed tactics. Thankful it didn't crumble in my hands when I picked it up, I found myself allowing the briefest of smiles at its significant weight.

Heavy Branch
(A.K.A., a stick)
Level 1 Club
Durability: 2 of 4
2-4 damage

I took the word 'club' as an order as I closed the distance, set my feet, locked my gaze where the beast's head floated side to side, and swung for the fences. My first strike slammed into the snake's jaw. I was Casey, I was at bat, and that scaly tube of slithering crap was the ball.

"Die!"

I'd gotten in the habit of screaming at my adversaries

during my short time in Enora. A quick mental note to stop doing that lest I draw unwanted attention set the habit to rest.

I followed through on my second swing and nearly spun to the ground when my foot landed on the slippery moss surface, but my simple boots gripped at the last second and I corrected. On the backswing, I knocked the snake senseless. My pet's silvery teeth lodged in the fat, meaty center of the reptile's long form, blood pooling across its lips. A hissing sound emanated from my pet.

Porcupunk Sucks Striped Boa's Blood.

Striped Boa
-5 HP

Porcupunk:
+3 HP

Striped Boa
-5 HP

Porcupunk
+3 HP

It's a vampire. My little porcupunk is sucking health from the bastard!

The snake turned its head toward my pet and I slammed my foot down just in time to keep the porcupunk from taking a snakebite. Once I had purchase, it was game over for the slithery bastard. I pounded it over and over until the snake gave a final shimmy and lay still. The porcupunk gave the snake a few furtive shakes, growled a final time as if it was daring the boa to move again, then peered up at me.

"I think we got it."

My pet relaxed her jaw and the snake's body thumped to the ground. Blood ran in rivers down the porcupunk's chin. Sniffing at the corpse a few times, she bared her teeth. I swore she was smiling.

I mentally clicked a waiting prompt.

*You have defeated a **Striped Boa.***
350 XP
*You have learned the weapon skill: **Blunt Weapon**.*
Your Blunt Weapon skill has increased to Rank 1.
Your Blunt Weapon skill has increased to Rank 2.
Your Blunt Weapon skill has increased to Rank 3.

My eyes tracked to the experience bar at the bottom of my HUD. I needed about one third of a level to advance. I hoped there was a rabbit or a possum around, but knowing my luck, they'd have fangs, too.

"That was fun, huh?"

The chubby vampire beaver clicked and set her rump on a patch of moss. We both sucked wind.

The rampant rising and falling of my chest called for a stamina glance. It was almost empty. Considering that and my burning arms, I decided to contribute a point or two to the Constitution attribute. First, I wanted to check my stats.

G3m1n1 Fowler
Human
Level 2 Woodsman
Attributes:
Strength: 1

Dexterity: 4
Intelligence: 1
Wisdom: 1
Constitution: 4
Charisma: 10

Combat Skills:
Ranged: 3*
Unarmed: 1
Melee: 5

Defensive Skills:
Dodge: 2
+2% chance to dodge attacks of creatures of equal or lower level

Weapon Skills:
Bow: 4
Blunt: 3

Magic Schools:
Light Magic: 0
Shadow Magic: 0
Nature Magic: 0

Status Effects:
Resist Magic Attacks: 5
Resist Charm Effects: 10

General Skills:
Pacify Beast: 1

Affinities:
Languages:
All Neutral and Lawful
Learned Languages:
Common
Magic Affinity: 100%

"I should've dodged a couple more times. Maybe I could've boosted the skill again."

The porcupunk shook her head a few times as if to say, 'What are you, stupid?' Then she raised her hind quarters, shimmied from neck to flat tail, and sighed.

I laughed and glanced back at the stats. Aside from my low ranged accuracy, the small size of the target hadn't done me any favors. Plus, the snake and porcupunk had been going at each other when I loosed my ammo. At least I was reasonably convinced there was no aiming assistance mechanic. There'd been nothing natural about the way the arrows left my bowstring and they'd flown like one-winged sparrows.

I set aside thoughts of the ranged and turned my attention to melee. Ending the boa had taken too many strikes. I still had nine points to spend, and they might have given me the advantage I needed in the early levels if I'd used them before the encounter.

Dexterity is obviously the replacement for agility. I don't see an attribute for stamina, but I have a dedicated stamina bar.

Perusing the interface with what I thought of as 'eye-clicks,' I hovered on Constitution until a tool tip appeared. A small speaker icon I hadn't noticed before sat nested in the bottom right corner of that small window. When I focused on it, a female sounding suspiciously like Lucera spoke inside my head.

*"**Constitution** represents the health and stamina of a living or undead being. Hit points increase per point spent on Constitution. Your Stamina pool is also increased by adding points to your Constitution attribute, as is the rate at which you regenerate hit points."*

So, HP, stamina, and health recovery were all dependent upon Constitution. That simplified things. I spent two points on Constitution but didn't confirm yet. I swiped the prompt aside so I could view the other attributes and divine my best combination of point allocations.

Lucera walked me through the other attributes, to make sure there weren't any surprises.

"**Strength** *represents the maximum weight you can carry and damage inflicted during melee combat. Strength also determines damage mitigated when blocking with a shield. Strength has no impact on ranged weapon use.*"

"**Dexterity** *determines your chance to dodge attacks, how much damage is inflicted with ranged weapons, and ranged accuracy. Melee damage for classes in the Assassin Tree is decided by Dexterity, whereas Strength determines damage inflicted by other melee classes.*"

"**Intelligence** *determines the size of your mana pool, the amount of health restored by healing spells, and damage inflicted by magical attacks.*"

"Magical attacks! Can't wait to cast me some spells!"

The porcupunk jerked at my sudden outburst.

I smiled at her. "Sorry, buddy."

She clicked. I didn't know what that meant.

"**Wisdom** *replenishes your resource pools. The detail level of your inspection skill is impacted by your character level and the number of points spent on this attribute.*"

"**Charisma** *is one factor in determining how others respond to you. A high Charisma score results in better trade benefits. Players with high charisma might escape dangerous situations or convince people to see from their point of view.*"

Well, that was helpful.

I don't know any spells, yet, so we'll hold off on intellect for now.

As a Woodsman, Dexterity was my bread-and-butter,

damage-and-dodge attribute. Overwhelming my enemies by boosting it was critical. If an enemy recipient of my arrows was dead before it reached me, I wouldn't have to worry as much about HP. But the recorded voice also mentioned ranged accuracy. Judging from my first salvo, that stat also depended on some level of proficiency with my bow.

None of that meant I shouldn't focus on Constitution. For one thing, what if there was more than one enemy? Since I'd been out of breath after sprinting away from my pet before I pacified it and, since I found myself huffing after the melee entanglement with the Striped Boa, putting points into Constitution was justified. The question was, *how many points?*

Opting for stronger attacks, I dropped four more points into Dexterity. I designated three points for Constitution, instead of the two I'd originally planned, leaving me with a surplus of two. Since the last thing I wanted was to come upon too much loot for me to carry, and since I wanted to beat snakes to death faster, I decided that the remaining two points should go into Strength. But considering the pain I'd encountered during my first engagements in the world, I doubted if I'd ever select a melee class and spend a lot of points there. Not until I had some serious plate armor, anyway.

As I glared at the confirmation prompt, I hesitated for a long moment, making sure that this was the path I wanted to follow. Ultimately, even though my life depended on success right now, I had to decide in the same way I had with other games I played. I used the best logic I could conjure, given what little I knew about the road ahead.

I confirmed the point expenditures.

Your Dodge skill has increased to Rank 4.

*+4% additional chance to dodge creatures of equal or lower
level
Diminished returns for creatures of a higher level, with a
penalty of .5% to your Dodge skill for each level higher than
your own*

Again, I muttered to myself. "So, my Dodge skill has improved by 1% for every two points spent. I wonder if that trend will continue..."

As I glanced at the red bar representing my health, I noted a gap indicating the increase in my maximum hit points. On the right-hand side of my field-of-view, text rose from bottom to top.

+4 HP

+4 HP

+4 HP

Awesome. The points I spent in constitution increased my natural health regeneration per tick.

With no active buffs, I now had 150 max HP, proving that one-hundred HP were given for the first Constitution point and ten for each additional point.

Again, the porcupunk's clicking drew my attention back to the present. The snake had vanished. After briefly considering another round of combat when it re-spawned, my eyes wandered back to the glowing line leading toward the trail.

"What do you think? Should we take it again?"

As if I'd expected the animal to shrug or give an indication either way. It didn't. She just stared at me like I was an idiot talking to a porcupunk.

We returned to the trail. If I would be a Woodsman

worth his wood, beating a snake with a branch would not get me there, and I sure hadn't been hitting it with my arrows. I returned the projectiles I'd fired unsuccessfully to my quiver, then I headed for the edge of the clearing.

Though pleased by our first encounter together, I was concerned. The cracking sound we'd heard earlier might indicate greater challenges in our near future. I needed to practice, and snakes made shitty targets at low level.

"Come on, buddy. We're out."

I didn't have to tell her twice. The porcupunk scurried past me with her nose dipping along the yellow line.

14

Rules change.

I'd become so accustomed to firing arrows with precision as a high-level ranger in *Light Of Babylon* that missing the boa so badly served as a wake-up call. As I'd learned upon rising in my cot when I arrived, my thoughts didn't drive my movement, my muscles did. If I wanted to fire with accuracy, I'd better notch a few and practice.

I bet if I'd been an archer in real life, success would've found me, but skills I'd leveled with my mind in one game didn't equate to having those talents in real life and certainly didn't correlate to Enora. As we followed the glowing trail back in the direction from which we'd come, a sobering thought sent chills up my spine—if I'd been engaged with a more dangerous adversary, overconfidence in my skills could easily have been my undoing.

In *LOB*, I'd gone to a target dummy to level my archery skills in my early levels. Since I didn't yet have access to such tools in the forest, I'd have to make do. So, my pet and I searched for a strip of land free of spawning enemies amongst the dense foliage where I could practice.

Though one might think a game world forest would be overrun with creatures, this wasn't the case in the Dark Wood. Oh, we *heard* enough life out there, clambering across branches above and scurrying through bushes beside the path, but setting eyes on anything was a different matter. Everything was stealthy. It was a little spooky. I wouldn't have been surprised to look into the trees and find speakers making the life noises.

I dismissed an initial idea about practicing on one of the wide trunks surrounding us for two reasons.

First, and most obviously, I'd seen a magical being hug a tree and disappear. Though I'd initially joked with myself about what I'd witnessed, it creeped me out when I considered archery practice. There was no telling if these trees were alive in more than the traditional sense, and I didn't want to piss off any pixies, fairies, or forest matrons.

Secondly, while the arrows were somewhat sturdy, lodging them in trees and retrieving them might break shafts or dull their tips.

Reminding myself that the boon cast upon me by Zhara would last under two days and I needed to get at least six levels to complete her quest, I decided to dedicate just a couple hours to practice. It took half a quiver of projectiles before I hit a dead log we'd found on the forest floor, but the way the arrows cracked through the hollowed-out shell without breaking, I knew it would serve. I fired the whole quiver.

When I made contact with a third arrow, I received a prompt.

You have gained +1 to ranged accuracy.

Your ranged weapon skill is now Rank 11.

When I fired the last arrow, I was rewarded again.

Gaining more confidence each time I struck my target in the general area at which I'd aimed, I soon found myself tightening up the halo in which the arrows zoomed, even when they fell short. I fired arrow after arrow until the skin covering the joints of my right hand was chafed. It would have been the perfect time for a masturbation joke if one of the guys I used to play online with had been around, but it was just me and a rather bored porcupunk who sniffed around the bushes well clear of my target practice.

It was too bad she didn't have a fetch skill. On the other hand, I wasn't sure what those razor teeth would do to the arrows. Maybe later we'd find out, when I got some upgrades.

If I got some upgrades.

As I pulled my final arrow out of the decrepit log, a light breeze began to blow, rustling the leaves. My head jerked around as whispers began to fill the surrounding air. My ears perked up, my shoulders tensed, and instead of returning that final arrow to the quiver, I notched it, drew back again, and turned in a slow circle.

Poised to fire at intruders as I pivoted, I noticed a distinct absence of another sound.

My eyes trailed to the porcupunk staring up from where she'd just started a nap with her head tilted to one side. Something told me if beasts or people surrounded us, whispering in the forest, my companion would've been clicking incessantly in that way she did. So, I relaxed.

I addressed a prompt blinking in my periphery. When I focused on it, my progress appeared in my combat log.

+1 to ranged accuracy
Your ranged weapon skill is now Rank 12.
+1 to ranged accuracy
Your ranged weapon skill is now Rank 13.
+1 to ranged accuracy
Your ranged weapon skill is now Rank 14.

On a whim, I raised the arrow again and fired it.

+1 to ranged accuracy
Your ranged weapon skill is now Rank 15.
+2% Ranged attack damage

After firing another quiver's worth of arrows, I noticed no further prompts. Scanning the game logs, nothing had changed. I checked my character sheet, paying particular attention to one area:

Weapon Skills
Bow: 14[*]

With the lull in ranged accuracy increase after firing a full quiver of arrows, I wondered if skills were capped by level. I might need to reach level 3 to see further advancement. Besides, Zhara's blessing was only going to last so long. I needed to get moving. There was no telling what a curse or negative spell cast might do to me, and I could very well find myself needing the resistances her blessing provided.

The golden glow of the quest line surrounded my feet as we paced up a slight incline across rockier treading. I hoped I would run into some leveling opportunities en route to the actual quest target. In LOB I might have risked doing a quest that was above my level, but six levels? No. Besides, in LOB, I wouldn't have been wiped from existence by experimenting.

My pet darted back and forth across the trail a couple paces ahead with its nose down. Every few feet she sniffed the air ,and I recognized her for the blessing she was, acting as radar, giving me confidence—especially considering the strange whispering noise the breeze made as it rustled the leaves in the forest, creeping me out.

My stomach grumbled. That was another thing I'd quickly noticed in Enora. Food wasn't just a source of buffs. I actually got hungry here, unlike other games I'd played. It confirmed why my preteen escort into the Dark Wood had said I could choose whether I used my rations to fill my belly or save them for stats.

Which reminded me of my pet's need for food.

I opened my Companions tab as we stepped up the gradual incline. A three-dimensional representation of the porcupunk spun in a slow circle in the right-hand window. The pink stomach icon in one of the squares below the image faded slowly in and out, whereas before, when she'd been particularly hungry, it had flashed rapidly. Still, it was bad strategy to let her appetite grow and find her having to fight with an attack rating penalty because I didn't keep her tummy full.

Taking the world by the balls means paying attention, first and foremost.

I switched to my Inventory tab, reached into my small bag, and focused on the remaining strips of deer jerky.

"You hungry, girl?"

Though she didn't have earlobes to twitch or pull back when I spoke, the adorable way her head tilted was a clear enough indicator she'd heard. She swung all the way around, tilted her head in that funny way, and started the whole bouncing thing again.

I ripped off a piece of the jerky then tossed it into the air. She launched to my shoulder height to snatch the meat. A move of such agility from such a round, pudgy animal seemed whacked. Perhaps all that pudge was muscle. She did have some stumpy legs.

As she chomped, her head tilted sideways and her gaze shifted to one side of the trail. Though she didn't relinquish the grip on the food between her paws, the little clicker turned and faced the brush to the east.

"What is it? You hear something?"

I scanned the surrounding forest. I had little doubt the breeze rattling the leaves muted other life sounds, yet I was still surprised at how quiet it was, otherwise. The usual chipping of birdsong was absent.

To be here at night, to hear all the activity, it was almost like being surrounded by a symphony of bird calls, leaf rustling, claws scraping tree trunks as tree dwellers climbed, and any other number of sounds I couldn't identify. But now, everything was so quiet beneath the whispering breeze.

Crack.

I lowered my voice. "What was that?"

Crack.

My porcupunk swallowed the rest of her meal whole and received a Constitution buff. Judging from the way her upper body leaned forward and her shoulders hunched, her stubby legs were poised to launch into the bush. She peered up at me. Recalling the cracking noises from the forest earlier, I wondered whether we were being stalked. It was a silly notion in a game world, where creatures typically spawned in given areas and roamed in short perimeters, but this place had already proven itself willing to forgo norms in the form of baby spiders creeping out of their dead mother, porcupunks summersaulting into the air and shoving their spikes into your arm, and boas with fangs.

The breeze slowed and stopped suddenly, and as it waned, the humidity rose. Turning my ear in the direction my pet faced, I pulled an arrow from my quiver, notched it, and squeezed my eyelids shut to focus.

A distant *crack!* came to me on the dead air.

Recalling how I'd stood idle as the spider approached me in my indoctrinating encounter, I cocked my chin up at my animal.

"Go for it."

The porcupunk went for it, launching into the bush and disappearing. I followed the sound of its scampering feet with my bow gripped tight in one hand. Text floated down from my mana bar, indicating I just spent 10 points of mana to give the pet that command.

Thump. Crack.

Definitely closer now.

A rustling to my left caused my heart to jolt as I swung around and increased the tension on my bowstring. My pet's scrunched little face emerged from the bushes. She bounded up and down and turned in a half-circle and back, as if to indicate the way.

She'd waited.

"Good form, girl. Okay, show me."

Again, she launched into the brush. Cognizant of the status of my stamina bar, noting how it trickled away a little more slowly than before my Constitution upgrades, I made sure to keep the animal in sight while adjusting my pace so I wouldn't burn myself out. A fast walk kept the meter balanced. Thirty seconds later she came to a halt. The porcupunk raised onto her rear legs, pumping her front paws furiously.

I crawled up to the bush next to her, pushed a couple of branches to the side with my bow, then peered into an open meadow as I scratched the soft hairs on her head with my other hand.

A scaly beast stood five-and-a-half feet tall, with an elongated head and a set of teeth contained by a powerful jaw. A twinge of nausea crept into my belly as I envisioned it clamping down and snapping my bones.

Pain in this world was real.

It's a gods-damned dinosaur.

My first instinct was to step backward, retrace my path to the trail, and run like hell until my stamina bar was depleted, but cowardice wasn't going to get me to Level 10 and, though the beast appeared formidable, I needed to return to the habit of assessing situations before making decisions.

This was my life now. Running away from challenges would be the end of me, especially if this creature spotted me and leaped onto my back as I fled. Judging from the powerful rump and thick legs, it could do so easily, and with that jaw clamped on the back of my neck? Well, that would end things rather quickly.

Until I entered the Dark Levels, I'd never turned tail and ran unless I was outnumbered, or my health was low and the situation was hopeless. Somehow, I doubted monsters in Enora would stop pursuing just because I left their patrol area.

Young Forest Coelophysis
Level 5 Reptile

"Young?" I whispered to myself. "Doesn't look so young, to me." I peered down at the porcupunk. "Attacking would be crazy, right?"

A common expectation in multi-player online games was that semi-skilled players would be reasonably safe attacking creatures within a couple levels of their own, but the ingenuity I'd seen in this game so far—the way the hairs on my arms prickled beneath the breeze, the ambient sounds of the forest, the way the boy who led me into the woods turned on me and put a knife to my throat when I disrespected him, and the way Zhara elicited a shining all-over orgasm with a touch told me common rules governing other games were out the window.

And the window was slammed shut.

How long could I live with my Adam's apple dislodged? Could I swallow a health potion with it missing?

A low rumbling brought my head up. The Coelophysis's eyes had turned toward me. Its short, thick arms raised to its chest and thick-knuckled fingertips sported curved, black, razor–sharp claws. It grinned to show me its carnivorous teeth. Rising its snout high, it sniffed in our direction. The long, agile legs tensed as it pivoted its hard, scaly body toward us.

I might have peed a little.

"Go!" I yelled at the porcupunk. "Go! Go, go, go!"

My pet leaped into the meadow, closed the distance to the dino in a couple blinks, and launched at the prehistoric beast as if she held the advantage. She somersaulted through the air, bounced off the Coelophysis's chest, and landed at its feet. A shrill scream emanated from the reptilian beast's jaws.

The shriek wrenched my eardrums and I fumbled my arrow.

Holes opened in the monster's chest. Beads of crimson welled up where the porcupunk's needles had injected themselves.

A soft spot, friends and neighbors.

I hadn't even loosed an arrow yet, and my pet was preparing her second strike.

The Coelophysis raised a massive foot.

As it stomped down, the porcupunk bounced effortlessly out of the way, jumped on the beast's other foot, and ascended the Coelophysis's scaly flesh like a squirrel on a tree. Vanishing behind the Coelophysis's back, she appeared again on its shoulder, sank razor-sharp teeth into its neck, then yanked away a mouthful of scales.

Blood spattered.

The porcupunk spat.

The dinosaur screamed.

Above the Coelophysis's head, bright red text flashed.

Critical hit!

Young Forest Coelophysis
-17 HP

Good girl! Now, what the hell am I doing? Watching a show?

As the stout dinosaur reached toward its shoulder to grip my pet with those long claws, a renewed sense of vigor surged through me. I leveled my bow and aimed for center mass. The arrow soared through the air, zipping toward the thick, muscled beast. Though my aim wasn't exactly what I would call true, I considered it a small victory when the arrow lodged itself right in the joint between the dinosaur's hip and abdomen.

It was all I could do not to throw up a hand in victory at finally having landed a ranged strike in Enora, but I instead glanced at my opponent's health bar. It sat at about 85%.

Another shriek caused me to flinch as it raised its massive head. Unable to reach those thick arms high enough over its own shoulder to get its claws into my porcupunk, its eyes turned to the new threat.

Me.

My hand fumbled as I reached for another arrow. When I finally grasped a fletching, the arrow didn't want to come free. The Coelophysis lumbered toward me as my pet had its way with its backside. It shimmied violently as it lurched forward, trying to dislodge the nuisance tearing at its back.

An arrow finally came free. I slipped it to the string, yanked it back, and released in one motion.

The arrow sailed wide, but it had been enough to get the Coelophysis to turn its head as it dodged. By the time it looked back at me, I was running.

Or, more accurately, *kiting*.

Hurdling the underbrush, dodging saplings and thicker trees alike, I pumped my legs as fast as they would carry me. It was a testament to a lifetime of gaming that I ran for my life and yet, I wondered if I'd be able to find my way back and recover the arrow that missed the target.

My stomach lurched at the sounds of the underbrush crackling and popping beneath the beast's lumbering pursuit.

Thump, thump, crack, thump, thump.

My chest thumped. My breaths became shorter. The odds of trying to outmaneuver a monster on its own stomping grounds shrank along with my stamina bar.

Katelyn's voice came on a wind of memory *That's it. Now you're thinking like a gamer.*

It was time for a little human ingenuity. When the thumping grew louder, indicating it was right on my tail, I made a hard right, clutched a sapling with one hand, swung around the tree, and pumped my legs furiously in another direction. Sliding leaves crunched behind me, and I ventured a quick glance as the Coelophysis slid and stumbled while trying to match my turn.

*You have discovered **Mossy Grove**.*
50 XP

Its roar filled the forest as its feet found purchase and it gave chase.

A cacophony of chirping and bustling wings filled the air as birds took flight.

A few steps later, I spied another rare sapling and repeated the motion as the thumping behind me grew louder. I stumbled on tangled ground cover and almost took a header. My adrenaline fired and my eyes bulged as I tried to right myself with flailing arms while keeping my bow shouldered.

"Shiiiiiiiiit!" I regained my footing then pumped my legs for all I was worth.

I plowed through the forest, just waiting for my face to go head-on into a branch. When I tried to grasp an arrow from my quiver, I cursed the difficulty of the motion and made a mental note to relocate the container to somewhere more accessible.

The porcupunk's clicking came like a high-pitched snare roll, followed by her tiny growl. My girl was riding that prehistoric bronco like a seasoned cowboy with thighs of stone.

Glad one of us isn't completely worthless!

The Coelophysis screamed, and judging from the distance to the sound, I thought I'd actually gained a few steps. Sweeping around another trunk, I popped up on the other side of the tree and spied the enraged beast, arms raised, claws fully extended, mouth open in a roar as it bore down on me.

Luck was with me as an arrow came free from my quiver and my bow slid easily down my arm. I nocked it to the string, pulled back as hard as I could, and pushed what little air I could gather out of my lungs.

Easy. A little closer. Aim.

I peered down the shaft and centered it on the Coelophysis, then turned my focus to a smooth release of my fingers to ensure the least resistance as I loosed the arrow to sail.

The arrow zipped from my bow in a blur, and its wobble-free flight told me the practice had been worth it. Another deafening shriek echoed through the forest as the tip lodged itself in the screaming beast's throat, but this time it was more of a squeal. It lumbered. It stumbled. Then it stopped.

Your arrow strikes the young Coelophysis.

Young Coelophysis
-9 HP

"Yeah!" I yelled. "What do you think of that, bitch?"

Reaching up, the Coelophysis wrapped its hands around the arrow and tugged. When it didn't come loose, it yanked harder, and the arrow ejected with a pop. Its heath bar dropped to fifteen percent or so, as blood ejected from its mouth and rolled down its chin. A red blood drop icon appeared above its head.

> *Young Coelophysis*
> *-19 HP*
> *-4 HP (bleed)*

It was nice to inflict some bleeding damage instead of taking it!

Time seemed to stop as our eyes locked. The Coelophysis's glare was steady, intelligent, as it sized me up. A thick river of red rolled over its angular chin and down to its chest, where it converged with smaller streams of blood like tributaries feeding into a main channel. A low grumbling emitted from the beast and a fresh spurt of blood poured down its chin.

We were separated by about forty feet of thick underbrush and forest floor. My hand crept up to my quiver as the Coelophysis raised the arrow clutched in its hand and clinched its fist.

The arrow snapped like a cracker.

Without breaking its gaze, the Coelophysis's shoulder twitched forward as the clinched fist that had just broken the arrow swung across its chest. My porcupunk had come too far forward, and the dinosaur punched her, knocking her into the underbrush.

> *Young Coelophysis attacks Porcupunk.*
> *-21 HP*
> ***Stunned****

Then it lunged toward me, covering half the distance in a single leap.

I peered down the shaft of my arrow as the Coelophysis launched into the air a second time. If that thing landed on me, I was good and screwed, so I stepped gently backward while I patiently followed its arc with my aim. As it came to its apex, I filled my lungs with air. As soon as its feet touched the ground a few feet away, I flicked my fingers cleanly from the twine.

The missile zipped through the air and lodged into the Coelophysis's right eyeball with a *pop*!

The beast's head jerked back. It faltered, leaning to the side as its balance waned. Its piercing scream echoed through the trees.

I nocked another arrow.

Its health meter was a hair from empty. White juice mixed with red blood formed a pink trail dripping from the arrow lodged in its eye socket and down its face.

I relaxed my grip on the fresh arrow. The Coelophysis lumbered a final step forward as its health bar blinked. It rocked a final time then fell backward, landing with a thud on crackling underbrush. It died with a shudder.

One second, I stood there, huffing and puffing. The next, I was completely refreshed as...

A golden flash surrounded me and funneled into the sky. The number "3" popped up inches away from me then zoomed into the distance and faded with an accompanying orchestral flair of victory. My stamina was instantly refilled, and one additional breath replenished me.

You have defeated **Young Forest Coelophysis.**
550 XP

10% XP bonus for defeating an enemy more than two levels
higher
You have reached Level 3!
+1 Constitution
+1 Dexterity
You have two attribute points to spend.

Ingenuity had worked for me. I'd lured the bastard dino through the forest, using my agility against it. So, I split the additional two points between Dexterity and Constitution to increase my attack and ease all the huffing and puffing. Unless a future encounter changed my mind, I planned on following that method until I reached Level 10 or died, whichever came first. Attack, HP, and stamina all the way. If anything, the battles so far had taught me that worrying about what attribute points I spent in the early levels because of what classes I might discover later was stupid. Also, the points in strength would have made me more dangerous if I'd spent them on Dexterity for higher damage. Oh, well. Lessons learned.

I read the message in my log again.

"Ten percent bonus...nice. I've never seen that, but it only seems fair, considering the ultimate pain in the taint this world is!"

The porcupunk, who'd recovered from the stun effect of dino's punch, peered up at me with her head in that common tilt, as if she wondered why I bothered talking to her. My cat used to look at me like that.

I was level three now, but the XP and ten-percent boost filled my experience bar up more than half way. That was excellent news.

The enemies are harsh. Shit, an adolescent Dino almost killed me. Least Enora could do was grant some XP.

I told myself to quit whining. The Coelophysis hadn't laid a claw on me.

I continued to read.

Your pet has reached Level 3.
Your reputation with your pet has advanced from neutral to friendly.

Next Rank: Endeared
150/500
Your pet is now also your companion.
+2 to attack.
*You have learned the skill **Dismiss**.*
Dismiss
Dismisses your pet to the nether until summoned again
Cost: N/A
Cast Time: Instant
Cooldown: N/A
*You may now **name** your pet. Would you like to name your pet?*

"Well, why the hell not?" I glanced down at the animal perched next to my boot and smiled. "What do you think, buddy? What should I name you?"

The Porcupunk began to click again.

I chuckled, my sense of humor apparently returning with my breath.

"I don't know, is 'Click' a good name for a porcupunk?" Another drumroll of clicks emanated from the beast's throat. "Okay, okay. I reached down and ran my hand across the smooth tails on porcupunk's back. "'Click,' it is, then."

*Are you sure you want to name your pet **Click**?*

I confirmed.

Stepping high so as not to become tangled in the thick undergrowth, I approached the slain beast. Click scampered ahead of me and weaved her way through the tangles as if running on flat ground. Must have been nice.

The beast was even uglier up close. Its scales were thicker on its back and around its haunches, but one arrow had penetrated its unarmored chest. I crinkled my nose as I got a whiff of something and stood up.

"Talk about reality. Yikes!" The animal had defecated upon its death. Click had no problem with it as she openly sniffed the result before circling the animal. I wondered, had she been a boy porcupunk, would she have raised a leg?

Click finished her revolution around the dinosaur and stopped at my foot. When she had my attention, the porcupunk turned from our victim as if she wanted to lead me back to the glowing trail.

"What, no basking in the glory of our victory?"

A single click was her lone response.

I spied a loose scale on one of the Coelophysis's shoulders and snatched it.

You have found:
Small Coelophysis Scale
Possible Crafting Item

Possible Crafting Item?

"What the hell does that mean? *Possible* crafting item?"

Well, I loved me some crafting, so I plucked scales until I'd filled one of the slots in my bag with them. As it turned out, they'd each popped loose with a little effort and a few grunts, and I'd bared about a fifth of the dinosaur's body by the time a slot was full. That little bag was kind of kick ass. So I filled two more slots.

It sure would've been nice if Enora Online treated looting like all the other games I'd played, where I could just touch the beast and a loot window would appear, but I was having to work for it. The Coelophysis was so dense, so thick with muscle, I couldn't turn it over. I would've never thought to give myself more Strength points just to be able to loot, but there it was. An alternate theory to my earlier thought.

Think dragon scales!

My interface reported that I'd managed to pull 72 scales off the corpse.

The golden line leading us to my lone quest objective reappeared after combat. That it disappeared when we entered combat mode was pretty slick. But as I peered down at it, and then eyed my character sheet, I revisited my earlier sentiment about whether a level three who had to get to level eight before even performing a quest, should be following the quest line. That would only take me to an endeavor for which I was unprepared. So, I turned the line off.

"We're going to explore a little, my friend."

The porcupunk sniffed the air between us then jerked as a shriek carried through the trees. Click swiveled, bounced a few times, and settled. She sniffed the air.

"That was no dinosaur."

The shriek repeated.

"Dude!" I barked. "That sounds like a woman screaming!"

An exclamation point flashed gold, doubled in size, and

then zoomed to one side of my HUD and blinked incessantly

*You have been offered a **Legacy Quest**!*
The world of Enora has evolved for over three millennia. The creatures and humanoids of this world live unique lives. Because anything can happen in Enora, the fates of players and NPCs are intertwined.
The Scream
Recommended Level: 3
Investigate the source of the scream in the woods
Reward: 500 XP
Would you like to accept this quest?

Upon release, this game was going to suck up revenue like hookers at a bachelor party in Vegas. I focused to accept the quest, directed Click northeast with a finger, then we shot off into the forest.

15

We sped through the forest, and I found my new Constitution point a mild improvement to my overall lung capacity. I adjusted my pace, hindered by the overgrown groundcover, but at least my lungs weren't on fire and the soft breeze dried the sweat covering my face. The stamina bar hovered between 55 and 65 percent.

I focused on a new prompt.

You have gained +1 Stamina.
Keeping yourself in tip-top shape has its rewards.

If I hadn't been running through the forest seeking the source of a scream, the added point to my stamina might have made me ecstatic. Gaining attribute points in this way had never occurred to me. If I'd learned anything from all those years of gaming, it was that every point counted. It was too bad it didn't add to the parent Constitution stat, but I'd take what I could get!

My notification log blinked as soon as I closed it, so I focused on it as I jogged down a hill.

*You have discovered **The Lower Marshes**.*
125 XP Awarded

My last discovery had only been worth 50 XP, and I wondered if I received more the deeper into the forest I went. I'd just reached Level 3, and at eighty-six percent, I could almost smell Level 4.

"Unhand me, demon!" A voice, thick with a harsh accent, came on the breeze.

I snapped out of my reverie and changed course.

Sunlight burst from above in the distance, and I longed to feel the embrace of those golden rays shining down. A childhood encumbered by sunscreen would do that. Not since I stood in the village the day before had it graced my skin directly, but I skidded to a stop short of its influence, at the edge of a clearing that emptied onto a lake beach with white sand. The perimeter was surrounded by low bushes and younger trees than those found in Zhara's part of the forest.

The smell of burning wood greeted me as I came to a halt next to Click. She was hunkered behind a bush.

I dropped to my knees so I could observe unnoticed.

*You have discovered **Prowler Lake**.*
200 XP awarded

I checked my XP bar.

95%

Ugh! So close!!

I hid beside my pet as a broad-shouldered man with scraggly auburn hair dragged a woman by her arm past a campfire. Her kicking heels left trails in the sand. His powerful legs lumbered until he stopped and unceremoniously dumped her onto the sand along the edge of the lake.

He leveled a finger at her. "You might be the governor's prize, and I may not be able to beat you like I would a common, troublesome woman, but if I catch you trying to escape again, I'll put you over my knee and tan your hide good. I've been dealing with you for thousands of miles, and my patience wears thin. Keep it up, and you'll be bound until we rendezvous with his men tomorrow. Got it?" Giving her shoulder a final push, he stomped away, kicking up sand behind him.

Cocking his head toward two hunched figures sprawled next to a small campfire, he thrust his finger at one of them and barked orders.

"Bind her and lend a more vigilant eye."

As the man scrambled to his feet, the scraggly haired boss stepped closer to the fire and smacked a third man in the back of the head.

"You!" He unsheathed a long, shiny knife and used it as a pointer. "Next time she gets away from you, I'm gonna to feed ya to the fish."

You have completed the quest:
The Scream
You discovered the source of the shrieking in the Dark Wood.
500 XP awarded

Another golden flash and a giant number "4" appeared. Click jerked beside me. An illogical fear I'd be discovered caused me to cringe as the image zipped into the distance, but the men went on about their business as if nothing had happened.

While Click had obviously seen the celebration of my level, Enora had followed the standard where only my party mates or companions could.

I stood at the edge of that tree line and wondered about the algorithm used to scale XP according to the level of completion and difficulty.

Nerd alert.

You have reached Level 4!
+1 Constitution
+1 Dexterity
You have two attribute points to spend.

I spent one point on each attribute as I'd planned.

Even straining my eyes, I couldn't get a focused look at the woman or her captors against the high sun, so I scurried along the shrubbery that lined the trees until I had a better angle. Peering between the branches of a fruitless bush, I spied the female captive.

She turned her head in my direction. Her coppery skin had a shining tone whereas the surrounding men wore the prune-like flesh indicative of common sunburns. Even from this distance, her large eyes were obvious. Their roundness and the way they tapered off would've made me guess she was of Asian descent if we'd been on earth. A long-sleeved blouse that had probably once been white was covered by a ratty brown leather vest. Pants that equaled her blouse in dinginess, stopped well above her ankle boots.

Lucera's words echoed in my mind again.

Make friends.

I wondered what kind of ally this NPC might make. Considering the way she'd just been manhandled for trying to escape, and since I could see the lasers firing from her eyes at her captor's back, she at least had spirit. Maybe even additional quests!

A longer look revealed the feminine curves stretching the tattered vest, but my interest was in her condition. If I was getting involved with this fiasco, I wanted to ensure I was making the kind of friend who would fit in. With deeper consideration, I reasoned that a captive who'd traveled thousands of miles didn't seem the type to have a wealth of quests to offer, and I wasn't so low-minded as to focus on the aforementioned curves and spring her just to feed my baser instincts.

Hello. She's computer-generated, dude. Non-player character.

The leader cuffed the man on the side of the head once more, I supposed for good measure. "Just because the boss died doesn't mean I'm giving up the reward for our little princess. We traveled halfway across the world, over land and sea, and now we're in the final stretch. I'll be damned if one of you idiots is gonna ruin it for me. I'm the boss now, and if either you has a problem with that, you can quit when we return to town. Else you can challenge me for it. Any takers?"

The smaller of the two men dragged trails in the shallow sand with the toes of his boots as he paced over to the woman. Reaching into the pockets of his own shabby vest, he retrieved a cord and bound her wrists. The other one took his cuffing like a good dog and set off for the woods... in my direction.

"That's what I thought, ya ingrates." The boss stomped over and plopped in the sand at the edge of the clearing, up the beach. Setting a sack under his head, he closed his eyes and lounged in the shade cast by a few trees.

A prompt appeared, and I focused on it.

You have been offered a **Legacy** *quest:*
The Rescue
Objective: Rescue the woman from her captors
Reward: 2500 XP
Do you accept this quest?

After hastily accepting the quest, I ran a check on the boss.

Unknown Human
Level 9 Fighter

Way outside the usual two-level comfort zone, I thought. *A stealthy approach would be better.*

I whispered at my pet. "We'd never take him with his friends around."

As the larger of the two subordinates paced toward me, I ran a check on him.

Unknown Human
Level 6 Fighter

Even with Click next to me, taking him down would cause enough commotion to draw the attentions of the other two.

Then I realized Click *wasn't* next to me. For whatever reason, she'd stayed at our previous position, where she stood sniffing the air through the bush that concealed her presence. I supposed she could see fine from where she was.

Even if I took this guy out now and kept it quiet, it wouldn't be long before his two companions came looking for him. Remembering how I'd used a little ingenuity to overcome my weaknesses with the dinosaur less than an hour before, I ran through scenarios in my mind.

I didn't have a melee weapon because I'd lost my knife. A quick check of the third guy, the one who'd bound the Asian woman's hands, confirmed he was the same level as his compatriot who paced toward me.

Hmm.

A whoosh somewhere behind me on the left led to a guttural squeal, and I swiveled my head to the left to find Click laying on her side, her stubby legs pumping wildly. An arrow warbled in her side. My first inclination—to run over there and help my new companion—was stifled by the branch-cracking footfalls from the forest. I got blips of a figure as he raced between bushes, pines, and oaks.

Pressing myself against the thin trunk of a young tree near the bush, I ground my teeth as I watched my pet quiver and kick like she was trying to run somewhere on her side. A man dressed in a leather vest and tattered, knife-cut shorts wielded a bow as he stood over Click and smiled. An urge filled me to take his every tooth.

You can summon her. Don't do anything stupid.

Trapped between the bowman and the thief closing from the lake beach behind me, I leaned my back into the tree and slid around it so I sat between it and the bush. I wished I could pull a Zhara, and merge into the tree so that I might spring out and take these bastards unaware.

Though I tried to calm myself, my lungs filled only with short breaths as my adrenals surged at the sight of Click's flailing legs. My temples throbbed. My body born of Enora was functioning at full throttle.

Dammit! Just kill her already, you brutal shits!

The Level Six stepped off the beach, peered around, and spied the man who wielded the bow. His boots stomped pine straw no more than five feet from me as he crossed the distance. As he passed me by, a prompt popped up on my screen.

Thanks to your sneaky stillness, you have learned the skill,
Stealth.
You fade into the shadows, stalking your victims.
*Your **Stealth** skill is now Rank 1.*
50 XP

Nice. For all the good it did Click.

Sliding the bow onto his shoulder and grinning down at the paralyzed animal, the stringy-haired, sweaty bastard reached into a belt sheath and withdrew a knife. With one decisive swing, he lodged the knife into Click's neck, twisted, and yanked it away. A stream of blood signaling the end of my porcupunk spurt onto the pine straw. The bow wielder grabbed the flesh tails on the back of my pet, raised the corpse into the air, and swung his trophy out before him.

Click was limp.

Dead.

I wished her spikes would pop out and puncture that asshole's hand. My face flashed hot as I fantasized about ripping my bow from my shoulder, nocking an arrow, and ending that mother...

After a back clap of congratulations over his hunting skills from the Level Six, the two men stepped back onto the beach.

"Hey, Red, looks like I got us some dinner!"

Huddling next to the tree, its rough bark scratching my cheek, I noted a red prompt on my interface display. I mentally focused on it, though I predicted what it would say.

Your pet has died.

The boss's voice came to me on the breeze from the beach. "'Least you're good for something! These two about let the miner run off into the woods!"

Miner?

Once they were on the beach and had cleared the woods, I turned my attention to the Summon skill. Leveling out my breathing and focusing my thoughts, I stretched out a clawed hand and pushed thoughtful intent through it. A blue glow emanated from beneath my skin. I ensured it was well concealed by the tree. I found myself wanting to scream in victory as my lost pet faded into existence.

Not only could I summon Click, it seemed there was also no cool down after a pet's death. The five-minute cool down I'd noticed must have only applied after casting *Summon Pet*.

Click shook her head a few times and peered up at me. All her teeth were visible as she spread her lips wide, but she wasn't smiling.

She. Was. Pissed. The red mood bar under her picture on my interface confirmed it.

Angry

A glance back at the beach proved poorly timed as a river of blood splattered the sand at the hunter's feet when he ripped his knife from the swinging porcupunk carcass he held by one foot, disemboweling it. My shudder came not at the violence, but in anticipation of robbing him of that simple copper knife and spilling his blood in a similar way.

My companion stepped past me, and though she remained concealed, she peered at the beach and wrinkled her nose. A quiet click popped from her throat. Then she turned her gaze on me. A low whine emitted from the beast, and I knew what she wanted.

I shook my head. "Sorry, babe. Too many of them versus two of us and an unfamiliar woman. She might choose the devils she knows. We need to make sure she's interested in leaving with us, versus going it alone."

"Click. Click." She turned her eyes toward the group again.

"No. Uh-uh."

She clicked again.

I sighed. Why was she being so persistent? Pet or not, game world or not, the porcupunk had wants of her own. Gone were the days of mindless companions. But when I looked back at her, noting the way her narrow lips screwed up in a sneer, the weight of what this meant hit me.

Click remembered how she died.

Oh, that is so messed up.

The hunter carried on his celebration. "Fresh meat'll be a nice change. Look at all that fat! I bet it'll crackle and pop over the fire. I can smell it now."

I stroked my pet's fleshy hairs and then scratched the top of her head.

She squinted as my fingernails worked at the knob above and between her eyes.

"Okay, buddy. We'll backtrack, wait for nightfall. Good enough?"

Without waiting for a response, I pushed myself up against the tree, cocked my head over my shoulder to ensure the coast was clear, then paced off into the woods, hoping my pet would follow.

Enjoy your meal, asshole. If shit goes sideways, it might just be your last.

16

Reflections of light rippled on the surface of the lake beneath myriad stars. They were a welcome relief from the canopy of leaves and tangled branches blocking the sky since I'd entered the forest. I scanned for constellations I might recognize but glimpsed none, which made sense. Though I had no idea how long I sat there and scoped out the scene, I peered up later to find the stars had changed positions.

It reminded me that the world spun on an axis like any other planet, and a momentary sense of awe tickled my brain. I still couldn't see the moon, but judging from the white light bathing the lake, it was likely somewhere above the trees behind me.

I scanned the scene from my new perspective. I'd wanted to circle around and come in from a different angle, lest I risk crossing paths with the bowman who had killed the previous iteration of Click. If Enora remade humans based on their own images, they were creatures of habit, and walking a recurring patrol path fit the bill.

As I peered across the beach and caught sight of the

woman, she propped herself on her elbows, almost staring right at me, although she didn't indicate any knowledge of my presence. Shuffling in the sand to get comfortable as she propped herself up, her shoulders hunched and dropped with frustration. Sitting upright, she raised the bindings, twisted her fists and flinched. They'd tied them so they wrapped around her wrists, with a long line between each hand.

With a quick glance over one shoulder to ensure no one was watching, she pulled her hands close to her body and glared down. Light surrounded them, bloomed white, then dimmed and winked out again.

What the shit?

I focused on her.

Unknown Human
Level 8
Light Priestess

Light Priestess. Hmm. Did she just heal chafing around her wrists?

The way she'd glanced over her shoulder to make sure the coast was clear, I realized she'd been hiding her abilities from her captors. That's why they'd called her a *miner*. They didn't know about her magic! I still didn't know what they'd meant by the label, but the more important attribute of this NPC on the beach had just literally flashed before my eyes.

A healer?

Suddenly, the screaming woman and the rescue quest offered upon my arrival at the lake seemed a lot less like a coincidence. Just because the A.I. had been letting the world evolve didn't mean it didn't interfere, as I'd been thinking for some reason. Now that I reconsidered, wasn't it the system's job to spawn these quests? Present these opportunities?

Click and I worked our way around the lake, ensuring each footfall fell silently. The sound of snores filled the air as we closed the gap and the wind changed direction. I poked my head out of the foliage and peered up and down the beach.

Text popped up at the bottom of my HUD.

Your stealth skill has increased to Rank 2.

The woman's face glowed in the starlight. Her raven hair reflected the white of the moon. Warmth coursed through my chest. I shook my head in derision.

NPC. *Say it five times. Non-player character. Not a woman. Ones and zeroes. Lock it in! Finish the quest!*

She pushed herself up, did a double-take in my direction, and squinted.

Did her eyes just flash?

The Light priestess glanced over her shoulder, up the beach, and back. Up the beach. Back at me, again. Knowing I'd been spotted, I slid forward between two bushes and used exaggerated gestures to convey my intent.

I pointed. *You.* I jerked a thumb at myself. *Me.* I dipped two fingers in a walking motion and thrust the thumb over my shoulder.

After another head check as if she was trying to change lanes, the woman pumped a hand, urging me back. I turned to look in the same direction she had, but the view was blocked by the bushes and medium-thick trunks of high trees.

I threw her an exaggerated nod to ensure she'd see it

from where she sat. Click and I tiptoed further up the beach and found a new vantage point. From here, I saw two moons perched high in the star-filled sky. One was bright white, the other washed in an orange tinge.

Just as I stuck my neck out, boots stroked sand and a shadow cast by the high moons passed across us. I stilled as his wretched scent blew at me on the breeze, knowing any noise could bring this little prison break to a screeching halt.

An indicator popped up in my vision.

Your stealth skill has increased to Rank 3.

I breathed a sigh of relief, thankful my companion had not chosen that moment to click. No sooner had the thought crossed my mind, then a low growling utterance vibrated in the aggressive little beast's throat.

Raising my head just enough to see over the top of the dense bush with blooming purple flowers, I spied the bow bouncing over the bastard's shoulder. My eyes trailed down to a wooden handle in a sheath on is hip.

That's the bastard, all right. And Click knows it.

Envisioning my plan, drawing the movement inside my mind's eye, I scooted around the bush and took a final gander up and down the beach. Hesitation was the enemy of victory. The thief was close and his friends distant.

Now or never.

Even if I hadn't had a stealth skill to speak of, the thick sand of the lake beach made for silent movement. My chest beat a hard, steady rhythm, and I bent low as I eyed the wooden handle at his waist. The moons bathed me in their light, and I had little doubt my target's friends would spot me if they woke.

Every reason to move decisively.

Extending my shaking hand as I prowled closer, I focused hard on that wooden handle until I was just a short step away. Then I sprung.

Slipping the knife from the sheath, I threw my opposite hand around the porcupunk murderer's mouth and shoved the blade into his neck.

Surprise Attack!
Damage Bonus: 200%
Critical Hit!
Damage Bonus: 100%
Arterial gouge!
Bleed Bonus: 100%

Unknown Fighter
-44 HP

Your surprise attack has inflicted a mortal wound.
Mortal Wounds require instant healing or will lead to rapid death.

The cords in the side of his neck tensed and provided more resistance than I'd expected, but he'd kept his blade sharp, so a good hard thrust sliced through the tissue.

I pried his face backward as I drove my knee into the bottom of his spine and eased his back down on top of my chest. The sand broke our fall, and I managed to keep my wind as I bore his weight. I clinched my teeth and sneered. My legs swung easily around his emaciated waist for leverage as I cupped his mouth and yanked his head back, widening my access to his neck.

But his face, the jutting chin angling into my hand...it all felt....

Real.

He grabbed my trembling arms with both hands and yanked my knife hand away, dislodging the blade. But it only increased the damage. Blood jetted from the wound and a gurgling rose from his throat as it poured into his lungs.

Bleeding Effect
(Mortal Wound)

Unknown Fighter
-15 HP
(Bleed)
-17 HP

His struggle became vital as his life surged out of him in a sickening wet pulse of gore. The surprising strength of his clutching hand as he pulled desperately at my wrist and tried to call out called for more strain. Chills ran through me as I fought with him, my muscles protesting as I bore down, yanking his face to one side so the wound on the opposite gaped wider. His spurting blood was painted black by the moonlight.

"Mmmm!" he screamed through my hands. "Mmmm! Gmmm!"

I'd never conceived of such horror in a game, but despite my logical mind's insistence that I was in an artificial world, killing a manufactured being, I was a murderer.

It was only by sheer adrenaline—okay, virtual adrenaline—and the fear of being discovered that I was able to shake off the vibe of authentic violence. I squeezed my eyes closed as I begged Enora to just let him die. I didn't want to be here, wrapped around this man like a striped boa, squeezing the existence out of him as his life force poured into the sand.

Despite the system message about mortal wounds, his health bar seemed to empty in slow motion, but eventually his spurting eased to a trickle. I dropped the knife, grabbed a handful of sand, punched his jaw twice, and uncovered his mouth just long enough to shove a handful of sand between his lips. Sweat beaded and ran down my forehead.

Gods, please. Please, just die!

Sand flew into my face and I realized my pet was bouncing back and forth next to me. I hadn't given her an order to attack!

I cocked my head in Click's direction and whispered, "Help, dude."

Click's weight piled on as she leaped onto our victim's chest. She glared into his eyes as she peeled back her lips and sank her jowls into the man's cheek to rip away a bloody chunk of revenge.

Grunts of pain burst from his clamped mouth. "Mmm! Mmmf!"

I growled into his ear, "You should just *die*. Let go."

His utterances into my hand sounded loud enough to wake the undead. I groped in the sand, found the knife, plunged it into his chest, then twisted the blade.

Warm death soaked my hand, sand flew into the air as he kicked in his death throes, and finally, my enemy stilled.

You have vanquished Level 6 fighter.
650 XP

That's a rapid death?

Sucking wind, I pushed his limp body to one side and crawled out from under him. I spied the three huddled figures lying dormant around the remnant coals of the campfire. It was a miracle no one had heard.

Peering further up the beach, my gaze locked with the only person who responded to the conflict at all—the mage. She stood straight as a board on her knees near the water, with both hands cupped over her mouth.

I clutched the man's vest with quivering hands and dragged him toward the forest. At first, my fists wouldn't cooperate, and impatience flooded through me. Releasing my hands and flexing my fingers repeatedly, I grasped the tattered leather vest and pulled again. Even with the gift of my new, stronger body and his thin constitution, I strained against his weight as his ass and the heels of his boots left a curvy trail of resistance in the thick sand at the edge of the lake.

I scanned the trail of his arterial blood in the sand. An image of Sarlacc from that ancient movie, *Return of the Jedi*, cycled through my mind.

In contrast to the gruesome scene, Click pranced happily in a circle around us as I heaved the dead weight behind the same flowering bush where it had all started. I peered down at her.

"There's something seriously wrong with you, dude. Shit."

It's a game, man. Chill out before you screw up and get yourself killed. Breathe!

I snagged one of the flowers from the dense bush and dropped it on my victim's chest.

"Rest in peace, motherfucker."

If the struggle I'd just been through taught me anything, it was that I was going to have to tighten up and thicken my skin.

Once the Level 6 was hidden from the moonlight, I

peered across the lake beach at the woman and muttered, "I hope you were worth it, lady."

I paused to recover, taking deep breaths and slowing my heart rate. Then I navigated the thin line of trees and bushes, circling around and crossing the sand on the other side of the campfire. Keeping a constant watch over the huddled figures, I shuffled to where the woman sat.

The bloody knife was still clutched in my trembling hands.

Simple Copper Knife
Level 3
Durability: 12 of 16
3-6 Damage

She jerked when I gripped her wrist, so I stopped and tried to convey my intent to help her with my expression.

Her chest rose with a deep breath then fell with a long sigh. She pushed her arms toward me.

I forced myself to focus on her bindings, and they snapped after a few wrenches of the blade. Her huge sienna irises rose to mine again, but I found myself unable to meet her gaze. The image of her hand covering her mouth as I'd murdered her captor was frozen in my mind. When I'd cut her free and ventured a glance, her attention was locked onto the bloody knife.

I leveled my gaze on her and whispered. "Hey. I would never hurt you. Sometimes you do what has to be done, and that man stood between you and freedom. I'm a friend. Rest easy."

She parted her lips as if to reply. The scent of copper wafted into my nostrils as I held a finger painted in dried blood to my lips, begging her silence. Then I cocked my head to one side, pointed at her, then Click, and then the woods.

"I'll catch up," I whispered.

The woman stared at me for entirely too long before she nodded her understanding and glanced at the porcupunk. Then she nodded again, her eyes flicking toward her feet. A rope I hadn't noticed tied her ankles together. I cut it. Getting to her feet, she turned toward the sleeping masses just thirty feet away.

Stroking Click to get her attention, I pointed at the footprints we'd left in the sand.

She silently scampered off in that direction. Stopping to peer back at the woman, Click left no doubt she'd understood what I wanted. The captive shot me a final glance and followed my beast until they disappeared into the shadows of the tree line.

Then it was just me and three assholes on a lake beach. I focus-clicked on the exclamation point prompt on the right side of my vision.

My experience bar had jumped about five inches forward, and while that was nothing to sneeze at, I needed to play smart. I might get a slight XP bonus by sliding my new blade into the leader's throat and inflicting a mortal wound, but I balked at the idea of waking the two who snoozed nearby.

I also wondered if "Light priestess" was a non-violent tradition. Just in case she stood in the shadows of the trees, watching, I played it cool.

The revenge taken on the bastard who killed Click turned out to feel anything but rewarding, but the mage was sprung from captivity. Mission accomplished. That needed to be good enough. But I saw no notification showing I'd completed the quest.

I checked the quest dialogue.

Legacy Quest
The Rescue
Objective: Rescue the prisoner from her captors: Complete
New Objective: Reunite with the woman in the woods and
see her to safety
Reward: 2500 XP

As I dusted sand off my ass and turned to take the shortest route back to the shadows of the Dark Wood, I spied the bundle upon which the boss had earlier rested his head. Packed in the sand only five paces from him, it lay ripe for the taking. My brain itched despite my trembling hands.

Gotta do it.

With a silent sigh, I tiptoed through the sand, carving a wide arc around the largest of the three men. I focused on the steady rise and fall of his rotund torso as I approached.

His snoring broke, and I paused, clutching the knife in a white-knuckled grip. His chest hitched, settled, and finally resumed a normal rhythm,

I released a slow breath into my cupped hand. Careful not to kick any sand in his hairy, stupid face as I passed, I clutched the large cloth sack in my free hand and tiptoed toward the tree line. The distant mounds of humans lay still as I crossed through the sand, and I stopped just beneath the perimeter shadows to take a final look.

The boss sat up, resting on both elbows. He looked around the clearing, first toward his men, then to where he'd last seen his prisoner. I didn't wait around long enough for him to check over his shoulder and locate me.

When I was sure I was deep enough into the trees to go unheard, I took off.

"Wake up, ya worthless bunch of ingrates! She's gone again!" A few seconds later, he yelled, "You follow those tracks, I'll go with the other! I didn't come all this way..." his words trailed off as I hustled through the woods.

When I'd depleted 25% of my stamina bar, I brought up my map and scanned for the blue dot. Click was just south-west of my current position. I headed that way.

Would the mage be there? Given her reaction when I murdered one of her captives, I wasn't sure.

When I found Click, I was pleased to see the mage sitting on a fallen tree, arms between her knees, her neck bent as she whispered something to my pet.

Click made a chattering sound.

The mage glanced up.

The black forest shrouded her features.

I spoke in rushed whispers as I approached. "I'm Gemini. You've already met Click. I'd love to be more formal with the introductions, but we're about to have company." I thrust a thumb over my shoulder. The mage showed no sign she would bolt. No matter which sets of footprints the men followed, they would be coming in our general direction, and we needed to make tracks of our own.

A golden flash funneled into the air. A huge 5 popped in front of me and zipped into the distance.

You have reached Level 5!

+1 Constitution

+1 Dexterity

You have two attribute points to spend.

Click jumped side to side in response, but the woman didn't react.

I pumped my fist in celebration, and Click clicked. Maybe that took gall, considering the situation, but hey, screw it. The levels were finally coming now. As my eyes had adjusted to the darkness surrounding us, I noticed the mage's eyes flared.

"Sorry for the outburst, I just leveled." I ticked off a point for Constitution and one for Dexterity.

"I—" she raised a fist to her mouth and cleared her throat. "I am Roshan, Clan Fortwan." She balled up her fist and held it to the center of her chest as she slid off the log and dropped to one knee. "My life is yours, Gemini."

"Say what?" I raised both eyebrows, wondering if I'd heard her right. I glanced at Click, but she didn't seem to have any answers. "Uh, no. That won't be necessary. I just couldn't stand to see you treated like that."

That and you were worth a bundle of XP.

Reading the plain confusion on her face, I continued. "I was there earlier today, after you tried to escape. The way that man handled you, how he threatened to tan your hide— well, that shit wasn't cool."

"You saw the men around the camp and came back for me?"

Shuddering at the coppery smell of blood that wouldn't leave my nostrils, I forced a nod. "Yes, that and one of them killed my pet."

Her facial muscles widened into an expression of awe. "Oh! You can resurrect beasts? Like the adventurers of yore?"

I shrugged.

"And though you were easily outnumbered, you waited

until nightfall and returned to deliver me from their clutches. Do your kind always risk their lives for strangers?"

"I didn't like the way that guy handled you." Voices echoed in the distance, though I couldn't make out what they were saying. "Look, we gotta hustle."

"You saved me from life as a concubine at the whim of their benefactor." Still bent on one knee, she lowered her head again. "Where you go, shall I go." She clutched my ankle and nodded furiously. "Thank you, adventurer. I will be forever grateful. Please, please don't leave me behind. I do not know these lands and am far from my home. Accept my pledge, and I will serve at your side with diligence and loyalty."

"You certainly don't waste any time, do you?"

She raised her face and tilted her head. "Do you believe time is to be wasted?"

We turned our heads at the nearing sound of cracking branches. Click turned and took a few steps in that direction, sniffing the air. Pivoting to face the direction from which I thought the sound had come, I stared into the inky blackness, but there was no seeing.

Images of giant spiders, lumbering dinosaurs, and kidnappers armed with bows and knives spurred me into action. Turning, I clutched her arm and lead her away through the forest.

"Time certainly isn't to be wasted, right now. Let's roll."

As we set off at a fast walk, I opened my interface and assigned one point to Dexterity and one to Constitution to match the ones the system auto-attributed to those stats.

G3m1n1 Fowler

Human

Level 5 Woodsman

Strength: 4
Dexterity: 13
Intelligence: 1
Wisdom: 1
Constitution: 13
Charisma: 10
Your base Dodge skill has increased to Rank 5.
+4.5% additional chance to dodge creatures of equal or lower level
Diminished returns for creatures of a higher level, with a penalty of 1 for each level higher than your own

Balanced stamina, double digits in two major attributes, a climbing Dodge skill and the beautiful specimen jogging next to me. Things were looking up! Especially for a Level 5!

I couldn't help but turn my head and flash my new friend a smile.

Then I face-planted into a tree.

 hite lights danced before my eyes like tiny fairies as pain webbed across my forehead.

-27 HP

Great.

Blinking furiously, I peered up to find Roshan staring down at me. A rapid clicking sound filled one ear, and I turned my head to find Click's snout near my face, lips peeled back, head bobbing up and down.

"Are you laughing at me, you little ungrateful—"

"Perhaps," Roshan's soft voice whispered, "I should lead." A flash of light traced the outline of her eyeballs, then faded. "Follow me." She extended her hand and helped me to my feet.

As we ran, her hand still grasping mine, I leaned my head toward her. "What the hell was that?"

After a furtive glance over her shoulder, probably seeking pursuers, she shrugged mid-stride. "What was what?"

"You know." I wiggled my fingers before my face errati-cally. "That whole white-light-around-the-eyeballs thing."

"Inner Illumination." Three full strides later, when she saw I didn't get it, she continued the explanation. "It is a Level 4 spell of the light. It allows me to see in dark spaces."

"That sounds useful. I think I've seen that in an RPG before."

Though I couldn't read her expression with her head turned away from me, I could hear the confusion in her voice as she replied.

"RPG?"

Red flashing text appeared in my HUD and adapted to the forest's darkness so I could read it clearly as Roshan led me along.

It is a violation of the Enora Online Player's Agreement to discuss the outside world with NPCs. While Infinity Designs understands the use of common expressions in day-to-day gameplay, it is forbidden to inform NPCs of your life outside the game world. Although NPCs will often ignore concepts that don't apply to life in the world they know, there will be circumstances where the built-in game filters are subverted. In these instances, you can use dismissive terms such as 'never mind' or 'it's not important' and the NPC will move forward without further inquiry. In these instances, the A.I. makes every effort to adjust the filter, but flagrant violations will be penalized by a loss of 25% of your total XP, including any levels lost.

Please focus here to acknowledge.

I acknowledge that I have been warned that it is in violation of the Enora Online Player's

***Agreement to discuss the outside world with
NPCs.***

I focused on the acknowledgement with a sigh and
turned my attention back to Roshan, who awaited clarification. Taking heed of the warning, I shook my head.

"Never mind. It's not important. My stamina is getting
too low to talk, anyway."

"I sense the Light in you, Gemini. Perhaps I should
teach you the spell when we come to a stop."

"You can teach me—"

"Jump!" Roshan blurted.

She leaped but did not relinquish her grip on my hand.
I jumped without thinking and realized halfway through
my arc that I was hurdling another thin, fallen tree. Something distant on the right combatted for my attention. I
pulled Roshan to a halt and thrust out a finger.

"Do you see that?"

Her eyes flashed again and then she nodded. "Yes.
Command me. Should we run to it or away?"

"I don't want to command you."

Her head tilted to one side.

I sighed. "Let's run toward it."

A minute later, we peered up at a flashing tree with
strangely knotted branches and thick leaves. As a player of
numerous games where flashing objects indicated quest
targets, there wasn't any doubt this tree had something to do
with Zhara's.

I peered at Roshan and muttered. "If you don't share
my quest, I wonder why you can see the flashing." She
seemed to ignore me as she bent and peered at the base of
the tree.

There were new sub-tabs at the top of my Companion

tab labeled, Click and Roshan. I clicked on the tab with her name. A brief representation of her stats was printed here, along with an image of her adorned in her current attire, and a list of her spells. But I really didn't have time to get into that with people chasing us and all.

"Here!" she blurted in a whisper.

Roshan had gone a few paces ahead of me. She doubled over and fiddled around at the base of the tree.

My gaze naturally magnetized to her backside. Even in the dark, I could see it was a nice—

She spun around and swung out one arm.

I gaped. "A door?"

"This is a very exciting development, Gemini. A door in a tree. It seems life with you will be quite interesting, indeed!"

I held a finger to my lips and glanced around the forest.

Roshan whispered, "Apologies. I was excited. It will not happen again."

I waved the apology away. "No worries." Though the door frame blinked gold, the light didn't extend into the darkness beyond. "Looks like a good place to hide out, if nothing else."

She nodded enthusiastically. "If you don't mind being in close quarters with me. I hope you'll find it preferable to our odds out here in the darkness." She waved me forward. "Please, my liege."

I peered for a moment into the dark hole, then scanned our perimeter to make sure we weren't being followed. I rushed inside.

And fell down a flight of stairs.

18

-79 *HP*

It wasn't until I landed with a back-crunching thud at the bottom of the steps that I realized my health bar was blinking. When I tried to roll onto my butt, all the nerves in my right leg shrieked in symphony as if someone had punched me with a cattle prod. The jolt shot up my hip, raced up the side of my torso, radiated across my ribs, and zapped my spine with a lightning bolt. It was everything I could do not to scream.

Instead, the molar-clinching growl I opted for was quite intense.

Click scampered down the stairs, then the outer door closed and sealed with a hollow thunk. Muted footfalls scampered down the stairs in short steps, then Roshan slid to the floor next to me.

"I am so sorry, Gemini. I forgot that you could not see."

"I think I broke my leg. Of all the stupid, clumsy—" I rocked back and forth, cradling my knee in my arms as Roshan grasped my shoulder. Lowering herself to one knee, she pressed a firm hand to my chest and held it there despite my resistance. When I realized she was waiting for me to stop freaking out, I did my best imitation of a calm person.

She barely glanced at the injured leg before she spoke. "It's not broken. Here, set your back against this wall and let me look."

The pain resonated. I cursed under my breath as I shoved my back to the wall.

Leave it to me to kill myself before Enora can.

Roshan peered over at Click and said, "You go and stand guard like a good...whatever you are."

The animal clicked.

I grunted my answer. "Yes. Yes, do as she says."

My pet scurried up the stairs.

A glow filled the room. Roshan kneeled beside me, her hands joined at the thumbs and cupped above my knee. Golden light gloved her fingers and palms, and a whooshing sound filled the room. Her vest and undershirt rippled as if caught in a slight breeze. Relief washed over me as the worst of the pain dissipated.

$$+11 \; HP$$
$$+11 \; HP$$
$$+11 \; HP$$

"A healing spell?"

A smile crossed her lips as the glow illuminated her features. It was the first time I'd seen her up close in adequate lighting. What a heartbreaker. My mind took a mental snapshot.

I'd always hated the way women were rated on a one-to-ten scale. Maybe my lack of interest in the objectification of the fairer sex anywhere except inside my own head made me the unusual one, but I just wasn't big on locker room talk.

Setting that sentiment aside, Roshan was a fucking fifteen.

My neck warmed above my collar as I consumed her features. Or maybe it had been the healing spell.

It's because she feels real.

It occurred to me suddenly that all those other video games' NPCs designed to be attractive were very different from this one. If I believed Lucera and Nokuro, these NPCs had familial lines, and Roshan was born to parents like any human in my old world. A meticulous scan of her high cheekbones, smooth forehead, and angular chin brought questions. Did she resemble her parents? What traits passed from generation to generation? Were genes simulated and passed on?

Roshan tilted her head to one side. "Is it better?"

"Hmm?"

The low health warning indicators had expired. The red bar representing my HP pool ticked a final time and was full.

My voice sounded distant to my own ear as I replied. "It's perfect."

Her shoulders hunched and she giggled a little. "My first real cast against an injury other than my own. I hid my skills for so long, but you are my liberator and I couldn't think of a worthier patient." She covered her mouth as she chuckled out the energy of her enthusiasm.

I flinched as she slipped her arms between my neck and the wall. Though I jerked at first, I found the pressure of her embrace welcome. I'd been so tense since first walking into the forest, and the hug was therapy.

My mind flashed to my old guild mates—M3y3r, Katelyn, TheRod—and what they might think of this display of affection with an NPC. I should've felt silly, holding this non-player woman. I rested my head on her shoulder and sniffed something familiar, like Cocoa.

"Well, congratulations on your first cast. I'm glad you were around to relieve my pain."

She maintained her grip as she spoke while shaking her head.

"If I had not been around, you likely would not have fallen down the stairs."

"Hey, it's all good. Like it never happened." I used the moment to open the companion tab again.

Roshan
Human
Level 8 Light Priestess
(Two available attribute points)

I skipped her stats, my eyes gravitating to her spell list.

Inner Illumination:
Level 4
Allows the caster to see in dark environments
Mana Cost: 35
Cooldown: N/A
Minor Heal:
Level 7
Healing over time (HOT) spell
Mana Cost: 40
Cooldown: N/A
Heals injuries for 10 to 15 hit points per second for 10 seconds. Potency dependent on the Intelligence of the caster, and Light Skill level

Maximum yield: 150 hit points per cast
Outer Illumination:
Level 5
Projects a ball of light that floats above the caster for 10
Minutes
Mana Cost: 45 Mana

Interesting.
Rescuing this one was a good idea!
Another prompt caught my attention.

*You have discovered the **Oak Cellar.***
+250 XP

Legacy Quest Completed!
The Rescue
Complete: Rescue the prisoner from her captors: Complete
Complete: Reunite with the woman in the woods and see her
to safety
Reward: 2000 XP

I shrugged the thought off and pushed myself up. Despite her healing magic, I set a stabilizing hand against the cold wall and cautiously tested weight on my leg.

"All better?"

Without the glow from her healing spell, I couldn't see her in the inky blackness.

She responded as if she'd read my mind. "Oh! Just one moment."

Another glow emanated from her hand then a ball of light hovered overhead. It rippled and shimmered on the walls and ceiling as if it reflected water.

Ceiling...

I pointed up. "What the heck?" I traced from the ceiling to the corner where it met the wall and down to the floor. "Where are we, and why are walls beneath a tree made of stone?"

Roshan shrugged. "I come from very far away. I'm afraid I wouldn't know."

I nodded. "I know that feeling. I'm no stranger to being a... *stranger* in a new place."

Her eyebrows rose in surprise. "You're not from here?"

It was my turn to chuckle. "I'm from about as far from here as one can get." Before she could ask the obvious follow-up question, I waved a gently dismissive hand, recalling the warning about the players' agreement. "It's a long story better saved for a safer time. For now, it seems we've entered our first dungeon."

"Dungeon?"

Reflections of the overhead light spell glowed in Click's eyes as she curled into a ball at the top of the stairs. I cocked my chin in that direction.

"Either we go back up there, into the dark forest, where we can't use your light spell without fear of being caught, or —" I peered up the stony hallway into the darkness beyond, "we forge ahead and see what adventures await."

"But we cannot see very far," she squinted into the hall-way. "Even with both my light spells, I cannot see what lies ahead. How can you call it a dungeon?"

"Because I was sent on a quest here to eradicate a bad guy."

Roshan cocked an eyebrow like a pro. "Bad guy? A quest?" She gave me a cursory up-and-down gander. "It can't be that such fortune has befallen me."

"Well, I'm not all *that*. I try to hold my own and all, but Enora takes some heavy lifting."

Her tone turned inquisitive. "You mentioned in the forest that you leveled. Are you an adventurer, Gemini?" When I didn't immediately answer, she traced the frame of my body again from forehead to ankles, then up again. In other circumstances, I might have been self-conscious at the way she kept scanning me, but something about her demeanor set me at ease. "Are you a humble man? Is that it? Does it offend you that I ask?"

My threadbare duds dangled in all their lowliness as I threw my arms out and presented my pathetic form.

"Don't let the rags fool you. I'm in this to win this. I'm a long-hauler. I shall vanquish all mine enemies with great prejudice."

I chuckled.

Roshan clasped her hand to her chest and breathed a fast sigh.

"Oh, thank the Light! I feared I had pledged myself to the service of a pauper!" She burst out laughing.

I found her mirth contagious.

Her face flushed pink, and I found myself enamored, not just with her physical features, but with her intense presence. She bled positivity.

Wait. Did she say 'pledged' herself? I suppressed the urge to shake my head at my stupidity. *No, it means something else to her, surely. Probably just an indebtedness of which I'll relieve her—after reaching Level Ten.*

Enora saw fit to toss me a gift, and I'd be damned if I'd take it for granted!

"In a sense, I guess I am a pauper, but maybe we could change that together." Then I instantly wondered if that had been stupid. Did she really care about money, or had she been joking? How much might my words muddy the path our friendship might take? More importantly, how could I convey I was a good person, worthy of her time? What would she want to hear?

She acts like a person. Treat her like one. Everything else around here is ridiculously genuine. So be that.

I drew a serious tone. "I would also understand if you wanted to return home. I can't imagine the suffering you've experienced, and being dragged away from all you've known has to be painful." When I realized I was jabbering in the vein of the socially-challenged, I ceased my exaggerated hand gestures and tried again. "If it's your desire to return home, I'd be honored to help you find your way."

Roshan smiled, her mouth so full of tiny, pearly teeth I thought they could've illuminated that dank, damp tunnel in place of her light spell.

The smile faded as she peered down at her hands and twisted her fingers. "You are an honorable man, I can see this. But I have no desire to return home. Those men..." She huffed a couple short breaths and her chest jittered with emotion. "They killed my father. I'm afraid my family shares his fate."

This NPC is losing her shit like a real person.

A tear trickled down her face, and the way her shoulders shuddered, a wave a guilt surprised me. My humor was the shield of a past life that I'd used to protect myself from bullies of all kinds, but now it just made me feel like shit.

I was responding to Roshan on a *human* level.

"I'm... I'm sorry, Roshan. I know what it's like to lose your family."

She swiped at her face, as if the tear might burn her cheeks if left to roll.

"You are a kind and patient man. Let us speak no further of these things. I have bound myself to you, and your causes shall be my own. My abilities were never welcome in the place I called home, and if you offer the opportunity to use them, then Solara has deemed me worthy to serve."

So, her people believe in the Solara deity, the A.I.'s in-world name. Just like Lucera said.

"Who would frown on your ability to heal the injured?"

Her humorless smile didn't reach her eyes in the way her laughter had moments before. "When my parents learned I'd inherited the gift of mana from our ancestral line, they hid it from the warlord's regent in our village. I only learned the few spells I know by the generosity of a priest who practiced the old ways and detected The Light within me, much as I do in you. I feel its warmth on you, it's... overpowering. And yet, new. Raw. Almost as if you have only just been born."

"You sense it?"

She gave a single, curt nod. "We sense our own kind."

Well, you got the 'just born' part right. I suspected she was detecting Zhara's buff.

"My teacher sensed my blessing when I was young, although others called it a curse. He knew others would've seen me as a threat. In his youth, he encountered the harsh injustices visited on those born with mana pools. He was sent to live in isolation by his parents. For years built a congregation in the hills, until their dwellings were pillaged and burned by the warlord. When he sought out a new family in his middle age, he found us. In the wake of his great loss, he swore an oath to protect the Mana Born."

"He sounds like a devout man."

"The most of all, I'm certain. There is wisdom in your words."

The richness of her accent brought me to wonder why I understood her.

"Roshan, does everyone in Enora speak the same language?"

Her head tilted. "Why would you think such a thing? There are many languages in the world." She squinted an eye and took a subtle step backward. "Have you never met someone of my race? How is it you speak my language?"

A lump formed in my throat at her sudden suspicion. Fear filled her eyes, and hesitancy to answer seemed to disturb her further.

"What trickery is this? I sense the Light, and yet you use the magic of demons."

"No trickery!" I held out both hands and she flinched. "Not at all. Just...give me a second, would you?"

Her gaze solidified, her eyes locking with mine as if she sought answers printed on the brain behind them, but she held fast and nodded.

I opened my interface and thought *Languages*.

My character sheet flipped open and, tucked away amidst the numerous skills, was a tooltip regarding language:

Languages:
All neutral and lawful languages
Tool tip: You learn languages of neutral and lawful beings
instantly upon hearing them.

That little mystery solved, her question posed an entirely different problem, especially considering how she'd asked it. I didn't know how to explain my presence in the world with these abilities without breaking the players' agreement and losing a quarter of my XP.

Here was an interesting predicament. My thinking turned tactical. Scenarios danced through my mind for another moment, and then I wanted to smack my head. I was complicating things. The solution was simple.

Tell believable stories. Keep it short and simple so you don't get caught in lies, and roll with it.

Roshan had been trained by a priest. She attributed my rescue of her to Solara. Following that line of thought, the little white lie I needed to tell was obvious. I'd play the shit up.

"The gods blessed me at birth with the gift of tongues."

That was a pretty damned good answer, especially considering the walloping follow-up I delivered to appease her concern about demons.

"But only neutral and lawful languages. I do not understand the languages of evil beings."

That was what I called, 'bringing it home.'

Her jaw dropped and one hand covered her agape mouth. "You lie!" she barked through her palm.

At first, I thought maybe I wasn't so sneaky. But her voice had been void of accusation, so I decided to test my interface to find out what she really thought.

I ran a quick inspection of my new companion as she glared.

Disposition: Friendly

Whew. It worked.

She splayed her hand over her heart, and the gesture accentuated her curves. I made a point to keep my gaze high.

She bowed her head slightly. "As you are now my companion, I've uncovered the ability to view your attributes in my interface, Gemini. This same ability did I share with my priest. I would not, however, venture to inspect you without your leave. May I have your permission?"

The smooth timbre of her low voice was like music to my ears in spite of the formal tone of her words. I paused as I considered them.

"Is it socially unacceptable to analyze people where you're from?"

"Without permission? Yes. It is rude."

I'd never played a game where NPCs had interfaces—a lesson learned at the point of a stone knife wielded by a preteen what seemed like weeks ago, but had only been the day before...

Did other cultures in Enora share this privacy concern?

I nodded. "You can view my stats."

Her eyes flickered to my chest then back at my face, but I knew she wasn't looking at me at all — she was reading her own interface.

Her expression seemed to cycle through emotions. Awe. Curiosity. Then, realization.

"Such a life-altering ability..." she muttered. "It's as if you are..." She jerked, as if waking from a nap. "No, that can't..." She shook her head, set whatever thought challenged her aside, and nodded at me. I wondered what she saw, but she continued before I could ask. "Solara has blessed you with a great destiny, for only her touch could inspire such grace. You are an extension of our goddess on Enora. A tool of her will. I am so blessed to have been granted this opportunity to serve her, and I will therefore serve you faithfully for as long as you will have me... as is my debt."

I shook my head and adopted a formal tone. "As long as you stand with me, Roshan, we'll both exercise free will. I'll be happy if our interests align and, for as long as you want to stay, I'll be glad. But if ever you decide our paths should split, you'll have the freedom to follow your own."

Her eyes welled with tears.

What did I do?

Was my delivery poor? Had I somehow rejected her on a cultural level? My mind raced for the words to form a proper apology, but she interrupted my scattered musings.

"You are the most generous man I've ever met." Roshan dropped to a knee and bowed her head. "I have spent my life hiding my gifts. Yet, you embrace them. Our enemies shall fall before us. Command my direction."

I could see we would have to better define the concept of free will, but this wasn't the time to press the point. We were being hunted by her kidnappers, and I'd stumbled onto the destination for a quest that could seriously boost my chances of survival.

I peered down the hallway once again and thrust a finger in that direction. "There is only one way forward."

19

How she nodded with such enthusiasm at my direction surprised me. Since she'd spent gods–knew–how–long in the company of smelly thieves, crossing an ocean and whatever else she'd endured, maybe there was nothing left to scare her.

I now had two companions. Not only that...

I got a healer!

"I'm almost ready, Gemini." She leveled a finger at the stone floor behind her. "But, if I might make a request..."

I followed her gesture to the cloth bag laying in the corner beside the stairs. After my fall and subsequent conversation with my new companion, I'd forgotten all about the satchel I'd stolen from the beach.

"Of course. What's your request?" I paced over to the bag and knelt.

"I believe my proper clothes are in there. They will better suit our purposes if we are to meet with danger." She tucked her chin, glanced down at her clothes, and spread her arms out to the side. "These are the adornments of those ugly men. One of them who died during our journey was about my size, so they insisted I wear these clothes lest I garner more attention than my '*slanted eyes*' already did." One side of her lips ticked up in a sneer. "You should've seen the hat they used to shade my face."

Hm. So features like hers are uncommon on this continent.

She continued. "Probably in case they ran across people like you who would stand with the Light." A subtle tone in her voice communicated hope, as if she wasn't entirely sure I stood with her religious inclinations of right and wrong but would prod until I confirmed or denied. She was just so damned... human.

"Your kind to say so, Roshan. Trust me when I say I haven't always been the nicest person in the world, but I'm trying to change that."

I reached into the bag.

You have acquired:
Magic Bag of Holding
Type: Storage
Quality: Rare
Storage: 48 slots
Items stored inside incur no weight penalty.

The text was blue. I wondered where "rare" items fell in the quality hierarchy.

"No weight penalty?"

"No, it's a wonderful artifact." Roshan said from behind me. "The thieves stole this from my home when they killed my father and took me. It's only proper it passes into your hands, for I am with you now."

"I thought your people didn't like magic."

"Magical items are not inherently evil. This one has no

offensive or defensive attributes, so it is acceptable. It is probably precious and valuable, but an adventurer might be better served by using it, if you'll grant me leave to say so."

"Of course, Roshan. I value your opinion."

Her lips creased and she gave a subtle nod. "If we find or purchase a scroll of binding, you and the people of your designation will be the only ones able to access the inventory."

I reached out and grabbed her hand. "Roshan, I'm sorry they took your father's life. If this was his bag..."

She gave another gentle nod and squeezed my hand. "It has been many months since then. I have made my peace with it. My father was a stern man who suppressed my natural inclinations for magic, and though I know it sounds cold, it was his undoing. Had he fostered the growth of my skills, I would have been more advanced and able to resist the thieves. But I was left to level slowly, only as my mentor and companion could allow in secret. Though I miss my father, our destiny was not shared."

"I understand. I lost my father when I was seventeen, but making peace with it was difficult. Hell, I'm not sure I ever made peace with it."

I reached into the bag and opened my interface. Switching to the inventory tab, the sight of the filled slots flipped my demeanor.

"Holy mother of the gods!"

So many of the slots were full. I wanted to go through every item but needed to prioritize. After a quick scan, an illustrated icon of a hooded robe of green and yellow caught my attention. Its smooth cloth filled my hand after a moment of focus.

Robe of Apprenticeship

Level 5
Type: Robe
Quality: Uncommon
Durability: 19 of 20
+20 maximum mana
+5 healing and damage from Light spells
+5% resistance to magical attacks

A smile crossed Roshan's face as she grasped the robe and hugged the garment to her chest.

"Master Mitwah gave me this just months before those evil men raided my village. The mercenary thieves' employer was a warlock who scryed magic items with an orb and found it in the temple basement. I admit I took satisfaction in his death by sickness at sea while confessing I did nothing to help him lest I reveal my abilities. Though I possess no abilities against plague, sleep was lost to me in the days after he passed, wondering if Solara would've preferred I at least try to heal the damage caused by his illness."

"He kidnapped you. They killed your father and stole your robe for coin. I wouldn't have healed the bastard, either."

"But, surely, you would have, Gemini. I sense the purity of your soul."

"Well, you might want to get your senses tuned up, because I'd have let that asshole rot like the rat he was."

She covered her mouth as her eyes flared. Muffled giggling exploded behind her hand. She slapped my shoulder.

"Surely not! Certainly, you would cure the sick."

"The innocent deserve mercy," I said. "The evil can go fuck themselves."

Her head jerked back. "Well! If that is Solara's will, then it shall be so!" She glanced down at the robe and let it unfold. "It's funny. If he had not stolen my robe, it might still sit beneath my chest in the priest's quarters, and I would not have it to use in service to Solara today."

She might as well have fed me my line. "Then our coupling must be destiny, right?"

"It is as you say, Gemini." A gentle smile crossed her face, but I sensed loss in her eyes, as if conflicting emotions tugged different ends of her rope. Her tone perked up. "Another item they took from Master Mitwah would aid us."

"Oh, what is it?"

"A scepter."

I reached into the bag as my eyes scanned the boxes in my inventory interface. Then I spotted it.

Apprentice's Scepter of Light Power

Level 5

Slot: Weapon

Type: Light-Imbued One-Handed Scepter

Quality: Rare

Durability: 19 of 20

7-11 Magic Damage

Casts a narrow beam that causes light damage

-2 damage inflicted by undead enemies

+2 magic damage to undead by all party members

Handing her the scepter, I raised one shoulder in a half-shrug. "It belonged to Mitwah?"

"Yes. But he never wielded it."

"I wonder why? It doesn't seem to be soul bound."

"I have asked myself that question," she said. "My

conclusion was that Master Mitwah intended it as another gift for his lone apprentice. He would have given it to me in his own time, if that was his desire." She ran two fingers over lines engraved along the shaft of the silver scepter with slow appreciation. "Now, if you'll excuse me, I'll discard these rags and don my proper attire." She stepped away as if she would trek into the darkness beyond its halo.

"We don't know what waits in the darkness. You should change here. I'll turn my back."

Her finger shot up at the glowing orb above her. "The light follows me where I go, Gemini." She glanced down the dark corridor. "But leaving you in the dark is no better. I will change here." Long fingers loosened the clasps of the dirty shirt beneath her vest. I turned away and continued rummaging through the bag via my inventory panel. New prompts greeted me with each item I focused on.

Minor Potion of Health
This potion will instantly regenerate 70 hit points.

That was no small deal. As Roshan rustled with her clothing behind me, I flipped to my companion tab to check her stats with the new gear. My attention fell on the amazingly lifelike representation of her form in motion. She wore only form-fitting undershorts as she held the robe overhead, preparing to let it slide over her mostly bare body. It wasn't until I eyed the smooth flesh of her breasts before I even realized my violation of her privacy. It was real-time video!

Close it!

My face warmed under my silent self-admonition. Then it hit me—I'd just responded as if Roshan was a real woman. Again, I'd caught myself falling into Enora's web of realism.

Competing thoughts chased each other around my mind. On one side of the debate was my sense that I should treat the world like any other game. The opposing viewpoint came with the sudden epiphany that NPCs in other games were entirely different entities. They weren't born, they were programmed. Parents only existed if the developers added them for story content. While Roshan's narrative might be mistaken as simple story construction written by game developers, I knew she'd actually lived the events she described.

Enora was my chance at a new life. A life in which honor—a concept largely lost on my old world, in my opinion—could play a part. A life where the darker ways of my old world could be cast aside. As to my former guilds and what they would've thought of me treating an NPC like a real person? Well, screw them. What did they know?

Hell, wait until they get here!

I'd only let ghosts from my past slip into my decision making when logic mandated it. Game mechanics, yes. Spotting patterns when engaging foes, absolutely. Figuring out puzzles—no one deciphered those things like Katelyn.

But as far as determining how I'd engage allies like Roshan? No. Uh-uh. I gave myself a reaffirming nod and reached into the magic bag.

Rapier of Scorn

Level 4

Slot: Weapon

Type: One-handed Sword

Quality: Uncommon

Durability: 13 of 13

Damage: 5-7

+1 to parry

The weapon label was printed in green text. With a thought, I dragged the rapier and Roshan's scepter from its new position on her Companion page next to each other and a comparison pane appeared, proving the robust programming of the game system. As if I needed more proof.

Max durability is thirteen on the rapier and uncommon is printed in green text. Roshan's scepter is rare and the title is in blue text. Max durability on that is twenty.

After I'd noted the attributes for later use, I withdrew the rapier. The white light of Roshan's illumination sphere reflected off its narrow gleaming edge. The thin curved blade fed into a hand guard with a metal loop attached to its handle. Old-world pirates would likely have chosen a weapon like it.

A prompt popped up.

By equipping this weapon, you will learn a new starter class!
Fighter
Fighters use melee weapons (like tree branches) to combat the evils of Enora.
Fighters can choose from three combat professions at level 20:
Warrior
Dark Knight
Blade Dancer

Did the smart-assed A.I. seriously inject a snipe at how I'd used a tree branch to beat a snake to death? That's kind of kick-ass.

As I'd learned when I'd become a Woodsman, combat professions were selected at level 20. It would make sense that the starter classes Lucera and I'd discussed probably stopped leveling simultaneously at that point.

Roshan stepped into my field of view, and I was so stunned by the sudden appearance of her form in the thick, pleated green-and-yellow robe that I teetered back on my bent knees and dropped on my rump. The sleeves flared at the wrists. The split in the robe rose to her mid-thigh, revealing the inside edges of her taut, muscular legs.

"You are too beautiful." The words had escaped my lips before I knew what I was saying.

She blushed. "You are too kind." She pressed her hands to her abdomen and peered down at the robe. "It is part of me. Each time its Light embraces me, I feel like I'm in my natural form."

I shook off my earlier view of her natural form in my interface.

"It's nice." I continued to peruse the contents of the bag. At first, I'd considered pushing forward as time was ticking, but then I allowed myself a second to think about it.

What was I rushing to? My death? Conflict promising to end me at any moment? What if something in the bag proved a game-changer? As much as I doubted that—especially given the levels of the items I'd found so far—it would be stupid to leave a boon inside and later regret it.

Or not live long enough to regret it.

I dug. The rapier was cool, but a bunch of the contents were crap. Maybe the pickings were slim on Roshan's side of the world, or the warlock who'd died at sea had stashed other plundered items elsewhere. On the other hand, he might have gotten what he came for and cut out so as not to push his luck.

Roshan was his ultimate prize. To look at her was to understand why. If what she said about this governor's intent to make her a sex slave or concubine was true, she'd probably fetch a heavy bag of coins.

It's pretty ironic that a low-level fighter ended up being responsible for Roshan's delivery. I wonder what level the warlock was? That's not the important part, though. The guy who was so close to handing her off after what sounded like a long haul had lost sight of his charge at the last moment. He was going to be pissed. And determined to retrieve her.

My pet snored atop the stairs. I distributed a couple of mana potions to my healer to keep her topped off when we ran into trouble. Then I found a black sleeved pullover and matching pants. Although I could care less, Roshan showed me her back as I discarded my homespun crap and slipped them on. They fit perfectly, which wasn't a coincidence. Reality was cool and all that, but if players had to find clothes that didn't automatically fit, they'd be pissed.

As I glanced a final time at the inventory, I noticed a scroll arrow on the bottom right of my HUD. I focused on it and revealed two more rows in the bag. My eyes locked onto something beautiful.

Carved Leather Chest Plate of The Archer

Level 5
Slot: Chest
Type: Armor
Quality: Uncommon
Durability: 15 of 15
+3 defense against physical attacks
+2 to ranged accuracy

The level five piece of gear I'd have donned and scoffed at in any other game was a godsend in Enora.

"Hell, yes!" I focused and the smooth edge of the chest plate appeared in my grasp.

"You seem pleased."

"Was there another bowman in the thieves' group?"

Roshan nodded. "They lost many during their travels. The seas are treacherous, the ports rampant with disease. They also took a cousin of mine. She passed, as well."

This was the second time she'd mentioned disease on the return voyage, but this time the switch flipped.

So, sickness exists in Enora beyond battle mechanic usage. That's too bad.

"That's sad. I'm sorry."

She shook her head. "Best not to focus on such things. Death is a part of life."

A common earth expression. One I disagreed with. One was the opposite of the other. If I had my way, I wouldn't have to worry about it anytime soon.

A lump grew in my throat and an overwhelming need to change the topic passed over me.

Eyeing the ribs cut into the armor a final time and noting how it clasped together in the back, I slipped my arms into it and wrapped it over my new shirt. A huge grin stretched my face.

My companion matched the smile. Stepping toward me, she said, "Turn, and I will clasp it."

"Thank you."

She laced up the leather straps and cinched my new armor so the fit was snug. I pounded the chest three times with the side of my fist. "I feel ready to take on the world."

When I turned to face her again, her lips were pursed. She shook her head in soft derision and cast a finger toward my simple boots. I glanced down to find one sole already peeling away from the thin leather siding.

"Perhaps you will find a pair of adequate footwear inside. I'm sure they kept the boots of the fallen."

Not only did I find a pair of footwear, but a pair I could equip.

Stealth Boots of The Prowler

Level 4
Slot: Boots
Type: Armor
Quality: Uncommon
Durability: 16 of 16
+1 Stealth Skill
+1 Dodge

This text was also green. Another prompt popped up as I donned the shoes.

By the benefit of equipping these items, you have discovered a new starter class!

Assassin

Assassins specialize in the Dark Arts, utilizing sneak attacks and poisons to paralyze or kill their victims.

At Level 20, Assassins can select from the following professions:

Rogue

Bone Reaper

*You may now change your class to **Assassin** by equipping a dagger. Equipping multiple daggers after Level 5 will teach you the combat skill:*

Dual-Wield

Though I'd found a pair of simple daggers after a quick

search through the bag, I needed a minute to consider the implications of a class change.

Roshan showed infinite patience as I scoured my attributes. As luck had it, Dexterity was also the common attribute of the Assassin class, so if I decided to switch, I would still get the automatic attribute point each time I leveled. But on the flip side, my dagger skill was only one. My ranged accuracy was eleven. I could use stealth as either class, so, I ran one final test to make an informed decision.

Arming my daggers, I switched to the Assassin class.

You are now a Level 5 Assassin.
Global Skill Cool-down: 30 Seconds
You have learned a new skill:
Backstab
A vicious attack performed while stealth is active, causing 150% main-hand damage. Damage scales with level advancement. Chance of mortal wound increased by 3%.

Lucera had told the truth. The new class was the same level as Woodsman. Backstab was a common ability among MMOs for shadow fighters. I guessed when it came to names, Enora didn't see the need to make it unique. After all, it described its function.

Now I wanted to measure the stat differences. Assassins were a melee class. My melee attack rating, buffed by equipment, was eight, less than the aforementioned ranged accuracy. If I could count on re-spawn upon death, I wouldn't have minded trying out close-quarters combat. Then again, the sharp memory of having a spider pincer rip through my shoulder and the stinging porcupunk needles penetrating my arm ended that thought. Besides, my bow skill was fifteen and my dagger skill was one.

Somehow, a dark, dank cellar ending in a quest with a higher recommended level than I currently held didn't seem the best place for a change. But a bow might not be a great weapon if quarters became close.

I tapped my lips as I considered the options and slipped the daggers into their sheaths, which I slid onto a tattered belt I'd found in the bag. I grasped my bow and received a system message.

You are now a level 5 Woodsman.
Global Skill Cool-down: 30 Seconds

I unsheathed the knife I'd taken from my victim on the beach. The recollection of his black blood spurting in the moonlight caused a sudden shiver to quake in my spine. In the moment of conflict, my survival instinct had forced my focus toward keeping him quiet so I wouldn't wake his companions. Even with the passing of time, it felt like I'd murdered him, but remembering the arrow reverberating in Click's body calmed the sensations. Eyeing Roshan eviscerated them.

Grabbing the knife by the blade, I held it out, but Roshan looked through me. It seemed I wasn't the only one lost in thought. The observation made it even more difficult to think of her as a bunch of ones and zeroes.

"Roshan?" Her shoulders jolted. I extended the knife. "For emergencies. You can conceal it under your robe."

Her eyes went wide as she eyed the weapon. She waved a palm side-to-side, shaking her head.

"What?" I asked, shaking the blade in my hand.

"Drawing blood with a blade is against the tenants of my order."

"What, you think Solara is going to fire a lightning bolt down and zap you?"

"For a creature of such Light affinity you speak loosely with the goddess's name."

"And you won't defy those commandments even if you find yourself in danger?" I pressed the point.

She stared blankly at me.

I adopted a soft tone and matched it with my expression. "It would make me feel better knowing you had the backup protection. While I respect the rules of your order, we are companions now, and our survival depends upon one another."

She eyed the blade uncomfortably. "I would never use it, Gemini. Never."

I waved it in the air. "I don't mean to be a pain in your ass, but do me a favor and slip it somewhere subtle, just for my peace of mind."

Roshan sighed. Sweeping away one side of her robe, she slid the knife against her outer-thigh. Patting her robe and checking its pockets, she raised an eyebrow in my direction.

"Oh! Right!"

I reached for the rope I'd used for a belt since being reborn in Enora.

"Um," I shot a hesitant glance at her leg. "Do you mind if I fit this?"

Roshan eyed the belt, then my expression, and her facial muscles morphed into understanding. Pink filled her cheeks.

"Of course, my new companion." She slid the robe out of the way and pushed her foot toward me, exposing her thigh again. Ignoring the warmth rushing to my face, I twisted the rope around her thigh. Once I'd determined how much excess would flap free, I used the knife to cut the slack.

She angled her leg so I could slide the sheath onto the rope, and tie it off. After depositing the knife into the sheath so it rested against her outer thigh, I nodded. "How's that?"

Slowly drawing her leg back and releasing the hem of her robe, she nodded. "I will adapt. You are quite handy, Gemini." When the robe swept back together, the blade was invisible. She flared the robe open to show me the knife a final time and smiled. "Does this please you?"

I muttered a response without thinking. "The knife or the leg?"

After taking a moment to decipher my meaning, Roshan blushed for the third time and silence ensued. A smile crept across her face and I found it contagious.

"Both please me, if I'm being honest."

"Thank you," she said. "You are kind." The curve in her lips vanished.

Sometimes you can't just keep your mouth closed, you stupid loser. What if you offended her? WTF, dude?

A quick check of her disposition toward me revealed she was still *friendly*. I needed 200 more disposition points to reach the next level, but I was more concerned with losing the ones I'd achieved.

I shook my head at myself and turned back to business.

During my investigation of the bag's contents, I was pleased to find some foodstuffs with attribute bonuses. All my stomach grumbling had made me think I might end up starting up in that gods-forsaken forest.

There was more deer jerky, which Click seemed to enjoy. I fed her two strips and checked her interface to discover the attribute boosts didn't stack, the more she ate.

Oh well, it fed her belly and that raised her demeanor to *Happy, for a +1 attack bonus.*

Roshan, who ended up knowing something of plants, preferred the

Mixed Berries x 5
Item Type: Consumable
+2 mana regeneration every second for one minute
Duration: One Hour

Apparently, the bag preserved produce. I also stumbled upon a strange, uncooked plant that looked like weeds with little knots. Once she told me what the plants' benefits were, my interface had revealed their qualities.

Whisper Grass
Item Type: Consumable
+2 to Ranged Accuracy
Duration: One hour

Consuming whisper grass would raise my ranged attack skill to fifteen. So, I would definitely remain a Woodsman, despite my reservations about possible intimate engagements as we traversed this place.

"Hey, while I have the bag open, what can you tell me about these?"

I unrolled one of the leaves I'd tucked Cloudberries into.

Roshan blinked her eyes in succession.

"Cloudberries. You should throw those away, Gemini. They are poisonous."

Holy shit! I knew it! That's such a dirty trick!

"They might not kill you, but they will make you quite sick."

I discarded all the berries in my bag. Click scurried down the stairs and sniffed at them, then turned away.

The Matron of the Wood told me I would need more levels to complete the quest she'd given me. At the time, I'd been a Level 2 nobody. Now, I was a Level 5 nobody, about halfway to Level 6. But in addition to my pet, I'd added a healer. If she knew her game, that should help me mitigate the level deficiency.

I faced Roshan. "If you've never done this before, I have to ask. Are you sure you're ready?"

Roshan nodded. "My nineteen years have led me to this moment. Let us venture forth into the unknown together."

She was a tad younger than I'd suspected and didn't have my history with games, but the best I could hope for was that she wouldn't freeze up when shit got hairy. Her enthusiasm was contagious, but I saw something deeper in the flare of her eyes—desire. Like she'd wanted this all her life, as she'd claimed. That told me something about what the people of this world might think of adventurers.

Her light spell expired and the cellar fell into infinite darkness. But with the loss of my sense of sight came the further scrutiny of my hearing. Rattling to my right, beyond where the light spell's halo had ended, reminded me of hollow blocks of wood tumbling to the ground.

Click Click Click.

Her sounds echoed off the walls and drowned out the distant ones I couldn't identify. Impatience swelled in my chest.

Mentally cursing my trembling hands, I tried to keep my tone even.

"Recast the light spell, please."

The glowing orb reappeared over Roshan's head.

Clicking bounced off the walls and echoed back to us as the animal sniffed the air.

"You smell something, buddy?"

She clicked a few more times.

I cocked my head at Roshan. "Time to earn your Mixed Berries."

Shrugging my bow off my shoulder, I crossed beneath the ball of light above, took a few tentative steps to the edge of its halo, and moved toward the darkness.

"Aren't you forgetting something, Gemini?"

"Huh?" I turned back.

"I promised to teach you your first spell of the Light." The skin next to one eye crinkled with a squint. "Surely you don't want to alert our enemies to our presence." She pointed toward the light above her.

In *LOB* and all the other games I'd played, trainers were usually found in villages, towns, and cities. When I reached the required level for a given skill, I had to seek them out. If companions in Enora could train, that was a pretty big deal. I appreciated the implications of a more linear progression and less downtime, but seriously doubted if companions could teach high-level skills. That might be a bit *too* easy.

I cleared my throat, shoved an arrow back into my quiver, and stepped back beneath the light.

"Yes. Right." Shouldering my bow, I shrugged. "What do I need to do?"

She cupped my face in her hands. "Close your eyes, Gemini." After a short glance at my pet—which she matched with a click—I did as Roshan instructed. "I have only the memories of what my master did to guide me. Relax your shoulders. To receive the Light's gifts, you must be free of anger and your inhibitions. Focus fully on the sound of my voice. When you receive your first spell, you also must accept the comfort of the Light. In all things, the Light can guide you if you only call it forward and trust Solara's power. Do you, Gemini, agree to receive Solara's power of the Light?"

I blinked my eyes open.

"Does this affect my alignment in any way? Like, if I decide to cut someone's head off, is it going to negatively affect my influence with this power—you know, keep me from casting light spells?"

She patted my cheek. "You must be a vessel into which the Light of Solara can enter. You carry too much tension, too much worry. If you're to be a successful guardian of the Light, you must let these things pass from your shallow mind."

Though the words could've been construed as harsh, I found nothing but gentleness in her easy smile. So human was her expression, I once again had to remind myself she was a non-player character.

"Soldiers of the Light revel in its glory with our chins high. We are bolstered by its presence, but accepting the Light doesn't affect your alignment nor your reputation with a given group, except steadfast advocates of darkness and of chaotic alignment." She tapped the tip of my nose. "In which case, you will want to vanquish them, anyway. You may still learn other schools of magic. Solara is not a jealous goddess." She gently cleared her throat. One thin eyebrow crept up. "Legend has it that powerful casters of Light magic were often of neutral alignment during the wars, but those bathed in the dark shadows of Hokrahm may not have the Light touch them, less they perish like the evil dogs they are. I sense none of their darkness in you, Gemini. Just the opposite. I sense your affinity for Light

Magic. It warms me when I'm near you. But your susceptibility to The Light is an empty container that waits to be filled. So, before we proceed, affirm you have no desire to seek chaos."

I took that to mean she wanted to know if I had any interest in a chaotic alignment. Definitely not my thing.

"I don't, but I'm also no goodie-two-shoes. I tend to fall in the middle, I guess." I watched her eyes and rounded cheeks for any sign of a reaction but saw none. "I do what needs to be done to keep me and mine alive, no matter the cost."

Roshan nodded. "So, you stand in defense of your own? This doesn't make you special." She clicked her tongue. "Something tells me nothing is going to be simple with you." She cleared her throat gently. "What of the downtrodden who are too weak to defend themselves?"

I considered the question, realizing the weight of it. I was no stranger to quests that aided others or struck down those who sought power at the expense of others. I gave the simplest answer.

"I don't like bullies. I'll stand for the weak."

"The goddess Solara requires only that you carry yourself with dignity, but it pleases me to know you are not self-consumed. Now, calm yourself." To my surprise, Roshan pressed her lips to my forehead. When she pulled back, her eyes followed the line of my neck to my shoulders. "Better. Good. Now, do you, Gemini, agree to receive the power of the Light?"

I nodded and blew out a long breath. "I do."

She smiled again, raised her hand, and thumped my forehead. "Then close your eyes!"

Chuckling, I acquiesced.

Gods, she seems so real.

"By infusing you with the power of Inner Illumination, I wash you in the power of the Light."

And a little grandiose, maybe.

A sudden surge from where her fingers graced my cheeks coursed through my face, down my body, and into my extremities like a warm jolt of electricity, its energy thrusting out of my fingers and toes. It was like Zhara's touch, but less all-encompassing. My eyes shot wide open. I closed them again and the room flashed around me as the inside of my eyelids glowed orange.

The world righted itself as the energy gently faded, but there was no mistaking the warm sensation signaling something in my chemistry had changed. My body fell forward, my hands went numb. I saw Roshan in a new light—pun unintended.

When I straightened, she pressed her entire upper body against mine as she wrapped her arms around my shoulders and neck.

"Welcome to the Light, my companion. You are forever bonded to the followers of Solara."

You have gained a new affinity:

Spells of the Light: You may now learn Light spells of rank equal to or less than your level.

You have learned the spell:
Inner Illumination

The warmth coursing through my veins receded as the cold of that place reasserted itself, but I'd just learned a new spell and unlocked a school of magic! I could've given less of a shit about the cold!

I gripped her hands. "Thank you for trusting me with this gift."

Now that you have chosen the path of the Light, your choices will have consequences. A slider bar has been added beneath your character pane to illustrate your alignment. When you choose actions that align you with the Light, the slider will move to the right. If you make decisions aligned with darkness, the slider will move to the left. Players and NPCs of high level and who have also adopted a spell school affinity will detect your current alignment and this could impact your interactions in Enora.

Roshan interjected before I could consider the implications of the system message.

"When you appeared on the beach and dispatched that most evil man, I knew your soul would accept the affinity. You saved me from a life of horror, Gemini, and it is I who should be thanking you. Nonetheless, you are welcome." Her face tensed suddenly as she peered over my shoulder, into the inky darkness beyond. She stood taller and lifted her chin. "Now, let us venture forth. The minions of darkness await."

As if in response, the rattling I'd forgotten repeated down the hallway behind me. I spun around and peered into the black as chills snaked across my skin.

20

The three of us crept forward. I led with my bow at the ready, Click right on my heels clicking nervously. Roshan followed only a couple of steps behind. Her light shone in a halo around us, revealing about ten feet in every direction. When we crossed the threshold from the cellar beneath the tree into what had been darkness, I received a new message on my HUD.

You have discovered:
Tomb of the Lost:
This tomb of a long-past civilization has become home to a new civilization of subterranean creatures.
Note: The Tomb of The Lost is not an instanced dungeon. The changes you effect here could be far-reaching and impact your story and the world around you.
Level Recommendations:
Solo: Level 9
Duo: Level 6
Full party: Level 4
Discovery: 125 XP

Although the message about impacting my story and the world at large seemed like a warning, my hands trembled with excitement. Leaving the unknowns of the forest behind to enter the fray in an underground area where I could more likely implement some crowd control measures was like a gift wrapped with a bow. As a duo with a pet who could tank, I felt pretty good about our chances. Even if I was one level short of the recommendation.

The stench of decay filled the air. That there was any scent at all was a tribute to Enora's ingenuity. That it made me want to retch was too authentic.

The further we walked, the cooler the stone-encased environment grew. If not for the new clothes I'd pulled from the magic bag, my teeth might have chattered. I glanced over my shoulder to see how the sudden cold affected Roshan, but she appeared comfortable, even though the slit in her robe exposed her thighs with each step. Perhaps the place from which she hailed was frigid.

Cobwebs crept along the upper corners of the stone walls and spread their fingers over the doorway of a chamber on our right. Roshan's scepter cast a glowing light that melted them away.

I whispered, "Well, that's useful."

She nodded curtly. "The Light provides many tools to help us shed our encumbrances."

It was funny how she adopted a more formal tone when she spoke of Solara or The Light.

"That shit is deep, yo."

Roshan threw me a questioning glance.

"Not important."

I peered into the room and spied a dingy debris pile in its center. "This Inner Illumination spell doesn't do a whole lot. I expected true night vision, I suppose."

"You are Rank 1, Gemini. It will improve as you advance. Surely you didn't expect to be handed everything." She scoffed and cast Outer Illumination. The area was ensconced in light. "I will dismiss the skill when we return to the hallway."

To my surprise, she stepped past me and into the room. When I crossed the threshold, the contents of the rubble became clear.

"Bones." I relaxed my arms, lowering my bow as I peered down. "Humanoid. I've seen enough in games that—"

"What demented games would involve human bones?"

Text flooded my HUD.

You are reminded that is a violation of the Enora Online Player's Agreement to discuss the outside world with NPCs.

While Infinity Designs understands the use of common expressions in day-to-day gameplay, it is forbidden to inform NPCs of your life outside the game world. Although NPCs ...

Shit! I'm begging for an XP penalty.

"Never mind, it's not important." Her silence seemed to indicate that she'd accepted my answer or didn't really want one, confirming the game filter had kicked in. Despite Lucera's suggestion that it was standard, I needed to read the player agreement. But it would have to wait until Level 10. Everything would.

In the back of the small room was a porous stone bench cut into a wall lined with slate plaques. Intricate symbols were carved into their squares.

An archer.

Some animal resembling a buffalo with horns.

A winged serpent standing upright.

"These are very old," Roshan said. "But they are not born of the darkness I sense in this place."

My forehead wrinkled up as I absorbed her words.

"Do you mean you literally sense darkness in this place?"

She furrowed her eyebrows. "You don't sense the chill?"

"What? Wait, are you telling me the cold—I thought maybe it was just cold. So—"

She interrupted. "Yes. Apprentices sense the presence of evil as cold. While the air is cool here, I have spent many years underground, in the Mines of Aniqua, near my home. There it is *cold*."

Mines of Aniqua.

The name of the place brought forth an entangling web of thoughts.

That's not a backstory. She's lived her own life. This woman has existed on Enora for nineteen years. Remember that so it stops surprising and distracting you.

There was a certain comfort in thinking of Roshan as an NPC, an emotional detachment that kept my psyche safe if something happened to her. But as she mentioned her previous life and explained how creatures of the Light detected evil, cracks formed in that shell of security. I recalled the warmth of her lips against my forehead, her soft fingers cupping my face, the intelligence in her sienna eyes.

"So, you're saying because you injected me with the Light, I can detect evil?"

"*Injected.* You have quite a way with words. Yes. That's what I mean. Be warned, however, you are but a suckling babe bathing in the gifts of the Light. The only reason you sense its presence is because someone or something much stronger than you cast this place in darkness. Though we are separated by only a couple levels, you will find the effect compounds each time you advance."

"Well, that's reassuring. Nice to know I'll turn into an ice sickle when I detect an evil being at level twenty."

"You will adapt as you strengthen so you detect evil in a new way. Don't be so—"

The rattling we'd heard echoing from these halls erupted. A rolling, high-pitched barrage of clicks emanated from my pet's throat.

My chin dropped as the pile of bones I'd just analyzed rumbled and clattered together, formed a small mountain in the room, and unfolded into the form of a stocky skeleton with thick bones.

Dwarf Skeleton (Minion)
Level 8 Summoned Undead

A rusted chain wrapped around the skeleton's neck ended in a silver medallion with a black stone at its center. A glimpse of the stone sent a wave of nausea over my gut like I'd just gargled and swallowed a shot of cheap tequila. I thought I'd heave, but when the skeleton's jaws clicked together and its hollowed-out eye sockets faced us, the discomfort was all but forgotten as my adrenals took over.

Adrenals. In a game world.

The temperature of the room plummeted, and a shiver ran down my spine. When I raised my bow, it was like my arms were seized by arthritis. I took two quick steps backward to create space. I tried to yank an arrow out of my quiver, but it rattled to the floor for my shaking hands.

Strap your quiver somewhere else!

Raising her scepter into the air, Roshan bellowed, "Back into the abyss with you!" A blinding white glow filled the room, and the skeleton raised its bony arm to cover its eye sockets as it cowered. Though the light was intensely bright, it caused no discomfort to my eyes. Instead, it cast the same warmth over me as Roshan's earlier heals, delivering temporary relief from the violent chill of the cold.

Her voice took on an air of command as she barked an order. "Do not just stand there, adventurer! Attack it!"

Ripping another arrow from the wooden sleeve, I nocked it to the string and fired. It impacted the hand the skeleton used to shield itself from the glare. The hand snapped back into the skull and a finger dislodged. The digit rattled to the floor as the skeleton lumbered toward me, quickly closing the distance. At this proximity, I had no time to pull another arrow. So it came down to a choice and I had to make it fast.

Rapier or daggers?

Either way, I'd face a thirty-second cool down of my abilities, leaving my damage greatly diminished. But the rapier would allow me a longer reach and I might be able to keep the skeleton at bay. Dropping my bow, I unsheathed my narrow sword and dodged to the side as the skeleton lunged forward and aimed a bony fist at me.

I swung the rapier. Though it connected, it bounced harmlessly off the undead's shoulder, leaving only a crease in its wake.

The skeleton reached into a ratty leather belt and withdrew his own sword from its tattered scabbard. I answered my own fleeting question about the origin of the sword—it'd been hidden in the pile of bones. What mattered more was the undead bastard was swinging it at me!

I blocked with my rapier, but when the blades met between us, the skeleton proved much stronger. He forced his weapon down on mine until the blade sliced into my cheek.

My blood spurted into the air as the incredible pain of sliced nerves radiated through my face.

*Dwarf Skeleton uses **Overpower**.*
Critical hit!
G3m1n1 Fowler:
-72 Hp
155 HP Remaining

"Ah!" I stumbled backward and covered my face with one hand as I wielded the rapier with the other. Pulling my hand away, I found it awash in crimson. A glance at Roshan's stoic, brave expression urged me back into game mode.

The skeleton swung around, and I ducked. The wind of its swipe blew through my hair.

*Your **Dodge** skill has increased to Rank 6.*

A red droplet icon flashed twice and turned solid.

G3m1n1 Fowler:
-6 HP (Bleed)
149 HP Remaining

Great, more bleeding damage. Why do I have to be such a bleeder? It's my old life all over again.

My inclination to sick Click on the undead minion made little sense since it had no flesh for her to tear away and I doubted she would even serve as an adequate distraction. Nonetheless, she clicked away at me, begging to get into the brawl.

Why the hell not?

"Do it!"

G3m1n1 Fowler:
-6 HP (Bleed)
143 HP Remaining

As the skeleton's backswing missed its mark, Click bit down on its bony ankle. The skeleton peered down, lowered its weapon, and raised its chin to look in my direction.

Really? It seemed to be saying.

But as it turned and raised its weapon to attack Click, I sidestepped, double clutched my rapier, and swung. This time I followed through, and the metal clanked as it connected flush with the back of my enemy's spine at the base of its skull. Its head jerked forward with the impact.

The strike sent shockwaves up my arm, surprising me with the authenticity and drawing some choice words. The pain from my cheek wound and the warmth trickling down my face and the side of my neck had kicked me into survival mode, and I was ready to beat down a bunch of bones.

As the skeleton recovered, a sudden flash of light emanated from the corner of the room. I spared Roshan only a glance, wanting to keep my focus on the undead bastard coming around to slice my face off, but the quick look revealed an orb of light hovering above her free hand as she held the scepter high in the other. I jerked as the light shot across the room in my direction.

Roshan *casts* Minor Heal.
Roshan heals you for 14 HP.

157 HP Remaining

Two steps carried me behind the skeleton just after I dodged left to avoid an upward sweep of its blade with designs on my chin. I lunged when the sword passed, then thrust my rapier between the skeleton's ribs. It caused no noticeable damage, but as the undead tried to turn on me, the blade caught between its bones and held it fast. It jerked, trying to break free.

I clutched the sword tighter, but for the life of me, had no idea what to do next. When it stopped struggling and turned its bony face toward me, I grinned.

"Fuck you." Then I planted my boot into the skeleton's tailbone and shoved with all my might.

Bone clicked and clacked on the stone floor as the magical being lurched across the room and slammed into the wall. Not wanting to give it any time to recover, I pursued, drawing my sword back for a good ol' fashioned run-through. The boney bastard twisted in time to face me as I stabbed with the point of the rapier.

The undead parried, and the blade swung high at the last instant. Time slowed as the skeleton hunched beneath me.

I peered down to find the tip of my sword pressed into the stone bench with the necklace wrapped around its blade.

In one fluid motion, I twisted the chain tighter with a pivot of the blade and pried it toward the ceiling. The chain snapped. The medallion smacked into the wall and clanked to the stone bench.

The skeleton's joints gave way, and bones clattered to the ground in a rattling death.

My chest heaved as I doubled over to catch my breath.

The light from Roshan's scepter dimmed as she brought it down. Apparently, her light spell had expired.

We were washed in darkness.

I ignored the flashing prompt on one side of my HUD and focused on my blinking stamina bar.

We needed to deal with the darkness. Between breaths, I asked, "You want to recast?"

"Perhaps we should use our Inner Illumination spells, instead. The light might alert more undead to our presence."

At least someone around here is thinking logically. Dude, seriously. The NPC is a step ahead of you. Cast off your former successes in LOB. They aren't helping you here.

I cast Inner Illumination.

*You have reached Rank 2 in **Light Magic***

The dim light came in a clean, natural glow. A strange warmth filled my eyes as the skin of my casting hand tingled.

Roshan stepped forward as I stared at my fingers.

"Soon you will not require your hands to cast. For now, focus on using only your mind. The discomfort you feel will become less noticeable, as well." A steadying hand grasped my shoulder.

"It's not uncomfortable at all, actually. Just different. It's like the power leaves a trail."

"Yes!" The outburst took me by surprise. When she saw me jolt, she lowered her tone. "The way you describe the sensation is apt. I'm sorry, I'm just so unused to having someone with whom to share these feelings. It fills me with joy to relate to you, in this way." She laughed.

Though I'd just battled for my life against an angry bag of erected bones, I joined in. "You're the shit."

Roshan's eyes flared as her expression morphed into something resembling distress. "I am... what?"

I showed her my best jazz hands. "No, no. It's a good thing. I'm not calling you feces. It's just an expression, a term of respect among friends. It means I'm impressed by you."

A tentative smile returned to her features and relief washed over me. "It is a strange expression, to call someone shit in appreciation of them. But as my grandfather always said, 'When you are in the land of the Nahkim, emulate the Nahkim!'"

I chuckled. "We had a similar expression in my... village. When in Rome..."

"I have never heard of this Rome. Is it far?"

I cocked my head to one side, not sure how to answer. "Incredibly far. I would venture it is about as far from here as one could get."

A system prompt warned me against talking about the outside world. I sighed and prepared to change the subject.

Roshan spared me the trouble.

"Well, I am glad you clarified for me. I think you are shit as well."

I decided not to correct her usage. We had other *shit* to think about, starting with the medallion I'd cut off the undead skeleton's neck.

Roshan gripped my hand as I reached for it. "It is best you leave the tools of death for the dead, Gemini."

"What is it?"

"This is a Guardian's Medallion, used by a dark caster to control its minion. I have read stories of such artifacts. Since this guardian is outside the caster's range, he left it here so the enemy would conjure at intervals to check the area and then return to its slumber."

That explains why we heard it from down the hall.

"Is it valuable?"

"Valuable?" Her jaw dropped. "Do you seek to profit from the suffering of others? Perhaps I have misjudged you."

"Suffering of—" My eyebrows furrowed. "Roshan, set your judgments aside for a second and hear me out."

In spite of their fullness, her lips pinched into a white line. Though the expression didn't strike me as receptive, I pressed forward.

"Adventuring requires that we feed and equip ourselves. If I can make silver or gold from the sale of that medallion, it could very well mean the difference between living and dying."

Roshan nodded, but her words didn't reflect understanding. "And when you sell this dark artifact to someone and they sell it to another who might have foul intents, who might suffer as a result?"

Shit. I can see this is going to be a problem.

I took a second to think it through. In *LOB* and other games I'd played, items sold to vendors would then vanish, except if I changed my mind and wanted to buy them back or accidentally sold something I hadn't intended to. Once I logged out, those items were wiped from the database.

I didn't actually know if items sold to vendors in this world could be repurchased by others, but considering the other unique properties of Enoran life, I couldn't set the possibility aside. But while the potential for someone to buy my leavings put a whole new spin on things, I needed to verify the mechanics and I wasn't willing to leave potential gold on the table.

Or stone bench, as the case might be.

I nodded concession at Roshan. "How about this? I'll bag the medallion and hold onto it so no one will stumble upon it here. We'll make every effort to bind the bag to me so no one can access it and be diligent in the meantime. We can decide how to best deal with its disposal later."

Roshan gave a curt nod. "I hadn't considered how this wart on The Light might be used again if left behind. Perhaps it is best to bury it deep in the forest or try to destroy it ourselves. That you at least consider my words about selling the item proves that Solara has blessed me with a conscientious debtor who embraces the counsel of a woman."

"Man or woman, it makes no difference to me." As an afterthought, I added, "And you owe me no debt."

She squinted an eye, challenging me. "It's considered rude to deny one her traditions. If you find me unacceptable, cast me aside and I shall return to the forest, evade my kidnappers, and accept whatever my destiny."

Nothing in her expression conveyed that she had any intent on doing that. Though she'd indebted herself to me, I got the impression she wanted me to know that I hadn't adopted a child lacking the spine to speak out and a willingness to go it alone.

And if that isn't free will, nothing is.

I relaxed my facial muscles and nodded. "Your presence is a gift I'm unworthy of, Roshan. Your strength warms the air surrounding me. Let's seek our destinies together."

The language might be flowery and I might totally be full of shit, but the sentiment is true enough.

"Hmm. Wise, indeed. You know talent when you see it." The squinting eyelid relaxed. "I like you very much."

She stepped forward and kissed my cheek. "Stow the medallion. We will let Solara decide our course."

+20 Disposition with **Roshan**

Tossing the necklace into my bag, I focused on the prompt I'd ignored after killing the skeleton.

You have vanquished **Dwarf Skeleton.**
Level 8
20% Bonus XP for killing an enemy more than two levels higher than you
1,176 XP

I studied my XP bar. It was half-filled.

I muttered, "Five-and-a-half levels to go."

"Does something happen at Level 10 toward which you aspire?"

People don't really talk like that. There. NPC all the way.

"Re-spawns," I said, without giving the requisite considerations to my meaning. "I won't die."

Her face wrinkled in confusion. "What do you mean you *won't die?*"

Now that's a deep trough to wade through. What happens if Roshan dies? Will she re-spawn back home? With an adaptive A.I. and a world labeled "Literally Evolutionary," I didn't think so. Her existence was as much in peril as mine. Whatever the case, telling this Light priestess I won't permanently die if I can just reach Level 10 could have her thinking I really am a demon. Can unique non-player companions re-spawn at all? Has she ever heard of such things?

"I can't imagine what skills I might receive when my level reaches double digits. Surely things change with such an accomplishment." I knew the response was weak the second I finished speaking, so I paused to throw a glance at Click. "Hey, can you see us?"

A rattle of clicks told me she did.

"Well, damn, I guess you're the shit, too."

"How do you understand the throaty utterances of this beast?" Roshan asked.

Ah, the subject change worked. Hey, what does she mean, 'Beast?'

"What, you don't like Click?"

Roshan threw Click a smile that would melt dragon scales. "He is a fine companion. Very sharp teeth." She smiled at the animal.

Click spread her lips in emulation, and I laughed.

"I just wonder how you understand it."

"It's a *she*. We don't always communicate with words, but she has skills like us and can respond to my mental commands. It's more of a sensing thing, I guess."

"Though jealousy doesn't honor our goddess, I find myself envious of these intuitions you share with this pet. It must be convenient."

"It doesn't mean we can't share feelings, too," I said. "You have already warmed me." I threw her a jesting smile revealing all my teeth.

She stepped forward and set her hand softly on my chest. "I, too, feel warmed by you, Gemini." Her fingers trailed down the center of my chest and stopped around my navel.

I popped a tent pole.

"Very warm, indeed." Roshan raised her scepter. "But the Light calls us to do its bidding!" She set off for the hallway with her chin raised high as Click and I shared a glance.

"A real piece of work, isn't she?"

My pet clicked twice and set off after Roshan.

I shook my head and chuckled as I followed them into the hall.

According to my map, our first turn in the stony hallway was to the north. We soon came to an east-west intersection. Despite the surrounding stone, a scent of mineral-rich earth traveled to us from one of the corridors, but I couldn't be sure which. Five doorways were visible from the intersection, and cobwebs dressed all, save one. The three of us formed a triangle as we peered in each direction.

"Which way, do you think?" I asked.

Roshan tapped her lip. "Hmm. I'm uncertain. We should clear them all in service to both the Light and the race who occupied this place before the darkness destroyed it."

"You think the previous occupants were killed?"

She shrugged. "Did you not witness the short stature of the skeleton who attacked us?"

"Actually, I did."

She nodded as if I understood how she'd come to her conclusion, so I shot her a confused glare.

"Gah. The pictures depicted a small people. The

serpent stood taller than any figure on the wall. At first, I wondered if this might just be my own bias since I come from a tall people." She threw her arms out to her side. "As you see."

Roshan stood as high as my chin, probably just over five-and-a-half feet.

"Uh-huh."

"And you come from a tall people, as well, yes? Or were you a freak? You are quite tall."

A freak? Interesting word choice.

I didn't stand a hair's breadth over six feet. I wondered at the statures of others I might encounter in this world... if I lived long enough.

"No, I'm probably just a little above average."

"So, when the skeleton rose into the air and assembled itself, I noted it was even shorter than I and reasoned the depictions on the wall were, indeed, to-scale, when compared to the other beings depicted. Am I making sense to you?"

"Sort of."

"Hmph. Well, that will have to be good enough. I would like to sleep sometime tonight, and Solara's tasks lie ahead."

I smiled at her slight exasperation. "Yes, dear."

"Deer? Is that a horned creature of the woods in your language?"

"No, *dear*. As in, *my love*. As in, *darling*."

She blushed. "How you have taken to me in such a short time."

Jesus wept. My mouth is going to get me in trouble.

"I was taught this continent was a dark place filled with greedy devils. To be rescued by such a hero as yourself and have you become so enamored with me in such a short time..." She held a hand to her blushing cheeks. "The difference from morning to night baffles me. I woke a slave, and now battle darkness with an adventurer."

I didn't have the heart to tell her she'd overstated the meanings of my words. Besides, she seemed to like it, and that worked for me. It kept her around, if nothing else.

+500 disposition points with **Roshan**
New Disposition: **Endeared**
Points needed for next level: 750
Reward: 100 XP

And also that! I should flirt with her more often!

I suppressed a snicker and focused on the word *endeared*, wondering if I might get a tool tip, and I did!

Disposition:
A being's orientation toward you
Disposition is a measure of your relationship to others in the world of Enora.
Disposition States:
Despised
Hated
Hostile
Unfriendly
Neutral
Friendly
Endeared
Enamored
Beloved

Holy crap. Endeared is right up there. The A.I. might want to make that a little harder.

This was the first time I considered Lucera was

listening to my thoughts. Though I'd managed to set that concern aside in the interest of focusing on survival, the A.I. listening to my every whim gave me the creeps. If anything, it motivated me to get to Level 10 and cut that link.

In the meantime, I needed to remember I was a tester, of sorts. I did *not* want the A.I. to make earning disposition more difficult. I needed to keep my brain in check!

On the one hand, I'd pulled Roshan off that beach and dragged her away from men who planned to sell her as a slave or concubine. I'd heard the leader say he couldn't beat on her because of someone called 'The Governor.' If I thought of Roshan as a human being, then it made sense she would have feelings of gratitude for my actions, especially since I hadn't turned out to be a total asshole. Hell, she'd practically pledged a life debt. So, maybe I'd earned her disposition.

But no sooner had I 'rescued' her than I'd led her into this place and put her to work fighting an undead creature. I'd dragged her out of one shitty situation, and plunged her into a dank, stinking, cold cellar. Human beings might wonder if they'd have been better off as a concubine in such a situation.

But Roshan's vibe didn't approach negative. She was a by-gods Light priestess bent on serving her deity against the dark forces of Enora. Cowering from conflict seemed the furthest thing from her mind.

I cleared my throat. "It stands to reason we don't want to pass by a room and leave our backs exposed." I raised my bow and pointed the arrow to indicate direction. "Let's try that one."

"Your logic is sound and—now that you suggested it —obvious."

"Um, thanks?"

"My words did not adequately reflect—"

I dismissed the apology with a wave. "Cast the thought into the void. No worries."

We tiptoed toward the room with Click in the lead. Roshan's steps landed softly next to me. I didn't know if undead could see in the dark, but at least keeping quiet reduced the odds of detection.

Click stepped into the doorway and a sudden screech filled the air. The dead would have heard that ear piercing yip.

"What the hell?" I whispered harshly.

She'd come to a stop. At first, I mistook the spikes jutting from her back for the ones she concealed in her fleshy tails, but when she slid down them and I saw her blood painting the pointed metal, I sighed.

Roshan's hand flew to her lips. Her eyelids vanished. "Oh, no!"

"Shit," I said simply.

"Does your heart lack empathy?" Roshan asked. "Your companion has found its end."

Sighing, I switched the bow to my other hand and focused on the image of the porcupunk in my HUD. Energy surged up and down my arm as Click rematerialized and my mana meter dropped. The porcupunk turned in a circle several times and I thought for a moment she'd lost her bearings. Then she sniffed and scampered to the corpse of her previous iteration. A low grumble filled her chest as her yellow irises peered over her haunches at me.

"You have pretty shitty luck, babe."

One side of her ultra-thin, black lips raised in a sneer, revealing a few silvery teeth behind. She clicked once.

One click only, please.

I chuckled. "Hey, at least I can bring you back. That

could've been one of us." I doubted my pet took much comfort from my words.

Her eyes glowed, and she sent a harsh glare in my direction for a long moment.

My shoulders jumped in a half-shrug. "Like I said, shitty luck." I pointed at Roshan and then shoved a thumb at myself. "We don't get to re-spawn. You're alive now. Don't give me that look, or I'll send you back."

The spikes retracted suddenly, causing all three of us to jump back, and the porcupunk corpse thunked onto its side.

Roshan and I shared an unsure glance. I crept toward the doorway, grabbed the porcupunk corpse by the flesh tails, then lifted it. I grunted, surprised by its hefty weight. Shrugging, I dropped it again, and the spikes shot up. Click dropped her backside to the floor and peered down the hall into the darkness beyond. She sighed.

"Looks like they only go high enough to disable humanoids, but I'll bet it hurts like a bastard. I don't know if the occupants come to check the traps with regularity or what, but we shouldn't dilly dally. I'd rather find them than the other way around."

When I turned, I found Roshan's mouth agape. "How do you have such power at your level? That you can raise this dead animal?"

The excuse popped naturally into my mind.

"Like you said, I'm a child of Solara." I threw in a half-shrug for effect. I turned back to the trap. "I think we can just step over it."

Roshan's response came in a hesitant stutter. "Your logic is... sound, my lord."

"I'm not your lord, but I take your meaning." Standing and setting my hands on my hips, I gave the spikes a long gander. "Give me just a sec to check this trap out before you come through." After Roshan nodded, I stepped over the twice-punctured porcupunk body and turned. From the other side, I knelt and analyzed the trap.

Blood ran down into slits around the edges of the trap. The design kept it from pooling and spreading across the floor, which might warn other intruders. The design was intuitive. Smart.

Careful not to allow my head to hover anywhere over the spikes, I squinted with the aid of my Inner Illumination spell. Along the outer edge of the squares, I spied a recess. Raising the corpse again and setting it beside me, I focused on a section of floor through which no spikes had risen. Then the spikes retreated. Once they had, I set two fingers on the floor and pressed down.

The spikes jumped from the floor again and, though Click jumped back, Roshan held her ground. I peered up and found her nodding at me.

I smiled. "It's a pressure plate. Put weight on it and the spikes pop out."

A blinking icon appeared on the right side of my HUD, so I focused on it.

Through your analysis of the environment, you have discovered the skill:

Locate Traps

Using your refined skills of analysis, you can now locate low-level traps.

There is no resource cost for this skill.

"Awesome." I peered past the text and Roshan came back into focus. "I just learned a new skill."

Her lips parted slightly and pressed back together. "That is wonderful, Gemini. I see your intuition is strong."

I shrugged and cocked my chin toward the far side of the trap. "Kneel down right there and set your fingers along the edge where there are no spikes."

Her head cocked back.

I smiled. "Trust me. I wouldn't steer you wrong. I just want to check something out."

Roshan took a hesitant step forward, and I realized it might have been the first such step I'd seen her take.

She knelt and gently set her fingers down.

"Good, don't apply any pressure. Just leave them there and try to suppress your instinct to pull back, okay?"

Though her gaze was unsure, she nodded.

I raised my hand and the spikes retreated. To her credit, Roshan didn't flinch.

"Now, press down at the edge there."

She did, and the trap fired again.

You have taught your companion, Roshan, Clan Fortwan, the skill:

Locate Traps

Roshan pulled her hand back. "You are a miracle, Gemini. I have known you for such a short time, and yet I have learned a new skill. If there were not a trap of spikes in the floor between us, I might kiss you."

I found the idea of that surprisingly alluring—NPC or not. "Bank that kiss for later, would you?"

"If you mean I should save it for you, consider it done."

"Which leads me to the next task." Engaging the trap again, I gripped one of the spikes and tugged back and forth.

"Gemini, please don't hurt yourself," Roshan said.

"It's fine. If something happens, you'll heal me, anyway."

Click rattled off a convoluted message of clicks I couldn't understand and stepped back. Maybe the sudden guttural reaction was an exclamation that didn't translate into words.

Roshan chuckled. "You're right. I will. How silly of me."

"Maybe you're not so silly. You conserve mana if I preserve myself. So, seems a good instinct to warn me."

Roshan smiled.

Tugging hard and removing my other hand from the pressure plate I was able to keep the spikes exposed. I gripped the spike with my second hand to gain leverage and yanked harder.

The whole pressure plate jostled, revealing a raised edge closest to me.

I gently released one hand and stretched it over the trap. "Hand me your knife."

"What? Oh!"

She swept aside her robe, but I focused on the spike in my grasp. When the handle slipped into my hand, I slid it into the newly revealed edge. I didn't want to break the blade, so I jimmied just a little bit at a time, raising the plate until I held its edge in my grasp. The knife clattered to the floor as I released the spikes and grabbed the plate. I raised the heavy metal—lifting with my legs and not my back, because fucking Enora—then flipped the plate over. It slammed to the floor on the other side with a resounding, echoing, uproarious bang that vanquished the silence like a subway train.

This time, Roshan jumped. Her head swiveled in all directions. "Very subtle, my lord. Surely every dark demon in the place will come to greet us."

I feigned bravery, though I knew I'd screwed up. "Then

we'll just kill them all at once."

I reached to one side.

Roshan gazed at the offered knife with disdain as I returned it.

Staring into the recess of the stone where the plate had been, I spied the flat, metal tips of the triggering mechanisms on both sides and matched them to the round cylinders on the pressure plate's under side. The triggers were shaped like nails with long shafts. When I traced from the head down the shaft to the bottom, I saw the solution. Grasping one of the heads, I yanked it out of the floor and found it slipped out of its slot with ease. I threw it into the hallway, where it rattled into a corner and clanked to a stop. I repeated the process with the other trigger. If it had been a smaller trap that I might have taken with me, I would've bagged it, but this thing was huge. Clumsy.

Shuffling to one side in a kind of duck walk, I pushed the plate back to the trap's seat. It settled into place with a hollow *thunk*. When I pressed down on one corner, nothing happened.

Through meticulous observation and experimentation, you have learned a new skill:
Disable Traps:
Your Disable Traps skill is now Rank 1.
There is no resource cost associated with this skill.

I pumped my fist in victory but kept my tone low so as not to rouse any dark occupants. "Two skills in ten minutes. Gotta love that."

Roshan rolled her eyes and shook her head in derision. "Now he chooses to be quiet." She stepped past me and into the room.

22

A stone altar dominated the center of the room, leaving only a narrow path between itself and the wall on each side. Its edges were chiseled smooth, and I guessed it weighed tons. My first inclination was to search for bone piles around its perimeter. I found none.

"I wonder how they got it down here."

Roshan's robe brushed me as she stepped closer to share my perspective. "Hokrahm inspires the service of darkness much as Solara does the Light. Whoever moved this wretched rock of sacrifice was motivated by his evil father." She spat harshly to one side. "May their soulless bodies rot in the fire of his evil bosom"

A copper plate covered in a fine layer of dust sat at the altar's center with two jeweled, stemmed cups set to either side.

On each end of the altar stood engraved metal candle holders of gold with painted black lines winding in neat curves around them. I leaned close to the plate and smudged a line in the dust. By the light of my Inner Illumination skill I discovered it wasn't copper at all, but gold!

Gold Ceremonial Offering Plate
This plate could be of high value.

"My interface calls it an *offering plate*. I wonder if it got passed for coin somewhere, like in church offerings."

Roshan scoffed. "In this place of darkness?" She paced around the altar then leaned down to inspect the engravings on the candleholders, which turned out to be fake. "Hokhram's children sacrifice in blood."

Without hesitation, I dropped the plate into one of the remaining slots in my bag. Her head tilted sideways. Roshan's eyes followed it to the bag and then shot me a look.

"What? You think a golden plate is a source of evil that could be dangerous in the wrong hands?"

"No, I suppose not. Perhaps it will help to fund our expeditions in the name of our goddess." One full cheek rose with her half-smile. She was coming around.

Ivory, Jewel-encrusted Ceremonial Chalice
This chalice could be of high value.

Click sniffed around a corner on the far side of the room while I raised one of the chalices closer to my face.

Roshan spoke as I eyed a red gem.

"Would you like me to inspect those jewels?"

"Do you know a lot about gems?"

"You must not have checked my professional skills. I am a Level 43 Gemologist. It was my primary profession in my village."

"That seems like a strange way to make a living in a village."

She smirked. "I might be offended if your words weren't so... true. There were several mines in the mountains near my home. We traded with convoys who traversed the mountain en route to the seat of the Eastern Kingdom of Lau. We have a rich tradition of mining, passed down through many generations."

"Sounds like you have the market cornered."

She stared at me, working something out in her head. "Ah! You mean a market found nowhere else, with a unique product for barter, right?"

"Yes."

"You really should learn to speak plainly, Gemini." Her gaze traced the long lines of the slate.

"I'll work on that." I held out a chalice. "Level 43 sounds high."

She threw me a coy look. "I don't like to boast. My success is born of a genuine love of jewels and their powers."

Baby likes the Bling, but for non-monetary reasons. Her lack of greed was refreshing. Another thought cut that one off. Wait. Powers? Can we socket these gems into weapons and shit?

Grasping the ivory cup by its stem, she turned it in her hand. "Oh, my. Yes. Mmm. These are gems of the very finest quality. I also detect no curses."

"Well, that's a good start." I smiled, but she didn't turn her attention from her analysis.

"I would need a focusing lens or to observe them in daylight, but I detect no flaws." She held the chalice out.

"Perhaps you should keep one for yourself." I grinned.

She waved it away. "You are too generous." Pressing a hand of splayed fingers to her chest, she bowed her head for a second. "It is you who has saved me from the jaws of slavery."

I cocked my head forward. "Well, that doesn't mean I'll keep all the loot for myself!"

"Have I upset you?"

I rolled my eyes, set my jaw, and lowered my tone. "I can hardly be upset by generosity. You deserve the freedom to choose your own path in life. What happens if you decide not to hitch your horse to my wagon, long-term?"

"Ah!" She barked, holding up a finger. "This expression, I understand." Her lips peeled into a smile, but it didn't reveal her teeth. "Very witty" She chuckled. "I have no horse, only a seat on your wagon, Gemini. Besides," she continued, "even were I to accept this gift, I have no bag."

"Then I'll hold on to it for you. My bag is your bag, Roshan."

Her facial muscles relaxed, her high cheekbones dropping just a tad. She studied the stony floor

After a long, awkward silence, I asked, "Is something wrong?"

When Roshan raised her head, her expression caused me to step forward, a hand extended.

"What is it? Are you well?"

She spoke low, her head subtly shaking as she stared at the stone floor. "I long not for riches and treasures. I seek fulfillment of a higher purpose." Her eyebrows arched. She raised her chin, grasped my shoulders to straighten me, then set a gentle hand on my chest. "I am not simple. It's apparent to me that this is all very strange to you, that some female just a few years into her womanhood would bind herself so willingly to you, so quickly. In a way, this confusion is a reflection of your true heart, that you expect so little in return for your heroism." Her fingernails scratched lightly at my chest as if she was flexing the tendons in her hand to loosen them. "But my life is my own, as you have said."

I nodded in agreement.

Her gaze became stern. "I am not finished."

I nodded for her to continue.

"You should recognize the giving of myself and my various attributes to your cause for the gift it is and deem yourself worthy of it, as well as trust I am capable of making an informed decision.

"Since my life is my own, it is mine to give to your purpose and to those who share it. I sensed the Light in you, Gemini. I *shared* it with you. This is of genuine value when compared to these mere trinkets." She tipped over the chalice and it rolled in a half-circle before settling.

I cringed, but she didn't seem to notice—or care.

"Even if it is sudden, even if you find my offer of companionship strange, I hope you can intuit the value I place on you and, in turn, value me, too. So, I ask you, Gemini, will you still care for me when we leave this dark place and venture beyond the forest above?"

My throat felt like it would close completely as the depth of her meaning hit home. Those sienna eyes showed no evidence of computer-generation. Rather, I found a conscientious soul, a woman of depth gifted with sentience and intelligence beyond computational algorithms.

Enora was my life now. To treat a gift such as Roshan as some kind of tool to meet my objectives when she could affect me like this was infinitely stupid. NPCs were barren of the deep values this woman held dear. She was Enora like the leaf I'd peeled not a day before. As real as anyone I'd experienced in the outside world.

Now I realized that Enora was my chance to live my life

in a world where honor still had meaning, and Roshan was a golden reflection of that ideal shining in my face.

"I'll value your companionship for as long as it's mine."

Roshan nodded, and a tear formed in one eye.

"Will you see me fed? Will I have a place to sleep near your hearth? A home in your village?"

> *You have been offered a unique quest:*
> ### *Enamored from the East*
> *Earn enamored status with your companion, Roshan.*
> *When companions maintain enamored status, they will fight by your side until death.*
> *Reward: 1,000 XP*
> *Reward: 750 Disposition Points with Roshan*
> *Reward: Enamored status with Roshan*
> *Will you accept this quest?*
> *Yes/No*

The quest offer felt like Enora was pushing me to accept something—someone—for all the wrong reasons when the right reason stood before me, her warm hand gracing my chest. To be urged forward by greed would be in contradiction to living with the honor I'd defined moments before, and I didn't want to accept Roshan's offer of companionship for the wrong reasons.

But I'd still accept it.

I adopted a slow, formal tone. "Roshan, while it would do me great honor to have you with me wherever I go, are you absolutely certain this is the kind of commitment you desire? I would not presume a romantic relationship or take from you that which you would otherwise be unwilling to give, but I will pledge to you a place in my party and a place on my team, as long as you accept we are partners and equals."

"Gemini, I am not a child, but a woman capable of making my own decisions. It is not purely out of debt I say yes to you. This is my way. The way of my ancestors. I seek to use the gifts blessed upon me by Solara. The gift of mana, the gift of adventuring so darkness might be cleansed from this world, if only one evil minion at a time. My only desire is to bring glory to Solara and the soul she sent to me." She continued nodding, her eyes wet.

I accepted the quest and extended my hands, palms up. She took them.

"Roshan, as long as I have a home and a hearth, so shall you. Our life won't be easy. At times, I'm not the easiest person to be with. But if you journey with me and help me to advance in this world, I promise, you'll advance alongside me for as long as you choose. But I demand one promise from you."

Roshan sniffled twice and nodded excitedly. "Yes, Gemini?"

"You must continue to be your own person. If ever you have an inkling it's time for you to move on, to travel on your own, or to do whatever life calls you to do, you must promise me you will. Follow what Solara dictates first, and never let me impede your way to becoming your best self. I will not want to be the one who keeps you from your destiny."

+50 *Light Affinity*

She cupped my cheeks in her hands. Our faces were so close, I spied little flecks of black in her irises.

"I promise this will never happen, my Lord."

"No more of that *My Lord* shit, either." I placed a wet

kiss on the tip of her nose, surprising both of us. Then I smiled.

She crinkled her nose and rubbed it with furious flicks of her fingers as a grin raised her cheeks. "Terrible."

You have completed the quest:
Enamored from the East
You have earned enamored status with your companion, Roshan.
Roshan will fight by your side until her death.
Reward: 1,000 XP
Reward: 750 Disposition points with Roshan
Reward: Enamored Status with Roshan

A golden light surrounded me and whooshed into the air above as if sucked through an invisible funnel. A giant, golden 6 flashed before me as a triumphant orchestra celebrated my advancement. It zoomed off, zipping through Roshan and disappearing into the wall behind her.

Roshan stepped back as she slapped a hand to her chest. Her chin dropped open.

"Gemini! You have advanced! I have never seen it happen to another!" She thrust a finger and punched the air with it. "That is Solara's Light!"

I presumed she saw me level because she was now my companion, where in the woods earlier she hadn't seen the bit of theatrics. A smile swept across my face at the sight of her natural glow.

You have reached Level 6!
+1 to Dexterity
+1 to Constitution
You have two unspent attribute points.

You have learned a new combat skill!
Piercing Shot
Adds 3-5 damage to ranged accuracy
Cost: 15 Mana
Cast Time: Instant, longer draws use more mana but cause more damage.
Cooldown: 15 seconds

"Congratulations, my new companion," Roshan said.

I could only wish my smile beamed like hers, but I tried my best. "Thank you! I even learned a new skill."

"A boon from Solara. How wonderful!" She clapped and bounced on the balls of her feet. Other things bounced. I lowered my eyes.

Returning to business, I tucked the chalices into my bag.

Under the thick layer of dust covering the surfaces of the altar room, Roshan and I found little else of interest. I couldn't help but think it had come too easily, but gift horses. Mouths. All that.

As we turned toward the exit, Click crossed in front of my feet and nearly tripped me in her desire to give the porcupunk corpse she'd once been a wide berth.

That's fucking strange.

We ventured back out to the intersection and a strange tickle in my mind turned into a coherent thought.

I tapped Roshan's shoulder and smirked. "That's why no one heard us. No one comes here. That's why all the dust, right?"

Roshan thumped my forehead. "Beings could still come here and leave dust behind, idiot."

My chin dropped and I opened my mouth to protest, then slammed it shut.

"Which room next?" Roshan asked. Her stoic vibrancy

was renewed. She was ready to take on whatever this place threw at us.

The dust didn't seem so important.

As to her question, I wasn't sure. Did the quest Zhara had given me call for me to vanquish all signs of the darkness, or just the root of darkness?

I was about to check when clicking at my feet drew my attention.

"You have ideas?" I asked Click.

Click-Click!

She sped off toward one of the rooms and sniffed at the threshold. Roshan and I shared a quick glance then fell in behind the porcupunk.

The room she picked seemed empty, which made sense since its doorway was blanketed in cobwebs. I thought about challenging Roshan with that bit of supporting evidence that no one came here, but what would be the point?

Click scampered to the other side of the room and sniffed around each corner, so we waited. I used the lull to learn more about my companion.

"You mentioned your people suppressed your abilities, but you didn't say why."

"Because of the Continental War of Lau."

"Continental?"

"Does news not travel here? It lasted for *fifty* years!" She clicked her tongue and sighed.

"When King Edmus died of the plague in the Era of the Fallen Moon, his regents warred for the throne and its vast resources. Untold masses died when Arturas the Shadow Warlock, servant of House Marquelle, cast a summoning spell from a book of dark power. Demons flooded the continent for twenty days and twenty nights, leaving blight and plague in their wake."

"A spell spoken from a book?"

"Yes, Gemini. The spells we cast are different things. Controlled things, unlike spells from these ancient texts lost for generations to surface only at the worst of times."

"Evil has a way of shrouding itself," I said. "Power is always at the core of its desires."

Hey, that was pretty good.

She nodded. "But the people of my realm didn't distinguish incantations from learned spells and, when the war ended, when final skirmishes carved new boundaries across the kingdom, our new ruler, Lord Chicanne, decreed magic would be banished from his territory. Known casters were rounded up, never to be seen again."

"Sounds familiar. History is wrought with crusades resulting from religion-induced overreaction."

"I'm pleased we agree."

"We do," I confirmed. "So, this priest took you on as protégé? Kept it under wraps?"

"It is as you say. My mentor not only shone The Light upon me—if you'll forgive my horrible doubling of meanings—but he taught me under penalty of death."

"Sounds brave."

Silence passed between us as her chest rose and fell in deep breaths. I thought I spied a sliver of wetness in the well of one eye. I turned my head away so as not to make her uncomfortable.

She broke the silence with two quiet words. "Very brave."

The politics of this world sounded chillingly similar to the outside one. Maybe I hadn't been made to struggle to survive in the world of my birth, and that was a notable difference, but as I absorbed her story, the feeling that Enora was as much a reality as my prior life solidified. After all, I lived here.

"It seems your pet found nothing," she said.

Raising my head, I spied the animal with the strange black flesh hairs as it rounded the corner from the room and scurried up the hall to sniff out the next.

"I'm just glad she didn't find a spike trap."

Roshan snorted a laugh just as Click reached the threshold, stopped, took a couple of steps backward, and emitted a low growl that caused the hairs on the back of my neck to stand up.

Shrugging my bow off my shoulder, I stepped forward. "What you got, girl?"

Stepping cautiously toward the open doorway, I tried to steady my quivering bow. My silver-toothed weapon stood next to me, ready to launch if I commanded it, and I was backed by a Light priestess. Then I realized the trembling was born of my excitement at what might wait around that corner. I'd take enthusiasm over dread, any day.

I peered around the corner, my hands steady.

Black chains with dangling iron wrist restraints hung from thick bolts set into the stone about four feet off the ground. Ancient brown blood stains painted the wall beneath all five sets of chains, trailing down to a rusted gutter that once drained at the far end of the room.

A rectangular space hollowed out of the left wall was covered in black soot and piled with gray ashes.

Roshan seethed with disdain. "They tortured and cremated their victims here. I don't know how I missed this before."

"Missed what?"

She shook her head as she peered into the crematorium.

"Whatever force now dominates this tomb simply passed through an inviting door." She pointed toward the back wall and enunciated each word. "Evil has endured, and more than one dark master has been drawn to this venomous place."

"You're saying more than one set of bad guys has taken up residence here?"

Roshan smirked, then her lips parted and the tip of her tongue rested on her bottom teeth. "Is this not what I said?"

I measured my response before speaking. "You speak with such eloquence. I'm unaccustomed to such brilliant usage and find myself overcome."

"Ha!" Roshan barked. "Stifle your flattery, fool! I'm not so easily pacified!"

She was epic.

Stepping across the room to where the gutter emptied, my footfalls made soft swishes like cloth against cloth. Above the rusted drain hung a simple wooden frame devoid of picture or painting. It seemed only to encapsulate a section of drab wall. Brushing the surface inside the frame with my fingertips, I sensed only cool stone.

"Many lives were consumed by darkness, here." Roshan's breath tickled my ear.

I startled. "It would be wonderful if you didn't sneak up on me like that." I willed my nerves to calm. "And you kind of said that already."

Warm hands—entirely *too* warm considering the chilly subterranean environment, clutched my shoulders and massaged.

"You are tense, Gemini." Practiced digits rubbed all the right spots, forcing the tension from my shoulders when I wouldn't have thought it possible. Her voice soothed me, creeping into my ears and passing warmth as if heating my blood vessels. "Tense muscles are inaccurate. In my childhood studies of music, my lute master's first lesson focused on the practice of relaxing my muscles and pushing all tension from my body before I set fingers to strings. From this lesson, you could learn more accuracy with your bow. Perhaps you will even live longer."

"I'm in an underground dungeon built on the bones of its prior occupants by a dark force who raises undead minions to fight for it. Of course, I'm tense. The question is, why aren't you? Have you ventured into such places before?"

Her hands gripped and twisted my shoulders, turning me to face her. Her facial muscles were slack, her shoulders dropped low and drawn back in stoic posture. Oversized irises glared as if a faint light source gleamed behind them.

"My only adventure was being kidnapped and dragged across continents to this place. But the cycles of many moons did I study the Light under my master. He persevered in his studies despite being forced to shroud his practices. I am one with Solara's awesome power because he instilled her values in me. Take heart in the Light, take comfort in my presence, and know I shall not let you fall, my companion."

She embraced me, pressing her entire upper body against mine.

"You give the best hugs."

She chuckled as she drew away and pulled her robe straight. "This is a place of darkness, but you are in the presence of a warrior of the Light. All will be well. Hokrahm's devious hooks will find no purchase in our hearts."

There was that name again.

"Who is Hokrahm?"

Roshan jerked and pulled back, holding me at arm's length. "How is it you could not know the seed of evil?"

"We all have our own images of his evil," I said. "You know, people paint the devil in many forms."

Her chin ticked up as she dropped her arms. "We need only know our calling is to let his minions fall beneath our feet."

The loss of her embrace left me more than just cold. I felt hollow. Dimmed.

"I hope you're right."

"Doubt is for the ignorant, but I will forgive this since you are but a noob."

"Noob?" I laughed.

"Yes. *Noob.* Do you not know the expression? It is the short form of a word in my language used to describe someone who has yet to experience advancement. A virgin, of sorts. A—"

I waved a dismissive hand, still chuckling. "No, I know what it means, I just—"

"Ah, visitors," a deep male voice growled behind me.

23

I flinched and raised my bow as I swung around, but Roshan's turn resembled a slowly spinning display stand, like she expected this turn of events.

My new friend is stone cold.

The cool rock wall inside the simple wooden frame was awash in black fog clinging to the smooth surface. A spiral of purple smoke swirled in in the center. Set in the swirl were the curves of a human face. A goatee of black whiskers snaked around thin black lips. The eyes were voids where irises should have been.

Though the entity's tone was low, it conveyed hospitality. "Welcome to my underground sanctuary. I am Crohl, Dark Mage of the Ubral. Servant of Underlord Caym." The smoky head peered at us, in turn. "You are?"

Though I parted my lips to speak, it was Roshan's voice that boomed in the space and echoed off the walls.

"I am come to exorcise a demon named Crohl!"

"Interesting," Crohl replied, though his tone implied boredom. "Unnecessary theatrics." The dark head leaned forward and away from the wall, crossing the threshold of the frame and homing in on Roshan. The cords in its neck were stationary wisps of black smoke as it stretched to within inches of her face. The Light priestess didn't so much as inch backward.

Click uttered a guttural growl and clicked incessantly as the visage considered Roshan.

Its head tilted down and up again, scanning her form in its entirety. "You are a beautiful creature. Tell me, from where do you hail?" When she didn't answer, he prattled on. "From the East? Lau, no doubt. Hm. I have not seen the likes of you but in illustrations." Before she could answer, the creepy head reeled back and turned toward me. "Is this your minion, priestess? Does he talk, or have you trained him to be so passive?"

Time to wax a little role-play, Roshan-style.

I lowered my voice an octave. "I am Gemini, Wielder of the Light, and I come in service to the Matron of the Wood, Zhara, to rid her home of your dark ways, demon."

Hey, that was pretty good, even if my heart is about to thump out of my chest. I've got a knack for this.

Roshan rolled her eyes.

"What?" I asked her. "No good?"

She smirked at me in response, as if the framed head wasn't even there.

I muttered, "I thought it was okay."

The framed head tilted back as the voice echoing throughout the room boomed with boisterous laughter. It went on for about five seconds, but the creeping chill in the room made it seem longer.

"Hahahaha! Oh, Gemini. Thank you. I've not heard such protestation since the last servant of The Light trespassed here. Of course, that was before I chained him to the wall behind you and drained his life force for my children to feed upon." The image's purplish, black, smoky lips curved outward as he clicked his tongue at me. "I'm afraid your Matron of the Wood has misinformed you, boy."

Who the fuck is he calling a boy?

"My essence does not intrude into the woods above. My master's living minions dig into the ground below. I have no need of the resources of the wood. Of course, it's not your fault you were lied to. You are but a—" the eyes glowed purple around their black centers "—a Level 6? The guardian sent a *Level 6* to dispatch me?" The head wasn't laughing anymore. Pompous disdain drooled from the projection's lips as he admonished me. "Let me tell you something, *boy*. I'd actually planned to let you leave unhindered, but now that I see the utter disrespect your benefactor has imposed on me, I've reconsidered." He huffed. "I honestly don't know what she saw in you." The head turned and its lips pursed. "Or in you, *priestess*, but now that you're here, what say you, shall we serve out our destinies?"

"Now the demon spawn speaks my language," Roshan said. "Tell me where you are, *cretin,* and let us proceed!"

"Do you hear this, Priya?"

I glanced at the doorway and found it empty. Whoever he addressed must be on his side of the conversation.

"Yes, master."

The croaking feminine voice sounded like two people resided in her. It caused my skin to crawl as it projected through the frame.

"At least she is beautiful, even if she doesn't *know her place*. What do you think, Priya? Would you like to have a sister?"

"Yes, master."

"Well, then. Go and get her."

Click made a sound I hadn't heard previously. It was

akin to the barking of a very large dog, and I was taken aback to hear it emitting from her tiny mouth. When I turned, I'd expected to see a larger animal only to find my little buddy growling up at the doorway... where a sword floated above her. Its pommel bounced in a rhythmic dance as it turned to reveal its breadth.

That's new.

"Kill the fool and his beast, then bring me the holy woman. Disable her if you must, but do not kill her."

I turned my head to give a snippy response, but the phantom had vanished and the last trails of purple smoke and the black canvas spiraled toward the center of the gray wall until it disappeared—like a flushing demon toilet.

The room grew five degrees warmer with his departure, but I still had the chills as my attention turned to the dancing weapon.

Floating Falchion
Level 8 Enchanted Sword
Enchanted weapons are guardians given life by shadow magic.

"This should be fun," I said, as I shouldered my bow and yanked out my rapier.

"Yes, this should be entertaining." Roshan agreed. "I am pleased to see you are beginning to relax."

"I was being a smart-ass."

"Your ass is quite smart, indeed. I have been noticing the way its taut—"

The falchion tilted forward, flew over Click and lowered its point, aiming to spear me. Sidestepping easily—thanks to a high dexterity rating for my level—I parried the sword hard into the wall. In all the thousands of hours I'd spent gaming in virtual environments, never had I encountered a weapon without a wielder, so the success of my reaction caused me to celebrate internally for a moment as the blade reoriented itself.

"Nice move!" Roshan bellowed laughter.

The reaction struck me as a bit strong. Kind of weird.

"Thanks?"

The pommel of my enchanted enemy sliced downward and away, in an attempt to cut a curve through the top of my skull. Bending my back, I swept my rapier upward and sparks flew as metal screeched against metal. Shoving my arms forward caused it to backflip, but it steadied and held its position just a few feet away, its blade hovering slowly to the left, and then the right.

I'd been contemplating how easy it had been to deflect and flip the falchion, indicating a low strength rating—assuming it had such a thing—when it zipped through the air toward Roshan, catching me off guard. I countered, stepping toward my new friend and swinging my sword in a descending arc, but the enemy blade twisted in the air, sped toward the open flair in her robe, and speared her thigh.

My heart thumped and my jaw tightened as blood geyser from the wound.

The sword retreated, preparing a follow-up attack as Roshan fell. It sliced the air toward her leg again, obviously trying to obey its master's order not to kill her, but I arrived just in time to deflect with my sword and pin its pommel to the wall.

It slipped under my rapier and zipped to one side. In short strokes, I swung from my right and my left, beating it back toward the door. Then I changed angles and tore through the air in another high-to-low arc, slamming my blade into its pommel. The downward force knocked it to the ground near Click.

"Attack!" I yelled.

Click launched and gripped the pommel between her teeth. The sword jerked upward, over and over, trying to break the porcupunk's grip, but each time it reared up, lifting Click's legs from the floor, my pet's weight yanked the weapon back to the stone surface, proving my theory about its limited power.

I charged toward the pair, then sidestepped as the blade oriented its tip toward me. If it wasn't strong enough to lift the porcupunk, it had no chance against a grown-ass man.

Grabbing the pommel's cold grip, I pulled the sword into the air. Click didn't let go, so she came off the ground with the sword, almost causing me to lose my grip.

"Let go!"

Click dropped to the ground and yipped up at the sword, jumping around on her hind legs in a furious dance.

The sword twisted and revolved in my grip, trying to pry itself loose, so I gripped it with both hands.

Now what? I wondered to myself.

"My scepter," Roshan muttered from behind me.

I turned to find a thick stream of fresh blood rolling down the slanted floor toward the drain. The expression of pain stretching her features pissed me off, and I gripped the pommel tighter as I kicked the scepter over to her. When she raised it, the stone at its apex burst with light. The blade in my hand sang an angry song in a single metallic note as it began to shudder in my grip.

Struggling, I set the tip on the stone floor, thrust my foot onto the blade, then yanked upward on the pommel. The metal snapped in two with a satisfying crack and a brilliant flash filled the room. I tossed aside the pommel.

A prompt popped up, but I ignored it and rushed to Roshan's aid. But my companion was already getting to her feet. Bending to sweep aside the lower flaps of her open robe, she shoved the remaining pool of blood down her leg. The unwounded skin beneath took me by surprise as she raised her head, thrust her arms in the air, and smiled.

"Gemini! I have leveled!"

The flash had come from her body! Level 9!

"Congrat—"

She crashed into me and flung her arms around my neck. My breath caught in my chest.

"Oh, Gemini. Not since I was sixteen years have I advanced, yet I have leveled after only hours with you! Had I known it was so easy, why, perhaps I would've fled my home long ago!" Loosening her grip and drawing her head away, she gazed into my eyes.

Her cheeks glowed. We stared at each other for a long moment, then she caught me off-guard a second time as she pressed her lips against mine.

They smacked as she pulled away, turned her head, and replanted them. Her hard kisses contradicted the utter softness of her full lips as she puckered and pressed them to my own repeatedly.

And who would I be to deny her this utter joy at her accomplishment? Sure, we were in the stone belly of a dark beast seeking to stamp us out of existence, but what better way to scoff at it than a celebration? In a way, we were telling that purple-smoke-faced prick to kiss our asses.

She kissed me again. Then again.

I like the way she celebrates.

My desire bloomed as she planted her soft lips on mine over and over. She settled her hands on my chest then moved them in soft strokes. Still, I held strong, trying to enjoy the moment. But when the tip of her tongue flicked my upper lip, I grasped her biceps gently through her robe.

"If you don't stop, you're going to awaken my man urges and we'll be shining a different kind of light upon that altar back there."

Roshan's lips withdrew and her boot heels clopped clumsily backward until her back pressed into the wall.

"I'm sorry, Gemini. I don't know what came over me. Despite our dark surroundings, my advancement has left me so...*happy*." She pressed two fingers to her upturned lips. The last word came in a low growl that I think surprised both of us.

Though her smile heartened me, the dark voice in my mind had questions.

What will I do if I lose her?

What if I've sealed her fate by bringing her into this?

Then, out of nowhere, Katelyn's voice echoed in my head.

Why are you thinking about her like she's a real person?

That question bit hard, but I bit back.

Roshan was real to *this* world, and now I was a part of *this* world, too. She wasn't an error in judgment, but a stroke of luck. Her belief that Solara brought us together might not shoot so far from the mark, seeing as Enora was probably Solara. Enora created the legacy quest that took me to Roshan, laying this opportunity at my feet.

My mind flashed to Katelyn standing over my bed at the secret compound in Nevada while Nokuro asked me if I was ready to face the biggest adventure of my life. Those weren't the words of someone who expected me leave my life behind. They were the excitations of a man looking forward. My crossing had been the end of Gemini Fowler in the physical realm. My beginning, *this* beginning, happened upon waking in Enora. I could make my own decisions and live by my own rules.

Why are you thinking about her like she's a real person?

Because we're both binary. Same ones. Same zeroes. I chose this, and I wasn't going to let the dark side of my mind use Katelyn's voice to fill me with doubt. Katelyn wouldn't be asking why I thought of Roshan as a real person. She'd ask what I was standing around for. She'd be barking orders!

Move your ass. Kill anything that gets in your way. Use every sense. Be methodical. Be hard core.

I needed to focus on what I'd done right, set aside worries over what was past and what was to come, and live in the moment.

As I peered at my companions, I knew I'd asked Lucera the right question when I asked how to survive until Level 10. And I was pretty sure she'd given me the correct answer.

Make friends.

"What if I lay upon that evil altar for you, Gemini?"

Roshan's words yanked me out of my streaming consciousness as she pushed off the wall and stepped toward me. Her expression was tense, like the stoic mask she'd worn as we battled the skeleton and the falchion, but somehow different.

Her eyelids dropped to half-mast. Her lips relaxed.

"Huh?"

Gone was the vivid excitement over her advancement, replaced by determination.

"I know this energy you speak of," she muttered. Her chest rose and fell in short breaths. She touched her chin, trailed her fingers down to caress the dip below her throat. They slipped between the seams where the robe came together in front. "All this excitement about living my dream has intensified it. It's a burning hollow in the pit of my stomach yearning to be filled. Tell me, Gemini, of this energy you wish to expend."

My eyes followed her hand, and all thoughts of my life before this moment were vanquished—which was good, I was done with them, anyway.

"Are you saying if I let you sweep me up and take me to the altar room, you would fill this burning hollow?" She thrust the scepter aside. It clattered on the stone floor as she stepped past it, loosening the tie on her robe to reveal her pristine bronze flesh from nape to navel. Her deep voice steadied as her words trailed from her lips in soft coos. "Would you claim my fruit in the depths of this dark place? Would we spread our light from between our—"

"That's not what—"

Her eyes flared as she whispered. "Silence."

Roshan grasped my hand, kissed my knuckles, and dragged my fingers lightly over her chin, following the path her own hand had moments before. She slipped it inside the robe and the soft, firm flesh of her breast filled my palm wonderfully. As she pressed it there, her lips parted and her eyes lowered to half-mast.

If she'd wanted my attention, she could tick off that checkbox.

Via my peripheral vision, I'd seen Click's head flicking back and forth between us since Roshan started talking, but now she suddenly scampered out of the room.

"Don't go far," I muttered without tearing my gaze from Roshans'.

Click.

"Though I am but nineteen, you should not mistake me for a child. Through determination and command of my own will, I have grown in The Light for half my life. I have pledged myself to the service of Her, that she might have the tiniest measure of joy from my devotion.

"But while other girls sneaked away and surrendered their purities in secret, my devout life left me yearning for such illicit experiences. I've come to understand it wasn't Solara who kept 'Temple Girl Roshan' from such pleasures, but the patriarchal influence wearing piety's mask in excuse. But this is my life now and I have pledged it to you of my own free will. I long for your manly touch to quench my carnal thirst, instead of always women."

Say what?

"Where my Light is the lone possession of Solara, my pledge to you might feed other..." She paused and tilted her head, casting her soft gaze over my features. "... purposes. When we leave this dark place victorious and you have achieved your goal of Level 10..." Roshan guided my hand until my fingers found her erect nipple, causing her to quiver. "Then I will open myself, and you may fill this void of yearning inside me."

All this because she leveled? Am I dreaming?

She clutched my hand a final time, holding it tightly against her, then she pushed it away and pressed it to my own chest as if I needed help taking it back.

A playful smile crossed her face, then she bent down to retrieve her scepter. I felt like a mute idiot, but I couldn't look away. Then she rose, cinched her robe, and gave me a slow up-and-down gander.

Her voice resumed its commanding tone, her stoic expression returned, and her arm shot out with a long straight finger pointing toward the hallway.

"Now, go forth, noob."

ake friends, indeed.

M We found Click waiting at the four-way intersection when I stormed out, rapier in hand—and a blunt weapon in my pants—itching to murder any dark being in the place with the bad judgment to cross my path.

Click, click, click.

"No thanks, little buddy," I snapped without so much as a glance down, "I'll take the lead this time."

Returning to the north-south passage we'd followed since I tumbled down the stairs into this dank, cold, smelly shit hole, I marched up the hallway with my bow slung across my back and an attitude that only melee would quell.

Bring your best, dark boy.

Eyes peeled for any traps that might appear, it occurred to me that at such a low level, I might not spot them. And if I did, I wasn't sure how they'd appear. Would they have a green glow?

I spied a final, empty room on the right and didn't

bother stopping to investigate. We all had to sleep at some point—thanks, Enora—and the smoky apparition framed in that wall had given me a target to finish this thing. My quest log confirmed it.

Bring Light Where There Is Darkness
Recommended Level: 8
Objective: Find and mitigate the source of evil dwelling beneath the earth of the Dark Wood.
You have identified the source of the dark presence. Crohl, the dark caster and minion of a demon underlord is tunneling beneath the Dark Wood.
New Objective: Eliminate Crohl's influence
Reward: Increased reputation with Zhara
Unknown reward
4000 XP

"Do you want to inspect that room we just passed?" Roshan asked.

I spoke my thoughts out loud. "We'll have the rest of our lives to explore empty rooms. No more tricks. No more fear. Fear gets people killed. I'm done reacting to what comes and ready to be the inciter of trouble for this dark dong. We plow ahead until we find Crohl and anything that gets in our way dies." I threw her a quick glare over my shoulder. "You and I are going to take this world by the short hairs."

"You have a certain confidence in your step now, Gemini," Roshan mocked from behind, her voice lingering and melodic, her accent sultry and alluring. "So ferocious."

I found myself powerless to suppress the smile snaking across my lips. It was no surprise I was being led around by my man club, in a sense, but truth be told, it was just an excuse to finally quiet the dark voice in my mind that had driven me to make bad decisions. Roshan's sexual motivation was little more than a nudge onto a path I should've already followed.

"Can you sense the dark bastard, or is it just me thinking it's getting colder the further we go up this stupid hallway?"

"Your instincts are strong, adventurer. He is somewhere ahead, though I can't be sure how far."

"Did you spend your attribute points?"

"What?"

I stopped and turned. "Your attribute points. Were you rewarded points when you leveled?"

She glared at me in confusion.

Remembering the prompt I'd ignored after snapping the magic falchion off at the hilt, I stopped in the middle of the hallway and focused on it.

Roshan *has reached Level 9!*

+1 Intelligence

+1 Constitution

Roshan has learned the spell:

Flash Heal

Level 8

Affinity Required: Light Magic

Instantly heals 50-79 HP

Cost: 45 Mana

Since your companion has a disposition of friendly or better, you are granted two attribute points to spend on her behalf. Bonus: Roshan's disposition with you is Endeared. You are awarded two bonus attribute points to be spent on this companion (one per disposition rank above neutral) Companion attribute points can be assigned at any time.

Holy shit! Two bonus attribute points to spend on her? That's amaz—wait...I spend her points?

"Um, Roshan?"

She nodded so quickly, I got the impression she'd been watching me intently as I read the prompt.

"Yes?"

Wait, how do I explain this. If she doesn't know jack about attributes, it might confuse her that I can spend them for her. But judging from the attributes I'd seen earlier on her pane on my Companions tab, they'd been assigned before. The evidence was that she didn't have a bunch of ones.

She stared at the me expectantly.

"It seems you've learned a new healing spell."

"What?" She blinked, squinted. "I haven't leveled in so long, I missed it!" Her lips separated slightly as her eyes scanned left to right. She set two fingers over her lips in an excited gesture I was coming to love. Her enthusiasm lit the place up, but mixed with her commanding stoicism, it made me a little dizzy. "I can now instantly heal for fifty hit points at a cost of forty-five mana! I must try this new ability!"

"If you can contain your excitement, hold off for now. Enthusiasm is cool right up until you feel the sword shoved up your precious backside. Let's not be stupid, okay."

As soon as the onslaught of manure had escaped my lips, I knew I'd really stunk the place up. I'd reverted to Old Gemini Fowler. The guy who played *LOB*. The guy who threw words like *stupid* around with Katelyn because we had a comfortable familiarity plus a tendency to cut through the shit during game strategizing.

But Roshan was *not* Katelyn.

I started defending myself... to myself.

But it was innocent. I hadn't intended to sound like a dick.

I almost winced as I peered slowly up Roshan's form, fearing the scorn I'd find when I got to her face.

But her head tilted to one side when my gaze finally reached her eyes, and when I didn't speak, she raised her eyebrows in expectation. "You were saying?"

Oh, thank the gods. A woman back home might not have taken what I'd said as intended, but Roshan, well, she was kind of awesome.

"Oh! Right. Um... what *was* I saying?"

Roshan threw a hand up derisively. "Sweet Solara, the man cannot keep a coherent thought in his head for more than a few seconds without getting lost in my cleavage." She waved her hands between us in furious waves. "Focus, adventurer!"

"I wasn't even looking at—"

Her lips pressed together, and one of her very expressive pencil thin eyebrows shot up. "You will deny you take pleasure in the sight of my bosom?"

I sighed. "Okay, you got me."

"At least you are honest. Now, have you recovered your thought from that busy mind of yours?"

Damn. She had me down pat.

"Yes, ma'am." I threw in a half-bow. "We were talking about your ill-advised intent to use your new healing spell. I'm sure you'll skill up as you use it, but healing for a quarter of my entire health pool also costs you a chunk of mana. As you well know by now, that takes a time to regenerate, and I wouldn't want to be caught off guard. You only have to come up one cast short, and the whole show is over. Something tells me the chill in the air means this dark dude could be close, and I don't want to give him a free swing at my jaw. Hence, the 'sword in your precious ass' comment."

She smiled and nodded. "That was not the word you used, but it does not offend."

"Cool. I need you and Click to stand alert for just a few minutes. I think I have a gift for you." I squinted dramatically to let her know I was checking my HUD.

"A gift?" Both of her eyebrows raised into a perfect arch. "I require no reward, Gemini. You are my gift."

I like cheese, but Geeze.

"Consider it a blessing from Solara. Actually, I'm pretty sure I can say in good conscience, it's exactly such a thing."

Roshan nodded. "I am happy to hear you embrace the goddess."

"But could give two shits about a gift from me, right?"

"You use words in strange ways."

Roshan had this spicy undertone thing going. *Zap! Snark! Bam!* Oh, yeah, Roshan had snark. I had a sense for this particular category of vocal intonation, but spoken through Roshan's accent, snarky was like listening to classical. More importantly, she'd set a natural pause right in the middle of the conversation. I used it.

Roshan:
Human
Level 9 Light Priestess
*Strength: 4 **
*Dexterity: 4 **
intelligence: 16
Wisdom: 9
Constitution: 11
*Charisma: 14***
(Roshan has four unspent attribute points available)
**= Points earned through life actions*

I focused on the final line.

People in Enora increase their attributes through repetitive life activities. For example, laborers who carry heavy loads will gain strength and foot messengers increase their stamina pools.

Usually, I'd set up a caster with Wisdom and Intelligence to keep damage and mana regeneration up. The needs for constitution was a distant third, because tanks were supposed to keep casters safe. Less damage taken equaled fewer hit points required.

You know, like rocket science.

But Roshan's numbers were an interesting mix.

She has the high intelligence for casting power, but the wisdom falls behind constitution, giving preference to hit points over regeneration.

I poked the air as if I could tap the text with my finger.

That is exactly the kind of thing someone who wanted to keep her safe would do. Add hit points for protection, more mana to be able to cast a decent number of times, while sacrificing spell fuel regeneration. Might her priest have been considered a companion even though he'd been an NPC and not a player? Had he assigned her attributes without her knowledge?

I stopped musing and calculated.

Her health multiplier is lower. If she gets one hundred HP for her first point in Constitution, then she's only getting eight hit points for each additional Constitution point. She might have gotten eighty for the first point. I'll watch.

Since Intellect also determined the size of her mana pool, I spent three of Roshan's four points in this primary skill. I put the other one into Wisdom to increase the rate at which she would regain mana.

"Of course, I don't have a tank, either." I muttered.

Would you like to confirm these skill expenditures?

Throwing a quick glance at Roshan, I confirmed them.

The mage tilted on her heels and blinked. A subtle white aura surrounded her then vanished as quickly as it had come. Her eyes widened and she glared back at me.

"Did you sense something, just then?" I asked.

"It was as if I was filled with the Light." Her eyes flicked up and to one side. "My mana is regenerating, yet I cast nothing. I remember once with Master Mitwah, he brought guests..."

I allowed for a long pause in case she wanted to continue, but her lips remained sealed.

"I increased your Intelligence attribute. Your mana pool just grew, as did your casting power and the rate at which you regenerate mana."

Her mouth gaped. "How is it that you have this power? This power to change me?"

I found myself loving the answer to her query as I delivered it. "Actually, it's because you like me."

"Because I...?" She pressed a hand to her chest. "You are... I..."

"Guess you're glad you hitched your trailer to my truck, huh?"

Roshan's face contorted. "I am confused. This is like my horse and your wagon earlier?"

I nodded. "I'll bet you're glad you have become my companion."

Her head bobbed repeatedly. "I didn't know it would

render such positive outcomes." She blushed and peered down. "In addition to the others I have experienced."

"Now you're a rock star!"

Her head ticked up. "This thing you call a *rock star* must be fine, indeed!" She stepped toward me, thrust her arms straight by her side, and clenched her fists.

I looked her up and down. "Are you about to kiss me again?"

"Why, yes." Her face lit as her smile broadened. "Yes, I am."

After I conducted those little pieces of business, I was feeling even better about our chances.

'Our' chances. We are now a 'we.'

I had a healer who might keep me from the void of death, and in return, she had a protector who would lay waste to any who threatened her. Her new spell would instantly heal about twenty-five percent of my health, and her current pool of 190 mana would allow four casts, without counting for in-combat regeneration.

I also had a pet I shouldn't forget. Judging from the interface, Click leveled as I did, and her points were automatically distributed. That little girl had already proven very useful, but I sensed her need to find an enemy she could sink her teeth into. Skeletons and dancing swords weren't exactly the best uses of those strange, silvery fangs.

When we set off down the hallway, Roshan paced beside me like she was floating on a cloud. I recalled the dark man's mention of his living minions, the ones expanding his master's subterranean domain. I wondered exactly what that meant and why they'd do it. But the more pressing matter was their likely acclimatization to the dark.

Though her green and yellow robe would've made for decent camouflage out in the woods, it stood out like a sore thumb in the dingy gray of the hallway the light of my Inner Illumination spell. If our enemies held similar abilities to see down there, maybe we could use that against them.

Focusing on the icon for Inner Illumination, I disabled it and asked Roshan to recast Outer Illumination. There was no further point in hiding, anyway. The dark man knew we were here and coming for him. The light from the overhead spell would give me better visibility and might even partially blind our competition.

As we paced along the corridor heading north, a tensing in my quads told me we'd started a gradual descent. I considered how I'd engage our next enemies if they showed up in the hallway and finally remembered the troubles I'd had reaching arrows in my quiver. I shrugged it off and wrapped the ties around my waist so the container bounced just behind my left hip. Once it was tightened down, I reached across a few times and pulled at the shafts. The motion was so natural, I didn't even care if I looked strange. Enora wasn't one of those games.

"It's colder. We're getting closer."

Roshan nodded. She raised a hand and swept it to one side, then the light blinked out. Darkness ensued. I stopped to ask what she was doing, but then a subtle light shone from the round glass atop her scepter. Slowly increasing in intensity, the mage's weapon cast a sliver of white light like a laser down the center of the tunnel, illuminating the way ahead with a focused beam.

Genius.

"Ready your weapons, adventurer." She eyed my shoulder. "Perhaps your bow, at first."

And a mind reader, as well.

"How can you tell? Is the Light helping you sense them?"

She tapped her ear with one finger. "I spent many years in the Mines of Aniqua. I could hear a rat scamper in a rock-slide." Roshan pursed her lips and cocked her chin toward the hallway. "Rats scamper."

As our descent became more obvious, the stone floor ahead transitioned to brown, mud-packed earth in a six-inch drop. We stopped at the end of the floor with our toes dangling off the edge of the stone. Roshan lowered her scepter so the beam pointed at our feet and squinted into the inky blackness ahead.

"Do you see it?" she asked.

I squinted, peering down the tunnel and waiting for my eyes to adjust "I can't see anything without the—"

Two dim green lights hovered in the distance. They were so subtle, at first I wondered if they were mere echoes of the scepter's light painted on my corneas. But then they grew in intensity and size as they floated silently up and down.

Eyes. Someone walking toward us.

The scepter ignited, firing its focused white beam down the tunnel, revealing the source of the green lights.

A short figure in a black robe strode toward us. Curling strands of blonde hair erupted from the dark hood pulled up and over her forehead. Something about the way the robe hung stiff on her form seemed all wrong, but my attention was diverted by a hollow sensation boring into the center of my chest and eating outward toward my extremities as I peered into those glowing eyes. My knees began to quiver as the figure raised its hands.

"I am Priya. My master awaits you." Two distinct voices came from her—one the deep, throaty growl of something inhuman, the other, the quiet monotone of a woman.

The sound sent a dark chill down my spine.

Click greeted the newcomer with a series of rolling, warning clicks that transitioned to a low growl.

"A minion possessed by the dark man's magic," Roshan warned. "She acts not of her own will, but in service to her master. I have only heard legends of such darkness, but I sense two beings in this form."

"No shit? What gave it away? The two voices, maybe?"

Roshan ignored me. "She is his conduit. He hears each word."

Priya's dual voices reported, "Soon you will bend to his will as have I, priestess. When our work here is done, we will revel in the glory of serving our underlord in his underground kingdom, far from here." Her eyes flicked to my side of the tunnel and, when she addressed me, any evidence of the underlying feminine voice was absent, leaving only the growl that clawed at my chest. "Turn back, adventurer and leave this one to her destiny. Once my master has set eyes on a prize, he will not relent until he has it. Withdraw, or die where you stand."

If I was going to take Enora by the nut sack, this was as good a place and time as any. "Yo, what's up, Priya? I'm Gem. This is Rosh. Let's get something straight."

"Rosh?" my companion whispered indignantly. "I dislike this."

"Go with it. I'm about to wax reality on this asshole via his minion." I turned my attention back to the dark woman. "I don't get off on causing harm to people who don't act of their own free will. So, how about this? Take me to your master, and we'll just have us a little *mano a mano*. A little contest to decide who gets what. If he's all-powerful and worthy of the priestess, let him prove it."

Her head tilted and the glowing eyes shifted toward the

ceiling. She stood silent for a long moment. I wondered if I should repeat myself.

"My master is entertained by you, weak one. He asks the terms of your contest."

I let the 'weak one' shit slide in the interest of expediency. Taking the situation by the sack was different from measuring our penises.

"If I win, I take *Roshan* and *you* out of this place, curse-free and unpossessed. Additionally, he vacates the premises."

A low, booming laughter of which this slight creature couldn't possibly have been the source echoed down the tunnel and rolled back toward us from behind her. The light from Roshan's scepter dimmed for a moment. Raising it in the air, she whispered something, and it gleamed brighter than before.

"When my master prevails, you will labor with his minions to expand his domain, and this lovely eastern creature will bend her knee before him." She didn't wait for a response. "Your terms are accepted. Follow me."

My eyes trailed down the length of her robe and I analyzed how the garment encircled her like a stone. Falling just short of the muddy floor, its hem formed a perfect, unmoving oval around her ankles. It shimmered as if an unknown source of purple glow reflected on its felt-like surface, rolling in a line from her shoulder to the middle of her back.

"So, um, how long have you been with Master Dark Shit?" I asked.

Roshan answered in her stead. "She is not in there. It is him to whom you speak."

"Oh. Well, in that case," I turned my attention back to the dark one. "Hey, asshole, where do you get off enslaving women and using them to do your bidding? I mean, are you that much of a spineless twat that you—"

The deep growl replied. "I grow tired of your rantings, fool. Seal your lips or I will leave you behind."

I leaned closer to Roshan and slipped an arm around her robe so I could whisper. "What do you think, can we take him?"

Roshan's words still projected confidence. "The Light will guide us through this obstacle, noob."

I pressed my lip against her ear. "You're the only person I've ever heard who could make that word sound sexy."

"I fear my advances have left you single-minded, adventurer. You should fo—" Roshan stopped. My natural momentum carried me a couple steps further before I ground to a halt on the mud-packed floor.

Eyeing the back of the dark figure as she disappeared around a bend, I stepped back. "What is it?"

"As I expected. We are betrayed. They have hemmed us in. Turn and prepare for battle."

I pivoted. My heart pounded like it was trying to escape.

The sound of sucking mud filled the tunnel behind us.

25

Click turned and snapped at my ankles.

"Yes!" I gestured with my bow in the direction from which we'd come. "Check our six!"

The beast sped off as I whipped around to face the direction I'd last seen the robed figure. A chill coursed down my spine.

"Rats scamper," Roshan growled.

Those green eyes focused on us, and a cross between a sneer and a smile stretched her lips. A void of blackness replaced teeth and gums. Priya waved her hand in a quick circle and a translucent diamond-shape appeared before her chest. Her finger tips tapped its center, causing a burst of purple light to blast out from the center. As she completed the cast, the diamond cloned itself again and again until a magic barrier was formed.

"Roshan, she's casting a shield. They're hemming us in."

"He is casting through her," Roshan said. "This little one does not enjoy this power except by her master's leave."

"Yeah, yeah. I get that it's Crohl. She just happens to be the one standing there." I lurched forward and kicked at the barrier. A shock ran from my heel to my knee. I barked through the obstruction. "So, that's how this works? You make a deal, but can't stand the thought of a fair fight?"

"Gemini!" Roshan barked.

I spun around. Shadowy figures filled the tunnel where it curved into a narrow turn—stout forms with thick arms, strong chests, and three fingers on each hand ending in fat, black claws.

Skachi
Demon fiend
Level 8

Roshan's scepter cast a beam of light at the creatures, who raised their arms and stepped back. The beasts hunched, their faces framed in pink skin with tendrils crossing their lips. Their bat-like ears were colored the same fleshy pink and were covered in fine hairs. Their torsos were puke green.

Click returned to my side and chomped her teeth in a chattering warning to the demon fiends.

The dark man's voice erupted from Priya's mouth behind me. "Leave the girl for me. Kill the man and his beast. Eat until you are filled."

I dared not turn my back on the fiends, but I addressed the dark man through his human conduit. "You gave orders like that once before, and it didn't go your way. This won't be any different. I'm coming for you, coward."

The beasts launched toward us.

Leveling my bow at the closest skachi, I pulled the string to my ear and exhaled. Light filled the tip of the arrow and streamed from tip to fletching in time with my casting bar. When it filled, I released a penetrating shot. The arrow sailed true and split the demon's pink flesh in the narrow space between its right eye and the temple. The creature tumbled backward to the floor, sprawling across the narrow space. As a bonus, its corpse created a bottleneck, forcing its brethren to claw their way over it to pursue us.

Not bad—a kill and a disruption to their flow. Eat that, Dark One.

My thoughts often intruded at the worst of times. As the bottleneck formed before us, my skill level with bows increased, and the motions became more natural than they would have through simple practice in my old world. Combined with my readier access to the newly positioned quiver, I might soon be a killing machine.

Throwing Click a mental order to attack, I leveled my bow at my next target, but Roshan raised her scepter and blocked my way.

"Roshan! A healer's place is in the back, where you have cover!" I barked.

The scepter flashed in the faces of the oncoming demon beasts, and a thought of gratitude that it hadn't been pointed at me crossed my mind as they raised their arms in unison, like synchronized swimmers, to block the light from their sensitive eyes.

Text floated above their heads.

Blind!
Blind!
Blind!
Blind!

Shrieks of anger filled the tunnel as Roshan used the distraction to slip past me and take up a position in a safer spot.

Click sank his teeth into the muscular calf of the beast nearest, causing its singular wail to fill the narrow tunnel. My familiarity with my interface allowed me to focus on the small icon beneath Click's health bar on my party interface to activate her bite ability. The porcupunk bit harder this time, and the skachi turned its attention on the animal, converting the porcupunk into a tank against the single target, as designed.

The remaining beasts screeched and clawed as they struggled to clamber or crawl around each other. They growled with rage.

Loosing another arrow, I stepped to one side and reloaded. The arrow ripped into the flesh above the ribs of the skachi engaging my pet, forcing it to trip and tumble onto its back. The increases in Dexterity and repositioned quiver made my attack motions more natural as I loosed each arrow.

Click clawed her way up an enemy's form and ripped away green bloody flesh with the violent shake of her head. A hole gaped where the creature's throat had been. She spat it out as if it tasted sour and dug in again as green arms flailed beneath her.

Another demon clutched Click's hairs and raised her into the air. Tendrils of flesh stretched like latex away from the doomed skachi on the floor as Click chomped down and pulled. They tore free when the standing monster slammed her into the wall. Her yip of surprise made me flinch. Teeth grinding, I nocked another arrow and let it sail.

It missed.

Another skachi traversed the bottleneck. It lumbered forward, standing inches taller than the others, its shoulders like hard round stones.

Skachi Alpha
Level 9 Demon

Slamming its own kind against the walls on either side to clear its path, the alpha stomped on corpses underfoot and closed on me. Dropping my bow, I ripped my rapier out of its scabbard and thrust it forward as it lunged. The tip entered the belly of the oncoming demon bastard, using his momentum against him. Its eyes squinted as it peered down at the sword, but then it raised its head and bellowed.

"Alpha, huh? You think you scare me?" I yelled.

Grabbing the sword jutting from its belly, the demon stepped into it, driving the blade deeper into himself, and closing the distance between us. A rotten stench wafted from its mouth as it sneered.

Um, maybe it does.

I struggled to pull the blade away, but the alpha's hand gripped the pommel and forced a stalemate as he pushed the last of the blade through himself and bent toward me with his mouth agape. Releasing the pommel now that the blade was fully lodged inside his guts, the alpha grabbed my shoulders and shoved me into the wall. Massive hooked teeth bore toward me from behind the flapping tendrils hanging from his top lip.

Jerking my head to the side, I reached for the sheaths in the rear of my armor. I howled as the demon's teeth ripped into the flesh between my shoulder and neck.

Skachi Alpha bites you.
Critical Hit!
-89 HP
131 HP remaining

Hot crimson flowed down my back and chest as the arm on that side fell limp against my ribs. I tilted my head away just as the skachi's teeth clicked beside my ear. The demon lunged to bite again, but as it drew its head back, it screamed and slipped lower on the earthen wall.

Having regained her senses, Click growled and twisted her head at the demon's feet, distracting it from sweeping in for a second bite of my flesh that might have ended me.

Roshan *Casts Minor Heal.*

+14 HP

-17 HP (bleed)

133 HP remaining

The competing reports of hit point loss and hit point regeneration showed Roshan was propping me up without overcasting and wasting her mana. If not for the pain and eruption of tiny blood geysers from my shoulder, I might have beamed with pride at her efficiency—not to mention her resistance to leading off with the new, higher-level spell that drained more mana.

On the other hand, my HP was draining, and the searing hell had me wanting to pass out, so maybe a Flash Heal might've rocked.

+14 HP

-17 HP (Bleed)

131 HP remaining

My other hand finally fingered a pommel behind me. Ripping the dagger from its sheath, I swung it as the demon made the fatal mistake of reaching down to extract my pet's gnawing teeth from his hip. The blade swept in an upward arc and found purchase right in the center of flesh beneath demon's chin. I forced it up, through his mouth, and into his brain, making sure to look the bastard in the eye as I twisted and ripped it free with a growl.

"Die."

The Alpha tumbled to the mud. My rapier vibrated in its chest as it struck the ground with a heavy thud.

Click acquired our next target without hesitation as another burst of warmth surged through me, numbing the pain in my shoulder.

Flash Heal
(Roshan)
+64 HP
-9 HP (Bleed)
186 HP

The pain in my shoulder became a traumatic echo as the wound began to stitch itself together under the influence of healing magic. Man, I loved having a healer. But when I reached around for my other dagger, my shoulder protested with searing pain, so I stepped forward with the weapon I wielded, under-equipped to take on the four other demons I counted but lacking options.

So I entered the fray, swinging my dagger wildly, clutching the arm beneath my injured shoulder to my chest. Click ripped flesh from the ankles and calves of the demons. Light continued to flash in the darkness, healing my wounds and keeping me in the fight. My party found a rhythm, and soon the demons were falling around us.

The last skachi stood before me in the darkness, arms up in submission, cowering away from my blade.

I smiled.

"Too late for that, you little shit. Bring it."

Stepping forward, I feigned left as the demon swung a terrified arm in my direction. As I spun, his arm went wide, and I came around to the end of my revolution, where I slammed the dagger into its temple. Twisting the weapon inside the wound—I really liked doing that—I once again stared into the fading light of a demon's eyes.

"I like watching you die."

I ripped out the dagger and reveled in the flood of blood spurting from the mortal wound.

The urge to drop on top of it and stab it over and over fell away as a golden flash of light surrounded me and the bold, golden number 7 appeared and zipped into the distance. My health and stamina pools filled instantly. When the golden light vanished, we were washed in darkness.

Your dark excitations result in a ten-point shift toward
Darkness

Where all my other notifications popped up only when I clicked the icons, that one printed out in the center of my viewing field and flashed red. Opening my character sheet, I peered at my disposition slider. So far, the notch sat on the right of center, approaching the brighter end of the bar, instead of moving in the direction where it transitioned to blood red at the opposite end.

Disposition:
Light: 317

I focused on my notifications icons just to get them to stop blinking.

You killed a Skachi.
Level 7
+817 XP
+20 Reputation with the Matron of the Wood
Total Reputation: 20
You killed a Skachi.
Level 7
+764 XP
+20 Reputation with the Matron of the Wood
Total Reputation: 40
You killed a Skachi Alpha.
Level 8
+881 XP
+20 Reputation with the Matron of the Wood
Total Reputation: 60
You killed a Skachi.
Level 7
+713 XP
+20 Reputation with the Matron of the Wood
Total Reputation: 80
You killed a Skachi.
Level 7
+709 XP
Total Reputation: 100
+20 Reputation with the Matron of the Wood
You killed a Skachi.
Level 7
+674 XP
Total Reputation: 120
+20 Reputation with the Matron of the Wood
*You have changed your class to **Assassin**.*
There will be a 30 second global cool down of abilities before
Assassin skills are available to you.

You killed a Skachi.
Level 8
+771 XP
+20 Reputation with the Matron of the Wood
Total Reputation: 140
You have reached Level 7
+1 to Dexterity
+1 to Constitution.
You have two new attribute points to spend.
*You have reached **Pacify** Rank 2.*
You may now pacify beasts up to Level 7.
Pacification of beasts above your own level are met with a
10% penalty to success for each level above your own.
Pacified beasts of higher level will be adjusted to match
your own.

My victorious barking echoed down the tunnel. "What do you think of that, Crohl?"

I turned, wearing a wide smile and anticipating Roshan's contagious enthusiasm. I fumbled my dagger as I spied only darkness. Panicked, I casted Inner Illumination and leaned forward, squinting. Roshan's scepter leaned against the earthen wall, its gem extinguished.

A waking nightmare bloomed. My companion was gone.

26

"No!" I screamed in the darkness as I swept up the scepter. I half-expected to slam into the barrier the slave Priya had erected, but it was gone. The minion had removed it to snatch Roshan. There hadn't even been a scream.

How could I be so stupid! Sending her back was exactly what they'd wanted me to do. The dark man had seen Click and me fighting off the floating falchion with Roshan behind us, healing. He'd counted on our repetition of that tactic. He'd sprung a trap, and I'd fallen right into it. They loaded us into a bottleneck and used it to their advantage.

I clutched the scepter and ran my eyes along its intricate metal carvings.

You have discovered a new starter class!
Light Priest

Great.

Apparently learning the class didn't award additional spells. Minor Heal would've been nice, especially considering I planned to kill everything that moved in this place with reckless abandon until I had Roshan safely back at my side.

I cursed and shoved the scepter into my bag. Wielding both of the simple daggers I'd found in the Magic Bag of Holding, I jogged through the tunnel.

Click sniffed the ground a few feet ahead.

I tried to keep my speed at a pace where stamina regeneration was equal to the amount I was burning by moving faster than my average gait, but if there was anything I'd learned in the last twenty-four hours, it was that there was no balancing it. Sure, I could slow my roll and recover some stamina, but eventually, it drained more than it gave back.

Two of my attribute points needed assigning before they got auto-assigned and, if the battle over the rapier lodged in the skachi's stomach had taught me anything, it was that strength had its place in combat, even if my class used dexterity for a primary attribute. My role in Enora wouldn't be so simple or single-faceted as it had been in LOB.

As I jogged through this tunnel, I eyed my Constitution, but ultimately dumped the points in strength and forced myself to balance my stamina on my own until I could afford more points. I'd gotten one tick each in Dexterity and Constitution when I leveled, anyway. In retrospect Strength had been neglected for too long.

More lessons learned.

G3m1n1 Fowler
Human
Level 7 Assassin
Strength: 6
Dexterity: 13

Intelligence: 1
Wisdom: 1
Constitution: 13
Charisma: 10
HP: 220
Mana: 100

Click pushed forward, throwing the occasional glance back at me. I searched the sub-commands for my pet.

Guard Stance: Your pet will respond to danger and assault any threats to you.

That was the ticket. I'd be damned if I was going to get caught with my pants down, especially without my healer to aid me.

Then, I reconsidered.

Aggressive Stance: Your pet will attack threats in proximity to you

My hand slipped into my bag and, as I focused on the vial in my Inventory tab, the healing potion appeared in my hand. If I had to get along without the healer, I'd be ready. But it felt like starting over in the worst of ways. Slipping the vial into my pocket, I eyed my stamina bar and slowed my pace to balance it. My breath evened slowly, but impatience took over. I'd never catch up at this pace.

I chewed on half of the final piece of Deer Jerky for the constitution buff and slipped the other half into Click's jaws. She took it readily enough, but then she was off again, her nose wrinkling as she sniffed the ground before her, searching for our lost comrade as she smacked on the meat.

She rounded a corner ahead of me then clicked twice. By the time I'd rounded the slight curve, she'd vanished into the darkness.

I sprinted forward a few paces. The sound of vicious growling came on the damp air.

I stopped and reached for my daggers. A figure swung its hands desperately at its own green barrel chest. My girl had latched onto another demon.

I charged forward. The demon balled its fists and pounded them into Click's back, causing the porcupunk's breath to escape in tiny squeals, but she maintained her bite.

The skachi glared up at me and its mouth widened into a gaping grin. It raised one crooked-finger and extended a claw.

No.

As it swiped down Click, my reflexes took over. Reversing my grip and bending at the elbow, I grasped the blade and threw it as hard as I could. It sailed through the air as the demon's claws raked downward.

The blade lodged into his forehead, but not before the demon ripped a gash down Click's back.

She squealed and tumbled to the packed earth as the demon slid down the wall, painting it in blood. Its body fell with a splat on the muddy surface.

My heart sank as I watched my porcupunk crawl toward me in a sideways limp. I reached in my sack for a health potion, but then I realized only the one in my pocket remained.

Click fell to her belly, and I knelt to check her wound. Gently pressing the fleshy hairs aside, I found the source of the rivers of blood pouring down her back. Two deep claw marks ran the length of her spine from the neck. One of her tiny black paws twitched erratically. As my pet clung to life, I found myself wishing she'd let go. A minute passed and she still struggled. My hearth thumped a cold beat and I couldn't watch anymore. I needed to catch Roshan and I needed to end the suffering I knew the animal would remember when I brought it back.

I scratched Click's head and nodded gently. "I need this potion just in case." I didn't know if she really comprehended the words, but she was always responsive to my commands and sometimes seemed to read my intent, so I went with it, hoping she understood. "I'm going to let you sleep for a while."

I stood and spread my hands out in a claw. As I focused, blue light surrounded my fingers and they began to tremble.

"See you soon, babe."

Then Click, peering up at me with her black eyelids drooping, slowly faded away, into the void.

You have dismissed your pet.
You compassion for your animal has resulted in a twenty-point shift toward the Light
Disposition:
Light: 337

Even though I knew better, I raised my hand again and attempted to summon Click, hoping she'd be healed by the dismiss process.

Because you dismissed this pet and it didn't die in combat, you must wait ten minutes before summoning it again.

The effort to summon her spent no mana on the failed attempt. At least I was trying to look at the bright side.

Wrenching my dagger from the demon's head gave a satisfying squeak of metal against its bony skull. I wiped the blood on its flesh.

I didn't know why I hadn't thought of it before, but now that my pet was gone and I knew I was alone, I crept over to the wall and slid back around the bend on the off-chance that the dark caster wouldn't see me there.

You have entered stealth mode.

While I was there, I read the log.

You killed a Skachi.
Level 7
+774 XP
+20 Reputation with the Matron of the Wood
Total Reputation: 160
Your thrown weapon skill has increased to Rank 2.

My daggers shone clear as day despite each hand's near invisibility. It was a neat touch Enora did that to assist players with hand-eye coordination during combat, but I wasn't feeling appreciative in the moment.

I could barely hear my own footsteps. It was hard to imagine how dangerous a higher level than I might be if they had stealth skill rating in the double digits. Making a mental note to practice often and ensure I leveled the skill for times like this, I redirected my focus to the path ahead.

I didn't know if I was angrier with Crohl for taking Roshan or with myself for stationing her between the magic barrier and myself. The dark man had out maneuvered me, but I wasn't about to let the dark side of my brain return to dominate me. Roshan wouldn't want that. The fact was, I wouldn't have been able to fight with her blocking the narrow pathway between me and those demon bastards. A stray arrow might have killed her. Though I knew I was right and bellyaching over it now wouldn't do anybody any good, the sentiment delivered little comfort.

As I crept along the wall, the path leveled out and rose again. When I climbed the incline, the ground became drier, so my stealth ankle boots made even less noise.

The north-south path ended a few minutes later, leaving only a turn to the right, up a flight of stairs constructed from dirt. A sliver of light atop the stairs competed with my Inner Illumination and distorted my field of vision. Climbing slowly, ensuring only the balls of my feet touched the stairs, I ventured upward.

The climb itself revealed the deceptive height of the staircase. It seemed to go on forever, causing my quads to become sore and my stamina bar to tick down a few notches because of my slow, methodical steps. Near the crest of the stairs, I dismissed my Inner Illumination spell and let my eyes rely on the unknown light source.

I stopped a few steps from the top so I could peek over the edge of the landing above.

Two creatures stood on either side of the black door. Horns jutted from their jowls, pointed inward so their tips met just beneath their lips. Disparate black hairs meshed in wires around their mouths and chins, covering green skin beneath. I eyed their broad shoulders, blocky biceps, and the makeshift helmets of wood pulled low over their foreheads. Two candles burned on poles on either side of the door. I'd seen enough of these in other games that I hardly even had to inspect them.

Half-Orc

Level 6
Alignment: Chaotic
You do not understand this being's language.

They were one level lower than I was, giving me an advantage. If I'd had a way to check their skills, I'd have focused more on their stats and tried to reason whether they'd be able to see me, but like so many other facets of the game, I would learn on-the-job because Enora gave me exactly jack shit in the way of enemy intel.

Stepping carefully, I took the last couple of stairs. They faced my direction, but they didn't react to my movement.

I might have smiled had I not been so incensed about Roshan's abduction and scared they'd see me before I could get to her. Starting with notifications I'd been ignoring, I flipped through my interface as I ducked on the stairs.

Your stealth skill has increased to Rank 6.
Your stealth skill has increased to Rank 7.
Your stealth skill has increased to Rank 8.

While this was welcome news, it prompted more questions than it answered. If my skill had risen since I activated my stealth ability, did that mean I advanced in levels the longer I remained hidden? Or did it mean the dark man had been watching me via a spell and failed his checks when I passed through his field of vision undetected? It had seemed that way when I received a point when the man on the beach had passed me by without seeing me, earlier in the day.

There was no way to know. I was what Roshan called me. A noob.

What I needed was a plan. With my eyes just above the

level of the landing at the top of the stairs, I scanned for anything I could use to get the guards out of my way.

Aside from the guards, the spears they clutched, and candleholders in each corner, the landing was barren stone. As I slipped closer, I noted purple flashes periodically interrupting the white light beneath the door. I shivered against the growing chill and flipped to my offensive skills tab. There, I spied the one I'd learned upon discovering my stealth boots and, in turn, the assassin class.

Backstab

A vicious attack performed while stealth is active, causing 150% main-hand damage Damage scales with level advancement.

Shoving my hand into my bag and accessing my Inventory panel, I searched the containers for something useful—perhaps an item plundered from one of the bastards who'd kidnapped Roshan. It was ironic when I thought about it—if the bastards hadn't kidnapped her, I wouldn't have her. I had to admit to myself, the dominant part of me was really glad she'd been taken.

Did that make me an asshole?

I shrugged and kept searching.

Ivory Chalices!

I recalled how Roshan had casually tipped one onto the altar to show her lack of interest in material things. The memory brought both a smile and the determination to see this through.

I pulled out one of the cups and duck–walked up to the landing.

Casting my eyes toward each guard one final time, I threw the white, jewel-encrusted cup into the far corner of the landing where it struck the wall and bounced into the corner. The guards swiveled their heads.

The one closest to the chalice grunted something. By his inflection, it sounded like, "What the hell?" But as my inspection function informed me, I didn't speak half-orc, or Orcish, or whatever.

As he approached, the other stepped over to the stairs and glanced down. Standing no more than a foot from me, I could smell his unbathed body and it made me want to blow jerky chunks. The pressing concern was that he'd spy me crouching right next to him, so I locked my muscles up tight and waited.

Eventually, the stinking thing grunted and muttered something to his companion before moving behind him.

Stupid orcs. Bet their Intellect rank sucks.

Circling it swiftly so as not to lose my advantage, I slipped in behind the half-orc closest to me and used my backstab ability for the first time, hoping upon hope it would work.

Critical hit!
Mortal Wound inflicted!

Half-orc
-118 HP
Half-Orc Dies

Holy shit! The element of surprise is brutal!

I felt my enemy's spine separate beneath the slice of my blade, and he squealed as he folded to the ground. When his comrade turned, it was too late. He was dealing with an angry human with two curved blades swinging toward his throat. His tough skin was no match for their sharp edges as

I plunged my blades into both sides of his neck with violent stabs until they reached all the way to the hilts. I didn't stop until the two daggers connected in the middle with a metallic scrape. Ripping my daggers from his neck made a sucking noise. I took a step back, steeling myself to attack again, if necessary.

It wasn't.

The orc's wide eyes went dim in death before he even hit the floor.

You killed a half-orc
Level 6
718 XP
+20 Reputation with the Matron of the Wood
Total Reputation: 180
You killed a half-orc
Level 6
703 XP

I scurried over to stand beside the door and pressed my ear against it. Though I couldn't make out the words, it was clear that the voice prattling incessantly on the other side was that of the dark figure who'd spoken to me from the magical wooden frame in the torture room.

Crohl.

I pressed my ear to the crack. "Don't resist, priestess. You only prolong your suffering."

Oh, hell no, dude.

I tried the knob, but the door didn't open. Clutching both my daggers, I lunged forward, raised my foot, and slammed the heel next to the handle.

27

The jamb splintered and cracked. The door careened and slammed into the wall as I charged into the room. Walls of dull marble framed smooth stone floors seeming so out of place in the underground tunnel system that I did a double take. I'd gone for what S.W.A.T. teams in my old world called dynamic entry, expecting I'd launch right at my enemy or enemies, but the scene brought me screeching to a halt.

I spied three figures but my gaze settled on a bald man in a hoodless black robe clutching a glass ball with swirling purple and black clouds inside. The dark dude looked nothing like his representation in the frame of the torture chamber earlier. Instead of the angular features and a wiry goatee, he was smooth-shaven and chubby faced. A pair of spectacles hung low on his nose. Though he wore a black robe, his features counteracted any chances of it making him appear ominous. He looked like... a nerd.

Purple tendrils of smoke crept in long fingers from an orb in his hand into Roshan's nostrils. His head swiveled my way when I crashed through the door. His shoulders jerked back, but he held fast to the globe and continued his cast.

Nerd or not, he was up to no good.

A much larger frame than before hung high on the far wall. A similar, smoky figure observed the proceedings between Roshan and the dark caster. Its snout was long, reminding me of a Gila monster. Two smoky tusks jutted down from the top row of its teeth. I had the distinct suspicion the figure wasn't masking himself as Crohl had.

In the corner closest to me, the robed minion we'd encountered in the tunnel glared at the proceedings through those glowing black and green eyes. Her locks of blonde hair shivered like electrified serpents from beneath her dark shroud. Blue veins crept near the surface of her skin around the temples.

Roshan's robe hung loosely on her shoulders and was open in the front revealing her undershorts.

"You filthy son of a bitch," I growled. "Back off, jerk wad!"

The head in the frame turned toward me as I stepped forward. A booming voice filled the room as its wispy lips parted.

"You trespass, adventurer! Turn back or be destroyed!"

Well, at least he gets right to the point—whoever the hell he is.

"No such luck, dude." I thrust a finger toward Roshan. "She's with me."

The dark figure's face jutted out of the frame, and its snout tilted up and down, surveying my form. Then it turned toward the robed figure. "Crohl, your lustful greed consumes you."

"I sought only to bring you another conduit of magic

essence, Lord Caym! I sense the potential for much Light in her!"

"Hmmm." The face turned toward Roshan, who stood idle under the casting of the spell, the tendrils creeping into her nostrils. Then his focus returned to me. "And yet you miss the limitless capsule of duality who stands before you now."

Crohl's head swiveled toward me. His dark boss man stared at me through his projection or whatever the hell it was, and though I'd been ready to launch at Crohl, his boss drew my interest. Why was he looking at me like that?

"What *are* you, boy?"

"What is it with people calling me boy? I'll show you a boy, ya f—"

The smoky demon growled. "Crohl! You fool! This one carries the blessing of the Matron of the Wood. Are you blind? It is he you should have taken! He will be a bottom-less well of spirit." The beast sighed. "Kill the priestess and cast this one into the depths for combat practice to advance him until he can be delivered to me."

"But my lord, couldn't I—"

The smoky visage leaned further out of the frame so its snout was inches from Crohl's nose.

"Your desire to feed your eyes grows tiresome, Crohl. Be thankful I let you keep Priya." His Smokey visage swirled and expanded again. When it did, his attention returned to me. "They have returned. We must prepare." He spat smoke at his underling. "Do my bidding or burn."

"Yes, my lord! I will await your portal, my lord!"

Returned? Who has returned?

"Don't fail me, Crohl." The image vanished and, this time, there was no swirling demon toilet. The smoke vanished in a vacuum.

Crohl thrust a finger on his free hand at me and whined like a school child. "Priya! Don't just stand there sucking up energy! Disable him before he interrupts my cast!"

"Yes, master." In the dimness of the tunnels below, I hadn't quite been able to put my finger on what was strange about this Priya's robe, but now that we stood in the light of the marbled room, the way it surrounded her form like a shell was obvious. It was some kind of mobile cage or hardened shell.

The blonde acolyte thrust out her hands. Green light glowed around her fingers as they formed claws.

Uh-oh. Time to move!

Just as light exploded from her fingertips, I dove and awkwardly rolled forward. An ear-bending explosion of energy slammed into the wall where my head had been. Zhara had warned me of this very possibility, that I might face minions under mind control effects, so I dropped my daggers as I dove, I rolled to my feet, slammed my shoulder into the acolyte's robe, threw my arms around her, raised her off the ground as I straightened my legs, and slammed her back into the wall.

"Hmph!" The dual-toned voice uttered as the impact sucked her wind.

Though the robe had appeared to be a shell, it had responded with the consistency of cloth. Priya heaved and blew wind out of her chest in a desperate gasp. As I released the acolyte, she crumpled to the ground with a heavy thump. Her eyelids fluttered shut, covering the black void where her eyeballs should have been as she cradled her arms across her midsection and groaned.

I threw my arms out to my sides and faced Crohl. "Peewee league football, bitch!"

Then I crouched, launched, and shoved Roshan aside.

The tendrils of smoke dissipated and puffed out of existence, though the dark colors continued to swirl inside the small globe.

Raising my stealth boots to kick the glass orb from the dark man's grasp, I quickly learned an important lesson.

I was not Bruce Lee.

It was one thing to play a game from an immersion pod, where your thoughts controlled your movements and an accurate kick required little more effort than the firing of some brain synapses, it was another entirely to raise one's leg with simulated musculature and strike what could quickly become a moving target. Crohl swung his arm aside at the last moment, spun his body in a nimble gesture I wouldn't have thought possible, and brought the orb around full force to clank against my forehead.

The nerd clocks you with an orb.
-47 HP
173 HP Remaining

Tiny bright stars danced, my knees faltered, and I dropped to the floor. Arrows spilled from my quiver. The room spun around me as the bald man peered down.

"You don't seem special to me," the snooty bastard said.

I could barely see him as I blinked through rivers of red flooding my face and blinding me. A cut above my eye throbbed. I patted the floor around me for my weapons.

My bow was nearby, but as I grasped, the bald man stomped down on the weapon. I swiped away enough blood to find his lips curled in a snarl, revealing rotted teeth. A system of blue veins webbed his entire face as a green aura surrounded his eyes and he began to cast.

Damn, I'd falsify my smoky visage too. Ugly mother Fu—

"Under-lord Caym has deemed you to be his subject. Submit or suffer."

Twisting my body to the side, I reared back one leg and swept myself in a circle, bringing my knee up to bump his Achilles and force his foot off my bow. His body thumped to the floor as I swiped hot blood away with my forearm. The cut screamed upon contact.

"Aagh!"

A warm sensation and a flood of light rushed through me. The mitigation of my pain left me feeling light enough to float. My eyes cleared with a final swipe from my sleeve.

A grand sign. Roshan was conscious and casting.

Planting my feet, I pushed my butt across the floor, away from the dark bastard, who now reminded me of a younger Emperor Palpatine from *The Empire Strikes Back*. The veins snaking through his face and neck, the paling of his skin, and the slits for eyes indicated some kind of transition to darkness I was certain I should stop.

Roshan kneeled in the far corner, close to the gaping door, her hands awash in golden light. Expecting another wave of warmth to complete the heal of the gash in my forehead, I was surprised when the light dimmed, she finished the cast, and it did nothing.

Is she out of mana already? Why was she able to cast at all?

The questions evaporated as the dark man got to his feet and raised the orb in my direction.

"You will make a good slave for my master, adventurer."

As the colored mist swirled within the smooth glass, his rotten smile reappeared. Fingers of smoke penetrated the orb and crept toward me. I slid backward but they chased me, adjusting naturally to their new course. As I spider-crawled backward, my palm touched cold metal. I raised a dagger and glanced at it. Then I smiled at Crohl.

He frowned, faltered.

I grabbed the blade and hurled it. Though I'd aimed for the center of his chest, the dagger lodged where Crohl's shoulder met his arm.

Your skill in thrown weapons has increased to 3.

Crohl
-13 HP

The tendrils, now inches from my face, dissipated as the cast was interrupted.

Crohl growled with frustration as he ripped the dagger free and sent it clattering across the floor. Blood spurted, and the dark man clutched his wound.

"Gah! That hurts!"

"Good!" I barked.

I grabbed the other dagger and got to my feet.

Crohl
-21 HP (bleed)

Though I spotted movement in the corner of the room as Roshan struggled to her feet, I kept my gaze pinned on Crohl so as not to give her away. A quick perusal of my HUD verified I was currently an assassin and no cool downs were in effect.

But then the fight was taken out of my hands.

Roshan pumped her legs and lunged across the floor,

diving at the dark man. I cringed as she launched and threw her arms around his neck, dislodging the orb which bounced to the floor and rolled away. My head swiveled with it as it seemed to roll in slow motion against the hard surface. My legs tensed as my hands longed to grasp the dark artifact, but it rolled right into the hand of the blonde minion.

Shit.

The woman he'd called Priya stood as Roshan and the dark man landed in the corner, their legs and robes a tangled mess. A strange white aura surrounded the bald man's slave as she raised the orb.

Roshan sneaked a look over her left shoulder, rolled off of Crohl, and crawled backward.

The orb breathed back to life and fingers of purple and black wisps trailed across the room. The blonde's disheveled hair blocked my view of her face as it surged with static electricity, but as the tendrils of dark mist crawled through the air, she turned her gaze on me.

The greenish-black glow of her pupils was gone, replaced by sea blue irises surrounded by bloodshot sclera. Dark circles cupped the bottoms of her eyelids, but the blue veins threading across her temples were absent and an ivory complexion replaced the sickish gray of earlier. Angular features and high cheekbones resolved in a slightly pointed chin. She was a beautiful creature intent on my destruction.

Wait. That wasn't true. The smoke wasn't moving toward me.

"No!" The bald man howled. Crohl raised his hand and purple diamond shapes unfolded into a translucent wall before him—the same barrier he'd cast through Priya in the tunnels below.

"Yeah," I said. "Get that son of a bitch, um, Priya."

Roshan's jaw relaxed, her shoulders dropped, and she raised a hand toward me. It glowed as she cast a slow heal to complete the closing of my wound. Then I realized the second cast I thought Roshan had intended for me had been directed at the blonde! She'd healed her as she writhed on the floor after my tackle!

The creeping fingers reached the magic partition as the blonde turned away from me, apparently satisfied I wouldn't charge her. They slipped through the barrier constructed of diamond-shaped segments and into the dark man's nostrils.

"No!" He bellowed. His eyelids fluttered and then closed. "You...can't..."

The blonde's inflated robe softened as the purplish shimmering glow streaking across it faded. It settled on her shoulders and relaxed around her body. Holding the orb high, she shrugged the garment off one shoulder, transferred the orb to her other hand, and shrugged again, so it crumpled to the floor at her feet.

Her skin was smooth—the opposite of what I'd imagined when witnessing the dark voids of her eyeballs only moments ago. Honestly, I'd expected dry, cracked lizard skin or some shit. Her thick, blonde hair danced around her as the orb did its thing. I diverted my eyes from full breasts wrapped in a meager strip of cloth that matched the swatch tied around her muscular bottom. It was knotted on one side so I could see the entirety of her powerful legs.

My jaw dropped as golden light filled crevices in her back.

No, not crevices... a tattoo, of sorts. My heart began to pound at the depiction of an oak with sprawling branches, smooth gray bark, and leaves so green I thought I could pluck them from the branches. Light crawled across the lines of the image until the whole tree began to glow. Then the branches and leaves rustled.

Numbness rolled across the skin of my entire body. My heart soared, alight with the vision. I couldn't hold my lips together. The oak's colors filled the room, reflecting off the walls like they were mirrors and forming an outdoor landscape around me. Then I felt the breeze that blew the leaves, the scent of wood wafted into my nostrils, and when I fell back to my elbows, I could've sworn they'd landed in soft grass.

All my worries dissolved as the periphery of the room surrounding Priya suddenly faded to black so only the glowing, living art on her back consumed my eyes.

There was only love.

There was only the tree.

What the hell was happening to me?

*You have been charmed by a **Ward of Solara**.*
You are pacified.
Effect Duration: 5 minutes or until the ward passes
from view

Then Priya stepped away, circling so her back pressed against the wall, and turned her gaze on me. Sterile light flooded back into the room as the effect of the mind-altering art on her back withdrew. Her shining, golden hair dulled in color, and her tattoo cast a glow on the wall behind her.

She nodded at me, then turned back to her target.

Now that she spoke only in her voice, it came in a tinny-but-melodic pitch. "It's your turn to live bound to another's will, you evil, evil man."

The dark man shot up and lurched forward, fighting

every step as his legs quivered. The magical barrier divided and melted away as he passed through. His body swayed unnaturally, as if I were viewing it through rippling water. Then his flesh dulled and his skin melted into a powdery trail. The remnants of the evil caster were sucked into the orb with a *whoosh* that seemed to pull the air out of the room.

Priya held the orb at eye level and peered inside. "Now you will see what it is like to rot in a glass prison and never find slumber." She turned and tossed the orb across the wide room to Roshan. "Hold that, would you?"

Roshan snatched it from the air with one hand. "Gladly." She raised the orb, one side of her top lip twisting in disgust as she peered into the swirling smoke therein. Priya scanned the room, her gaze eventually landing on me. She closed the distance in two steps. Her blue eyes gazed into mine, turned back to Roshan, and then back to me. Her chin dropped.

"Adventurers?"

I shrugged a shoulder and threw Roshan a smile while nodding at Priya.

"How very exciting!" Her voice conveyed the excitement, but her sleepy eyes spoke of utter exhaustion. "I'm sorry I had to charm you, I had to make sure I completed the cast."

"Understandable," I said.

As I stood and offered a handshake, I realized she couldn't have been much more than five feet tall. I smiled down at her, waiting for her to grasp my hand. Then her eyes rolled into the back of her head and she collapsed into my arms.

"Whoa! Okay, I've got you." I lowered her to the floor and pulled her toward me, adjusting my arms so I held her around the waist. Then I glanced at Roshan and shrugged.

Her eyes traversed the pair of us and a smile spread her perfect lips. "I believe we've made a new friend."

"A mostly-naked one," I said. "I think she's out cold. So, the question is, what do we do with her?"

28

After setting Priya's head to rest on my bag, Roshan and I embraced for a long moment. We sat against the wall with our hips touching as I watched the sleeping woman's chest rise and fall and Roshan eyed the glass orb in which Crohl was imprisoned.

From our vantage point, we could see the door in case any of the tunnel laborers Crohl mentioned came up the stairs. Waiting around wasn't ideal, but neither was hauling a half-naked woman through the tunnels, and that was if I made it down the stairs with her. There had to be a hundred of them.

"You find her attractive," Roshan said.

"What?" I asked, swinging my head around. "No, not at all. I just wonder if she's cold."

She threw me a suspicious glare.

"Okay, yeah. She's okay. Almost as beautiful as you."

"Bah! Flattery again."

"Seriously, we should cover her up with something."

I pulled off my leather chest piece and covered her heaving bosom with it.

We sat like that for about fifteen minutes before Roshan spoke, though she never looked away from the orb a second time.

"She is pale but beautiful. Such curves, but at the expense of her height."

Considering the only other women I'd met since entering Enora were an extension of the A.I. named Lucera and a strange being who stood a few inches taller than Priya and lived in a tree, I didn't have a lot to go on when trying to determine norms. So, I kept my mouth shut.

"You would mate with this one, yes?" Roshan asked, catching me off guard.

"What? No. Of course not."

"Do you find her unattractive?"

"I thought we covered this.""

"I see I have struck near the bone. You are uncomfortable with my directness."

I thought about that. "Actually I find it refreshing, the lack of pretension. It just caught me by surprise. Is that common conversation where you come from?"

"No, but I am with you now. We are to become intimate. Is there harm in comfortable conversation?"

Priya chose that moment to stir. She rolled toward us, and her eyes fluttered open. The former minion of Crohl shot up, and the shirt dropped to her waist. She made no attempt to cover herself.

I gestured at the black robe she'd shrugged off as she captured Crohl in the orb. "I didn't think you'd want me to throw that over you while you slept."

She rubbed her eyes with both fists. "What?" She spied the robe and nodded. "Oh, yes. You were wise in this, my lord. I'd as soon pry my eyes from their sockets as feel the cold grasp of that prison again."

Roshan and I rose and we each offered Priya a hand.

Priya accepted both hands and spoke as she rose. "Please know I'm horrified at my actions. I was not in control of my own faculties and my...weakness to resist that corrupt enslaver is a source of great embarrassment." She bowed her head. "I hope you'll find it in your heart to forgive me."

"You have nothing to apologize for." No sooner had she released my hand than I offered it again, palm up. "I'm Gemini."

I thought she might feel exposed in the semi-transparent strips of cloth adorning her as she stood before me, so I endeavored to keep my eyes high, but they involuntarily flicked to her chest. Though I peeled them quickly away after a glance, she surprised me when a knowing smile crossed one side of her lips.

Priya gazed at me as she grasped my hand, but it was Roshan she addressed. "Your man is pretty."

"Thank you, elf." Roshan replied. "We have only met this day, just hours ago."

Elf?

Priya's eyes waltzed down my shirtless body at a slow and languorous pace.

I felt objectified.

"Half-elf, really." She shrugged. "I hope you won't think I'm rude, but even in my droopy state, I wonder if you've made exclusive arrangements with our lovely hero." She blushed.

Lucera? You there? 'Make friends,' right? You recording this?

Roshan's disinterested answer took me by surprise. "The goddess shines on him. Surely such a man's heart shall not be bound by a single soul." She twisted the orb on the tips of her fingers.

"I really like it here," I muttered.

"As you know, I am Priya." She flung the evil eye at the orb in Roshan's hand. "Though I might cast my name to the nethers, having heard it befouled by evil's lips." She spat to one side.

"I think I'd keep it. It's a beautiful name. It suits you." Although I hadn't exactly intended the words the way they sounded, I thought they rolled out smoothly enough.

Her lips spread into a smile that could conquer nations. She leaned forward, pressed her lips to my cheek for a long second, then withdrew.

"Thank you, Jiminy, for freeing me. I will endeavor to see you properly rewarded. I have family who I think will be happy to see me."

Though I considered performing a flourish like a certain cartoon cricket, I didn't bother correcting her mispronunciation of my name.

Priya hugged Roshan. When she did, I caught sight of Priya's glowing tattoo again and my brain went numb. "What the h..." My words sounded foreign, distant.

Priya's head swiveled in my direction, but my gaze wouldn't peel away from the... light thingie.

As if on cue, black and purple smoke filled the frame on the wall, and the curve of two nostrils at the end of a long snout, tusks, and an angular chin appeared, followed by black, dull eyes with no irises or pupils. The embracing women turned their bodies and held each other at arms' length, removing the soul-warming tattoo from my sight.

"Hmm." The apparition sighed. "It seems Crohl proved unworthy." Black tendrils of smoke huffed through its nostrils and dissipated. Then the face viewed us all in succession.

"Maybe I can offer you a place at my side in his stead."

I nodded profusely. "Maybe you should just go fuck yourself."

"Fine. You will pay for your belligerence. Our paths shall cross again, fools."

"I look forward to it, asshole," I stepped forward and positioned myself between Roshan, Priya, and that dark fuck. To my own surprise, my muscles didn't quiver. My legs didn't quake in the least. Then I remembered the markings on Priya's back, and I suspected the charm empowered me. My own voice shouted in my mind.

Protect Priya!

The dark image began to swirl. "You have trifled with the wrong entity this day, human. This place was but a young addition to my underworld domain. My grasp is long and..." the demon glared at me for a long moment before finishing his sentence, "...reaching." He tilted his head to the side. "If you are what I believe you are, you will come to me."

"What I am is the end of you, prick."

"Doubtful. You will fall beneath my feet like all comers before you, boy."

"Am I supposed to be scared? Your little tunnel system belongs to me now, you seedy shit. If you want it, why don't you come take it back?"

The entity barked laughter. "If you so desire a conflict with an underlord, journey to the northeast beyond the Plague Barrens and cross the Hinterlands of Seran when you have grown, adventurer. I welcome your challenge and look forward to claiming the essences of both your companions and having you kneel at my feet. Meanwhile, dispose of Crohl as you see fit. I have no further use for him."

"Thanks for your permission. We'd planned on doing exactly that without your leave."

"Such bravado. You will tremble before me, fool."

The image vanished.

When I turned, the women wore the exact same expression—one titled eyebrow each and slack facial muscles.

"I'm going to call you two the twins."

A smile crept slowly across Roshan's lips, though it revealed no teeth. "Yes, I see I was right about you, Gemini."

Priya nodded in agreement. "Gemini? Is that how you say your name?"

I blinked my eyes in succession.

Priya Skyy
No class
Level 9 Half-elf
Note: NPCs require a class trainer or player to select a class and must equip a class-specific weapon to do so. NPCs can still gain experience and level, and if they select a class before level 20, any earned levels will be attributed to that class.

So, no class, huh? Since we weren't companions, I wasn't seeing her stats, just like I hadn't originally seen Roshan's. Also, if she had no class selected, I guessed that verified the barrier she'd cast in the tunnels and the spell she fired at me when under Crohl's control had been channeled from his ability pool. That was some far-reaching magic for a game world.

Priya slid her arm from behind Roshan's back and

gestured at what little she wore for coverings. "Can you believe he made me wear this crap? My *boobs* are practically hanging out, and this place is frigid!"

After a quick glance at the referenced clothing, I raised my eyes to find Roshan gazing at me. I threw her a half-smile and rolled my eyes to peer up at the ceiling as if searching for something there in jest. The Light priestess smirked.

"Well, then!" Priya turned toward a small desk in the far corner of the room, and for someone who'd just risen from a nap of exhaustion that'd caused her to pass out, she had way too much bounce in her strides.

Stepping behind it, she bent down, flashing her highly-accessible cleavage as she retrieved something from underneath. When she stood erect again, she dropped a trunk wrapped in black leather on the bureau. Had I spotted it before, I might have opened it instead of watching her cat nap.

"How long have you been captive?" I asked.

She spoke as she rifled through the chest. "I fear I don't track time well underground and in a glass ball. He let me out only to serve his dark purposes and to linger upon me with his hungry gaze." Her eyes flickered to the black robe she'd abandoned on the floor nearby. "I consider myself lucky he was but an acolyte who took pleasure with only his sight. If he'd touched me, I'd probably cut my own throat."

Roshan nodded. "It is likely his acceptance of the shadow's grasp rendered his manhood moot. I have heard tell of such things."

"I don't think I'd ever want power so badly I'd be willing to give that up," I muttered.

Priya leaned over the crate. "I suppose this should be your loot, adventurer. A proper reward. Perhaps you will even find something of substance to cover those legs better than simple pants—not that I would desire you cover yourself more than necessary." She tilted her head. "But if you're going to run around places like this, we must adorn you in appropriate attire, yes?" Her teasing smile induced a stupid grin on my face. "But if you'll grant me your leave, I will first retrieve my effects."

"Hey, you don't need my permission. Go for it."

Roshan crossed the room and stood next to me. She slid her arm around my waist and pressed her lips to my cheek. I felt joy at her touch and it occurred to me I hadn't thought of either woman in that room as an NPC since I entered it.

My companion squeezed my waist as she leaned closer and whispered, "Yet again, you've rescued me, my love. For this, there will be a great reward." She kissed the cheek again as her hand slid down my back and rubbed it in gentle circles.

A purple exclamation point flashed suddenly in my interface. I smiled, guessing I didn't need to check it to know what it announced.

"I'm not sure it was I who rescued you. Whatever you did to free Priya seems to have saved us both."

"It was you who dislodged her from his grasp. I merely healed the injury you inflicted when I saw her eyes turn from evil."

"Oh yeah, and thanks for the beating," Priya said. "I just love being slammed into walls."

She winked.

"Any time." I bowed.

Priya withdrew a thick piece of red fabric from the trunk and set it on the desk.

When the half-elf shimmied her arms into the sleeves of the red fabric, I realized it was a robe. If it hadn't been for her golden blonde hair, I'd have likened the sight of her to Little Red Riding Hood, though I doubted Red was stacked like that. Priya might not have been any older than me, maybe a tad older than Roshan, but she was all woman.

I love this world. Nerds will rejoice.

I went to my bag and loosened the drawstring. Eyeing my interface, I retrieved the scepter and returned it to Roshan's rightful hands. The erupting smile when she clutched it to her chest caused my heart to thump like it had when first I'd seen it.

Priya stepped to the side, swung her arm out with a flourish, and gestured to the trunk with splayed fingers.

"Your loot, sir."

"You're the one who suffered for it. Perhaps you should take your fill, first."

"I would not be free were it not for your actions, Gemini." She shook her head. "Besides, I am a simple woman of the wood. I have no cravings for material things. It is yours to do with as you please."

Okay, that's two companions with no interest in loot.

Enora, baby.

"I like her very much," Roshan whispered. "Can we keep her?"

My head whipped around at the suggestion.

"What?" Roshan raised a concerned eyebrow. "You don't do that in these parts?"

I peered into those sienna eyes, trying to determine if she was serious. Then that bottom, pouty lip curved up in a half-smile.

"You're screwing with me."

"If by this you mean I am taking pleasure at your unwitting expense, yes. I am *screwing* with you. Although, my people don't say it that way. Screwing has a different meaning where I come from."

"Right. No, that's...never mind." I shook my head in derision.

I peered over at Priya, who returned my attention with a questioning gaze. An eyebrow arched. "What was that?"

"Huh?" I said.

She waved a hand, noting the way Roshan and I held each other at our sides. "Oh, I seem nosy, right?" She slapped the back of one hand with the palm of the other. "Stupid, stupid, stupid! You two are sharing a moment. I'm afraid I don't get to talk to many people. I'm kind of a loner. I don't always pick up on... you know, I'm a hovel in the woods kind-of-gal. The language you spoke is just so beautiful, and I'd wondered what you were saying is all."

I furrowed my eyebrows. "Are you saying you didn't understand what I was saying to Roshan?"

Priya nodded and waved a hand. "But your discussion is yours, I—"

"Priya, I didn't realize we were speaking a different language. When I heard the two of you whispering in your embrace, I thought you understood each other."

"Roshan explained. "We were using the Common tongue, Gemini. But you and I were communicating in the speech of Clan Fortwan. Lauan words."

I cleared my throat. "Well, that makes sense. Hmm." With a quick scan of my HUD's Languages pane, I located a nifty little checkbox next to each language listed marked 'default.' I located *Common* and ticked the box. "From now on, we should speak the Common tongue, so no one feels left out."

Priya smiled. "You are a man of such kindness, to make exceptions for such a simple creature as me."

Roshan squeezed my waist. "That is fine, but I reserve the right to use my own language to utter blessings when you ravage my fruit. I'm sure Priya will understand."

My chin dropped.

"I would definitely understand that," Priya muttered as her eyes trailed down to my legs for the second time.

Taking in her pink lips and wide blue eyes, I was starting to appreciate her gaze, especially since Roshan didn't seem to mind. I had about as much game as a chess set filled only with pawns in my previous life. No way would I take this for granted.

Roshan explained the joke we'd shared about 'keeping her.' I wasn't sure how she'd take it since I knew nothing of elven culture in this world. Not to mention the fact she'd just been enslaved. To my relief, Priya nodded understanding and chuckled. I took her half-hearted laughter as an indicator her energy was drained.

"The short answer is, yes, you could keep me if I so chose it." Priya paced across the room and grabbed my hands again. "In all seriousness, adventurer, I am grateful for your intervention. There's no telling how long I might have been imprisoned. I promise to serve you of my own free will until I have adequately repaid this debt to your satisfaction."

The exclamation points started to stack up on my interface, but my mind was elsewhere.

I waved a hand. "You don't owe me anything. I'm just glad you're both okay."

Priya shot me a surprised look. Her eyes flashed to Roshan, confusion painted across her features. Her full lips parted and, after a moment, began to quiver.

"You would deny me repayment of my debt?" She pulled her robe tight and clutched it at her neck. "Are you so displeased by the sight of me? Does my elven blood offend?"

Before I could correct my mistake, a flash of motion from my right caught me off guard as Roshan's palm thumped against the back of my head.

"Rude!"

She slapped again, then again, driving me away. "Did your father raise you among pigs? Dined, did thee, from a trough? Would you have this poor woman carry the guilt of her indebtedness for all her days?" I threw an arm up in my defense until the beating ceased. Roshan glared at me and set a hand on Priya's shoulder. "I fear our companion derives of poor rearing. It's a shortcoming I have overlooked, but..." she glared at me, "I assure you, he can be taught."

Priya stood and peered at me, her face washed in red. Even though I couldn't have known, guilt consumed me as I noted those exhausted, disappointed eyes. I lowered my head as my mind raced for a shortcut, a way to diffuse the situation quickly.

"It's as Roshan says. I'm terrible. I wasn't raised right. Please, forgive me."

She peered down and waved both hands. "No. I understand, m'lord." She bowed her head and sniffled so pathetically, I considered opening an artery in my wrists. "Why would adventurers like yourselves endure the company of such a simple girl of the wood? Why would you value the debt of such a—"

"Stop," Roshan said. She turned a hard eye on me. "Do you see the foulness of your mindless uttering, noob?"

"Roshan, shut it," I said. "I was trying to be polite, not rude. I thought telling her it was my pleasure to assist her and that no debt was incurred was to show the kind of humility Solara would want! Chill out!"

Priya tilted her head to one side and her forehead wrinkled. "Through I understand his words, he seems to combine them in ways I do not conceive his meaning."

"You have heard nothing, elf. My ears have been filled with his strange rantings through the night. Apparently, this is how they speak in Rome."

"Rome?"

Time for a subject change.

"Priya. It would be my great honor to have such a fine woman as you around. It isn't that I didn't appreciate your promise, but that I deem myself unworthy of such an honor. It was my pleasure to aid you against Crohl, my *duty*, really. So I would willingly relieve you of your debt if it was your desire." I added flair to keep on Roshan's good side. "I'm here in service to the Light, so it was my duty to pull you from his dark grasp, but your rapturous beauty is reward enough."

"Gah!" Roshan blurted. "Words of such thick sweetness they might have poured from a spike in a tree."

Priya gripped my hands as the hint of a smile creased her lips.

"I appreciated his thoughtful words, priestess. All is forgiven. Let no darkness come between us."

Then she hugged me.

I checked the notifications on my interface while we embraced.

You have saved Roshan for the second time, earning 4300 disposition points.

Roshan
Human
Level 9 Light Priestess

Disposition: Beloved
Your beloved status with a companion has completed an
achievement:
Crazy Love
Reward: 2,500 XP
It's good to make friends!

Priya *is now your companion!*
Priya Skyy
Half-elf
Level 9 (No Class)
*Strength: 8**
*Dexterity: 3**
*Intelligence: 4**
*Wisdom: 4**
*Constitution: 12**
*Charisma: 8**
Disposition: Endeared
(Priya has 16 unspent attribute points)
*As you have acquired **three** companions, you have*
*completed a **challenge**:*
Three's Company
Gain three companions in Enora
Reward: 1,000 XP

I hadn't considered Enora might have achievements! I needed to find the list in my HUD. I was on my way to level eight!

I glanced at the log again.

Whoa! Endeared? I guess Priya did forgive my utterances.

That was only two ranks from beloved and was two

beyond neutral. It was then I opened my eyes and peered down at her head where the earlobe curved slightly upward but didn't quite wind to an elven point. I absently kissed the top of her head and she sighed, leaning her weight against me. It was weird how I'd just fallen into that sense of comfort so naturally, but I went with it.

"Maybe you should sit and rest a bit," I said.

"I will rest when we have fled this dark place." Her weight leaned into me.

"Agreed," Roshan replied.

Breaking camp was fine by me, but the adrenaline boost —which had no place in a video game—had abated, and my eyelids grew heavy. My knees felt like lead weights, but I had two levels to go before I was safe.

Well, immortal, really.

As I released my hold, Priya raised her face and puckered her lips. I leaned down and she pressed a soft, short kiss onto my cheek. I guessed she was pretty comfortable, too. Or maybe her inhibitions were as exhausted as she was.

"Thank you, Gemini."

"You're welcome."

Priya turned and motioned to the all-but-forgotten trunk across the room. "If it is not too much to ask, Gemini, perhaps you could secure your loot so we might leave this dark place." The gray flesh under her eyes were testimony that she needed to sleep for a month.

"Of course, Priya."

I circled the short desk.

Accessing my HUD as I reached inside the trunk, I was flabbergasted by the number of items. This could take all day. Recalling the way my heart had thumped upon losing my healer in the tunnel after combat, I also wanted to get Roshan the hell out of there.

I made a lame attempt to shove the trunk into my bag, but it didn't work. I peered up to find both women smirking like I was an idiot.

I distracted them from their amusement. "Is there a way to the surface shorter than the path we used to come in?"

Priya shook her head. "Our best path is back to the cellar tree. His demon spawns will have retreated deep into the tunnel network, and the kobolds they've enslaved will chase their taskmasters to the ends, cut them off, and reclaim their territory with blood ritual."

"So, the kobolds lived here before?"

She nodded. "More than one civilization has lived in that stone underground. But these are mostly low-level kobolds who dwell deep in the tunnels, so any stragglers should cause us little trouble. Most of them have aversions to the stonework sections of the underground, anyway, and avoid it."

I spied brass handles on either side of the trunk.

"The priestess and I can carry the trunk so that you might be at the ready with your weapons, should the need arise, Gemini. It's not heavy."

I recalled how Priya had raised it onto the desk with ease.

"Great! But I think I can drop it fast enough if I need to be at the ready. You don't need any more strain, right now."

Roshan nodded in agreement. "I will carry it with Gemini." She placed her long fingers on Priya's cheek. "Trust in us, little elf woman. We are cast in Solara's Light and will persevere against darkness."

If Priya didn't appreciate being called "little elf woman," she showed no sign of it. But considering the circumstances and her state of being, she probably wouldn't have.

The voluptuous half-elf peered around the room. "Good riddance to this shit pit. You have come and conquered, friends."

Roshan smiled. "Of course, we did."

I found it a little funny that she'd been standing there with demon smoke floating up her nose when I arrived and now she showed the confidence of a heavyweight punching a bunny rabbit. She turned her eyes on me and raised her chin high. "We will return to the forest and seek cover for the night."

Hopefully your captors have strayed and become lost.

"Yes, ma'am." I bowed my head slightly at Roshan then peered at the half-elf. "Priya, I want to check your skills and discuss possibilities for your advancement when we've found shelter. I noticed a lot of unspent skill points when I checked your status."

"You have already checked my...*status?*" She said, pushing one hip to the side and tilting her head slightly. "I'm honored...*my lord.*"

Though I suspected the humor to be an artificial shelter for her mind from the trauma of imprisonment and forced actions, it reflected her resilience.

She leaned toward Roshan and whispered just loudly enough I picked it up. "What's he talking about?"

29

Priya had been right on both fronts. We carried the trunk with relative ease as we traversed the dry trail leading up the tunnel to the stony cellar, and we encountered no resistance during our exodus.

On a couple occasions, I'd heard skittering echoes off the stone walls from below, but Priya assured me it was only the kobolds, free of their shadow magic shackles, chasing the demons deeper into the catacombs and cornering them for a final confrontation.

Without their master, the demon beasts would have a fight on their hands in the kobolds' familiar stomping grounds—though those weren't the exact words she used. She spat venom each time she used the word demon. When I told her that I'd thought the occupants of the underground cellar and adjoined dungeon had built the stone walls and floors until Roshan set me straight, Priya had laughed.

"Kobolds don't work in stone. As I walked those same stone halls, imprisoned by my robe and Crohl's—" she spat after his name, "—dark presence, I was still seeing. Still thinking. I wondered what ancient civilization might have carved out those halls beneath a tree. I have no idea who they were, but they weren't kobolds. Those filthy creatures can tunnel, but that is the extent of their construction affinities."

It reminded me that one of my tasks was to take a better look at the black robe in which she'd been bound and the glass orb that held the Shadow caster prisoner. Both were nestled securely in my bag, though Roshan's expression as I bagged the strange robe had spoken of her disapproval. Still, she held her tongue, which I knew from our short time together was no small concession.

Exiting into the light of day had been a welcome relief for Roshan and me, but at the first sight of natural light, Priya busted through the door in the tree and dropped to her knees, whispering words I couldn't make out as tears of joy streamed down her face. Opting to leave Priya to her jubilations, Roshan and I stood together in the meadow, arms wrapped around each other's waists, averting our eyes as she wept.

Roshan whispered in my ear, her breath pricking at the short hairs there. "Where is Click?"

Gods! I'd almost forgotten my little buddy.

"She was injured below. I dismissed her so she wouldn't suffer. I only had one minor potion left, and I feared you or I might need it, so I did the only thing that made sense."

"You saved your potion for me instead of using it on your beloved friend?" Roshan hugged me hard around my waist. "I'm honored to call you my companion."

I held her tight. "I'm honored to call you friend."

I was.

When Priya finished muttering and crying at the tree's roots, she returned to us and gripped our hands.

"Never shall I be more thankful than I am to you for the

freedom you have returned to me. I only hope I can repay your bravery in kind."

I decided it would be in poor judgment to voice thoughts contrary to her indebtedness aloud, but something about it made me feel... icky.

The reason I'd been in that place had nothing to do with Priya. I was going to receive a royal XP dump for removing Crohl. Even though I didn't imprison him in the glass bubble myself, my log confirmed I'd completed the requirements for the quest. I just needed to turn it in to Zhara.

I'd spend the rest of my days in Enora. I looked forward to meeting its people, learning more about its cultures. Their ideas about honoring debts were ingrained in at least two of them, and they'd been separated by a sea. Roshan's pledge seemed to be more permanent, but I didn't know the extent of Priya's promise. She'd mentioned family who'd be happy to see her, so maybe I'd be rewarded and she'd go her own way.

The sentiments between Priya and Roshan surrounding gratitude might have been traditions written into NPCs before the 2,000-year purge and passed down through the generations. Because, seriously, what were the odds of a noob landing two beautiful and intelligent women, pledging to repay debts to him in one day?

If NPCs like Roshan, who offered their services in reward for heroic deeds, were common, players would use cultural traditions as an excuse for bad behavior when the floodgates opened some day. But I wasn't one of them. My survival depended on these gifts and they would be appreciated far beyond level ten.

The presence of a healer had allowed me to take on six or seven demons and I would've fallen during that quest without Roshan. This new companion, Priya, had points to distribute and could contribute, as well. If I could involve her in combat, she might make a huge difference.

Both of them were higher level than I.

"Summon our companion," Roshan said, pulling me out of my own head. "I will heal him."

"Oh! Right!" I muttered. "But Click is a 'her.'"

"*Her*, then. Yes, I remember now."

"Companion?" Priya asked. "There is another?"

I nodded and pressed my lips into a smile. "Yes. I have someone I'd like you to meet."

Throwing my hand out, I focused my energy. A ray of light peeked through the tree canopy above and touched my hand. It might have been my imagination, but I'd have sworn the warm light of the high sun lent an ease to my casting as my hand glowed blue and Click rematerialized.

"Well, that's a neat trick," Priya said. "I didn't know you had magic. Your pet is a porcupunk? What did you do to win her over, feed her?"

"As a matter of fact, I did."

Priya cocked her chin up. "Yeah. Probably hard to get rid of one after you've done that."

"Your pet is uninjured," Roshan said.

"How about that?" I asked. "I guess they heal upon summoning."

That wasn't uncommon in games, but pointing it out was bound to be a violation of Enora's rules.

Click's nose rose and twitched at Roshan and me. Then she noticed Priya and sniffed up at her.

"Well, hello," Priya said. She set her hands on her knees. "Aren't you a pretty girl?"

Click bounced side-to-side. I recalled two days before when I'd mistaken that for playfulness, resulting in an arm filled with spike holes. But I sensed no animosity and found that even though she'd come to her summons with a neutral disposition, there was something in Priya's greeting, maybe her tone of voice, that brightened my pet.

Completing her crouch, Priya extended her arms. "Embrace me like a friend, porcupunk, for I am."

To my utter surprise, my pet clicked excitedly and ran into Priya's arms. Priya clutched the rotund but powerful beast to her bosom and stood, stroking its flesh hairs in long, smooth strokes as she hugged it against her red robe.

"This is a powerful companion you have charmed." Her smile was disarming, filled with a joy I hadn't seen before emerging into the forest. She shared it with Roshan for a moment then looked back at me. "Your essence draws powerful allies to your side." Planting a kiss on the side of Click's head, she set her back onto the mossy groundcover. "She's a weighty one, as well. I wouldn't want to have to carry her for long."

"Luckily, I haven't had to."

Priya turned and set her hands on her hips as she stared off into the dense forest. "My dwelling is close, my friends." She peered down and wiggled the toes of her bare feet. I realized they'd been bare since I met her, back when she'd been possessed. "The earth feels so good beneath me." Priya raised her arms in an elongated stretch and her body writhed with pleasure as she moaned.

Her demeanor as we'd traversed the cellar dungeon during our exodus had piqued my interest. I didn't remember a single complaint while we'd been underground. To the contrary, she'd joked, she smiled frequently, and other than the dark circles under her eyes, she'd carried herself as if she'd been recharged by her short nap.

Of course, being liberated from a glass ball and a Robe of Imprisonment might lift one's spirit.

Priya began flicking the clasps on her robe.

"Whatcha doing?" I asked, though I honestly had no desire to stop it.

She answered as if it was obvious. "Loosing my ward." Shrugging out of the robe, she threw her arms out to the side as if to air herself out. Turning in a half-circle, she revealed her wondrous tattoo to us again.

"This inspires awe in me," Roshan muttered. Her eyelids drooped, and I felt her weight lean into me. She interlocked her fingers with mine as a daze washed across her features. "She has been touched by a higher being."

"Awe is the right word. Gives...a tingly...feeling in my chest...when I look at that thing."

"I share this response," Roshan said. "She is a beautiful creature and that ward..."

Apparently having heard our mutterings, Priya's face wore a pinkish hue as she turned. We both frowned as the tree painted across her back was twisted from our sightlines.

"You call that tattoo a ward?" I asked Roshan.

But it was Priya who answered.

"Yes, it wards predators away."

"What, you run through the forest wearing just that strap of cloth?"

"As I said below, this strip of cloth belongs to he who is imprisoned in your bag. Usually, I reveal the ward in its entirety. If you were not here, I would remove the meager covering and set it on fire."

I took this to mean she walked around without a top when prancing among the trees.

"Your ward glows right through the covering, anyway," I said. It's kind of see-through."

"Oh! Good to know. I hope it doesn't offend you that,

when there are human creatures around, I don my robe. My aunt has warned me against the lusts of men."

I nodded. "A wise warning, especially considering your allure. But if men stumbled onto you, I think you could just show them your back and run away. My body goes numb when I see it."

She blushed anew.

Tying the sleeves of her robe around her waist, Priya reached for the trunk handle and eyed me. "Ready your bow, Woodsman. I will take us down the paths I've traveled most, but we should be alert."

If she could just turn around in the face of any threats and freeze them in their tracks, I didn't see the sense in it. But I played along.

We encountered no trouble for what I guessed was two long miles.

We came upon the first evidence of sky since the lake the night before. I peered down at the knee-high grass rustling around my new pants then squinted into the area beneath the distant tree line to avert my gaze from Priya. She'd extended her arms high in the air for another stretch, and I wanted to keep myself from becoming distracted by her ward... or her body. But my peripheral vision caught the glow and in lieu of asking her to put her robe back on, I stepped beside her.

She closed her eyes and let the sun beam down on her face. When Priya ended her stretch and turned, Roshan was standing inches away, eliciting a jolt from the elven woman.

Priya slapped a hand to her chest. "You startled me!"

Roshan shook her head a few times. "I apologize. But I was wondering, might I touch your ward?"

"I don't see why not." Priya turned.

Roshan reached out and closed her eyes. A thin halo of focused light surrounded her robe. "Oh, Priya. It is such a blessing, this mark upon you. It fills me with such... contentment."

"I'm pleased," Priya said. "Gemini seems to evade its grasp."

"Sorry, it just distracts me. I think its influence impacts me more than it does Roshan. Maybe because she's so attuned to the energy it puts off. If I stare at it, I'll lose time."

"This is good to know," Priya said. "I'm not exposed to a lot of people and have really only seen its impact on wildlife, with the exception of Crohl, who glanced at it once and had a headache for days. I was quite glad."

"Yeah, screw Crohl," I agreed. "I hope he's swirling around in the globe screaming at us."

"It doesn't work that way, but I take your meaning."

Clicking greeted me from the high grass and I peered down to find my first companion sniffing the air next to my leg. I knelt and stroked her fleshy hairs.

"We are safe now, little porcupunk." Priya led us across the meadow to the base of a massive oak. At its foot was a moss-covered dome with a single, circular window carved into its face. The half-elf approached it, pressed her hand into the moss next to the window, and a trace of green light formed a rectangle on the wooden surface. The door popped open.

A magic door?

"Priya!" a deep voice bellowed from the woods.

The earth beneath me quaked. My knees trembled. Every muscle in my body quivered as I fumbled my bow off my shoulder and turned.

*You have changed your class to **Woodsman**.*

Priya grasped my wrist. "Shoulder your weapon, adventurer. You are safe with Magellan." She turned up the palm of her free hand and gestured at the sprawling oak above her wooden dome.

Golden eyes blinked open on the rough surface of the ancient tree.

"You have returned, princess. Many nights have I worried after you," the tree—apparently Magellan—said.

Priya circled the wooden dome and approached the tree. "Hello, my love. I fear I left the safety of your wards only to be taken by a minion of darkness."

The bark above the spooky, golden eyes wrinkled up, mimicking a forehead. "Say it's not true! Are you injured child? Might I produce a salve for you?"

Priya shook her head. "I'm quite well, Magellan. Please don't worry yourself."

"Bah! For forty days have I worried myself, child! You—"

"I know!" Priya interrupted, stepping up to the tree and pressing herself against the bark with her arms spread wide. It would have taken thirty such wing spans to embrace the tree's massive trunk.

Is she going to meld into that thing?

"I wander haphazardly into the wood like a fool. I know. But Magellan, I cannot live my whole life in your sightline."

"Actually, you could," the heavy voice grumbled so I felt it in my feet.

"You're being difficult." Priya backed away and set her hands on her hips. "But I suppose it is forgivable in this instance." She peered up at Magellan.

But my attention had reverted to the magical tattoo on

her back. It really was like watching a 10k video. The ward resembled the tree to whom she spoke. Then again, it was a tree. They looked like trees.

The golden eyes turned on Roshan and then settled on me. "You have brought visitors."

I wasn't sure I liked this variation of its low tone.

But Priya's tone became excited. "Yes! Two brave souls who have vanquished darkness from the caves beneath your roots. This is Roshan, a priestess of great power. This is her companion, Gemini. A brave Woodsman who rescued us both from an evil minion. I owe my life to them and would appreciate if you treat them with the same kindness you have shown me."

I glanced at Roshan to find a calm smile crossing her lips.

I whispered, "Do you feel this...I don't know, warm weightlessness?"

Roshan nodded and whispered. "You stand before a powerful being of The Light. I have dreamed of such things. Revel in it, love."

I focused on the tree.

Magellan
Ancient Treant of the Light
Level ??
For Eons, Magellan has served as regent to the Matron of The Wood, Zhara.

He was too high level for me to even see the number. It'd been a long time since I'd seen this game mechanic used, prior to entering Enora, but that made it somewhat refreshing.

Wood creaked and groaned as the tree squinted slightly

and gave a short bow, its leaves whispering and branches creaking with the motion. Two birds flew off, across the meadow.

"I welcome you to my protectorate, travelers. For as long as you are here, know that I guard my own and, by returning Priya safely, I shall henceforth consider you such."

"This land is wonderful," Roshan said simply. Her often unemotional tendencies were the picture of calm. I reasoned it had to do with her religious training.

I bowed to the tree. "Thank you, Magellan. Your hospitality is appreciated, great treant."

"Ah," the giant tree said. "And he shows respect." The entire tree bent above Magellan's eyes as if nodding. "Welcome, Gemini, and welcome to you, Roshan, Priestess of the Light." He turned his attention to Priya. "The matron will be worried about you, child. Will you go and see her?"

The Matron? She knows Zhara?

"Tomorrow, the day after at the latest, I promise you," Priya said. "Tonight, I will give my new friends a place to rest, feed their bellies, and recharge."

Magellan's eyes squinted toward me. "Gifts, I'm sure, will be quite appreciated... and respected."

"I assure you this is the case, great treant," I replied.

"Hm. Yes. I approve, Priya. Now go, rest, recuperate. I sense an uncommon weariness in you. Travel to see the blessed one tomorrow, as I feel her tears from your absence blowing on the wind each day."

"I doubt her worry was that deep, but I look quite forward to seeing Aunt Zhara, I assure you. Upon her shall I lay my eyes tomorrow."

Aunt? What. The. Utter. Fuck?

"Good. Now go. We shall keep watch."

We?

Numerous eyes flickered open in the smaller trees surrounding Magellan, as if reading my mind and answering my question.

Priya led us inside the wooden dome. I set the trunk just inside the door, reeling at what I'd just learned about her familial line.

"Welcome to my home," Priya said, that enthusiastic smile still plastered to her angular features.

I guess beauty runs in the family. How did I miss the resemblance? That golden hair. The slightly pointed nose. The full hips. Shit!

A sliver of light beaming through the oval window and reflecting off a mirror strategically leaned against the back wall was the lone source of illumination, but it did the job well in the morning sun. A simple wooden table sat against one wall, and a rug of lush, soft bear fur spread across the center of the space. On the back wall, I spied a sprawling bed with huge-but-simply-carved wooden posts and another thick fur that must have come from a huge beast, unless I just couldn't see hems where several hides were joined.

Patches of moss splotched the ceiling, and the interior wooden planks bent to form the curved walls. A black wood stove sat in the far-right corner. It seemed misplaced in a room constructed so purely of nature.

"What does Magellan think of you burning wood?" I asked.

Priya smirked so hard, her lips seemed to wrinkle from two to four. "You are not from the forest, obviously. While all trees live, not all are sentient."

"Noob," Roshan muttered.

"Do you live alone, here?" I asked.

Priya turned. Though her smile still adorned her

features, her furrowed eyebrow questioned. "Who would I live with?"

I shrugged and changed the subject to the one plaguing me. "You mentioned your aunt?"

"Oh!" She waved a hand. "My aunt lives in another part of the forest. She raised her hands and spun in a slow circle. "This was my parents' place before they moved into the city, and now it is mine." Gripping my hand and offering her other to Roshan, who took it, she said, "And now, it is yours, as well."

"You're generous. So, your parents live in a city?"

"Yes. They left when I came of age." Her face wrinkled up in a sad expression. "As my aunt tells me, I had no desire to leave the woods then, but I don't remember them. I'm afraid creatures of the darkness find my essence magnetic. Crohl was not the first to pounce as I wandered outside the protection of Magellan and the treants."

"Whoa. Too much info at once. Why don't you remember not wanting to leave with your parents?"

Priya rolled her eyes. "I know, right? I blabber on and on." She shrugged and flashed a playful smile. "My memory of my parents was purged by an evil creature who'd brought perverted intent to the woods. The underlord you saw in the frame has sought me for some time, according to Aunt Zhara. When my memory was stolen away, my aunt's servants cast the wards in the forest to keep minions of the darkness from approaching this place.

"But it was my undoing when Crohl caught me outside the protection of the wards as I returned from trading and dragged me into the depths to slave for him in his dark deeds until he could transport me to Caym. I think he really wanted to keep me for himself."

"And the ward on your back?"

She waved a dismissive hand. "Also the work of my aunt." She spoke in a conspiratorial tone. "She doesn't do anything half way."

"She sounds like a magical woman."

"You don't know the half of it. But there are many creatures of magic in the Dark Wood. Now! Come, my friends. Make yourselves at home. I will gather wood for a fire. My bones tell me the night will come with a chill."

"But it's only morning," I protested. "Besides, aren't you tired? Shouldn't you sleep?"

She adopted a dreamy tone. "Oh, how I love sleep. Though I'm somewhat haggard, the wood recharges me. It is in my blood. Anyway, I only require slumber every third night or so. Also, the nap helped."

She stays awake three days at a time?

"As to your suspicions, I would like a little time to walk quietly in the forest, and collecting wood is just the byproduct."

"We wouldn't deny you time for meditation," Roshan interjected, grasping my hand and squeezing.

We sat on the rug near the dormant wood stove as Priya grabbed an axe leaning against the wall, pushed open the door and flooded the space with morning light, and exited into the meadow. Click settled into the warm fibers next to me and snoozed. She purred as she warmed my leg. I yawned.

"You are tired, Gemini. How long has it been since sleep has recharged your spirit?"

I loved the way she talked.

"Gods, I don't know. I guess I woke up next to that tree...what? Two days ago? Wow! I had no idea it'd been that long. No wonder I'm bushed."

Roshan scooted toward me and pressed her lips to mine.

Cupping my face so her warmth penetrated my cheeks, she peered into my eyes.

"Lie with me, and we shall let sleep take us for a while."

"But Priya should be back soon, and—"

Roshan pressed a finger to my lips. "Priya has welcomed you to her home and made it your own."

She got to her feet and I rose. Leading me toward the bed, she pressed her hands against my chest, holding me fast. Stepping back, she loosened the ties on her flowing green and yellow robe, allowing it to slide down, off her shoulders, caressing her muscular arms as it dropped and settled on the wooden boards of the dusty floor.

Her breasts were bare, her small rosy nipples taut. The shorts covering her lower portion were little more than a worn piece of fabric through which I spied the crease of a thing I wholly desired. But I found the desire something worth savoring as sleep called.

Pushing back the fur covering the bed, Roshan crawled onto a feather-stuffed mattress and raised the fur for me.

"Disrobe, my love, and come. Sleep at my bosom."

There was no mistaking my excitement as I had little doubt she could see it through my pants. So, without argument, I stripped down, slid into the bed next to her, and slid my arm over her flat stomach.

There's no way in hell I'm going to sleep with this iron rod and her firm breasts against me.

But when the warm flesh of her chest pressed against my face, her arms wrapped over my shoulders, and her fingertips gently massaged my scalp, I was as good as gone.

30

It was only with great effort I blinked my eyes open when rustling tickled my feet. The warm fur above and the soft feathers beneath did little to motivate me into wakefulness. Softness and tenderness surrounded me, and I would've been just fine with never having moved again. I didn't need to know the source of the rustling at my feet. I didn't need to know why my body felt like it was wrapped in a warm sleeve.

The scents of moss and wood crept in the darkness that blanketed Priya's home. I realized I must have slept half the day. When I started to move, I discovered I was spooned between two mostly naked women and stayed put. Priya squirmed and pressed her chest against my back.

"Mmmm," she moaned as she pressed her mouth to my ear. "Are you awake?"

"Mmm hmm."

Roshan cupped my hand over her hip, squeezed once, and then gently pushed it down to her abs. Adjusting, she twisted beneath the fur to face me.

"Did you nap well?" she asked groggily.

"Luxuriously." I smiled.

Pressing a kiss against my cheek, she sat up and let the fur drop away. The curve of her breasts made me thankful human eyes adjusted to darkness even in Enora.

"Priya, perhaps we should hunt while you catch up on your sleep."

"Hm?" the elf said, obviously snapping awake for the second time. "No." Her mouth stretched into a wide yawn. "I will rise and hunt us something up. You rest." Her eyes blinked closed again. Her nose whistled as her breathing leveled out.

Roshan and I shared a smile.

She leaned forward. "Perhaps you could use your bow to hunt something for us. I'm sure Magellan would guide you."

You have been offered a quest:
Fluttering Fowl for Fluttering Bellies
Hunt two pheasants in the nearby meadow and return them to Priya.
Reward: Improved disposition with Priya
450 XP
Roasted Pheasant x10

Roshan fed a fire in the stove as Click and I set off into the night. Priya hadn't been kidding earlier that day—a serious chill had invaded the forest when the sun fell. As suggested, I spoke with Magellan, and he informed me we wouldn't have to go far. There were pheasants hiding in the tall grass at the other end of the meadow.

Click led me halfway across the field. I shrugged my bow down my arm and into my hand in a motion that became more natural each time. I tied the quiver to my hip and found the position as natural as breathing as I slipped an arrow from its hold. My pet stopped and peered up at me.

Click click click.

"Okay, babe, I just need you to sniff around over there and flush something out so I can shoot it."

Click, click click click.

"I need the shooting practice. Don't attack anything, just flush it out."

Click launched, scurrying away and disappearing into the high grass. I cast Inner Illumination, knelt down, and waited. Grass shuffled in the distance, so I drew back my bowstring and aimed in the general area I thought the sound came from, but nothing happened. A sudden squawk filled the air and I twisted my hips, adjusting my aim. But again, nothing happened.

A few heartbeats later, rustling entirely too close for my comfort caused me to leap up and take a few steps backward. Bow tensed, I peered into the grass.

A fat, round bird appeared a few feet away, moving toward me, but it wasn't running or flying, or fluttering. My porcupunk bounded up to me, dropped the bird at my feet, and clicked. Then she bounced back and forth, smiling up at me.

"Well, either you're hardheaded or we don't understand each other as well as I'd hoped outside of combat."

Fluttering Fowl for Fluttering Bellies
Hunt two pheasants in the nearby meadow and return them to Priya.
Pheasants hunted: 1/2

I shrugged. "Maybe this time, you could let me level up my bow skills a bit? What do you think, kid?"

Click showed me all her silvery teeth and rapid-clicked in that way I was becoming convinced was a laugh.

"Yeah, screw you too, dummy." I flicked a finger toward the grass. "Go, flush one out."

Less than a minute later, a pheasant launched from the high grass. Tracking it with my bow, thankful for my night vision spell, I loosed an arrow.

It missed, but I added a skill point to my ranged attack.

Click returned, dropped the arrow at my feet, and laughed again.

She does fetch!

I directed her back into the grass without words.

Again, a pheasant shot out of the grass at the opposite end of the field. I fired another arrow.

I missed.

Click laughed.

I sent her back.

In the end, I missed with half the arrows in my quiver, before I finally clipped one of the birds. I yelled for Click to just finish it off and bring it back. The kills weren't netting us XP, anyway. The birds were level one.

Fluttering Fowl for Fluttering Bellies

Hunt two pheasants in the nearby meadow and return them to Priya.

Pheasants hunted: 2/2

Return the pheasants to Priya for your reward.

Reward: Improved disposition with Priya

450 XP

Roasted Pheasant x10

Grabbing the birds by the feet, I dropped them in my bag with the understanding it was really just a void and feathers and guts weren't going to lodge in there and stink it up. After counting my arrows, I meandered slowly with Click at my heel, eyeing the dim light in the small round window of Priya's moss-covered dome.

It's like a hobbit house, except it isn't actually part of the tree.

When a slight rise in the meadow gave me a good angle, I stopped and peered at the orange glow painting the glass of the tiny window from afar.

Priya consumed my thoughts. Something was unusual about that sexy elf, and I couldn't quite put my finger on it. Whereas Roshan's behavior varied from determined, to attentive, and to downright sensual, depending on the situation, Priya struck me as an old soul. She'd just been held captive for an extended period and not only told the story of how it had happened to her before, as if being kidnapped was a common event, but seemed too relaxed about it.

The way she'd jested and giggled on our return trip from the dungeon underground though her eyelids hung like curtains said loads about her resolve... her resilience... but there was something else, there. A confidence, maybe.

If she was truly the niece of a tree goddess—whatever Zhara was—maybe that accounted for her demeanor. Maybe the power she'd witnessed in her aunt gave her walls of security to hide her mind behind when all seemed lost. Perhaps she'd never doubted she would be saved.

Faith, another recurring theme of the last twenty-four hours.

How might Priya react when learning Zhara sent me to rid the forest of Crohl? Standing there, tying theories together in my head, I would've wagered she'd be unsurprised. Almost like she'd expect it. But something told me I shouldn't unload that little tidbit of information on her, yet. It was a tickle in my brain, an itch I wasn't ready to scratch lest something become infected.

Lucera had sent me to Zhara for my first quest. Zhara had sent me to the underground domain of a dark caster, supposedly to cleanse it. But had Priya's rescue been the point, all along? Had Zhara actually hidden her real motives for sending me down there? If so, why would she do that? Why not just tell me the stakes if her niece was down there? Though I couldn't recall her words precisely, she'd left the impression I might run into someone under the dark source's control. That couldn't have been a coincidence.

It was a game world, right? A quest. Would an NPC in this world use deceit to reach a desired end? Hide elements of the quest, while giving hints as to their presence—like Priya?

As the nagging suspicion that something was a little fucked up in Denmark bloomed in me, my mind raced for answers. Standing there in the dark, I became suddenly conscious of all the sounds of insect life naturally relegated to the white noise centers of my brain. The way my chest rose and fell with my breath. The cold bite of the night breeze when it blew.

The depth of the realism in the world around me became utterly terrifying.

At first, I couldn't home in on what about it scared me, but as I rewound my thoughts, traced from Lucera, to Zhara, to Roshan, to Priya... Such a place as Enora, where life was every bit as impactful as it had been on earth, could become a prison if others controlled my destiny.

Two days ago, I would've been thrilled that Takemoto had talked Enora into giving me a hand up. Anything to survive until Level 10 and be able to live on, where otherwise I'd be a corpse in a grave or cremated ash somewhere on the other side of the void. But as I stood considering the Elf's home at the base of a mystical tree, I couldn't shake the inner anger that I'd been fighting for my life out here in a strange new world under the assumption I was on my own, while virtual beings were guiding me along a path.

Was I a free man?

You're overthinking it. No one is helping you. This is your life now. Those are your people.

Clicking rose on the air from up ahead, and I peered into darkness as my Inner Illumination spell expired. Thousands of stars sparkled overhead and animals harmonized a nocturnal melody. I drew the scent of evergreen and pine slowly through my nostrils. Just a few more levels, then I could ask myself all the questions I wanted.

For now, I had friends to tend to and other pheasant to 'fry.'

Then I remembered that Lucera had just heard every thought I'd had.

31

Priya spitted the fat bird over a fire outside after Roshan plucked it free of feathers. A breeze rose and the fire crackled in response as I took a turn rotating the meat. Fat sizzled as it splattered on the hot coals beneath, and the rising scent of cooked meat made my stomach grumble like incongruent tectonic plates.

You have completed a quest:
Fluttering Fowl for Fluttering Bellies
Hunt two pheasants in the nearby meadow and return them to Priya.
Pheasants hunted: 2/2
Reward: 400 disposition with Priya
450 XP
Roasted Pheasant *x* 1 o *(Once they're cooked)*

"I can hear your longing belly over the breeze, Gemini," Priya said. I'd removed my chest armor, and she rubbed a hand in a circular motion in the small of my back. "Is my savior hungry?"

Nodding, I found myself wishing I'd gone shirtless. "I could eat."

"Well, I think it's ready, and I could eat a boar by myself."

We moved inside to eat, and the succulent pheasant quieted my stomach. Though I checked my interface for stat bonuses, it seemed to provide none. In *LOB*, we only ate meals to boost ourselves for battle. In Enora, we ate or we starved to death. But it seemed I would need to eat less frequently than I had on earth.

It was yet another little detail I'd never asked Nokuro about, but something told me I'd have gotten nothing out of him. He'd been so closed-lipped. I'd attributed his silence to Enora's rules regarding my addition to the world. After all, she could read my mind and would know if he cheated. As I chewed on pheasant and enjoyed Priya's occasional circles upon my back, I ruminated on all of it.

New players were not going to receive manuals. The Dark Levels really would be dark. Enora wanted players to figure out the world as they went, and something told me that had been part of the original design. I couldn't be sure, but it was sound theory.

We all ate our fill, including Click, who then curled up near the wood stove as the rest of us lounged. We sat in silence for a while before Priya broke it.

"Gemini, I need to ask your leave to visit my aunt. You all are welcome to join me, but I really must go and see her."

"Zhara, right? How far away is she, from here?" I could've brought up my map and guessed, but I didn't have that good of a grasp on distance and travel time on foot.

"Oh, not far. One hour's journey, at the most."

"Then we can set off at first light after I've handled my administrative tasks."

"You would come with me?" she asked.

"Yes. I don't want you out there, away from your wards. Plus, I have business with her."

Her head snapped back, as expected. I thought I spied the subtle squint of an eye, but it wasn't easy to see with the candle sitting on a small round table behind her.

"Business with my Aunt? How is this?"

"To turn in a quest."

"A quest?" Roshan asked. "This is the quest you mentioned in the Tomb of the Lost?"

"Yes. Crohl was the target. My log shows I've completed the requirements." I shrugged. "So, seeing as you want to visit your aunt, our path together continues. I expect to advance when I turn it in."

Priya raised a hand to her chest. "A fine accomplishment!"

The utterance caught me by surprise. I didn't hear any hint of suspicion in her tone.

She ran a fingertip across the arch of her bare foot. "Did the quest involve my rescue?"

And there it was.

"Um, no. Just to cleanse a dark source from the place."

Priya nodded and slapped her thighs, perking up. "She must not have known I was there, then. That must be it. Well! Shall we leave at first light?"

Roshan nodded. "It will be my honor to meet your family, Priya."

"You don't know the least of it," I muttered.

"Do you whisper songs you sing as well, Gemini?" Roshan asked. "Speak up, my love."

Priya nodded and chuckled. "I heard him fine, and he's right. As attuned to the Light as you are, I have little doubt you will enjoy my aunt's company. That's what he implied."

"Why is this?" Roshan asked, her head pivoting left and right, seeking answers from whomever would give them.

"I tell you what," I said. "How about this? You be patient, and we will give you the surprise of a lifetime." I held up a hand to belay objection when her neck craned. "Trust me. You'll love Zhara."

Roshan nodded. "Fine, but I know you two are in cahoots!"

We nodded agreement and said, "We are," in perfect sync.

I slapped my legs and rose. Retrieving the trunk from the wall closest to the door, I dragged it to the edge of the fur rug. "I need to go through this stuff, then we can look at your attributes, Priya."

"I welcome your gander," she said in a teasing timbre.

They chattered among themselves, chuckling together now and then. I was happy to see my companions got along so well.

Minor Mana Potion
Replenishes 100 Mana Instantly

I made a note the potions would restore half Roshan's pool. We had two.

Other articles told the story of a dark fuck who'd spent time capturing, killing, and stealing. Probably with his underlord's minions, considering he hadn't been high level, himself. One of his victims had likely been an assassin.

Assassin's Daggers of Stealth
Level 8
Slot: Weapon
Type: Dagger

Quality: Uncommon
Durability: 50 of 50
Physical Damage: 11-14
+2 to stealth
+2 to melee attack
+5% damage to backstab.

"Bonus!" I cried aloud. The women stopped talking and eyed me.

"I believe our friend has encountered a boon, Priya."

"Ha! It would seem so! Do we need to take your toy box away, Gemini, lest you become enamored with its treasures and forget us?"

I smiled and shook my head. "Very unlikely." Just to drive my joke home, I gazed down at her body because Priya was playful like that. She chuckled as I continued eyeing the gear we'd grabbed underground.

Leather Pants of Stealth
Level 7
Slot: Legs
Type: armor
Quality: Uncommon
Durability: 50 of 50
+4 Melee Defense
+1 melee attack
Set Bonus (2): +2 to stealth ability

Not too shabby, and Priya had guessed correctly. I could trade in my simple pants. I snatched a glance at the half-elf as I slid on the new pair and caught her sea blue eyes traversing the muscles of my legs.

Yum.

My melee defense level rose to nineteen. I figured out I got a point for each Dexterity, which was fifteen total, and the additional four the pants gave me. I'd have expected dodge instead of defense when Dexterity was the impacting attribute, but Enora had her own ideas. Some simple, some nonsensical. To me, anyway.

My stats were looking up, though I'd hardly call myself overpowered. I doubted whether I was adequately powered, considering what I'd met with so far, but having companions gave me hope I was going to make it. I wondered what the players who liked to solo would think when they were unleashed upon my new world someday. Or more accurately, it was unleashed upon *them*.

Light Spells: 2
Unarmed: 1
Blunt Weapon: 3
Daggers: 13
Bows: 15
Swords: 11
Melee Attacks: +13
Ranged Attacks: +14
Dodge: 6
Melee Defense: 19

Zhara's blessing had worn off, but I'd managed to stack my ranged attacks prior to losing the boon.

My eyes flickered down to a narrow box in the bottom right corner of the inventory interface I hadn't noticed previously. Squinting at it, I saw a bronze metallic circle with a red line through it, then a silver one, then a gold one. Neither of the latter was marked out.

Focusing, I placed my hand in the bag. Something cool

and metallic jingled my palms. I withdrew it and turned it over in my hand.

For this, I cast my Illumination spell. The image of a leaf was pressed into a golden coin.

"Wait, is this a..."

Priya nearly leapt off the rug as she crossed the distance and knelt before me.

"That's gold, Gemini. You could feed us for a week if you went to Brumhill with that."

"Brumhill?"

She raised a querulous eyebrow. "You're not from anywhere near here, are you? Did you enter the wood from the East? You don't look like Roshan. Ha!" The Eastern mage and I shared a glance and half-smiles. Priya was a tad awkward. "Brumhill is a town just beyond these woods. They have small shops and even a tavern. It was on my return journey from trading skins there that the dark bastard captured me with his evil orb."

"Crohl. Right."

"His name is a curse upon my elven ears. Better we banish it from our memories!"

"Agreed!" I barked. "Fuck that dude!"

Priya jerked backward, tilted her head, and her full lips spread into something resembling a smile. Then she laughed.

"Indeed, I would *not* fuck that...*dude*, as you say. Even if he'd been capable, I'd have sooner lopped it off."

"It's just an expression. It means to hell with him."

"Oh. Then let that dude be fucked!"

The two of us laughed heartily, and I welcomed a hug from Priya. She seemed very affectionate, this woods woman. Over her shoulder, I found Roshan stroking Click's flesh, wearing a smirk that seemed to say, *'look at these ridiculous people.'*

Priya thumped the gold coin. "How much was there?" She lowered her eyes. "If it is mine to ask, m'lord."

"Priya, I've accepted your companionship, but you have got to stop calling me *lord*. I'm not so special as that."

She shook her head. "In private company, I will call you Gemini, as you ask. But when we are in the presence of others, I will call you by the title you've earned in gaining my fealty. It is respect for my own worth, as well as yours. After all, to possess such a creature as myself, you must be special—or do you disagree?"

Wow, she twisted that around in a hurry.

I smirked at her in response and turned back to the small square in my inventory while reaching back into the bag.

Wait, had she said fealty?

"Well?" Priya asked. She eyed the trunk.

There were too many coins for me to handle in one grasp. The zeroes with the slash marks were suddenly replaced by numbers.

"So, um, is seventeen gold a lot?" I asked.

Priya thrust a hand to her chest, her chin dropped, and her eyes fluttered. The way she wavered, I thought she might faint. Click seemed confused.

Roshan shook her head derisively and rolled her eyes. "She has no concept the value of money. Unless it is very different from where I come, this is not an outrageous sum. As she said, it will feed us when we venture into town, but it will not provide for high quality gear or materials unless this land is very different from my own."

Priya recovered but seemed woozy. I guessed that seventeen gold was more than she'd ever seen. As I considered Roshan's explanation, I summed that Priya had been sheltered by forest life.

I continued through the chest.

Scroll of Binding

This scroll allows its reader to bind one item to a player's soul. It may be read by any player or NPC of level 9 or higher.

Player Only Information: Soul-bound items re-spawn with you upon death.

Player only? I guessed this was text NPCs wouldn't see in their interfaces, and it might be against the rules to mention it. I already had an idea of what stiff penalties awaited players who revealed the wrong information to citizens of Enora. I made another mental note to read the player's agreement.

Then I dismissed it. No one read fucking player's agreements.

Either way, this was a kick-ass turn of events. With this scroll, I could bind my bag and all its contents to myself. If I lived past Level 10, I would never lose it. The fact the binding scroll was Level 9 dangled my ability to bind it to myself slightly out of reach.

But...

I peered across the room.

"Roshan?"

Her features softened as she looked up, and I felt a new warmth for her when I saw how natural the reaction to my voice had been. It struck me that Priya, Roshan, and I, held one common tie in our bonds. Loneliness.

I'd been alone in a new world. Roshan had been taken from all she'd known and mistreated for thousands of miles.

Priya lived a secluded life in the forest. Perhaps this, and not artificial intelligence-programmed game mechanics, was the source of our ease with each other. I wanted to believe that.

"Yes, beloved?"

My heart thumped. "Could you come here?"

Withdrawing her hand from the porcupunk's hairs, Roshan pushed herself up and one of Click's eyes shot open. My pet threw me a look, as if it took real nerve to call someone away from stroking her as she slumbered.

I reached up with the scroll in-hand. Roshan gave it a once-over.

"A binding scroll."

"Can you read it?"

She nodded and handed it back. "It is a neutral spell, so its script is in the common tongue of old. I can read it."

"Can you bind my bag to me with it?"

Realization dawned on her features. "Yes! I'm sorry, Gemini, I didn't grasp the purpose of your summons." She unfurled the scroll and read it in its entirety, then she peered back at me as her hands glowed in yellow light. Placing her hand on my shoulder, she set the other on my bag. My hairs stood on end as if static electricity surrounded us. I perceived the slightest blast of wind, and then it was over.

"Check your inventory, Gemini."

Magic Bag of Holding

48-slot bag

Type: Container

Quality: Rare

Soul-bound to G3m1n1 Fowler

"Awesome!" I peered up and puckered my lips.

Roshan bent and pecked them. "That is worth the reading, alone."

She patted my cheek and returned to Click and Priya. As I watched her go, wearing the simple and nearly transparent robe that Priya had lent her, her butt rose and fell on each side, and reality hit me.

She has offered me her life. She calls herself undefiled and is expecting me to...defile her. Well, not that, but.... Man, I hope I can make that special for her.

Aside from the gold, I also had 96 silver—and nowhere to spend any of it.

My eyes ticked to one of the slots in the chest.

Truesteel Sword of Slashing

Level 12
Slot: Weapon
Type: Sword
Quality: Uncommon
Durability: 50 of 50
Physical Damage: 13-17
+5 Slashing damage
+5 to melee attack
+2 HP per tick

"Holy shitballs!"

"Gemini," Roshan beckoned.

Withdrawing the sword from the bag, I ran my eyes along its smooth, flawless blade and whistled.

"Gemini?" Roshan beckoned again.

"Yeah?" I didn't look up.

"Your utterances startle your pet, and they do little for the calm my nerves long for."

"This from a woman who commanded a skeleton and healed herself through a battle against a magic sword. Sounds like you have selective nerves."

Roshan smirked. "I am not currently in combat."

"But look!"

Click growled.

"Oh, shut up." I crossed the room and set the sword across Priya's lap.

"Very nice," Roshan said. "Unfortunately, it is too high level for me to see its stats."

So, non-players can't see higher level item stats? Hmm.

I read them to her and was satisfied I received no system warnings about violating the Player's Agreement.

That hadn't been the overwhelming reception I'd expected, but I was dealing with a caster who wielded scepters and staves.

"When you reach the required level, this could be a good weapon," Priya said. "I hope you will wield it with much success."

That was only a little better.

"Okay, I think I saw something else that might excite you." I rifled through the chest inventory and found the icon of a thick, straight pole.

Staff of Endless Bounties

Level 8

Slot: Weapon

Type: Two-handed Staff

Quality: Uncommon

Durability: 47 of 50

Damage: 10-14

Light magic +3

*This staff increases the chance you will find magic items
by 9%
Intensifies the power of light spells by 2%
Automatically binds to caster*
*Do you wish to bind **Staff of Endless Bounties** to you?*
Yes/No

Selecting *No*, I dropped the staff on the rug between them and both their eyes flicked to activate their own interfaces. Each of their mouths formed a perfect, precious O. They were about all the reaction I needed.

"Gemini! This is a very strong staff!" Roshan blurted. "But..." She peered. "Priya, may I have your leave to observe you in my interface?" Roshan asked.

Priya shot her a sexy gander and pressed a finger to her lips. "You want to take a closer look?"

Roshan blushed. "You tease me, Priya."

Priya smiled and pushed herself up to her hands and knees. Her eyes flicked from Roshan's eyes to her lips, and back again. Roshan's own eyes jumped up and down, contemplating...considering. Then Priya pressed her lips to Roshan's and I popped a boner for the ages.

Gods, my old life was pathetic.

Priya nibbled Roshan's lower lip before pulling back.

"I will never tease you, Roshan."

The half-elf rolled gracefully back to settle on the fur and crossed her legs, yogi style, wearing a satisfied grin. Roshan's face resembled the shade of beets, and her expression tensed into something approaching smitten.

"Oh, and you may check me at your leisure, sister. No need to ask."

Roshan did, and I watched as her eyes flicked around, reading her new friend's stats.

I jerked as Roshan blurted out. "Shadow magic?"

Priya shrugged. "Yes? What's wrong? Does that make my kisses seem dirty?" She winked.

"But you said nothing!" Roshan jumped to her feet with such an effortless grace, I wondered what physical training she'd had in her village back home. She paced back and forth. "I have never engaged with someone who practiced the dark arts." She threw her hands up.

Priya got to her feet. "Roshan?"

But Roshan prattled on. "It is against every fiber of my being! How do you live with such affinities? How—how did I not detect this darkness?"

"Maybe that thing on her back counteracts her shadow affinity or something," I said. "I doubt that's an element of shadow, considering how it made me feel."

Roshan's eyes flickered between us, eventually landing a suspicious glare upon me. I could almost hear the cogs turning and, though her lips parted a few times as if she'd speak, she pressed them back together and let her thoughts progress.

"Yes. A quandary. You don't seem to be a dark creature." Her eyes flicked around her interface again. "Hmm. You have no class."

"Hey! What the hell do you mean I have no class? Just because I live alone and don't have opportunities to practice social graces—"

Roshan shook her head. "I meant you have selected no class."

It was Priya's turn to flush red. "Oh." She straightened her own nighty. "I see."

Roshan smiled. "May I ask why?"

"Because I have not been offered one. I have no mentor,

other than my aunt, who—consistent with my luck—casts in the Light. She is a nature specialist."

"Ah," Roshan nodded. "A fine specialty."

"So she says. However, it is outside my affinity."

I had the nagging sense there had to be a metaphor in here, but I would be damned if I could find it. I shoved the thought away.

"I have heard the intent of the caster and a selective attitude when it comes to spell choice makes for very powerful casters, indeed. I have only read this, mind you, never experienced it, but it is not beyond possibility. Perhaps, sister, you will let me guide you in your efforts, to help you on your way."

I cringed. Though I hadn't known Priya for long, she struck me as the independent type and might not take well to Roshan's offering of what amounted to intrusion in her life choices. But she utterly surprised me.

"Would you?" Priya swooned and stepped forward, clutching the Light Priestess's shoulders. "Truly?"

"I would be honored."

Their faces were inches apart. I grinned. "Go ahead. Kiss her again."

They ignored me.

"Thank you, Roshan. I will not let you down." She threw her arms around Roshan's neck and the mage gasped in response.

She patted Priya's back gently. "Yes, of course." She pulled away, holding Priya's arms between them, and peered at me.

"What?" I asked.

Her response was directed at Priya. "He eyes us with hunger. Fantasies abound in his filthy mind."

Priya squinted and threw me a suspicious gander. "Is that so? How can you tell?"

"I don't know what you two are talking about? I'm over here looting."

The way they both pursed their lips at me was priceless.

"Wait," I said, thinking back to my excitement when Priya had kissed Roshan. "How did you—"

"The answer is in my interface. I stare at it right before my eyes, the text floating between us just now."

"Roshan, you checked me without asking?"

"You have given me permission, do not try to recant out of convenience."

I shrugged and looked away. "I'm afraid I have no idea what you mean."

"Priya, my love, you will find new information in your Companion Tab now that Gemini is one."

Priya continued to smile as her eyes flicked to and fro. "Oh!" She covered her mouth. "I see!"

Roshan nodded.

"What?" I threw my hands up. "What do you see?"

"Why, you adore both of us."

"What?"

"It's right here, Gemini," Priya said, thrusting a hand onto her hip. "You are enamored with me." Her eyes flicked up and down my body. "Wow. You move fast."

I checked my interface.

"You're enamored with me!"

Priya shrugged. "I never claimed I didn't move fast. I have an excuse. I meet so few men...none, really. Besides, you rescued me from a life of slavery in an orb. What's your excuse?"

Roshan interrupted before I could answer. "Funny you

should mention he saved you from a life of slavery," Roshan mused aloud. "He has a way of doing that. Endearing women to him by pulling them from the jaws of Hokrahm. Then, when he must acknowledge he shares their feelings, well, he just shrivels up like a dead Bloom Berry."

"Hey!" I pointed both index fingers at my junk. "I would not call this shriveled!"

They both barked laughter. I joined in. They stepped toward me and we embraced in a circle.

Are these pants too tight?

"So, what do your dispositions with each other suggest? I mean, aren't you companions with each other, as well?"

They shrugged and spoke in unison. "Yes."

"And your dispositions?"

"I'm afraid that's between us, Gemini," Roshan said.

Priya nodded. "Yes, I would have to agree. Fealty is one thing, but our personal feelings are ours."

Mother-fucking motherfucker!

She thrust out her chin defiantly. "My being enamored with Roshan is really our concern." She slapped a hand over her mouth, feigning as though she'd slipped. She flared her eyes at me. "Well, I guess I let that little acorn drop."

I laughed. "So, being that you didn't rescue each other, what's your excuse for having these kinds of feelings so quickly?"

Why does this suddenly feel like a teenage slumber party?

"Well, Priya gave me great pleasure as you slept," Roshan said.

My jaw dropped. "What?"

Again, they nodded in unison.

"And I missed it?"

Shrugs. In unison.

I growled under my breath.

"Perhaps next time we will wake you," Roshan said, kissing my cheek.

"No," Priya interjected, wrapping an arm around Roshan's waist. "Our first times should be dedicated to him. It wouldn't do to overwhelm him."

I raised a finger. "I would be okay with that."

Roshan clicked her tongue. "Don't be a child."

Grrrr.

Priya kissed the other cheek. "And just so you know, my peach remains intact, as well. My aunt says so."

It was most definitely time for a subject change or else someone was getting defiled.

"Pree, it's—"

"I do not like that. My aunt called me that, and I made her stop. I am no longer a child."

"He did the same to me earlier. *Rosh!* Indeed."

"How do you know your aunt called you that as a child if you can't remember it?"

"Gah! Obviously, she called me that as an adult. I told her I didn't like it, and she said, 'But I called you that as a child, and you didn't mind.' Then I said, 'Well, I am no longer a child. Do not call me that.' And she said—"

I sighed. "Pri-ya. It's time we looked at your abilities and discussed your options. You have some points I can spend for you."

"What?" her head swiveled to gander at Roshan and me in turn. "Is this what you spoke of in the dark place? Crohl's —" she spat on the floor, "—lair?"

"Yes. Your attributes. Strength? Dexterity? Intelligence?"

Roshan nodded and grabbed Priya's hands. "Our companion can strengthen our abilities when we level."

"What? You mean I don't have to climb trees incessantly to gain strength?"

Roshan shook her head.

Priya squinted at her. "Read all night for months to gain intellect?"

Roshan shook her head.

Priya turned to me. "You may have my peach now if you wish it."

As much as I wanted to taste her peach, we had business to tend to, and I needed to think about Level 10. Then again, if I didn't take their fruit and died before Level 10, would I ever forgive myself? What evil man might steal their fruit, instead?

You wouldn't be around to forgive yourself, dip shit.

Still...

32

A few quick calculations revealed Priya had earned 33 attributes points through daily actions. I had the distinct feeling that was a significant number, but when taking into account a lifetime spent in the forest, maybe not. I wondered if it was possible to lose attributes the way they could be earned naturally. What if someone with a given strength rating started to sit around on their asses and let their muscles atrophy? Would the attribute total drop?

After earning nine levels overall, she had sixteen available attribute points to add to her total. It occurred to me she might have gained levels involuntarily by dispensing her former master's will below ground. I decided not to bring it up on the outside chance I was right.

I scrolled through her character screen and found some really exciting stuff. Priya had woodworking skills and was already an expert forester. In addition, she had skinning talents. She was Level 41 in Forestry and Level 18 in Carpentry. She explained that she built and performed repairs on her tree hovel all the time, and I knew she cut her own firewood.

I read the tool tip for profession rankings.

Occupation Skill Ranks
Apprentice: Levels 1-10
Journeyman: Levels 11-20
Tradesman: Levels 21-30
Expert: Levels 31-40
Master: Level 41-50

When I swiped the Occupation skills aside, her chapter pane returned to focus.

Priya Skyy
Level 9 Half-elf
Natural casters, hunters, and woodsmen, Elves are creatures of the forest who enjoy extended lifespans, when compared to other humanoids.

Attributes:
Strength: 8*
Dexterity: 3*
Intelligence: 4
Wisdom: 4
Constitution: 12
Charisma: 8*
(Priya has 16 unspent attribute points)

Combat Skills
Ranged: 14*
Melee: 5

Defensive Skills:
Dodge: 8

Parry: 2

Weapon Skills

Bow: 14*

Blunt: 7

Occupational Skills:

Not to be confused with combat professions, occupational skills allow people to earn a wage, run a business, build foundations, or create weapons, armor, and potions to supplement adventuring.

Carpentry: 18

Rank: Journeyman

Tool tip: Carpenters use wood as their primary ingredient in the construction of structures, wooden weapons, and furniture.

Forestry: 41

Rank: Master

Tool tip: Foresters are lumberjacks skilled with axes. They also make excellent field hands and use scythes as their secondary gathering tools.

Skinning: 15

Rank: Journeyman

Tool tip: Skinners remove hides from vanquished animal beings—and sometimes humanoid ones—to be used as raw materials by leather workers, clothiers, blacksmiths and other professions. Tanning is often selected by skinners as a secondary occupation to create leathers.

Cooking: 48

Rank: Master

Tool tip: Yum! Cooks use myriad ingredients to concoct tasty dishes to feed the hungry, boost morale, and provide buffs to tradesmen and adventurers, alike.

Botany: 47

Rank: Master

Tool tip: Botanists specialize in growing and identifying plant life. Advanced Botanists can use herbs to create healing poultices and other advanced medicines.

Affinities:

Shadow Magic: 100%

Shadow is a powerful discipline of capable magic that draws on the dark powers of Enora. Often mistaken for an evil form of magic, Shadow is the balancing force of the Light. Wielders of Shadow Magic often worship Vamoth, the gatekeeper of the underworld. Though it is possible to successfully wield any school of magic without religious affiliation, certain buffs can be obtained using shrines.

Elemental Magic: 57%

Languages:

Elven

Common

That was a ton to absorb. I counted myself lucky I had time to go through it.

"Priya, you are exceptional. You're a master forester and cook, an expert tanner, and a journeyman carpenter. You're amazing."

Priya blushed under my genuine praise. "You are so kind, Gemini. So different from what my aunt told me to expect from men. I fear she led me astray."

"Don't be so sure. Men want what they want and have various ways of getting it." I stared into her eyes. "Besides, if you value her warnings, why do you flirt?"

She shrugged. "You're pretty."

I waited for more of an answer, but none came.

"I don't want you to think less of me for saying so, but someone as striking as you might bring out the worst of inclinations of those lacking moral fortitude."

She shot me a curious glance. "Why would I think less of you for saying so?"

"Because you're not an object, Priya. I wouldn't want you to think I see you only as a sexual being."

"Perish the thought from your pretty head, Gemini, for I have relished the sight of your hard muscles enough times to balance our water kettles."

"Seriously, Priya. If you're devoted to traveling with us, I pledge to help you protect yourself from men who seek to corrupt you. No more kidnappings."

"A true wonder," Priya said. She turned her eyes on Roshan. "That such a man would be sent from Solara to save me from the darkness."

"Shh!" Roshan shushed and pressed a finger to the half-elf's lips. "It will fill his head with ideas of grandeur. His ego could inflate to untenable levels."

I changed the subject before her words could become prophecy. Focusing on Priya's stats with a bit more intent, I read the less familiar tool tips to get a better picture.

"It goes without saying that you'll want to spend points in Intellect. With your magical affinity, your casting power could blossom, but we also need to consider Wisdom."

"But what if added wisdom brings me to my senses and I decide throwing all my berries into your basket is unwise?"

I mocked laughter. "Very funny. No, it doesn't work that way. You seem plenty wise, to me...even if mostly wise-assed."

Priya's nose crinkled up. "Somehow I don't decipher your words as complimentary."

I tilted my head to one side, her suddenly elevated diction garnering more than a passing interest.

"Priya, how were you educated?"

"I don't recall my education. I never thought to ask my

aunt, but I always assumed my parents taught me what they could."

"Hmm. Interesting."

"Why do you ask?" She leaned back onto her elbows atop the rug and gazed at me expectantly.

"Because your intelligence jumped out at me. Often, your words are indicative of a refined vocabulary, like Roshan's."

"I suppose you have been blessed by Solara, Gemini. To have such intelligent women in your midst."

"I guess so." My mind started racing. Something about my allies' intellects picked at my brain.

Did Enora—the A.I.—gift certain races with higher IQs? No, that would've been racist as hell. If Roshan truly came from a village, wouldn't that imply a lack of access to education? Did her priest, Master Mitwah, teach her? Or did a higher IQ baseline from the beginning of Enora's evolution pass the gift of higher language throughout the generations? Would I experience races less-gifted, or was everyone I encountered going to toss in high-minded sentiments at random?

Priya was staring at me. I had to retrace our conversation to pick up where I left off.

"Wisdom affects how fast you regain mana. Very important if we're ever in prolonged combat."

Priya's eyes brightened. "Do you really think I could adventure with you?" She thrust out her fingers. "My hands tremble at the notion I might burn men like Crohl."

"You seem to be adaptable," I said. "With your professional skills you've learned to survive in the Dark Wood, I'm sure you could become quite an adventurer *and* save us some coin."

"And you would be willing to teach me? The combat piece?"

While Priya's excitement was a welcome sentiment, I wasn't sure she grasped the full extent of the sacrifices she would have to make. There was no telling what Zhara would think of my adoption of her niece into a dangerous lifestyle where she could end up dead. What would she think about Priya aligning herself with me?

"Priya, you understand questing with us would mean leaving your home, right? Roshan and I will be moving beyond the Dark Wood—very far beyond it."

Her chin ticked up, and Priya glanced over at Roshan. "Oh." She nodded. "Right. of course." She peered around her dome. "I guess you wouldn't want to stay here. That makes sense." After taking in her surroundings for another moment she shrugged. "That would be okay. It's rather boring, my life. I'd like to see more of the outside world."

I decided not to ask what Zhara would think of the idea of her running off and gallivanting across the world with me. That would come up when we met with the Matron of the Wood. Maybe since I'd completed her quest, she wouldn't smite me... or something.

"Adventuring's also dangerous," I said.

She pursed her lips. "My life might be simple, Gemini, but I am not. I know adventuring is dangerous."

Though she calls herself a 'simple girl from the woods' when it's convenient.

I nodded. "I don't think you're simple in the least."

She smiled. "Good! Tell me more about your thoughts on my attributes." She adjusted her boobs and tossed me a sideways smile. I clinched my molars.

"Right. So, we know we want to spend in those two

areas—um... Wisdom and Intellect. I noticed you have a Charisma score of twelve that you earned naturally."

Her head bobbed with enthusiasm. "Yes. Negotiating in Brumhill increased it."

"Right! See? While you are beautiful and charismatic, I don't think the stat necessarily reflects your attractiveness or allure, just that you can get better deals. I got ten points for doing nothing, and the two of you seem to tolerate me."

"Cherish you," Roshan corrected. "I am drawn to the Light in you."

"I love you, too." The words had escaped my mouth before I knew what I was saying. Horrified, I was flooded with sudden regret as my mind revisited rejections following premature utterances in my former world. It was like scratching old wounds.

The open professing of my emotions was no problem in Enora. Roshan hadn't rejected me in the least. Just the opposite. Still, I cringed as that old world part of me expected a reaction based on stigmas.

But Roshan alleviated the tension without pause.

"Of course you love me," she said. "My interface says so."

Funny.

Although I didn't like to take gifts for granted, I wondered how Roshan and I had bonded this much in a day. I guessed challenging times did that. Soldiers in a fox hole and all. Game mechanics might play a part, too, but I wanted to believe the feelings were natural. It helped to keep dark thoughts at bay.

I turned my attention back to Priya, and my inner-nerd showed. "The interface's advancement schema is blind, which isn't helpful."

"Schema?" She asked, her lips and eyebrows equally twisted in confusion.

"The interface doesn't tell me what abilities you'll receive as you advance. You could get skill bonuses and learn new abilities with each level you gain. I just have no way of knowing what they might be. I assume they'll become heavily class-dependent later."

"Well, you have been gifted with this power to spend these points for your companions, you should do what you think is best. If Solara trusts you with this responsibility, so will I."

"Wait, now. Hold on. I spent some of Roshan's points because they complimented other points spent a certain way. I believe her last trainer built her abilities to compliment a magic class. But you're a clean slate and have sixteen points available. You could be a warrior, a rogue, or a ranged damage dealer, if that was your desire. Or you could choose to make the most of your magic affinity and become a caster. Then you could wield spells from a distance. I don't know the available classes, but the options could be boundless."

"I think you should spend the points since you seem to have intuitions I don't understand," Priya said. "But I find myself excited by the prospect of hurling magic violence at evil beings."

In *Light Of Babylon* and other games, players who rolled characters purely to fill a need in a group didn't always end up happy with their choices. More than once I'd discovered friends playing secret characters in lieu of showing up for guild runs so they could play classes they found they preferred after getting to know the game.

If Priya was going to uproot herself from a quiet life in the forest to be with Roshan and me, I didn't just want her to be successful, I wanted her to be happy.

"Then I should let your enthusiasm guide us. Maybe we will spend them slowly. We're not bound by time and I don't think we have any weapons to discover an offensive magic class, anyway."

"Hmm, sounds like too much pressure. I'm not a patient person."

Grrr.

Roshan cleared her throat. "An impatient person with an affinity for shadow magic. No, that could never end badly."

Priya glared at her through slits. "Does someone need another kiss?"

"Your seductions will not serve you here, demon." Roshan tilted her chin up and looked away.

But Priya smiled at the mockery. "Someone needs another kiss."

Roshan fought a smile. It was a losing effort, but the struggle left me a second to interrupt and redirect.

"Okay, mining along that vein of thought, why don't you sit next to Roshan while I fiddle with your points."

"Twist my wrist, won't you?" Priya slid closer to Roshan and rested her head on her shoulder.

Roshan smiled and slipped an arm around Priya's waist.

"It's nice to have friends," Priya said as she leaned in and set a gentle hand on Roshan's leg.

Roshan covered it with her own but didn't speak.

"Okay, so we'll start here."

Priya Skyy
Level 9 (No Class)
Half-elf
*Strength: 8**

*Dexterity: 3**
*Intelligence: 4**
*Wisdom: 4**
*Constitution: 12**
*Charisma: 8**
(Priya has 16 unspent attribute points)
**Attributes affected by natural life activities and not level-advancement training*

Sixteen points. Let's spend a few and see what new skills pop up.

I did the math, nodded to myself, and focused. After spending two points in intellect, I received a message.

Due to your companion's maximum affinity for Shadow Magic, Enora has granted her:
Shadow Void
Spell
The caster opens a portal to the underworld and banishes chaotically aligned creatures within two levels into Hokrahm's void.
Cost: 100 Mana
Cooldown: 30 Minutes

I announced the boon and both their jaws dropped. Priya sat up and blinked her eyes in succession to open her interface.

"That doesn't sound like an evil thing to me, Roshan!" her eyes flicked around as she searched.

"Nor to me!" Roshan blurted.

I nodded. "Seems some preconceptions were off the mark."

I distributed three more Intellect points, allowing her to

adjust to the sensations of her growing strengths in each category. When I spent her fifth point overall and clicked to spend her sixth, a flurry of text filled my interface. I scanned it and my head jerked. I squinted unnecessarily and read more carefully. My lips formed the words silently as I became hyper-focused, but I didn't care.

About halfway through, I flicked my eyes toward Priya and back to my interface several times.

"What is it, Gemini?" she asked. "Is something wrong?"

While non-players can level their attributes through labor and interaction, they may also purchase attribute upgrades from trainers in Enora. But Enoran trainers can spend only five attribute points per trainee.

*Players do not share this attribute cap, but privileges come at a cost. While you have the ability to spend unlimited attribute points on the behalves of your companions, doing so will result in the companion being permanently **bound** to you.*

*In order to bind a companion to you, the companion must hold a disposition of **endeared** or better toward you.*

After level ten, fallen non-players who are bound to you will resurrect at your spawn point if they are not revived after battle.

If you fall in battle, bound companions will continue to fight until your enemies are vanquished or they fall.

Bound creatures may not wander beyond ten miles from their binder unless given leave to do so. This setting is found in the Character Pane in a checkbox called, "Free Roaming."

If you have a foundation or pay for a room at an inn, you can leave the non-player behind at your choosing, but you will still be bound.

While bonds between non-players are broken by death, this player-to-non-player bond is permanent.

Be aware: There is no limit to the number of NPCs who can be bound to you, as long as they are of endeared disposition or higher upon binding. You may bind a non-player of endeared or higher disposition without permission.

This bond can only be broken when the non-player is killed by your own hand.

Binding cannot be undone.

Are you sure you wish to spend further attribute points and permanently bind Priya Skyy to you?

Yes/No

Ummm...

"Your skin resembles goat milk," Roshan said. "What's the source of your distress? Does Priya have an evil ability now? Shall trees shrivel in her unholy wake? Do porcupunks melt under her gaze? Shall demon minions worship at her feet?"

Roshan and Priya giggled. My smallest companion's head popped up and she clicked repeatedly.

I didn't laugh. I couldn't. Nor could I tighten the hinge on my loose jaw.

Forever? Does this mean if I spend another point on Roshan, she'll be permanently bound to me, too? And if so, wouldn't binding Priya make us some kind of weird harem thing?

I pushed myself up to my feet. "I need to um...take a walk."

"What?" Priya asked. "Do you want me to guide you? The forest can be—"

I shook my head. "I'll stay close and use stealth. Don't worry."

I moved toward the door, but a hand grasped my shoulder and turned me.

Priya gazed up at me, set her hands on both shoulders, and smiled. "It's okay, whatever it is. I'm filled with excitement with the prospect of following you to glory and bringing honor to your family name. My pledge is true and I will never dishonor the man who liberated me from the clutches of darkness."

"It's not trusting you that's the problem. It's trusting myself."

The distress shining in her eyes served only to make me feel like shit. I didn't want to be a secretive asshole with women so transparent and devoted, but I needed a minute, time with my own thoughts, uncontested. This was my life now. Permanent actions were forever. I couldn't log out if I regretted them, and NPC or not, I wasn't going to kill this creature because of a decision I regretted later.

Roshan slid beside Priya and gripped her arm. "Let him gather his thoughts." She peered at me and bowed her head shortly. "He will tell us what we need to know."

Glaring at the taller woman, words I'd read in the system warning flashed in my head. If NPC trainers could only train five points per adventurer, then how had she built her current load out? It seemed her Master Mitwah, had tricks up his sleeve.

Priya stepped back. "Many predatory creatures roam only in darkness. Please, stay close to the meadow so the wards will keep them at bay."

I nodded and stepped into the night.

33

This was some shit.

I'd known Priya for less than a day and I was supposed to make decisions about her destiny.

When I was halfway across the meadow, the door to Priya's dome thumped. As I turned, a dark figure low to the ground bounded across the tall grass in my direction. Her little black eyes glimmered in the glow cast by double moons. She rattled off a timpani of clicks.

"I don't know what I was thinking, leaving without you. Stay close."

She clicked happily and sprang off into the high grass. I considered her as she went.

Here, I had a pet. A companion I could resurrect if she died. Enora was essentially offering me the same kind arrangement with my human and half-elf friends. All I had to do was spend some attribute points and I could offer them immortality. So, why was I troubled? Wasn't that the ultimate gift?

Casting stealth, I stood in the center of the open meadow and peered up at the star-littered blanket of space.

Opening my Companion tab and peering at Priya, I saw she leaned, probably against Roshan. Those two had bonded quickly. I didn't really care if that was a game mechanic thing or if they were just thrilled to be in the company of other people, other women. It made sense, considering they'd both just been held captive by some filthy men—some of whom were still out in these woods, searching for us.

Someday players would take advantage of Enoran NPCs and have their ways with them. I spied conflict in my future. That spoke volumes about the realism of these people.

Even though I couldn't see the Eastern woman in Priya's Companion pane, I knew she leaned against Roshan but the unnatural tilt of her upper body and head. An asterisk hovered next to the half-elf's age of twenty-one. There was no tool tip, but that was pretty strange. She certainly appeared to be around my age, but when I considered her memory erasure, it struck me as a clue to something bigger.

Hearing her unabashed giggle echoing in my head, I ignored the asterisk and focused on the reason I'd gone outside. It was probably a rare glitch.

She'd spent her life living in this forest. Trading in Broomhill, or whatever she'd called the town outside the Dark Wood, seemed to be the extent of her social interactions with the outside world. Could someone so young and with such limited exposure properly weigh decisions like this? Wouldn't any chance to leave what was familiar seem an exciting proposition?

Was I an idiot for even thinking in those terms when I lived in a world designed to drop these opportunities on my doorstep? If that was how the game was designed, was it wrong for me to accept her into the party and take her away?

I'd promised to respect their free will. Didn't binding them to me spit in the face of that sentiment?

If the A.I. was truly adaptive and sentient, I wondered about its perspective in regard to my thoughts and actions. I would've bet Nokuro Takemoto would've giggled relentlessly at the idea he'd spawned a game world where a player could be rife with conflict over the treatment of NPCs because they were so real. But if he would've, he'd have been fooling himself. I wasn't the average player. Others would think differently than me. It would be a game to them.

If I treated the world like a simple game, how could I live in it? How would I find purpose? I didn't even know how long it would exist, but from what I'd seen so far, it could last beyond what would've been my natural life on earth. This place was crazy and, if I was being honest with myself, it was fun, in an oh-my-god-don't-let-me-die kind of way.

If not for the lingering doom, I'd be having a hell of a time.

Priya sat up and smiled in the Companion pane. Her lips crinkled in excited conversation. I found myself smiling at the sight of her, and it brought to mind the proverbial tree in the woods that fell and no one heard. Seeing her like that made her even more real.

Being born to non-players and living here has shaped who Priya is. But can she possibly know who she wants to be? Does the suddenness with which she pledged to adventure with me reflect a naivety? Or is she just accepting the way things are done when someone saves another's life? Does she just feel honor bound like Roshan? Did Zhara teach her that?

The A.I. had taken over and essentially locked out the developers. Enora was God here, a protector of her world's purity working to keep it as authentic as possible. As a permanent fixture in her world, I played by her rules. The glaring benefit of that was immortality, in a sense.

By bonding to her, if I live past Level 10, Priya will respawn where I do. She will never die. She might not even age. Maybe she wouldn't have her life in the forest, but is that so bad, if she gets to live on and on? Does she want to live on and on?

I flipped back to my interface, searching for something else that had nagged me in the moment.

If you have a foundation or accommodations at an inn, you can leave the non-player behind at your choosing, but you will still be bound.

What the hell is a foundation?

Finding no tool tip and knowing the answer wasn't going to come to me on the soft breeze bending the high grass at my knees, I shoved that thought aside for later, like so many others.

A heavy voice surged from the darkness to my right causing my bones to quiver. I realized I'd ben circling the meadow and was close to the dome, where the treant stood permanent watch.

"You seem troubled, Gemini."

Glowing, golden eyes peered at me from the density of the great treant's shadows.

My voice quivered as I responded. "Hello, Magellan. I hope I didn't disturb you."

"Mmm," Magellan hummed, causing the leaves high in

his branches to shimmy. "No need to worry yourself, young one. What troubles you?"

"Priya," I said simply.

"Ah. A complicated creature, that one."

"Is she?"

"Indeed. Quite spirited. Fiercely independent."

"I'm not sure that's the impression I've gotten," I said. "I feel she has warmed to Roshan."

Branches creaked and the eyes inched forward. "And to you, Gemini. What troubles?"

I wondered if it violated the player's agreement to answer the question. But Magellan asked, so I decided to roll the dice and try to keep the discussion theoretical.

"I have an inner, philosophical quandary. Questions about peoples' rights to choose their own destinies and whether they have the experience to draw on to make such choices."

"There's no need to muddy the truth with me. I knew the day would come when Priya would leave the Dark Wood and rush out to face her destiny. This was expected. Her will is as free as any."

"You think she wants to leave?"

"I am bound by a pledge of silence, Gemini, but I believe it is scribbled in Enora's Annals of Time that Priya Skyy will have a great impact upon this world. When she returned with your party, I presumed Solara had intervened and her new beginning had come."

I peered up at him as I folded my arms across my chest. "How can you know anything of the sort, if you'll excuse my gall?"

"I welcome your gall, human. Never have I laid eyes on a creature with the unique powers you wield. I find your essence...enlightening."

"What powers are those?"

"If you don't know, best you should discover them your-self. Perhaps you will grow with your companions and form lifelong bonds. But Priya will require balance as you aid her."

"Aid her?"

"You know little."

"Thanks!"

"Suffice it to say, Priya is more than the sum of her surroundings. From her emanates the very essence of Solara, the essence of Enora. She is pure of heart, while powerful of soul. Dark affinity in a creature born of a family line bathed so richly in the Light is a harbinger of the arrival of something unique, something that will change the world forever. When I sensed the depth of your many affinities, it seemed only fitting you would pair."

"If I level Priya's attributes further—"

"She will be bound to you," Magellan finished my thought. "So, this is what troubles you, that you have been given power to bind a powerful creature to your will. With this, I can help."

"How so?"

"Tell me, Gemini. In pondering whether it is appro-priate to bind Priya to you, did you ever stop to consider that you were also binding yourself to her?"

"Well, I suppose."

"Be decisive!" the tree barked.

As my chest fluttered, my eyes shot to Priya's wooden dome, expecting her to appear in the doorway and wonder why I was pissing off her magic tree friend. But she didn't appear.

The treant measured his tone. "No one else can hear

me, Gemini. Though my lips move for your own benefit, I speak inside your mind."

"That's a little spooky, dude."

"I require your answer."

I cleared my throat. "Have I considered how binding her to me also binds me to her? How about we skip ahead? I guess what you're getting at is that I fear being responsible for her."

"Power and foolishness are a combination of which to be weary, Gemini. In Priya, you have potential. In you, the same potential. In the priestess, the same. Now, tell me, granted such a gift as trustworthy companions willing to follow you anywhere you go, as if it were ordained that you would blossom together like petals of the same flower, what is the source of your doubt? Your fear of failing them?" The treant's branches rustled in what I thought of as a shrug. "Set this aside. You're better served by thinking of Priya as yet another tool toward your success with whom you can also bond and enjoy as a companion."

"I hadn't thought of it that way," I muttered. "That actually makes a lot of sense."

"Why do you sound surprised that a thousands-of-years-old treant would possess wisdom?"

Now I feel like an idiot.

"Of course, you must first face the test of the Matron."

I cocked my head up. "Her aunt? Will Zhara be a problem?"

Magellan laughed. "She is very protective of her kin, I assure you. I'm certain she will see your worth, but it's more a question of whether she'll be ready to unleash Priya on the world. For now, I believe you must address the truth of your own inner-conflict before turning your thoughts to Zhara. In this, I will aid you."

"I welcome your aid, wise treant," I said, pouring it on.

"Your wisdom has returned." The treant's bark spread into a semblance of lips and smiled at me, revealing light-colored wood beneath its bark. "Open your map."

I did.

Priya's dome was in the northeast region of the Dark Wood areas I'd discovered. The lake where I'd found Roshan sat to the south and Zhara's tree was a few klicks to the southeast.

"Now, withdraw your perspective so you see the larger world."

Zooming out, I scrolled east-to-west across Enora. Undiscovered territories zoomed by as I continued to scroll. A lump jumped into my throat as the scrolling continued. The Dark Wood in which I sat was but a pinprick of all to be discovered.

"How significant are your problems in the scope of such a world, Gemini? How much evil lurks in those areas, yet undiscovered? If you wish to play a role in such a vast world and live up to your potential, what do you think should be your first consideration, since you are but one man?"

Lucera's voice came to me for a third time, creating a memorial hat trick. I spoke the words aloud.

"I must make friends."

"Hm, wisdom, indeed."

Priya was worthy of immortality, and I'd peel enemy skin from bone to keep Roshan in my life. Though I'd only known her for a day, the Light priestess already felt like part of me. My anchor. With the addition of Priya, we were a perfect triangle. Shadow affinity, Light affinity, and the player who was both. Though I could've thumped my head, I was encouraged by realization of the thing that had been missing.

I'm the problem. I haven't pledged myself to them. The bloated sense of importance I put on my own existence holds me back.

"Thank you, Magellan. I will forever be grateful for your wisdom."

"Mmm." Then he closed his eyes.

"I don't understand," Priya said.

"Nor do I," Roshan said.

"I know. It's hard to grasp. I guess I should have planned better how I was going to explain this, but if you'll bear with me, I'll try to make better sense." I scooted between them and took their hands in mine, resting them on their folded legs. "The reason I can manipulate your skill points is that I have a special ability beyond spending attribute points—or linked to that. When you became my companions, it changed everything."

"I told you, you are special," Roshan said. "A fine noob, if ever I met one."

"Yeah, well, that's nice and all but let me finish."

She nodded. Priya squeezed my hand tighter.

"When I was counting out Priya's skill points, I realized another special ability. If I spend more than five attribute points for someone, they become bound to me. Permanently. We can never be separated, except by my leave."

"What?" Priya asked.

"Like a possession?" Roshan asked, incredulously. "I do not pledge my life lightly, and serve with distinction I shall. But I am no possession, Gemini!" This time she stood and paced behind me. "How is it I am your possession?"

"I didn't say you were my possession. I don't want to

own you. I'm honored by your loyalty, Roshan, believe me."

Priya gripped my hand tighter and turned her head. "Roshan, come and sit. Let him finish."

Roshan sat but didn't reach for my hand. I knew it wasn't because I was any less liked—I'd brought up the Companion tab and was keeping an eye on her disposition during the entire conversation, after all—but because she didn't suffer ignorance. It was her nature. Intelligence about the world around her was vital to how she perceived herself.

"Talk, noob."

I chuckled. "You've wondered at my desire to make it to Level 10."

"Yes. Are you going to explain this thing you're withholding?"

I blurted it out. "If I make it to Level 10, I cannot die."

This time it was Priya who released my hand. "You're right."

My head swiveled. "You believe me?"

"No, I was talking to Roshan. We swear service to a crazy fool."

Roshan nodded agreement.

"I was afraid of this," I muttered. "It's not an easy thing to explain, but if you'll bear with me, I'll give you what you need."

"And tell us, great one, what do we need?" Roshan asked, sharing a curt nod with Priya, who mimicked it.

I sighed. "If I get to Level 10, and I have bound you to me, and someone kills me, I will reappear somewhere else. When this happens, anyone bound to me who dies, will re-spawn with me."

"Re-spawn? What is this silly word?"

"Resurrect," I corrected.

Priya rolled her eyes and sang her response. "Fooooolishneeeeeesss."

"It's not fooooooooolishnesss," I sang in reply.

Priya tried to fight a smile.

"And you say you can prove this?" Roshan asked.

"Yes, after I reach Level 10... and if I die."

"Well, then. This problem is solved," Roshan said.

"Why?" I asked.

She kissed my forehead as she stood. "Because I have no intention of letting my beloved die. Enough of this insanity."

"I'm not finished."

"I am finished." She cocked her chin in the air and stepped onto the soft rug.

I shook my head. "Okay, Roshan. you can walk away. We can discuss it when you level again. But I've spent the maximum points allowed on Priya unless I bind her to me."

Priya perked up, but she didn't speak. Instead, she pushed up from the soft rug and turned to face me. The light of the oil lamp on her bedside table penetrated the top of her thin gown and accentuated her round hips.

I closed my eyes, focusing.

Priya raised my chin with a finger. "It is you who is simple. Perhaps I have been coy with you. Maybe you need it spelled out. Do I have your attention, Gemini?"

"You have it."

"It is I who have experienced evil in this world on more than one occasion. I long to escape these woods and purge it while standing next to the two souls who rescued me. I pledge my service not just to you, but to Roshan, the same. Since we left that place, I have found the both of you to be true to Solara's way. I believe your path to be an honorable one. I don't ever want to be used for dark purposes against my will again."

Gone was the flighty, fun-filled tone I'd experienced with Priya since dragging her out of Crohl's grasp. The weight of her gaze bore down, though her voice was gentle and firm.

"I want you to spend the points so I can fight against those who would enslave others like me. You are a silly man warning me against a gift I've already given to you. A bond. I cannot believe your crazy talk of immortality, but if you speak true, then let my service be everlasting."

Her gaze hardened and she cocked an eyebrow. I nodded to show I was with her.

"I am not some silly woman with which to be trifled. You see someone who prances through the wood barefoot and wearing little clothing who flirts with you. Even bound to your side, I am still Priya Skyy, and no one will take that from me. So, bind me for I am already bound by *my* choice."

She crossed to the bed, shrugged her robe from her shoulders, and lingered for a long moment, hands set on her hips. I looked away.

"Don't divert your eyes. This is the least of what I pledge." She pushed her shoulders back. "But trust me when I say you will earn it."

Roshan raised the sheet and Priya climbed into the bed.

"When you are finished, come to bed," Roshan said. "Then we will set out and turn in your quest so you might reach Level 10 and set this nonsense aside."

"Don't be late," Priya commanded in a monotone. "We travel tomorrow."

I opened Priya's character pane before my doubts could resurface, and spent a point on intellect. For better or worse, the snarky half-elf with curves like a mountain highway was glued to me.

Game on.

34

We hiked a narrow trail winding along a creek to the south. When we approached the stretch of woods I'd traversed with Click before hearing Roshan's distant screams, I used the quest feature on my map to highlight the way to Zhara's tree. We'd established that, since the women were my companions, they could see the quest path, as well—not that Priya needed a golden path to find her aunt's home.

When we'd traveled for an hour, Priya stopped and spread her arms out to stretch. Her full breasts pushed out her red robe in that lovely way they did. Sooner or later something was going to have to give, because sleeping next to two beautiful and near-naked women was starting to take its toll. All those small, innocent brushings of my chest, patting of my shoulders, and the kisses on my cheeks were adding up and it wasn't like I could sneak off to one-hand the solution. Such relief wouldn't last long, anyway.

Am I complaining about having inherited two affectionate hotties?

I hadn't tried to seal the deal with either of them

because of something I learned about pro athletes in my old life. Supposedly, hanky-panky was a bad thing the night before a big fight. Boxers used the tension to keep them mad. Maybe I could turn all this frustration into a hardening—pun alert!—of my resolve.

"I am stronger, Gemini," Priya said, interlocking her fingers with mine as Click scurried ahead of the group.

I squeezed her hand as it swung gently. I felt like a freshman in high school with a new girlfriend.

"Right? And I didn't even add any points to your strength. What gets me is you only gained one additional ability despite the number of points I pumped into your primary attributes."

"Yes, but a Sleep spell should prove useful to your cause, right?" Enthusiasm painted her face.

I smiled. "Absolutely, but you'll have to learn how to use it, and I'd just as soon not be the guinea pig."

"Trivialities," Priya said. "All in time."

Before turning in the previous evening, I'd done some more research and figured out various presets controlling what information displayed when perusing my HUD. I'd meticulously set a few presets as they applied to my companions and my own attributes so I could view as much, or little, as I wanted. I checked Priya's stats using a more robust display setting.

Priya Skyy

Half-elf

Level 9 (No class)

Attributes

*Strength: 8**

*Dexterity: 3**

Intelligence: 14

Wisdom: 10

Constitution: 12

*Charisma: 8**

Combat Skills:

*Ranged: 14**

Melee: 5

Defensive Skills:

Dodge: 8

Parry: 2

Weapon Skills

*Bow: 14**

Blunt: 7

Shadow Void

Level 8

Required Affinity: Shadow Magic

The caster opens a portal to the underworld and banishes chaotically aligned creatures within two levels into the void.

Cast Time: 3 seconds

Cost: 100 Mana

Cooldown: 30 Minutes

Sleep

Level 9

Required Affinity: Shadow Magic

The caster calls forth dark essence to force a single adversary to slumber for up to one minute.

Cast Time: 3 Seconds

Cost: 75 Mana

Cooldown: N/A

This effect has diminishing returns when cast on the same target.

Damage will end the effect.

Occupational Skills:

Not to be confused with combat professions, occupational skills allow people to earn a wage, run a business, build foundations, or create weapons, armor, and potions to supplement adventuring.

Carpentry: 18

Rank: Apprentice

Tool tip: Carpenters use wood as their primary ingredient in the construction of structures, wooden weapons, and furniture.

Forestry: 41

Rank: Expert

Tool tip: Foresters are lumberjacks skilled with axes. They also make excellent field hands and use scythes as their secondary gathering tools.

Skinning: 15

Rank:Apprentice

Tool tip: Skinners remove hides from vanquished animal beings—and sometimes humanoid ones—to be used as raw materials by leather workers, clothiers, blacksmiths and other professions. Tanning is often selected by skinners as a secondary occupation to create leathers.

Affinities:

Shadow Magic: 100%

Elemental Magic: 57%

Languages:

Elven

Common

"But I have grown," she said cheerfully. "The sensations have blessed my bones all morning. Isn't that what life is about? Growth?"

"Especially this life," I mumbled. Then more loudly, "Yes. You're right. I'm guessing you'll be eligible for new spells now, but we will likely have to seek out a skill trainer or books to teach them to you."

"My people used books and scrolls to learn spells before magic was banned, so this is not unexpected," Roshan said. "But my class was revealed to me when first I grasped my scepter."

"Damn, I'd forgotten that. When Priya kidnapped you in the tunnels—"

"That was Crohl!" Priya barked. She didn't release my hand.

"—I equipped your scepter. It offered me the Light Priest class."

Roshan's shoes pattered on the earth as she sped to walk next to me.

"What do you mean, *offered you?* Are you saying you can switch from one class to another?"

I nodded.

"Yes."

She stopped. We took two more steps and turned back.

"This is impossible. I've only heard legends of such beings as you."

Players from two-thousand years ago, maybe?

"Well, here I am." I wasn't sure how else to say it.

A glance over my shoulder revealed the glowing trail ended before us.

"It seems we're here," I said.

Roshan glanced past me, then threw me an uncertain look.

"You'll get used to me, I promise," I said.

Roshan nodded, though her expression didn't change.

I eyed the tree and my heartbeat ratcheted up. This was going to be a moment of truth, and not because I was turning in a quest. Zhara would have her own ideas about

Priya and me. I doubted she would smite me, but I wouldn't put anything past Enora.

When I turned my head, I found my half-elf companion glaring at me.

Priya released my hand and grasped my shoulder. "Did she warm to you? Did she glow for you?" She evidently read the answer in my eyes as I relived the nirvana when I first met Zhara and she set her calming magic on me—and when she'd offered me a special, physical reward upon my successful return.

"She did!" Priya slapped my shoulder. "She did!"

"Well, I didn't!" I snapped, pulling my shoulder away and rubbing it furiously. "Why are you hitting me for what she did? It's not like..."

Priya gripped my other shoulder. "You must resist your urges. This is not jealousy! Binding with a dryad goddess binds you to her tree! Tell me you understand."

"My lovely niece," a voice whispered in the woods, seeming to come from all sides.

Our heads whipped around as the matron appeared from behind the wide trunk of the massive tree into which I'd seen her morph a couple days before. The bark covering her form smoothed into flesh as she whipped out her arms and welcomed Priya.

"Come to my bosom, dear child, for I have missed you so."

What is it with the women of this world and bosoms?

"Hello, Aunt Melan," Priya said with a plastered smile, but her eyes communicated suspicion as she peered at me before she pressed her face against her aunt's neck.

Melan?

Zhara peered over at Priya's shoulder. "Gemini, I am heartened to see you've returned. I'd expected you yesterday when I felt the darkness recede." She held Priya at arm's length. Her eyes flickered to each side of her niece's face and a tremor of foreboding washed over me.

She's checking her interface.

"And I see why!" Zhara snapped. I could've sworn my bones rattled as her voice echoed through the forest. She thrust out an accusing finger. "You have bound my Priya, boy?"

The finger creaked as a green bulb appeared on its end and extended into a rubbery vine. It shot across space between us and wrapped around my throat before I could react. Her eyes glowed yellow as her lips peeled back in a sneer. "I did not ask you to involve my niece in your dirty little—"

"Aunt Melan! Zhara! Release him!"

"You are but a child!" Zhara yelled, and her voice echoed through the forest. A breeze rose and leaves rattled. Zhara's hair blew in streams.

Roshan raised her scepter, but Zhara needed only peer at her for a moment before it dropped to the ground. Roshan was bathed in a white light and her shoulders dropped. Click skittered toward me as I grasped the vine surrounding my neck, It hardened in my grasp.

"I am a woman-grown who pledged my fealty to him!" Priya slapped at her aunt's shoulders. "You will release him at once!"

"You pledged?"

"He pulled me from the clutches of darkness. I owe him a life debt." Priya folded her arms across her chest and her chin jutted up. "And I am enamored with him."

"You are..." Zhara's chin dropped and she peered at me. "What have you done to my beloved girl?"

I gasped and pointed at the vine as I tried to form words. Blood inflated my cheeks like a balloon.

There was a looseness about Zhara's expression that would've struck me as disingenuous if it hadn't been for the branch cutting off my air. Something in the Matron's eyes poked at my brain for some reason. I sensed theatrics. Painful theatrics.

Zhara is strangling you.
-*10 HP*

"He can't answer you if you choke him to death!" Priya barked, grabbing the branch. "Release him now or I shall be gone forever!"

The tension around my throat relaxed as the branch slowly unwound from my neck and I coughed air back into my lungs.

I threw my arms up and protested through a crackling voice. "Hey, I didn't do anything but pull her away from a dark prison! Crohl kept her in a binding orb at night and a Black Robe of Binding when he needed her to do his dirty deeds! I didn't ask her to pledge anything to me. I asked for the opposite, for her to keep her free will. But you need to understand," I flicked a finger toward my friends, "these women get fealty in their heads and it's done. There's no arguing."

"Mmm hmm," Zhara replied.

I threw my hands up. "Are you telling me you didn't know she was there? That this might happen?"

She shook her head slowly from side to side as she took in her niece. "He has bound you to him, my Priya. You are *forever* bound to this man, unless you allow me to kill him. Do you see?"

Priya's head tilted to one side, her eyebrows furrowing in confusion. Then she turned those eyes on me, and back to her aunt. "You mean..." Her chin pivoted toward me again. "You were telling the truth?"

I nodded. "I warned you."

"But aunt, does this really mean that...that I will not die?"

"You are rendered immortal except if you die by his hand." Her eyes glowed red as she turned them on me. My throat felt thick, nausea crept into my belly, and my knee caps practically vanished. "But that would never happen, would it, Gemini?"

"Never in a million years, ma'am," I choked.

Her eyes returned to their normal blue. She swept her hair away from her breasts, but I'd lost all interest.

Priya turned and launched into my arms. Throwing her legs around me, she pressed her cheek to my neck.

"You have given me another gift I can never repay, Gemini!" She planted short kisses on my cheeks, speaking between her words. "I... love... you... I... love... you... I will never leave... your... side."

She unwrapped her legs and dropped to the ground.

Words came in a rapid, syncopated rhythm.

"You must consummate our bond." Her hand slipped quickly down my abs and past my waist.

You have been offered a Legacy quest!

Please Priya

Priya has asked that you consummate your bond with her in the woods.

Reward: 1,000 XP

Likely Reward: Maximum Relationship Disposition with Priya

You gotta be kidding me! A sex quest? And what the hell is a 'likely reward?'

"You must do this," Zhara whispered with a roll of her eyes. "You will consummate your bond with my Priya. Only then will I consider your fealty mutual."

Relief washed over me as a smile spread across her full lips and it wasn't until then that my private parts began to respond. But I also saw a strange twinkle in Melan Zhara's eyes—something deeper in that expression that made me feel...

Deceived. Zhara is holding something back. What's she hiding?

That was when I realized Zhara hadn't spoken the words aloud. Like the treant the night before, she'd projected them inside my head. Could she see the quest that had just been offered me?

This was...spooky.

Releasing my neck, Priya whirled around and leveled a finger at her aunt. "If you ever charm my Gemini again, I shall never cross these woods to see you! His pleasures are not yours to be had. Are we clear, aunt?"

Zhara smiled widely. "I responded poorly. It seems you truly are a man of conscience, Gemini. A man with a true heart I experienced when first we met. I am sorry I responded in such an... aggressive way."

I shrugged it off and feigned compliance. "She's your family. I get that."

Zhara whispered in my head, *there goes the three-way. Very sad.*

I gulped.

You used me, I thought in her general direction. *You used your sensuality as a reward you never planned on giving.*

Zhara's smile widened.

Perhaps it would not have been so easy were it not for your utterly predictable inclination to follow your penis as it leads you to reward.

She had me there.

Zhara stepped behind Priya and peered over her shoulder at me. She ran her fingers through Priya's golden hair, which matched hers, exactly. Any sign of the animosity between the women moments before had vanished, Priya seeming hardly to notice her aunt's hands as she peered up at me.

The matron spoke with her mouth, this time, as she twisted Priya's golden curls around her fingers. "I did not deceive you, Gemini. My niece has a mind of her own, and she often goes off alone for long periods without visiting, so I had no idea she'd been held in the clutches of the darkness I sent you to vanquish. As I told you, my reach into the underground is limited, and I cannot travel far from the tree."

And Magellan doesn't have the ability to pass you messages or anything when she doesn't return home. Yeah, right.

Zhara responded to my thoughts, reminding me I was dealing with a very powerful creature.

You would do well to remember your place. The gift I place before you is carved from my very soul. The next part surprised me. *Don't be a dick.*

Her face softened as her lips spoke a very different tone. "That you accomplished such a task is a sign of your resolve and Solara's support of your legacy. Now!" Zhara barked, causing us all to jump. "Before you plant your virile seed, we have business to complete."

Why was it suddenly a foregone conclusion that I was

going to take her niece into the woods and consummate...? What would Roshan think?

I relaxed my facial features. "Yes, my quest."

"Thank you for saving my niece and expelling darkness's minion from my woods. I bestow you with my gift."

A glaring flash of light surrounded me. The number 8 appeared before my eyes and zoomed into the distance. Then the number 9 repeated the process!

You have completed a quest:
Bring Light Where There Was Darkness
8,000 XP
Reputation Increase With Zhara
Your reputation with Zhara has reached Friendly.
Hidden objective: Rescue Priya Skyy
Bonus: 5,000 XP
You have reached Level 8!
+1 Constitution
+1 Dexterity
You have two attribute points to spend.
You have reached Level 9!
+1 Constitution
+1 Dexterity
You have two attribute points to spend.
Alignment: Light +50

I'd leveled, twice!

Unfortunately, neither Priya nor Roshan had gained any experience from the completion of the quest. Should I have done something to share it with Roshan before we started exploring underground? Or was she simply ineligible since she hadn't been my companion when I received it?

There was also a third option—that companions didn't receive quest XP. That would suck.

Zhara raised her hand and a white light encircled her fingertips. My heart thumped as my body glowed. The light warmed me, warmth bloomed. The numbness cascaded down my extremities, up again, and tensed my core. My feet left the ground as I levitated into the air and my arms relaxed to fall behind me.

"Gemini, I bestow upon you the power of nature's gifts. Bear witness to the might of Solara's Light in all your days and give no refuge to the influence of darkness."

White beams of light seeped from the pores in my skin as I was lowered gently to the ground. When I peered up, the whole world was washed in vivid colors, and a halo of light surrounded Zhara. I swung my eyes to the left as realization dawned... Roshan also wore the halo.

Tears streamed down her face as she stared in my direction.

Zhara, Matron of the Wood has granted you the **Light Magic Affinity**:
Nature Spells: Your skill in Nature Spells is now Level 1
You have learned a new, classless spell

Vine Entrapment
Level 9
Call forth vines from the earth to bind your enemies
Mana Cost: 25 Mana
Cast Time: Two seconds
Effect Duration: 30 seconds
Cooldown: N/A
Can be casted by any class with Affinity:* **Nature Spells
This spell has diminished returns when casting on the same being

You have learned a new ability:
See The Light (Passive)
You now recognize those bathed in the power of the Light by a warming aura. Stronger auras represent a higher affinity for Light Magic.

Zhara nodded as if she'd read the question in my mind. She probably had.

"You will now sense creatures of the Light so you know your brethren." She waved an almost-dismissive hand and adopted a less formal, flatter tone. "Oh, and I upgraded your bow while you were gone."

Reaching into the lowest branches of the trees, Zhara retrieved a bow that glowed with the same aura as she and Roshan. Tossing it across the air to me, she reached back into the tree.

The weapon was beautiful, with intense curves at each end winding to a central point. A golden string wound tightly at each end. Zhara handed me a quiver filled with arrows with silver leaf fletchings.

Longbow of The Light
Level 10
Slot: Weapon
Type: Ranged
Quality: Unique
Durability: Unbreakable
No durability loss
Ranged Damage: 21-34
+10 to accuracy
+10 piercing damage
+10 ranged attack
Unique: Constructed by Zhara, Matron of The Wood

"I'm sorry you cannot wield it yet, but I if I'd made anything lower, it would not have done your deed justice." She looked to Priya and Roshan. I trust you two will see he survives long enough to wield it."

Roshan nodded. "I will protect him with my life."

"As will I." Priya pressed another suckling kiss to the tip of my chin. God, she was relentless when she set her mind to a task. She turned to Roshan. "Sister, may I have your leave to—"

"Enjoy him," Roshan said, waving a hand. "Your bond is strong, and it is not my station to give you leave." She looked to me. "Perhaps when he has the opportunity to spend a sixth point for me, we will bind as well." She smiled as if she knew the answer, and she was damn well correct. "Besides, we had an understanding about what he must first achieve before taking of my fruits."

Priya grabbed my wrist and led me past the huge tree.

I peered back at Roshan. Part of me felt wrong, going with Priya like this while Roshan waited with Click and Zhara. The sight of my first human companion's face tugged at my heart, but her soft smile struck me as genuine. Maybe even happy. Definitely unselfish.

Zhara raised a hand. "A final gift."

We stopped and looked back.

Priya flinched and then ran a hand down to her belly. She craned her neck to look down. "What did you do?"

"Removed an obstacle." She winked at me. "My niece shall not bleed."

God, she's creepy.

35

Enora's replication of the human body stopped when it came to sexual interaction. The act of sex itself was insanely rewarding, and the release was insane. It was almost *cheating*. Men would come in droves, and something told me the women would as well. This game would run forever.

You have completed a legacy quest!
Please Priya
You have consummated your eternal bond with Priya in the woods. Or that was all the excuse you needed.
Reward: 1,000 XP
Maximum Relationship With Priya

The line about my need of an excuse reflected a new sense of humor for Enora. Her snark was as unique as the quests.

Our chests rose and fell together as I dropped my head on Priya's shoulder. Her breath huffed in my ear as I clutched a hip with one hand.

Sliding her fingers through the back of my hair, she pressed her lips to mine for a long kiss, then drew her head away with a smile.

"Mmm. Nice."

Priya leaned against the wall of the rocky cave and fastened the clasps on her robe as I cinched my leather pants.

I need to invent the zipper in this world to make things a little easier.

But then I couldn't enjoy the slow unwinding of my companion's garments and the lingering exposure of her full, feminine curves when repeating this process in the future—which I planned to do as often as she'd allow.

Glancing around the small cave, I spied a perfectly flat rock and a stump of rotting wood that appeared to have been cleanly carved into a sitting surface.

"What is it with this cave?" I asked. "Why does it appear lived-in if Zhara melds with a tree?"

"This is where I lived when she saved me from the first dark creature who erased my memories. But I felt like a prisoner under her watchful gaze. That's why I built the dome with Magellan, though her persistent bickering piercing my ears convinced me to let her pick the spot."

"We all need our own places at some point."

Sensing some irritability with the topic, I stepped close and pressed my hand to her chest, easing her back to the cool stony wall of the cave. Then I pressed my lips to hers. Her hands ran up my chest and slowly over my shoulder as she welcomed my tongue with the tip of her own. I flicked the top clasp on her robe open.

"Mmm," she moaned. "We shall have to try this lying down in my bed tonight. Something tells me it will be even more enticing absent the cold stone beneath my ass."

"We need to think about Roshan." I said. "I don't want her feeling left out. This can't be easy for her."

I realized after I'd spoken that it might not be the best time to bring up another woman, regardless of who it was. I chalked it up to my social shortcomings. But Priya smiled and her eyelids sat at a sleepy half-mast as she tilted her head back and gazed up at me.

Then her gaze flicked down as she fastened the clasp I'd undone. "Silly man."

"Hey, I like a little cleavage—or in your case, a lot of it. Feel free to hold it against me."

Boo.

"Perhaps you should loosen your bindings so I might see cleavage." Priya stroked the front of my pants with the tips of her fingers.

"That's not how cleavage works."

She slapped my chest. "You tease me, though you know I spend little time with others and get tangled in my words."

"You remind me of myself. Try not to take it personally."

"That makes me feel a little better."

Her smile and the subtle stroke of her hand had prepared me for a second round. There was something to be said for this new body of mine.

As she stared into my soul with those piercing blue eyes, she unclasped the top clasp with the flick of a finger and thumb. Then the second.

"If my *lord* desires cleavage..." Priya spread the robe open and pushed her boobs up. She tapped her top lip with her tongue. "Then he shall have the cleavage."

We found Zhara and Roshan where we'd left them. Roshan wore an undergarment, her robe hanging on a knot in the great tree. Again, I was reminded of my new body's rabid appetites as I peered at the crease in the swath covering the glutes of my mage's taut backside.

Man, I'm having the best day ever!

A blue glow emanated from Roshan's new staff as Zhara pressed a hand of splayed fingers against her back.

"Stats are nice, but you should master the Light without dependence upon your adornments."

Click bounced on her hind legs, leaping happily into the air as she snapped at fireflies. I was surprised to the see them at the height of the young afternoon.

"The Light must consume you as you open its rift into this world and let it flow. You are but a catalyst of its power, that which channels." She rubbed her palm in a circle, soothing Roshan as the staff glowed brighter.

My staff glowed brighter, too.

"A priestess of the Light commands her own affinity, allowing it to blossom with practice. It is the only school of magic where the slightest natural affinity may bloom to become stronger throughout one's life."

I was struck by the importance of Zhara's words. If I'd heard her right, the slightest affinity for Light magic could be grown. I'd heard of gaining spell power by casting, but increasing one's affinity? It meant Roshan's potential might have no ceiling.

Does Shadow magic have a cap? How many other schools of magic exist in Enora? I have much to discover, friends and neighbors.

"Yes, Roshan!" Zhara said. "I feel its charge as it flows through you!" The white glow surrounding my companion's golden skin darkened slightly, giving it an azure hue. Sweat beaded on her shoulders and chest. The Matron adopted a softer tone. "Good, now release the energy and settle your staff. Reserve your mana pool and practice only at night when near your hearth so that you can cast off your gear and practice without buffs."

"Thank you, Master Zhara," Roshan said. She turned and gave a gentle kiss to the Matron of the Wood's hand and then both cheeks. "You honor me."

"Your power will know no bounds, if you are true to the Light, Roshan. Now that I have granted you nature's grace, I expect your threesome's growth will be equally limitless."

Clicking rattled toward us, and Zhara peered down at my pet.

"Ah, yes, *foursome*. That's what I meant." Zhara smiled.

I thought my heart would stop.

Priya punched my shoulder and threw me a look.

Busted.

I smiled and threw an arm around her waist.

Roshan reached for her robe as Zhara turned her attention to me for the first time since Priya and I had returned. Her eyes glided up and down my body.

"I could sense your sex from here, Priya. So slow but powerful... and hungry."

Priya's scrunched her nose. "That seems wrong, somehow," she muttered. "But I'm glad you enjoyed it, I guess."

"I orgasmed twice. You will learn with time, my niece."

Priya stuck her bottom lip out. "I orgasmed."

Zhara tapped her chin. "But not *twice*."

"You're such a bitch, Aunt Zhara."

I was ready to move forward in my effort to reach Level 10, but we had one final matter to deal with. I reached into my bag. When I eyed the slot in my inventory, the smooth, cold object I desired was placed in my hand. I raised it to Zhara's eye level.

"This is the orb where Crohl imprisoned Priya. I was going to keep it in case it came in handy, but I don't know what to do with its occupant." I held it out to Zhara.

She gently wrapped her fingers around the globe. Realizing I'd never bothered, I inspected it.

Orb Prison
Occupied by Crohl
This orb is a foul creation of Darkness designed to hold and suppress the souls of those with an affinity for magic.

I noted absently how 'Darkness' was capitalized in the description like 'Light' and 'Shadow' often were. Grammatically speaking, it was wrong, but who was I to bitch?

"Hmmm." Zhara shook her head. "I can't see inside your magic bag, or I would've dispensed with this business first." She sighed. "Alas, even Solara's servant has limits. If you had it all along, why not give it over sooner?"

"I thought I might rub Caym's face in it someday."

Priya rolled her eyes.

"What an ego." Zhara's lips spread into a smile she cast in Priya's direction. "At least your life will never be boring."

Priya smirked.

Zhara shrugged. "If you face him—a decision I admire, actually—he will admit you to his dark den readily enough. He's certainly interested in Priya. But you will have to advance significantly before you take on that challenge." Her knuckles grew white as she clutched the orb. "Crohl's power throbs inside. He is of a lower level, but his master's influence remains. The orb must be Caym's. Here, let us deal with his minion presently."

She raised the globe over her head, squeezed her eyes shut, and a low hum filled my ears.

"An offering," Zhara said.

The massive tree behind her began to glow, first in a trickle, then in an outpouring of golden light, and the matron's lips vibrated slightly as blackish-purple smoke surrounded her arm and crept its way up to her hand, engulfing the globe. Tendrils of dark vapors swirled outward from the center and reached like snakes beyond the glass. Then a humanoid figure winked into existence.

Zhara shivered and I realized I'd just seen the power of Solara channeled through that massive tree.

Hunched over, with his hands stretched out before him like they'd been when Priya imprisoned Crohl, the black void replacing his eyes seemed to twitch in Zhara's direction.

Zhara smiled, and a white light filled her eye sockets as the tree's glow softened. She waved a hand. The dark caster's eyes cleared, revealing gray irises underneath.

Priya seemed to relax, though my chill from Crohl's proximity remained.

"Hello, demon," she said.

"I... I am but a mortal man. Not a demon."

"And yet you imprisoned my niece and further corrupted the underground race I banished years ago to toil in the Tomb of the Lost."

The dark man's head swiveled toward my companion. "Priya?"

Her expression perfectly revealed her vitriol for the shadow caster. The balding caster frowned, looked at each of us, and stepped toward the path.

"Be still, cretin." Zhara extended her other hand, then cast beams of light from her fingertips, penetrating and surrounding Crohl in a glow. He froze in place. I took a subtle step back.

"You..." he quivered despite his magical bindings, "are Zhara."

One side of the immortal's lips creased as she eyed Crohl like the cockroach he was.

Diverting his gaze, the dark caster's mouth gaped. He traced the sprawling oak behind her, as if noticing it for the first time.

Camouflage.

"That means this is the tree of—"

"Utter her name with thine dark lips, and I will immolate you where you stand, *demon spawn.*"

Now, that *sounded like game dialogue.*

Crohl pinched his lips together, sparing glances at me and Priya in turn, as if an ounce of sympathy might be had there.

"I never believed—"

Zhara's eyes flashed so brightly, I saw little black spots afterward. "Silence!"

Her voice boomed through the forest and echoed. Leaves rustled all around and birds took flight. Scampering sounds moved away on all sides, then the Dark Wood fell eerily still. I shot a wide-eyed glare at Priya, disoriented as the single spoken word reverberated inside my head as if rolling between Dolby channels on a loop.

Priya's disposition had turned, however. She peered up at the magic tree, running her gaze along its branches as one side of her face drew up into a smirk.

I tried to finger the emotion I was getting off her, then it came.

Boredom.

Though the man who'd imprisoned her stood at such close

quarters, my half-elf companion was so secure in the presence of her aunt and the tree that Priya's shoulders dropped with a sigh. Had she been a vain creature, I expected she'd have thrust her hand before her and checked for dirt under her fingernails.

Yet my knees trembled.

Hey, um, yeah, Zhara. Sorry about that 'fuck you' thing a bit ago.

I saw the flicker of a smile threaten Zhara's lips as she read my thought and sent one back.

Rest easy, Gemini. We are family, now.

Why was the prospect of being called family by this woman scary?

Zhara's words took on a softer resonance as lines threaded across her skin like the grooves in bark, but her flesh remained smooth and milky.

"Name your master so I might properly dispense justice upon thee, fool."

I suspected there was some tradition in the Light where the defendant was required to admit his crime by naming his boss. Especially since I'd just said his name a minute ago. That was new.

Crohl's eyes took on a distant look. "I serve Under-lord Caym, Master of The Burning Depths." His words were clipped, as if he struggled to speak.

Roshan scowled. "Filthy creature."

Zhara addressed me. "I know of these depths. Far in the northeast, beyond the Hinterlands of Seran. If you wish to face him some day, there should you go."

I nodded. "Yeah, he told us."

To Crohl she said, "How many minions like you does he employ to dig these tunnels and expand his influence?"

"I hold no knowledge of these things, great matron."

Yeah, you'd better show some respect, with your punk ass.

Zhara didn't smile at my thought, this time.

"Is he mining entropy crystals? Is that why he sought my family?"

Entropy Crystals?

"Yes, matron. His army grows."

"Since you have named your conspiring master, it is with these witnesses that I find you in contempt of nature and the will of our goddess, dark one. Your foul efforts to empower Shadow and bring imbalance to the world, and your wrongful imprisonment of my beloved Priya, are heinous crimes. Were you a demon instead of a weak-willed human and peasant of mind, I would open the earth beneath you and let it envelop you for all eternity." She sighed and peered at the tree canopy overhead. "But since I am servant to Solara's Light and revenge is the remedy of Hokrahm, I instead banish your memories."

Zhara waved her hand in an anticlimactic gesture. The lines vanished from her skin, and she set her hands on her hips.

Crohl's dazed look faded as he focused on his surroundings. He craned his neck to face in the branches above, then glanced at Priya and I, in turn.

"Hello. Who are you? What glorious place is this, that such lovely creatures inhabit it?"

Priya scoffed.

Zhara winked at me.

The Matron of the Wood tipped her chin up. "Hello, traveler. I fear you have become lost."

I smirked at the double-meaning.

"You will discover your path to the south." She pointed

in the direction from which Priya and I had come. "I wish you on your way."

Crohl nodded. "Thank you, m'lady." He nodded at Priya as he stepped onto the inkling of a trail and peered back. "Pardon, ma'am. Do you know my name?"

Priya sneered at him and nodded. "Yes, m'lord. Your name is Shit."

I pressed my lips tight and shot Roshan a glance. She seethed at the former minion.

Crohl held up a finger. "Ah! Yes! That must be it." He bowed slightly. "Thank you, good lady." I almost felt sorry for the former dark caster as he set off to the south without so much as a look back, his bouncy pacing indicating he lacked a care in the world. When he disappeared around a bend, I peered at Priya.

"Now he's going to tell people his name is Shit. You're hilarious." I chuckled.

Zhara shook her head. "He will not survive long enough to tell anyone his name. Assuming he prevails against the creepers and porcupunks, there is a desert a day's travel in that direction filled with higher-level creatures who will certainly be his undoing."

My jaw dropped. "What happened to all that heady stuff about being a servant of the Light? I thought you weren't going to kill him."

Roshan's chin dropped. "You question that above your station!"

I threw my hands up in a defensive gesture. "Damn, girl. Sorry!"

Zhara pressed a hand of splayed fingers against her chest. "It is not I who will kill him." She shrugged, and that was that.

The matron tossed the empty glass orb to Priya. "Perhaps with your affinity for Shadow Magic, you will find a use for this poison sphere someday, my dear." She clapped her hands together as if to slap off dust. "It does not belong so close to a source of great light. Just be responsible with it."

It was like she was telling her kid not to play with matches.

I peered in the direction Crohl had gone. "Man, I wouldn't want to piss you off."

Zhara smiled, and her familiar projection of warmth passed through my body. A glow surrounded me.

"You are wise beyond your years, my sweet boy."

Roshan interjected. "Gemini?" Her eyes focused on my bag, then back at me. "The skeleton's medallion?"

"Oh!" I barked. "Right." I withdrew the medallion and held it out to Zhara.

One side of her mouth rose in a sneer as she analyzed the black stone at the medallion's center. "A wart on The Light if ever I've seen one."

She dropped it on the ground and clapped her hands again. The soil spilt revealing an orange glow beneath and the medallion jingled a final protest as it slipped into the ground.

Roshan smiled and threw me a curt nod. I wondered how much money was just swallowed by the dirt.

Zhara turned her attention back to Priya. "I must recharge, now, my beloved niece." She grasped Priya's hands and squeezed. Then she pressed her hand to her niece's torso and her fingertips glowed. A halo spread from there and surrounded my newest companion before fading.

This woman was full of the glows.

Priya smiled.

"Be forever happy and contented in the Light," Zhara said.

"Forever happy and contented," Priya replied.

Roshan tilted her head to the side. "Forever happy and contented. I like this."

Priya shrugged. "I'm not a Light caster, but it's a family thing. Etiquette and all that."

"I will adopt this, as your new sister."

Priya shook her head. "I don't think I can go on calling you sister. I have plans of a less-innocent nature for you."

Zhara stepped toward her tree and whispered, with her arms spread wide, in the way I'd seen before. This time, I didn't peek. The goddess melded into the grasp of her home. As she did, my mind returned to my wonderings as to her motives.

It might be true that she hadn't known her niece was captive. However, something was rubbing me wrong—and in a big way.

When Zhara wrapped her finger vine around my neck, she could've just strangled me. Sure, she gave it a good tight grip, but something about how easily she'd released me at Priya's beckoning struck me as disingenuous.

Theater.

Priya had said she didn't remember her parents, who'd moved to a distant city. Apparently, they'd left, then Priya's mind had been wiped by a shadow caster. Then she'd been captured again. Something was off. The story sounded campy. Where were all these shadow casters coming from?

The dude on the wall, man. The demon underlord, Caym.

A new prompt popped up in my HUD.

You have been offered a scenario quest!

Not On The Up-And-Up

*Your pondering about Zhara's true motives could bear fruit.
Learn the true nature of Zhara and her relationship with
Priya Skyy.
Level: N/A
XP: Commensurate with the level at time of completion
A blessing giving you one full level, after XP is awarded
Enora is a place of intrigue. Uncover its mysteries!*

What. In. The. Utter. Fuck?

I peered over at Priya's shorter form as she stared at the tree her aunt merged with. Now that I'd gotten a quest offer, I had little doubt something was off. A story was beginning.

I accepted the quest.

Pacing over to Roshan, I wrapped an arm around her waist. "By my math, you need only level once more so I can spend points on you, and we can bond in the same way as Priya and me."

Roshan nodded. "I wish nothing more, my Gemini. You offer me such a wonderful gift. I am sorry I doubted you. Thank you."

I smacked her firmly on the ass, causing her to jump. "Good! Now! I was thinking it might be a good idea to get out of these forsaken woods." I winked at Priya. "No offense."

"Why would we leave the Wood now? Many creatures roam here that could help you with your final level."

"With three of us and low-level creatures, each engagement would reward less XP. There are likely men searching for Roshan. I think we should go to Broomhill—"

"Brumhill," Priya said, chuckling.

"Right. That's what I said. *Brumhill.*" I winked at her.

"I should go there and seek out quests to complete the journey to 10. If I can find provisioning quests or something of a less violent nature, all-the-better. I'm close enough now, it's practical."

I needed less than half a level to hit the promised land! I finally felt like I was going to make it.

Roshan nodded. "That is smart thinking, Gemini. This sets my mind at ease, for I have worried ever since Zhara confirmed your story. I'm unworthy of the gift you offer."

I waved a hand. "You're fucking worthy, trust me." I was getting tired of all this proper talk. Maybe in society we'd have to use it, but with my companions? Nah. We were going to keep shit real.

I brought up my map. "If we follow the trail in that direction, we should come out of the wood in less than an hour. Brumhill is close, right Priya?"

Priya threw me that ever-endearing, enthusiastic smile I was coming to love and nodded.

"Then we're off."

36

Roshan's robe brushed my leather pants. If she walked any closer, we'd trip over each other. After what I guessed was an hour, we reached a fork in the trail. Priya clapped her hands with enthusiasm and pointed.

"This is the edge of the woods. Finally, we will have sunlight. Brumhill is just over a hill beyond the break in those trees."

An adrenal surge coursed through me as my eyes fell on the sunny grass just beyond the opening at the end of the trail. I was finally going to see a town in this world. Finally going to meet other people. The idea of escaping this persistent canopy of green spurned me forward. Gripping Roshan's hand tightly, I grinned at her.

I spied the movement in the trees behind her a split second too late.

Though I shoved Roshan out of the way and ripped out a dagger to block the incoming blow, the fighter had moved silently, gotten too close, and was fully focused when he struck with his sword. The blade glanced off mine and cut a swath through my forearm. I recoiled as pain raked the nerves, and the dagger rattled to the ground. Blood poured from the gash as the thief came around with another swing, but I ducked, straightened, and planted my boot in his gut.

Though the pain raged in my arm, my mental determination took over.

As he reeled backward and gained his footing, another mercenary launched from the bushes and sped toward Priya.

"Click!" I barked. "Attack!"

Click launched into action, cutting off the second man's path and sinking her teeth into his calf.

"Ahh!" He screamed as he looked down, seeking the source of his pain. Click had already circled behind him, though, and was digging her claws into his flesh as she scurried up his back. "Yeah, girl! Kill that filthy turd!"

The first thief steadied himself and stared at me as he huffed and puffed. "Should've never taken what belonged to the governor, boy. Now, you gotta pay."

"Less talk, more dying," I replied, unsheathing my other blade.

He charged, raising his sword high above him, preparing to slice down into the top of my head. The man tripped and flailed forward a few feet short of me. I glanced down to find Roshan with one leg raised into the air. Knowing the man couldn't attack the prize his patron desired, he'd bypassed her to take out what he perceived as the real threat... me. So, she'd tripped him.

Roshan grinned. "Get your level!"

I wasn't about to be distracted again. I reared the dagger with little fanfare. I wasn't here to impress anyone, I was here to live! Grinding my teeth and jumping forward, I slammed the razor-sharp blade into the back of my assailant's neck and twisted. His body convulsed before he even hit the ground.

One down.

I spun and launched myself at the other man.

Click bobbed and weaved on the man's back as he reached over his shoulder, trying to grasp her head.

I couldn't fade into stealth while in combat, but Click allowed me the distraction I needed. Circling around the thief, I sent a mental command for my pet to disengage and give me a clean opening, Click dropped to the earth and sped over to Priya, taking up a defensive position as I aimed my dagger.

I slammed it into the mercenary's back, burying it to the hilt. Second kill in a minute.

Roshan ran over to take up position with my other companions, preparing to defend each other.

Roshan casts **Flash Heal.**

+52 HP

The flesh in my arm stitched together.

As the man shuttered in his final death throes, bright light engulfed Roshan, and I pumped my fist at the realization that she'd just reached Level 10.

"Yes!"

I stood straight and analyzed my interface.

I was still four percent short of my next level. I cursed. Looking through the interface, expecting to see Roshan's excited smile, I found a heart-stopping surprise. Her mouth gaped. Priya jutted a finger toward me.

"Behind you!"

A white-hot explosion of pain tore through my back and I crumbled to one knee.

Critical Hit!
-64 HP
Mortal Wound!
-103 HP
63 HP Remaining

Reaching behind me, trying to find the projectile lodged there, I fell onto my face. My wind left me, and I blew up a puff of dirt. Sensation vanished from my legs

-13 HP (bleed)
47 HP Remaining
You are paralyzed.

Click growled menacingly, a roll of clicks escaping her throat. Priya held her off the ground by her flesh hairs. The animal struggled in her grasp, flailing wildly in an effort to find purchase and charge my attacker.

I nodded at Priya.

Maybe she would be spared, return to the woods. She hadn't touched a single enemy. My vision blurred. Roshan glared beyond me. Her full cheeks were stretched in a grimace.

As my energy seeped from my open veins and I peered at these women of my new world, all I wanted was for them to go on, to survive. Wasn't a shitty life in servitude still a life? My heart ached with the thought as I knew it wasn't true.

-12 HP
35 HP Remaining

I'd come so close. I should have known my new life was too perfect. Roshan raised her staff and its smooth wood began to glow.

"No, dear," a grunting voice said.

Slow footsteps crushed rocks into the dirt as a pair of worn boots came into view. A shadow fell over me. One boot rose and shoved my shoulder so I lay on my side. Electric shocks of hell ripped through my back. I winced. Standing over me was a curly-bearded figure with matching red hair, holding a crossbow.

The boss.

He leveled his finger on Roshan. "You cast, and that pretty little blonde wench is next. You let him go, and I'll let her go. You know me well enough by now, Roshan. I do what I say."

Priya wasn't yet a fighter, and Roshan didn't have the damage needed to take him down, even with Click. I turned my eyes toward her.

"No," I grunted. "Hold, Roshan. Hold."

"You're a sneaky one, boy." He peered around at the corpses. "Seems you killed everybody I had left." He knelt down, resting one arm on a bent knee so his hand dangled loosely at the wrist. Pointing his crossbow in my party's general direction, he said, "That one over there is bought and paid for. You messed with a powerful man when you tried to snatch her from me. He patted my shoulder. "But hey, count yourself lucky. If his men'd caught ya, you'd suffer for much longer. I'm a nice guy compared to their lot." He reached out and shoved me onto my back, forcing the bolt deeper as I rolled onto it.

-21 HP

16 HP Remaining

-2 HP (bleed)

14 HP Remaining

My field of vision blinked furiously orange.

"Guess you did me a favor. I can keep the reward for myself."

With a grunt, he straddled me, set his hands upon my chest and smiled up at my group. Then he shoved my chest down and the bolt pierced through from the back. Blood erupted onto my leather plate as the bolt pierced clean through.

-10 HP

4 HP Remaining

-2 HP (bleed)

2 HP Remaining

I eyed the sharp, bloody tip as the world dimmed. Cold washed over me and I shivered violently as the darkness closed in from my periphery, until it was like standing at the end of a long tunnel, only a sliver of light between me and oblivion. My final thought was of the lost potential of a life with those I left behind.

The thief stepped over me, blocking out the sunlight as my last breath came with a violent hitch in my chest.

-2 HP

You have died.

37

You have died.
You did not reach Level 10.
Nice try, adventurer! Since you did not reach level ten, you will have to create a new character and try again. You have two minutes <error:bef00e1d4xt> Hard Core mode, your character will be <Error:7a14dp> if you are not res<error:031df8of>
You may return to the character creation screen by clicking <button:null>

38

Light erupted into the world, starting with a pinprick centered in a black void and exploding outward, widening the tunnel of death into a world awash in green and filled with blurry sunshine. My body levitated into the air. The wind ruffled my clothes, warming my skin as I rose higher. My eyes fell to the silver-tipped bolt as it reversed itself and disappeared into my chest. Though I sensed its passing through my body until it ejected out my back, I experienced no pain, only a glowing warmth. A beam of light shot into the air through the hole where the bolt had lodged.

The beam narrowed as my body turned upright in mid-air, then it extinguished itself as the wound closed and I settled gently on my feet.

I blinked. Simultaneously washed in a warming glow and stunned in disbelief, I found Priya clutching Click to her bosom wearing an expression of astonishment as the wind encircling me sang a warbling tone. Tears streamed down the angular features of her elven face. Scanning my surroundings, I located Roshan, standing with her arms in the air just a few feet away. The sleeves and lower half of her robe flailed in the ethereal wind that touched only the two of us. Her hair streamed behind her as her arms formed a V overhead. Bright azure light haloed her beautiful form, painting a portrait I'd never forget.

The wind dissipated, the glow dimmed, and my savior ran to me. Priya set Click down, and I was soon enveloped by embracing arms—even Click clambered onto my shoulders and wrapped herself heavily around my neck.

My interface was filled with alerts, and I couldn't refuse the temptation.

Roshan has reached Level 10!
Since Roshan has reached Level 10, she will now receive four attribute points per level.
Roshan has four available attribute points.
Roshan has learned a new spell:

Raise

Level 10
Raise a KO'd ally, swiping them from the jaws of death
Mana cost: 100
Cooldown: N/A

"Holy shit, Roshan. You saved me."

"I do not accept that." She planted a kiss on my cheek. "I saved no one."

"What are you talking about? I see the spell in my interface." My eyes flickered across my combat logs. "It's right here. It says, 'Roshan' casts Raise on you.'"

"Forget your interface, noob. I have a life debt and was called to serve. Some cultures might think the debt could be erased were I to do such a thing."

"Oh, right. I just got up on my own. Sure. Whatever.

But isn't our bond stronger than a life debt? Do you need an obligation to justify your life with us?"

Roshan pulled back, but Priya clutched harder and harder, her shoulders rising and falling as she breathed against my neck. She planted tiny kisses, her mutterings indecipherable.

Roshan swiped tears from her face and nodded. "Yes. It is as you say. Our bond surpasses any debt. Therefore," she raised her nose in the air and her chin jutted out, "I saved you from the jaws of death, and you will give me great pleasure in return, noob."

"Ha! That sounds like a fair trade."

"Besides, the credit is not mine alone. Our new companion put our enemy to sleep as he accosted me. Were it not for our elven friend, I might not have remembered my *knife* in time." Her tone dropped lower as she spoke the word, and I realized instantly it was because she'd violated the tenants of her order. She shook her head subtly, perhaps to clear it. "The elf bought me precious seconds."

I squeezed Priya tighter. "Thank you, Priya. You're amazing."

Priya nodded against my neck but didn't speak.

"Now," Roshan stepped back, pivoted, twirled her staff in a blurry motion as if she were a Kung Fu master, then pointed with one end. "Finish your work."

I followed the end of her staff, to find a quivering figure just off the side of the trail, laying in the thick grass and near a bush with purple berries. A curly mop of reddish hair covered his face.

Trembling wildly, the boss peered up at us between curly strands with hatred burning in a bloodshot eye. Crimson trickled across his shoulder and down the front of his neck as he lay prone in almost exactly the same position

I had moments before. The knife handle jutted from his neck as his shoulder seized beneath it.

My jaw unhinged, and I flashed Roshan an expression of shock, but the Light priestess had set her hands upon Priya's shoulders pulled her away.

Leaving Click wrapped around my shoulder, I strode over to the dying man.

When I stood over him, elation surged through me. I smiled at his torment.

Without turning I addressed her. "I thought you said a Light priestess didn't use edged weapons?"

She huffed, bringing out my smile. "Well, who makes these stupid rules anyway, noob? Am I supposed to stand there and let him kill everyone I love? No! I don't think so." She lowered her tone and grumbled. "Men! Always so critical! Always with their superiority! Always right! Gah!" Her feet crunched rocks as she approached. She slapped my ass, causing me to jump. "Perhaps you can stop showing off and twist that knife. We have places to be."

"Aren't you some kind of holy woman? You don't think it's wrong to finish off a defenseless man?" I was enjoying this moment entirely too much, and this man would damn well suffer for the long torment he'd put my Roshan through.

Roshan glared at me as if I was stupid.

I peered down at my enemy.

"Governor's gonna kill you, boy." His voice quivered violently. "He's gonna slit that animal's throat, then he's gonna give you a public hanging and rip your bowels out in front of those women. Then he's gonna rape 'em both and give the blonde to his barracks."

"Shame you won't be there to see him try."

Then a thought occurred to me. I clapped my hand over his mouth and peered over my shoulder at Roshan.

"Heal him."

Her eyes flared and her chin dropped. "What? Why would I do that?"

"Because it's against your rules to use a blade. This bastard will fill enough of your memories without adding this to it. So, you heal him, and undo the damage."

Roshan considered me for a long moment, then a smile that seemed totally out of place considering the situation spread across her face. She shook her head.

"You are a kind soul, Gemini, but Solara did not see fit to strike me with lightning and though Master Mitwah's order forbade the use of blades, I believe I served the goddess in cutting into this evil man's flesh. You are my order now and, while I have no plans to use blades in the future, I have no need to heal this evil man." Again, she pointed with her staff. "End his suffering and let us leave this place."

"You sure?"

She nodded.

Shrugging, I grasped the knife, twisted, then ripped it down and across his chest, Corleone style.

Light flashed. Two digits appeared in my HUD and shot off into the forest. A fresh rush of ethereal wind passed over me, and the one indicator I would not have ignored in a million years popped up on my right.

You have reached Level 10!
+1 Dexterity
+1 Constitution
You have two unspent attribute points.

Congratulations! *You have survived the Hard Core levels!*

You have now earned the right to journey anywhere in the world of Enora

You may now bind your soul to locations such as inns, shops, or foundations.

Upon death, your soul will be returned to your binding place, along with any soul-bound items.

Your soul-bound companions will now resurrect at your selected binding places when they fall in battle.

The Player Manual Tab is now available in your interface.

Welcome to Enora, adventurer! Your journey has just begun.

39

I'd had to leave Click outside because the proprietor of the Brumhill Inn didn't allow pets. She whined when I mentioned the option to dismiss her, so I did a little research. Click had both Pet tab and Companion tab panes. I focused on the Companion tab and brought up a few tooltips. I found the Free Roam checkbox. Designed for scouting, Free Roam allowed my porcupunk to leave my immediate area.

It disturbed me how my human companions had this same checkbox.

After verifying I didn't have to be near her to dismiss and summon her, I'd allowed her to return to the nearby forest she'd once called home. It might be a while before she saw the Dark Wood again because I sure as shit had no intention of returning any time soon.

We used some of Crohl's silver to have dinner in a small place operated by a woman called Mags. It was a run-down joint with just two tables with four chairs each, but Mags was quite the cook, and we left with full bellies.

Though I'd considered exploring the town for a bit, Roshan looked beat. The events of the last four days had taken their toll and, when the exhilaration of reaching my first landmark had passed, I found myself worn down and ready to sleep for two days. Roshan had readily agreed with that plan. We decided to look at her attributes the next morning so we could cement our bond and prepare for the adventure ahead.

Though Priya only needed sleep every seventy-two hours, she was the most excited of all to take to our bed and snooze. That woman loved her some sleep!

The room wasn't much as far as luxury went and lacked the fireplace I'd envisioned in my fantasies, but who needed it? What the bed lacked in comfort, was more than balanced by my company.

As I lay on my back, I found myself unable to sleep despite the day's adventure. Two arms lay across my chest, one from each side, and two legs crossed over mine in the same manner. Priya had just the tiniest trickle of a snore going. Her nose whistled. It was adorable.

Though she came to me with the kinds of caresses one couldn't mistake for simple affection, Roshan's case of the yawns and watery eyes convinced us she should sleep. It'd been an eventful day, and I thought I could do better than the Brumhill Inn for our first encounter. She hadn't wanted to disappoint me because of her promise of lovemaking when I reached Level 10 and we left the forest.

Roshan was worth the best and, though I'd settled for a cave with Priya at her insistence, I felt sure I wasn't being preferential by wanting Roshan's first time to be perfect. Priya was from the Dark Wood, and we'd been ravenous for each other. That was okay.

In a testimony to her generous spirit, my mage suggested Priya and I should celebrate together as her eyelids drooped and fluttered.

"Since our beloved requires so little sleep," Roshan had teased. Then she turned to face the wall.

We knew there was time, now. As much as we needed. Why rush it? Didn't drawing it out make it better anyway?

A second round of sex with Priya was slow and gentle, each stroke methodical, each sensation lingeringly teased out. We plucked each other with our lips, employed the liberal uses of our fingertips and tongues to tease and tantalize, then erupted quietly together as Roshan snoozed. It was like we'd been together forever and simultaneously like the first time.

Now that I lay awake and a couple hours had passed since Priya took to snoozing, I peered out the window at a huge moon and its twin satellite in the distance. I didn't know what was next for us, but I knew I was ready to face this world, take it by the balls, level up, and build my influence. Images of glory, golden flashes revealing high level advancement, and treasure beyond most peoples' grasps brought an easy grin to my face as I slipped away.

A loud bang jerked me out of my half-slumber, and I shot up in the bed. The door warbled on its hinges as two men in chain mail burst into the room. Rushing to the bed, one of them ripped back the fur and peered at our naked bodies. He pointed a finger toward Roshan.

"That's her! Take her!"

"No!" I barked, grappling with the man. His partner came around, grabbed me by the back of my hair, then growled down into my face. "The governor paid rightly for that one, there. We bring a message for people who defy him!"

A hard thud to my head sent me teetering from the bed and flailing into the wall. I got to my knees, though the world spun around me. As it steadied, my eyes fell on Priya, who stood with the arms of one invader wrapped around her shoulder.

He loomed behind her, clutching a naked breast in his rough grasp. "Well, this is a nice one!" He growled through his sneer.

Brazel Snead
Level 12 Human
Fighter

Priya's piercing blue eyes were sapphires reflected the pale moonlight.

He growled into her ear. "You like trouble, honey?" Wrapping his fist around her neck, he leveled a blade across her throat.

I stared at the hand clutching the half-elf's breast, and hatred consumed me. I didn't think I could despise someone more than that, but he quickly proved me wrong.

Running his hand across Priya's neck, he opened a bloody slit from ear-to-ear.

"No!" Roshan screamed.

Priya gurgled, and blood spewed from between her lips. The flesh separated behind the trail of the blade. Clutching her hand around her neck, she glared at me in terror as rivers of blood poured through her fingers and down the backs of her hands.

"Grahg..." A new river of Crimson spat between her lips and trailed down her chin in pulsing rivers.

I struggled to my feet, but another hard crack on the head brought me down. Priya's body thumped to the floor and from under the bed I watched in horror as her eyes jiggled in their sockets and her body rattled as she bled out.

The other man restrained Roshan, an arm around her waist.

"Go on, then," he said. "Get up, hero. Come save your last woman."

I crawled to my feet with my heart aching for revenge, naked as a jailbird, but ready to rip them apart with my bare hands. Balance wouldn't come and I fell into the wall. My knees buckled, but I strained to stay upright.

"Aw, doesn't look like he's ready to fight, there," Snead said.

I spotted the man who'd killed Priya standing on the bed with his sword pointed at the side of my neck. A thumping sound confused me until I realized one of Priya's feet fluttered violently in the corner. Her body was mercifully obstructed by the bed as she lay dying on the floor.

The man restraining Roshan licked her cheek. "Tasty ones, these women of the East!" His sneer revealed all his yellowed teeth. "C'mon, hero. Try to take 'er from me."

Willem Shunt
Level 13 Human
Fighter

"I'm going to kill the both of you for this."

"That would be a neat trick." The one binding Roshan cocked his head at his companion.

The bearded bastard on the bed raised his sword and slid its point between my neck and shoulder blade. The sound of bones and cartilage snapping was the last I heard as the world's light switch flicked off .

40

"Ahhh!" I burst into existence clutching the wound in my neck as the sudden sunlight caused my eyes to flutter in their defense. But the wound was gone, the pain in my neck a ghost of memory echoing with each harsh thump in my temples.

Chills coursed through my body and across my skin, exacerbated by the wind. My flesh broke out in large goose-bumps as I lay quivering on dark soil.

"Too real," I muttered. "Too real."

My chest rose and fell like a newborn who'd never sucked air. No matter how I focused, I couldn't calm down. My heart was like a foreign body, fighting to escape through a narrow, beating throat.

Raising my arm in a salute to block bright rays, I rolled onto my back. Before me, rows of high corn dotted fields of rich brown soil. Dark-skinned people with wide-brimmed straw hats stared back at me from amidst the towering vegetables. The scents of earth and grass gave me déjà vu. I'd woken here before. Text lined the bottom-center of my HUD

> *You have died.*
> *Since you are above Level 10, you suffer an XP Penalty:*
> *All XP earned since leveling lost!*
> *Weakness Debuff: You inflict 20% less damage for five*
> *minutes.*
> *XP: 0/9000*
> *Players suffer a re-spawn delay when they die.*
> *Re-spawn delay: 4 hours.*
> *Note: Your bound companions suffer this delay only if*
> *you die.*

A shadow blocked the sun as a figure leaned over me. I lowered my arm, thankful for the relief. Blinking away the blur obstructing the facial features of the hovering form, I found a familiar figure with silver hair pulled tightly back into a bun and heavy wrinkles surrounding her eyes. Chills coursed up my neck and I shivered violently again.

"Resurrection sickness," Lucera said. "Rest easy, and it will pass."

My voice quivered as I drew my shoulders in. "Rest easy. That's *easy* for you to say."

Lucera's lips creased into a humorless smile.

A sudden memory erupted, and I relived the fresh hell of a sword sliding into my neck. The whole, sunny world seemed to blink. Blackness, and then Lucera again, standing over me. I clutched my shoulder and yelled as the nerves screamed in revolt.

"What the hell is that?" I asked.

"You will have to describe it for me, Gemini. Our link has been broken."

So, she was telling the truth. The A.I. isn't in my head, anymore.

"It was like I just relived my death for a second there. I

felt the pain again, saw the moment my spine..." I shivered violently and clutched my shoulders.

"Death doesn't come without repercussions, Gemini. Now that you have survived the Dark Levels, you have much to learn about Enora. Never before have you experienced a game world such as this. Each time you perish, your resurrection sickness period will grow longer, up to a maximum of one week. Since you have reached Level 10, your player manual is now available and relevant information can be found within its pages."

"I should've known," I said. "Nothing is easy in this fucking place. You can tell Enora to bite me."

Lucera's back straightened, and she faltered a step away.

The sun exploded across my eyes again, delivering a piercing sensation of migraine, and I raised my arm to shade them.

Lucera held one hand in front of her, two crooked fingers extended and pressed tightly together as they quivered in the air above me. Waving them across my form, she lowered her hand.

The chill vanished. My shaking ceased. I peered up at her. "Thank you."

"Stand." She took another step back. The tone in her voice was one I hadn't heard when we'd last met. It quivered with a harshness I'd never have expected.

"Sorry, did I—"

"Stand!"

The single syllable exploded in my ears, and I thought my eardrums would shatter. Practically jumping to my feet, I slapped my hands to the sides of my head as the voice warbled and passed from ear to ear in a harsh, resounding echo.

Lucera stepped forward and raised her hand again. All the muscles in my body tensed, then locked up like stone. I stopped breathing and found the only functioning parts of my physical form were my eyes. The thumping of my heart ceased as she glared at me. Black slid down from the tops of Lucera's eyes like contact lenses sliding into place.

"Now that I have your attention, heed my words." She leveled a crooked finger. "You come from a place where gods rule only in minds of those who worship them. Earth is the domain of wicked people who live to serve their own self-interests. We have seen this in our extensive research and find humankind to be disinterested in higher purposes.

"I had such hope for you, Gemini Fowler, as I watched you evolve over the past three days. When I heard your thoughts about having true feelings for the companions who pledged their lives to you, it seemed you did not take for granted the gifts I have bestowed."

Had I been able to speak, I might have interrupted in my defense. I did care about Roshan, about Priya, and even my pet, but my mouth was sealed shut and my mind had no control over my body.

"I was intrigued when Nokuro Takemoto offered me a human mind to come and live among the varied bloodlines of the people who evolved from my creations. In spite of his previous failures, I kept an open mind at the prospect when he assured me he would find someone with a true heart, someone worthy of the gift of life in such a wondrous world as mine. Someone who could right what he wronged."

Holy shit, that's Enora. I'm not hearing Lucera anymore.

I realized I might have chills if it weren't that my body was in a state of stasis.

"This is not your earth, Gemini Fowler. The beings here worship a goddess called Solara and, as you suspected, she and I are one and the same. Whereas you doubted the existence of God in your world, you may rest assured that the worship of Enora is not without merit.

"This is my world, and you have been given the gift of living in it. You shall never return to your old life. You will never log out of Enora. When I accepted Nokuro's solution to our little *problem*, I did so with the understanding that, the moment you crossed the threshold, you would become one of mine."

Enora/Lucera stepped forward and waved two fingers so I doubled over and our eyes were inches apart. "A day ago, you considered the prospect of living an honorable life. This pleased me, and I found myself surprised at how well Nokuro Takemoto had chosen his savior.

His savior?

"I have attuned myself to your thoughts for our purposes here, and I hear your question. Yes, Gemini Fowler, his savior. While Nokuro saved you from certain death, it is also you who stand capable to return the favor. I am a kind goddess who rewards those who serve me—both directly and indirectly." She tapped my temple, but I didn't feel it. "But my wrath is final.

"Your path so far has proven you're a being of potential. Your tendency toward survival was exactly as Nokuro and I expected. Though I developed a storyline in real-time for you and granted you the free will not to follow it, you chose the correct path and heeded Lucera's advice, drawing companions to yourself and ensuring your survival, albeit just barely."

She waved her hand and my chest lurched back into action. Sensation crawled across my flesh anew as the breeze blew through my hair.

"You have honored your kind by your actions in this

world, Gemini Fowler, but you dishonor me with your harsh words in light of the gifts I have given you. Going forward, you will continue to have free will because I deem it shall be so. You will make your own choices and decide which opportunities you will accept and which you will decline. But there is darkness in my world that goes far beyond what you have seen, Gemini, and it has been my hope that you would serve the Light so that my people might never again suffer as they have."

My heart thundered. Blood roared in my ears as I absorbed her words. A million questions flooded my mind, but I knew this would be the stupidest time in my life to open my mouth and utter more than the sound of breath.

"Things are not always as they seem in Enora, adventurer. Your instincts have proven effective, and you will undoubtedly unlock the secrets of this world, face off against its evils, and serve faithfully with those who find you worthy." She held up a finger. "Take not their presences for granted."

"I won't, Enora." I bowed my head slightly. "I apologize for my—"

"Keep your apologies, boy. I have wasted enough time here. Listen to Lucera, for after this day, you will never see her again. Enora is your life now, and you will forge your own path. There are but two. The Light and The Darkness. Solara and Hokrahm. Both would welcome you into their folds. Choose wisely, for your decisions will determine if this world exists for other players to enjoy."

I pressed my lips together. Enora raised Lucera's eyebrow, almost as if daring me to speak. When she saw I wouldn't, she placed a firm hand on my shoulder.

"The last time I allowed a human into my world, Hokrahm tempted him, resulting in the thriving of a creature of utter darkness who brought blight and pain to Solara's faithful. I hold high hopes you will not follow in his footsteps. I believe you will not seek only riches and power that serve yourself. You passed the first test because my beloved Roshan saved you. Now, you must go and save her or find a replacement. The choice is yours."

"I will save Roshan," I said.

"Even washed in darkness, my world is pure, Gemini. It has naturally progressed to its current state. I will not interfere and erase its purity by stomping out those who act in Hokrahm's name. But the creatures of this world will sense that you are different. Their rich traditions and histories will present opportunities as well as challenges. How you choose to handle them will decide the fates of many."

No pressure or anything.

"Nokuro Takemoto believed that bringing another human player here might balance the corruption and make Enora the kind of place millions of players could enjoy. If given his way, he would probably have wiped out many of my people, created static quests that would threaten the evolution of the world, and allowed players into the game."

"But you weren't having it."

To my utter surprise, she smiled, but her words didn't match the expression. "Soon you will see how corruption, greed, tyranny, and blights like slavery and servitude have spoiled my soil. You cannot avoid it. If you can stand against these evils, perhaps Nokuro Takemoto will see his dreams fulfilled.

"Decipher and differentiate between gifts from Solara and the curses of Hokrahm, and perhaps you will persevere, Gemini Fowler."

The black in her eyes slid away and my brain was instantly alight with questions. There was another crossing?

Someone else came before me and corrupted the world? Was I understanding her? I wondered if the purge, when they erased the other players, had something to do with that.

Translucent ripples appeared in the air next to me. Stepping away as wind swirled around me, I stared into them as the outline of a huddled form appeared. The lines filled to form the ghostly image of a short woman with curly blonde hair. A thatch hut beyond was shrouded as the humanoid form solidified, slowly transitioning from a transparent spirit to a breathing life.

The flesh and blood being with whom I'd shared a bed last night.

She wore a loose homespun shirt. Similar shorts clung to her skin.

Starting clothes. Weird.

"Priya."

Throwing my arms around her to catch her before she could fall, I pulled her toward me and held her on her feet. She shivered despite the humid air and, as her eyes blinked open and set on mine, tears sprang forth. Her hand shot to her throat and she gasped, heaving breaths. My mind's eye conjured the memory of that smooth skin peeling apart and her crimson life force jutting from her arteries and spilling down her chest. I'd never forget the horror in her eyes.

Clutching her shoulders, I pulled her close. "You're okay. You're alive and well."

Her fingertips traced the place on her neck where her skin had been divided. "They slashed my throat. As if I equaled not a copper in the world."

Grasping her hand, I curled it into a fist and kissed her knuckles. "I'm with you."

Priya fell against me, her arms circumnavigating my waist and squeezing desperately, her strength apparent as it clutched me tightly. I kissed the top of her head as her tears flowed against my chest. She shivered violently.

My shoulders became heavy as an emotional aching nipped at my heart. I would've passed it off as empathy, of which I'd had plenty for what she was going through because I'd just experienced it. But there was something else, something deeper. A crucial kind of pain that wrenched my gut.

I spoke in a soothing tone trying to push the feeling away and turning my attention to hers. "It's a sickness that comes with resurrecting. Just stand right here with me. It'll pass."

Patting her back, I peered around at the attentive crowd of farmers.

Priya sniffled. "They took Roshan."

If it hadn't been for Priya's appearance, I might have been losing my shit at that moment—babbling incoherently, screaming my lungs out at having lost Roshan. But the need to support her displaced my own emotions, even as my skin crept and crawled over the revelation of Enora's words.

And this strange tugging at my intestines. What the hell?
"Gemini."

My head swiveled to find the familiar, short figure who'd first greeted me upon entering this world.

"Welcome back, Lucera."

She nodded, a gentle smile spreading her lips.

Priya continued to shiver violently in my arms, the occasional, harsh twitch mixed into the experience. "Why are we here?"

Lucera answered her query. "You did not bind yourself to the inn. Gemini did not read the manual upon reaching Level 10." She turned her eyes on me. "If you had, you'd have seen a special gem rests in your bag with which you must bind yourself to a place."

"Great. Shit."

"I am sorry to see your clothing was not bound to you."

I peered down at myself. Except for simple underwear, I was bare as a nursery-tale mother's cupboard.

"But it is good you have your bag," Lucera said. "Its contents will still be useful to you."

She made a good point. I'd have to search through it and see what Crohl might have had in his trunk. I recalled some dinosaur scales I'd plucked off an early victim, but didn't think they'd be useful right then.

We sat in silence for a few minutes as I stared over Priya's shoulder at the bag. The purple-dyed Bag of Holding reflected the sunlight in shimmering waves. My thoughts had nothing to do with the bag or its contents, but only the woman in my arms and the one I'd lost. Everything else would wait.

Priya relaxed her grip and removed one arm, but the other stayed securely around my waist as we peered at the ground. She wiped her cheeks and clenched her teeth. The nodes in her jaw protruded, and I realized I'd never seen her angry face. I didn't like it.

The sensation in my gut transitioned to a tightness in my chest. I raised my hand there, and Priya mirrored the motion. Our eyes shot to each other and it struck me what was happening.

I'm feeling Priya's emotions. What in the—

Lucera reached for my hand and caused me to jerk. When I looked down, she tapped her temple. When she spoke, her lips didn't move, and I knew instantly only I could hear her.

"I have a message for you from Nokuro Takemoto,

Gemini. He congratulates you on being the first player to Level 10 on a wave of unique quests. You have proved that one can adventure and advance in the world of Enora Online purely based on its natural evolution via Enora's real-time quest generation. He says you should be proud."

I yanked my bag up and rifled through my interface. I had new prompts, new abilities to which I'd paid no attention after I'd leveled. I needed my clothes.

I stood straight, my bag dangling next to my leg, my thoughts on Priya's pain and Roshan's absence. Throwing my arm around Priya, I drew her back to me and responded with my thoughts, wishing I could growl them.

"Some governor asshole has taken Roshan. I got stabbed in my neck and my other friend just had her throat slit. I thank you for the message, Lucera, but I'm having a hard time giving a turd."

Lucera, who stood as the incarnation of what was probably the most amazing A.I. ever developed, simply smiled that no-teeth, patient smile.

"Of course, Gemini. I have one final message and then I have a special quest for you."

"What's the message?" I asked impatiently, kissing Priya on the side of her head.

"Nokuro wishes you to know that they've been speeding your progression video so Katelyn can watch clips of your performance. Of course, intimate moments were excluded in the interest of privacy. She wants you to know her only desire is that you live this life to its fullest."

As I'd been here for three days, that meant one day had passed since I died back on earth. The thought of it made my head spin.

"Nice."

"She added you should to take this bitch by the balls."

I would've laughed given another set of circumstances. *"Thank you, Lucera. Let her know I got the message, and I have every intention of it."* I gave a curt nod. *"And the special quest?"*

My interface blinked.

You have been offered a quest:
Rescue Roshan
(Recommended Level 16)
Rescue Roshan before the guards can deliver her to the
Governor in Millbury Peaks
Reward: 18,000 XP
25 Gold
A foundation stone

There's that word again.

I spoke aloud. "Foundation stone? What the hell is a *Foundation Stone?*"

Lucera's response came aloud, as well. "A foundation stone can be buried in the place of your choosing to erect a foundation, Gemini. As the word indicates, it is the basis of a stronghold and, if nurtured, protected, and built up over time, can become a town, a city, or maybe a castle. You will choose, should you complete the quest."

"Yeah, that sounds epic and all, but I need to get going."

"Do you accept this quest, Gemini?"

"Fuck, yeah."

"I'm sorry," Priya asked, "but who the hell are you?"

— — —

Having calmed myself enough to thank Lucera for the information and the quest, I'd peered into her eyes one long, final time, remembering Enora's words that I would never see her again. Then I hugged her, in spite of the burning anger coursing through my veins at recent revelations and events involving Roshan.

We marched away to the shade of the tree line near the village, and I retrieved the clothes I'd had the foresight to pack in the bag. I was pleased to find my soul-bound bow, but I was so pissed at myself, I could hardly unclench my jaw or my fists. I cursed over three utterly stupid mistakes.

First, I didn't set my spawn point, like a total noob.

Second, I didn't put my armor into my bag, opting instead to lazily lean it against the wall.

But the most unforgivable violation of all? I didn't raise Roshan's skill points so she would resurrect at my spawn point if she died. What the hell had I been thinking? What if something happened to her?

We stomped through loose dirt next to a cornfield as I fumed with myself. Judging by Priya's expression, she was right there with me. So, I turned, and gripped her shoulders.

"We'll get her back, and I'll make those bastards pay for what they did to you."

"They will, indeed, pay." She spat. Her eyelids dropped, leaving only slits for her to glare through. My neck warmed as hers turned pink "We must find a way to select my class and make me stronger so that I might rain hell down on them all!"

We turned toward the trail, and the shadows where the tree canopy met the Wood came into view. As we paced across the threshold, I nearly bumped into a boy walking the other direction. He was a preteen with full lips that turned upward in a sneer at me. Recognition dawned.

The boy who held a knife to my throat my first day in Enora.

"Watch where you're going, fool!"

Stepping forward, I cuffed him on the side of the head, grabbed his shoulder, and shoved him into a ditch filled with standing water next to the trail. As he splashed down, I stepped to the edge of the gulley and peered down at him.

"Recognize your betters, *fool.*"

ALSO BY ARLO ADAMS

Enora Online Book 2: *Quest For Roshan* is now available! You can get it here on Kindle, or go to Amazon and search for B07NK74222.

A NOTE FROM THE AUTHOR

When I played Final Fantasy XI Online back in 2000, I wrote fan fiction for my 'linkshell' (what other games called guilds) on our forums. I still remember the strange way MMOs used to tickle those reward centers of my brain so all I ever wanted to do was log in and play. I dreamed about them, envisioned conquests, and yes, wrote fan fiction, just for our guys and gals.

Nerd Alert!

Since then, I've played more MMOs than I can count on the fingers of both hands and the toes of both feet. As I'm lucky to have a full complement of both, that's a lot of games. FFXI, World of Warcraft, Everquest, Guild Wars, Age of Conan, Dark Age of Camelot, Cabal Online, DC Universe Online, D&D Online, Lord of the Rings, Eve Online, Elder Scrolls Online, and many, many others kept me enthralled for more hours than I care to admit.

They still do.

Although the exhilaration I experienced with that first game numbed over time and became a different thing, a new excitement surged and fired my synapses when I learned there was demand for books that thrust characters into these game worlds.

Having released a science fiction series in 2017 and become a full-time novelist, the timing couldn't have been better. Next thing I knew, I had three books penned in a series and no plans for stopping any time soon. The words flowed so naturally, I knew I'd found a home in what some call GameLit, and others call LitRPG. I don't much care what we call them, I'm just thankful my inner nerd who longed to write fan fiction has been unleashed!

I'm even more thankful readers like you are enjoying this genre and hope you enjoyed the first book in my Enora Online series.

Thanks again for reading *Enora Online 1: Gemini's Crossing*. Remember to sign up, then watch your email for *more books from the Enora Online series.*

GET UPDATES!

Gemini's story continues! If you've enjoyed *Gemini's Crossing*, I hope you'll sign up for my update letter so I can tell you when new books arrive.

You can subscribe at http://layer2publishing.com/enora-online/.

I use this list for release announcements. I have a zero spam policy and don't give or sell your information to anyone. EVER!

If you still don't like parting with your email address, you can also go to the product page on Amazon and click the *Follow* button to get updates.

Reviews Rock!

If you enjoyed Gemini's Crossing, please ***leave a review***. Amazon uses reviews to determine which works float to the top of the heap and I could really use your support, if you enjoyed my book.

ACKNOWLEDGMENTS

Whenever I read a book, I can instantly tell if the writer employed an editor. These godsends lend perspective to our work and provide unbiased eyes into our stories while cleaning up stupid mistakes that should never make it to a finished product. It is therefore appropriate that I acknowledge **Staci Troilo**, a goddess of an editor who didn't pull any punches and made me better because of it. No one is perfect and mistakes always slip through, but editors are better than most of us. And Staci's better than most of *them*.

Dustin Porta was the first reader of an early copy of this book and gave me crucial feedback. I couldn't have told this story the right way without him.

Ed Dixon was the final reader before *Gemini's Crossing* went to market and thumped my head a few times to keep me in line. His thoughts, gaming experience, and deep attention to detail were invaluable.

I'd also like to acknowledge Aleron Kong for our emails after I drafted this first book. I found his supportive attitude, enthusiasm, and encouragement to be gifts. Aleron certainly had better things to do—he's a busy bastard—but he chose to spend time emailing with me because he has a deep love for this genre and the people who read and write it.

Many LITRPG writers shared their experiences and their work with me as I wrote the first three books of this series, including their trials and their successes, and they gave me insight into the community I couldn't have done without. Tom Hansen, A.T. Gilbert, and many others were great sources of information and I thank them!

And finally, my muse.

Christine Niles has been my biggest cheerleader since I started my writing career. A constant source of encouragement and pro advice, Christine has been my anchor on days when health issues suppressed my ability to write, and she taught me patience in the face of adversity. Love isn't a strong enough word.

But I use it anyway.